MADAM LOVE, ACTUALLY

RICH AMOOI

Copyright 2018 © Rich Amooi
http://www.richamooi.com
Edited by Mary Yakovets

Please consider asking a surgeon to remove the part of your brain that makes you think something in this make-believe story is not believable. This book is a work of fiction. Seriously. References to real people, crystal balls, clucking geese, companies, dead people, restaurants, baked ziti, events, products, electrocution, services, cupcakes, businesses, corporations, soulmates, organizations, or locations are intended only to provide a sense of authenticity and are used fictitiously. Characters, names, story, locations, incidents, and dialogue come from the author's imagination and are not to be construed as real. Reading a romance novel while dating may lead to marriage and/or pregnancy.

No part of this book may be reproduced, scanned, recorded, eaten, or distributed in printed or electronic form without permission from the author.

To romantic comedy lovers around the world.
YOU ROCK!

CHAPTER ONE

"I want a man who looks like Gerard Butler, has deep pockets like Bill Gates, cooks like the Barefoot Contessa, and has the fashion sensibilities of a gay man." The woman tapped her fingers on Madam Love's reception counter, obviously not finished with her impromptu Build-a-Man workshop. "Oh! And he needs to be a diehard fan of Dolly Parton and David Hasselhoff."

Emma Wright—known as Madam Love to her clients in San Francisco—was used to people with unrealistic expectations when it came to soulmates. Her job was to find them their happily-ever-afters, and she was good at what she did. The best. But somewhere along the way many of her clients had gotten the idea that they could custom order a soulmate easier than crown molding from Home Depot.

Emma cleared her throat. "It doesn't work that way, but you're about to find someone *very* special."

Brenda's eyes lit up like one of Madam Love's battery-powered candles. "Let's get this party started then!" She glanced toward the purple beaded curtain hanging in the doorway behind the reception counter.

Emma gave Brenda a knowing smile and pulled the beads to one side, waving her through. "Come in, darling. Your future awaits you."

Brenda slid between the beads and walked to the room in the back. She looked around and nodded her approval before taking a seat on the red loveseat with the oversized cushions.

Emma liked to keep the room cozy and dim, except for the light coming from the candles. Everything including the curtains, the furniture, and the floor rug were red and purple. She had done her homework years ago and knew the psychology of colors. They had a powerful impact on moods and behaviors. Madam Love's clients needed to be relaxed and open to her readings for the best chance of success. The color red evoked emotions and was associated with love, warmth, and comfort. It also heightened awareness. Purple was more exotic and sensual. It had a calming effect on the mind, which came in handy when she needed to tell her clients something they didn't want to hear.

Brenda reached over and squeezed the heart-shaped pillow twice. "This is *so* going to happen. I'm going to have love!"

That was a good sign.

It made things a lot easier when Emma's clients were open to something happening—when they believed they would meet their soulmate.

Emma slid into her leather chair across from Brenda, closed her eyes, and took a deep breath. She exhaled slowly, opened her eyes, and smiled. "Ready?"

Brenda nodded. "Yes, but I want to make sure you know

how important it is for my man to have very large feet. You know what they say about men with big feet, right?"

Emma knew exactly what they said, but she wasn't going there. "It's hard for them to find shoes in their size?"

Brenda's high-pitched laugh was like the clucking cry of a goose in the middle of an egg-laying marathon, but the psychotic euphoria was short-lived when she choked on her own saliva.

Emma handed her a water bottle. "Here. Drink."

Brenda twisted the top off the bottle and took a sip. "Thank you."

Emma settled in to get started. Her customers had their expectations, of course, and she didn't want to disappoint. Everyone wanted the stereotypical fortune teller they had seen portrayed countless times on television and in movies. They expected a vibrant, sensual, gypsy-type woman with long flowing hair, so Emma always covered her short blonde hair with an auburn wig that made her head itch on warm days. They wanted someone mysterious, so she did up her eyes in dark, smoky colors and always wore a matte red lipstick. She wore a scarf over her head that tied on the side and hung down just over her right shoulder. And she had enough gold jewelry around her neck and wrists to make Kanye West feel insecure.

Emma looked nothing like her real self, but she was okay with it. Really. She could help people find love, plus it paid the bills. Well, most of the time. Business had been slow for Emma due to heavy competition from live Internet readings. She had no way to compete with them because she was unable to get visions through the Internet.

"Oops," Emma said. "Almost forgot . . ." She walked

behind Brenda, grabbed the crystal ball and pedestal from the light-proof box in the closet, and set them gently on the table between them. "Here we go, darling."

That was another thing.

She called her clients *darling* because they loved it, for some reason.

Truth be told, most of the time Emma felt like an actress, dressing up in costume, putting on a show. She was okay with that. As long as what she was saying and feeling were the truth. The one thing she wouldn't do was tell her clients something just because she knew they wanted to hear it. Emma had true gifts and loved sharing them with people, loved helping them. Her vibrations—her feelings—weren't one hundred percent accurate, but they were darn close.

"Okay," Emma said, sitting back down in front of the crystal ball and closing her eyes. "Let's begin." She took a deep breath and let it out slowly. She held the crystal ball in the palms of her hands for a few moments to energize it, and then placed it back on the pedestal, leaning over to stare at it intently.

Emma kept her gaze there, not blinking. She loved this part. It was a form of meditation, and it rarely took long before she started feeling things. *Seeing* things.

A minute later images appeared in her mind, coming and going, replaced by more images. All the images were connected to Brenda's destiny—she was sure of it. After another minute, Emma took another deep breath and smiled at Brenda.

Brenda slid to the edge of the loveseat. "What is it? Is it love? Tell me it's love."

Emma nodded again. "It *is* love. As clear as day."

Brenda pumped her fist and let out another raucous goose cluck, but then gagged like a Persian cat trying to clear a giant hairball from her throat.

They were always this excited at first.

But once Emma told her clients what they had to do to meet their soulmates, the seas usually parted. Half of her clients followed her exact instructions and were able to meet someone special. The other half resisted, complaining that Emma must have gotten her signals mixed up. Like she had bad reception or was tuned in to the wrong radio station.

Brenda rubbed her hands together. "Does he look like Gerard Butler? Look, I'd even be okay with an older man like George Clooney, just so you know. I'm not picky!"

Right. Not picky at all.

Emma held up her palm to silence Brenda. "As I said earlier . . . it doesn't work that way. Pay attention—this is important."

"Sorry, Madam Love. You go ahead and work your magic."

"You need to do three things to meet your destiny," Emma said.

"Hold on . . ." Brenda pulled a pad and pen from her purse and began writing. "Three things. Got it. What's the first thing?"

"Number one, you need to visit Napa. I saw clear images of the wineries there. Go. This weekend."

Brenda looked up from her pad, rolling the pen back and forth in between her thumb and index finger. "Napa? But I don't drink."

"I didn't tell you to drink. I just told you to go there."

"Right. Okay . . . which winery?"

"I can't tell you that."

"Oh . . ." Brenda sat up straight, then grabbed her purse. "I get it. That's an extra charge."

Emma stifled a laugh. "No. You need to choose the place yourself. Listen to your intuition—what your gut is telling you. I have a feeling you're already being pulled in a certain direction."

Brenda nodded and set her purse aside. "What if I choose the wrong place?"

"You won't, darling."

"But how do you know that?"

Emma raised an eyebrow.

Brenda giggled. "Of course, you know that—you're Madam Love. Okay, what's the second thing?" She dropped her gaze back down to her pad, ready to write.

"A hot air balloon ride."

Brenda looked up again. "Pardon me?"

"You need to take a ride on a hot air balloon while you're there."

"No, no, no, no, no. That's not going to happen."

"Why not?"

"Let's just say I had a terrifying balloon-animal incident with Clunky the Clown as a child and leave it at that. I stay away from all things related to balloons."

"Let me be very clear with you, Brenda. I see a husband in your future. The man will make an appearance this weekend when you go to Napa—I'm sure of it. Your soulmate. It will be up to *you* to do something about it—nobody can force you. You need to make that decision for yourself. But be warned, if you go against what is meant for you, if you try to fight it, you'll continue to live a very unhappy life."

Brenda set the pad and paper on the table, got up, and

paced back and forth as she mumbled to herself. "Napa. Hot air balloon. Napa. Hot air balloon." She stopped and turned toward Emma. "Wait. You said I had to do three things. What's the third?"

"Oh, that's the easy one," Emma said, sensing that Brenda was coming around. "I want you to bring me back a bottle of the 2013 Cabernet from Black Stallion Winery."

Brenda let out a sigh of relief. "I'll bring you back a case if I meet my soulmate."

"You're going to follow my advice then?" Emma asked.

Brenda thought about it for a beat and then nodded. "Yeah. I'll do it. Even if it kills me."

"Good. You won't regret it." Emma smiled. "And it definitely won't kill you. In fact, I see you having one of the most memorable weekends of your entire life."

Brenda yanked Emma into a rib-crushing bear hug, then patted her on the back like she was trying to burp her. "Thank you, Madam Love."

"My pleasure."

After Brenda left, Emma slid into her chair in the reception area, satisfied with helping another client. She opened her laptop and checked her schedule for the rest of the day, hoping someone had used her online appointment system to grab one of the many open slots on her calendar for that afternoon.

Nothing.

Things were getting tight money-wise. She had two months' reserve cash for emergencies, but she didn't want to use up all of it. Things would change for the better. She had a feeling an opportunity would present itself soon, but even with her gifts she had no clue as to what that opportunity was.

The one thing she wouldn't do was look into her own future. She promised herself that.

The front door flew open, snapping Emma out of her thoughts.

It was her landlord Randy, eating a decadent cupcake.

He was always eating cupcakes.

Randy was a cupcake connoisseur, and even more surprisingly, he made them from scratch, almost on a daily basis.

Emma loved cupcakes but tried to stay away from them, knowing she couldn't eat just one. Especially since those cupcakes always seemed to have a one-way ticket to her thighs.

"Hey," Randy said. "This is for you." He handed her a small Tupperware container and then took another bite of his cupcake, closing his eyes and moaning as he enjoyed the flavor. It was a miracle the man was as skinny as a rail. It also wasn't fair.

Emma took the container from Randy, knowing what was inside, and knowing she had no willpower whatsoever to resist such a temptation. "I told you to stop bringing me these things." She pulled the cupcake from the container and smelled it. "What kind is it?"

Like it mattered.

Randy smiled and pointed at the cupcake. "White cake with brown sugar and maple frosting."

Emma nodded. "And the little brown thingies on top?"

"Bacon bits."

That was all he had to say.

Emma dove into the cupcake. It melted in her mouth and was completely gone in five bites.

Randy laughed. "I guess you liked it?"

She nodded, continuing to enjoy the flavor in her mouth.

"Glad to hear it. Someone suggested that I get a food truck and sell them, but I prefer to start off small, maybe a booth at the farmers' market."

"That's a great idea, but you're a cruel person for bringing these things around here. I just can't say no."

Randy shrugged. "Well, if you think I'm cruel for that, I don't want to know what you'll think when you read this." He pulled an envelope from his pocket and slid it on the counter toward her. "Sorry. I truly am."

Emma had a feeling she knew what it was, but before she could say anything Randy had walked out the door.

She opened the envelope and pulled out the official document that said, *Notice of Rent Increase.*

The timing couldn't have been worse, but Emma knew it was coming.

Randy had raised the rent on everyone else over eight months ago, but had been letting her slide because he knew her situation. In the beginning she had been sharing the space with two other fortune tellers, but kicked them both out when she found out neither of them were truly gifted. Emma had taken a chance by renting a space in the strip mall in the first place, but Randy had given her a great deal since it had been vacant for so long. Plus, it was easy dividing the payment between three people. She had never been able to find anyone else to take their places.

Now that vacancies were filling up and rents were increasing across the city, Randy was getting pressure from John, his brother and business partner, to raise the rent.

Emma dropped the letter on the counter and stared out the window, deep in thought. She shook her head at the thought of paying more for rent. She didn't have any appointments for the rest of the day and only one appointment for tomorrow. She needed more than that to survive.

Much more.

The ping of her laptop let her know a new email was in her inbox.

She slid behind the reception counter and sat in front of the computer, hoping the email was good news. A new client was just what she needed to get her spirits up. Or maybe a Nigerian prince wanted to transfer millions of dollars into her account and all she had to do was give him all of her personal banking information.

No such luck.

She glanced down at the email she didn't want to see, a cancellation for tomorrow's only appointment.

Reason for cancellation: Found someone else online.

Of course.

People were finding excuses not to leave their houses, and it was costing Emma.

She stared at the email for a moment and then closed her laptop in frustration. She needed to get out of the office. Some fresh air and exercise would do her good. The plan was to drive to Golden Gate Park and walk the loop around Spreckels Lake, enjoying the wildlife and the Monterey Cypress trees. Then maybe something would come to her.

Emma slid into her 1998 gold Toyota Corolla and turned the key.

"Yes!" she said, a little embarrassed that she got so excited when the car started.

Emma tried to not to drive her car often—not only because it was on its last leg, but also because it was almost impossible to find an open parking spot in the city. Today she had to drive, though. She needed to get gas and put some air in the tires.

After a pit stop at the gas station, Emma drove down Fulton Street toward the lake, looking forward to the walk. Now all she needed was one good, positive song to take her mind off things. A song to give her hope or to at least make her relax.

She pressed the radio button with her index finger, but the first station was playing a commercial. She changed the station, and the next one also had a commercial playing. And the next two stations after that.

"What's with all the commercials at the same time?"

Annoyed, she jabbed the next preset button with her index finger and hoped for a song she liked. Actually, any song would do at this point.

"Welcome back!" the female radio host said. "I'm Elaine Stewart and we've been talking with bestselling author Lance Parker about his book *Your Soulmate Doesn't Exist*. This seems to be a controversial topic with the ladies, Lance."

"The truth hurts," Lance said, laughing.

"Sure you want to take another call? Marie was not too happy with you last hour."

"Not a surprise," Lance answered. "I'll be blunt—most women are living in a dream world when it comes to love. What they see in the movies and reality are two different things altogether. Love is not some fantasy like serendipity or destiny or soulmates. None of that exists and don't let anyone tell you otherwise. You can just ignore the psychologists, the relationship experts, the matchmakers, the dating websites, and especially those so-called love doctors and fortune tellers."

Emma jerked her head back. "Who is this idiot?"

"Well, there seems to be plenty of people who disagree with you," Elaine continued. "We're talking about love and soulmates on the program this afternoon. We have a line open if you'd like to call in and join us. Do you believe in soulmates? In Lance's opinion, there is no such thing. What do you think?"

"I think Lance is full of bull," Emma said at the car radio, shaking her head in disgust. "Just what I need to hear, someone who's knocking what I'm selling." She moved her finger over the button to change the radio station.

"Patty is on line two and has a comment about fortune tellers."

Emma pulled her finger away from the radio.

"Patty, you're on the air with Lance Parker. Go ahead."

Please say something positive. Please, please, please.

Positive or negative, it could have a direct impact on Emma's business.

"Thanks, Elaine," Patty said. "Long time listener, first time caller. I just want to say that I disagree with Lance one hundred percent. I met my husband at the bowling alley in the Presidio, and it's all because of a fortune teller. He's my soulmate."

Emma pumped her fist in the air. "Yes! Take that!"

She pulled her car over near Thirty-Sixth Avenue, miraculously finding an open spot across the street from the lake. She killed the engine, but left the radio on.

Lance laughed. "You believe because of the fortune teller you met your *soul*mate, and now you're happily married?"

"Yes, actually," Patty said. "And there was no way that could have been a coincidence. She's the one who sent me to that bowling alley."

"Really?" Lance said. "And you didn't stop to think maybe it's not that difficult to meet a man at a bowling alley? It's a place with beer! The odds were in your favor that you were going to marry *someone* from that place. I'm surprised you didn't walk away with three or four proposals at the end of the night."

"You're not very nice," Patty said.

"And you're not very realistic," Lance said.

"Don't take that from him!" Emma said, talking to the radio again.

"Uh-oh," Elaine said. "Looks like another person hung up on you, Lance. You're not making any friends today."

"Like I said . . . the truth hurts." Lance laughed.

"So, you're not buying the whole fortune teller thing?" Elaine asked.

"Not even for a minute," Lance said. "You can stick fortune tellers in the same category as soulmates. Fantasy. In fact, just stick them in the garbage while you're at it."

"What a jerk!" Emma said.

She wanted to reach through the radio with her foot and kick Lance where it hurt the most.

"We're going to take a break for the news at the top of the hour, but we'll be right back to take more calls with bestselling author Lance Parker," Elaine said. "Do you agree or disagree with Lance? Do you believe in soulmates? Give us a call."

Emma glanced over at her cell phone on the passenger seat as Elaine gave the phone number of the radio station.

She tapped her fingers on the steering wheel, deep in thought. She turned her head to look across the street at the entrance to the lakeside path, and then back over to her phone on the passenger seat.

She was tempted to call the radio station and give that man a piece of her mind.

So tempted.

His harsh words were really eating at her.

You can stick fortune tellers in the same category as soulmates. Fantasy. In fact, just stick them in the garbage while you're at it.

Emma knew she would regret it if she let him get away with being so rude.

She blew out a big breath and then reached for the phone, tapping in the phone number of the radio station. "I'll show you who's garbage, Mr. Parker."

CHAPTER TWO

The radio host Elaine pulled her headphones off and set them down on the console, turning and shaking her head at Lance. "Do you really have a problem with fortune tellers or was that just a way of stirring things up?"

"Yeah, I've got a problem with them, all right," Lance answered, leaving it at that. No way he would get into a discussion with her about how a fortune teller ruined his life. In fact, he preferred to drop the topic. "How long is the break?"

"We're back live after the national news and the local weather and traffic, so about eight minutes, including the commercials." She gestured outside the broadcast studio. "Feel free to grab more coffee from the break room. If you're lucky there may be some cookies left. I can have someone come get you when it's time to go back on the air."

"Thanks," Lance said, exiting the studio and walking down the hallway to the break room. He refilled his mug with coffee and then added sugar and creamer. As he stirred his coffee he heard footsteps behind him. He was sure he knew who it was.

"I told you to behave," said Peter, Lance's agent. "But did you listen? Noooooo."

Lance tossed the wooden stir stick in the trash can and spun around, grinning. "What did I do wrong this time?" He grabbed the last chocolate chip cookie from the box on the counter and snapped off a piece, popping it in his mouth.

"You said fortune tellers belonged in the trash!"

"And? What? There's not enough room?"

"Not funny." Peter poured himself a cup of coffee and took a sip.

Peter was not only Lance's agent, but also his best friend. They had had their fair share of disagreements over the years, but there was one thing that had never changed: Peter always had Lance's back and vice versa. But that didn't mean Lance couldn't have some fun at Peter's expense.

"I think my next book will be about the downfall of marriage and how we should all become monks," Lance said, trying to keep a straight face.

"Nice try," Peter retorted, without missing a beat. He picked up the cookie box and eyed the crumbs at the bottom. "You ate the last cookie."

"Someone had to." Lance took another bite of the cookie and washed it down with coffee.

Peter flicked Lance's shoulder with his finger. "Be gentle with the callers. Don't call them crazy if they don't agree with you and don't say anyone belongs in the trash, even if you believe they do. It's offensive and this is a business. Got it?"

Lance threw his hands up in the air in defense. "I'm just telling it like it is. Do you want me to lie? And I don't see what the big deal is. We're trying to sell books, right? A boring interview won't sell books. Any publicity is good publicity. You told me that."

"Yes, I did, but people aren't going to buy your books if they don't like you. Argue your point in a respectable way. Play nice and remember that you have a lot riding on this."

That was the truth.

Lance's publisher wanted something controversial to publish, so he came up with *Your Soulmate Doesn't Exist*. Many people were convinced the book was Lance's knee-jerk reaction to a bad breakup with his ex-fiancée, Karla. Yes, he wrote the book a few weeks after she had left him heartbroken, but what had happened to him was proof that soulmates didn't exist. But Peter was right. If this book flopped he would have a difficult time convincing the publisher to give him a contract for another book.

A few minutes later, one of the producers came and gave Lance the two-minute warning. He and Peter headed back to the on-air studio.

Elaine smiled at them as they both entered the studio. "Looks like we have a surprise caller for you, Lance."

"Who is it?"

"You'll find out soon enough."

Lance blinked. "Did I tell you I don't like surprises?"

"This ought to be good then." Elaine laughed and swung back around to face the control board.

Lance didn't like that devious look on her face. She was up to something for sure. He placed the headphones back over his ears as the *On Air* light illuminated.

"Welcome back! I'm Elaine Stewart and we've been talking with author Lance Parker about his new book *Your Soulmate*

Doesn't Exist. Let's get right back to the calls," Elaine continued. "Madam Love is on line three. You're on the air with Lance Parker."

"Thanks for taking my call," Madam Love said.

Madam Love? What the hell kind of name is that?

"I was hoping Lance could help me," Madam Love said. "I'm a little lost."

Lance had no idea what she was talking about. "How's that?"

"Well, darling . . . I'm really not sure which garbage I belong in, you know, me being a fortune teller and all. I just want to make sure I place myself in the proper receptacle since tomorrow is pickup day in my neighborhood."

Peter covered his face with the palms of his hands.

"Do I go in the regular garbage or in the recycle bin?" Madam Love said. "Compost, maybe? Unless you think I'm radioactive."

Lance chuckled. "First . . . should I call you Miss Love? Or do you prefer Madam?"

"Madam Love, actually."

"Okay . . . Madam Love, *Actually*. Tell me—"

"You didn't answer the question."

"Feisty. I like that. But I need to know . . . how do you sleep at night?"

"On my side with a full-length body pillow. I snore less that way."

Lance sat up in his chair and ignored her answer. "You claim to be a *real* fortune teller? That's what you call yourself?"

"Yes," Madam Love said. "I'm also known as a human whisperer, a psychic, a clairvoyant, and a medium. They're all basically in the same category, although our gifts can vary depending on the person."

Lance smirked. "Gifts or scams?"

"Gifts," Madam Love said. "Sure, there are people who give us a bad reputation, but I assure you there are plenty of us who have genuine gifts and use them for the greater good of mankind."

"The greater good, meaning your bank account gets filled with lots of money for taking advantage of insecure people searching for answers?" Lance said, trying to make sure he had plenty of sarcasm in his voice.

"No!" Madam Love said.

"I didn't know that the gifts could vary depending on the person," Elaine jumped into the conversation. "That's fascinating. How much can they vary?"

Lance wondered how the topic got shifted from his book to fortune tellers.

Oh, that's right.

It was his fault for opening his big, fat mouth.

"My gifts are specific," Madam Love said. "I don't read minds or see dead people or predict upcoming catastrophic events. I specialize in finding people their soulmates, their destinies."

"What a crock," Lance mumbled, shaking his head in disbelief.

Peter poked Lance's arm and mouthed the words *be nice*.

"I'm curious how you can claim to find someone their destiny," Lance said. "Shouldn't that happen naturally? If something is meant to be, it doesn't need anyone's help to materialize."

"That's what you think?" Madam Love asked.

"That's what I *know*."

"Then let me ask you this . . . were you destined to become an author?"

"What does that have to do with soulmates?" Lance said.

"Yes or no."

Lance hesitated and then said, "Yes. I was destined. It's my calling."

"Okay, then. Did you have any help along the way? Any guidance to achieve your destiny? An education, maybe? Financial help? A mentor? Inspiration? Anything at all? Or did you snap a finger and you were an author?"

"That's different. One is a career. The other has to do with relationships."

"Destiny is destiny, no matter how you slice it."

Lance adjusted his headphones, not enjoying the conversation at all. "You're a former lawyer, aren't you? You like to twist words and try to confuse people."

"Awww," Madam Love said. "Is Lance Parker confused? Well, don't you worry—we'll get you some help. You hang in there."

Lance stared at his microphone.

Madam Love was trying to piss him off.

And it was working.

The woman was a con artist and Lance needed to say something.

He also needed to stop grinding his teeth.

"I take it by your silence that you had help," Madam Love said. "Hey—nothing wrong with that. We all need help. Things don't magically happen on their own. You have to take action, otherwise everyone will just sit around waiting to win the lottery. You have to play if you want to win, so to speak. I help people find their soulmates every day. Most of them just need a little nudge or have to be pointed in the right direction."

"I don't buy it," Lance said.

"Well, you don't have to *buy it*, Mr. Parker, but it's true. And you may find this hard to believe, but there's even a soulmate for someone as arrogant and impossible as you."

"Arrogant?" Lance said. "I don't believe—"

"Let me jump in here for a moment," Elaine said. "Madam Love, how do you know Lance has a soulmate? How do you know he isn't married or already in a relationship with someone?"

Madam Love laughed. "It's my job to know."

Lance hated that she was right about him not being married, but he wasn't going to say a word. All it takes is a simple click on Google to see if a famous person is married or not.

"You're saying it doesn't matter who the person is or what their personality is like?" Elaine asked. "Every single person in the world has a soulmate?"

"Yes," Madam Love answered. "Every single person. Even someone as childish and bitter as Lance Parker has someone special. Someone willing to put up with him and all the things that would drive the average woman insane."

Peter snorted, but his hand wasn't quick enough to cover his mouth.

Lance held up his fist in Peter's direction.

Elaine laughed. "This is fascinating. Can you actually see the woman, Lance's soulmate?"

"What does this have to do with my book?" Lance asked.

"This is related, if you think about it," Elaine answered. "You don't believe in soulmates and Madam Love does."

"Yes, but the difference is I *also* don't believe in Madam Love. She's a fraud."

Peter shook his head at Lance.

This was a nightmare.

All Lance wanted was to talk about his book. Where had this Madam Love come from? Maybe she worked for a competing publisher and this was a set-up to discredit him and lose book sales. Whoever she was, he needed to get rid of her. She was going to cost him lots of money.

"Madam Love?" Elaine said. "Can you see Lance's soulmate?"

"My gifts don't work that way."

"Of course, they don't," Lance muttered, but loud enough that his microphone picked up the words.

"I only give in-person readings," Madam Love replied, ignoring his comment. "I have visions when my client is in the same room. I can see a person, their soulmate, but not clearly. I know where they are and what my clients have to do to meet them."

"How long does it usually take?" Elaine asked.

"Most of my clients will meet their soulmate within two weeks."

Elaine winked at Lance. "Well, sounds like we need to get Lance out of our studio and into your office for a reading, now don't we?"

"No!" Lance and Madam Love said simultaneously.

Elaine laughed. "We need to take a commercial break, but if you don't mind, please stay on the line with us, Madam

Love. I would like to continue this fascinating conversation with you. Would that be okay?"

Please say no. Just hang up and go away forever.

"Of course," Madam Love said. "I'd be happy to stick around a little longer. Someone needs to put Mr. Parker in his place."

"Great," Elaine said, eyeing her computer monitor. "This should be fun since my producer just informed me he put a poll on Facebook and Twitter, asking our listeners if Lance should visit Madam Love for a soulmate consultation. Please vote now and we'll be right back with the results!"

During the commercial break Elaine swung around in her chair. "What do you think?"

Lance glanced over at Peter and then back at Elaine. "About what?"

"About you going in for a reading with Madam Love. We'll give her two weeks to find you your soulmate. This would be a ratings bonanza."

"No way," Lance said, pulling off his headphones and finger-combing his hair. "Out of the question."

"Think of the publicity. This show is simulcast on over a hundred radio stations across the country. We have more than a million followers on social media."

Peter sat up in his seat. "This is a great idea."

Lance shook his head. "It's a *bad* idea."

"Hear me out," Peter said. "Prove her wrong and your sales will go off the charts. That's pretty much a guaranteed contract for your next book. You can choose whatever you want to write next. Thriller, mystery, a children's book . . ."

"No," Lance said. "I would rather be dipped in honey and fed to the bears."

Elaine laughed. "I think you're missing a golden opportunity. Thirty seconds until we're live." She swung back around in her chair and slipped her headphones back on.

"Do it," Peter whispered.

"No," Lance snapped back.

"I know what's best for you."

"You're deranged."

Elaine held up her index finger to quiet them both down as the *On Air* light illuminated.

"Welcome back! I'm Elaine Stewart and we've been talking with bestselling author Lance Parker about his new book *Your Soulmate Doesn't Exist*. We also have Madam Love on the line with us. She's a fortune teller who specializes in finding her clients' soulmates. Are you still with us, Madam Love?"

"I'm here," Madam Love answered.

"Great. Before the break I was chatting with Lance about the possibility of visiting Madam Love for a consultation to find his soulmate. He doesn't believe in them, but Madam Love is confident he *does* have one. They both said it was a bad idea. Funny, but our listeners disagree with both of you." Elaine scrolled down the page on her computer monitor. "We have a poll on Facebook and Twitter asking if Lance should visit Madam Love. So far, ninety-nine percent of our listeners say yes!"

Lance let out a nervous chuckle. "Out of how many people? Three?"

"Over four thousand people have weighed in so far." She kept her eyes on the monitor. "Hang on . . . it's up over five thousand and climbing."

What the hell?

Peter scribbled *DO IT!* on a piece of paper and handed it to Lance.

Lance pushed the paper aside and mouthed *no* to Peter.

"Madam Love, you mentioned there was a soulmate waiting for Lance at this moment," Elaine said. "How sure are you?"

"I'm certain," Madam Love answered, then laughed. "Hard to believe, right?"

"Not funny," Lance grumbled.

"The truth hurts, darling," Madam Love shot back.

Elaine was watching her monitor. "We now have over twelve thousand listeners who want Madam Love to give Lance a reading and find him his soulmate. That's ninety-four percent of those polled."

"Twelve thousand people?" Madam Love said.

"Yes," Elaine answered. "Amazing, considering the poll hasn't been up on Facebook and Twitter long. Wait, we're up to almost fourteen thousand listeners in favor."

"I'll do it," Madam Love blurted out. "I'll take the challenge."

"Wonderful!" Elaine said. "Lance? What do you say?"

"I already told you I'm not interested," Lance said.

"Chicken," Madam Love said.

"Not at all. I don't want to waste my time with something so ridiculous."

"Bawk, bawk, bawk."

Lance adjusted his headphones. "Are you clucking at me?"

"You of all people should recognize that sound," Madam Love answered. "Chicken."

"I can't believe we're having this conversation live on the radio."

"You're scared. Admit it."

He chuckled. "Don't be ridiculous."

Lance wasn't scared. He knew true love didn't exist. He'd been deluding himself when he thought he had been in love with Karla. He didn't believe in soulmates and he especially didn't believe in fortune tellers. Madam Love was a nut job.

Peter stood and pulled Lance away from his microphone. He lifted the headphones away from Lance's right ear and whispered, "Are you crazy? We couldn't pay for publicity like this. Take the challenge and reap the rewards when you prove her wrong. Just do it." Peter let go of the headphones and they snapped back against Lance's right ear.

"Ouch!" Lance said, then threw his hand over his mouth when he realized that yell just went out over the radio.

Elaine scanned the monitor in front of the control board. "Over twenty-seven thousand listeners want this to happen. Amazing. I've never seen such listener engagement like this before. They clearly know what they want! Let's take another call. Steven is on the line. Welcome to the program."

"Lance, buddy!" Steven said. "What are you doing over there, man? You're giving us guys a bad name. You talk the talk, but you're not walking the walk. Take the challenge and prove Madam Love wrong. If you do, I'll buy your book."

"Thanks for the call, Steven," Elaine said. "I wouldn't be surprised if others feel the same way, Lance. What do you say? Are you up for the challenge?"

Lance wondered how many other listeners were like Steven. Would they really buy his book if he proved Madam Love wrong? Even if ten percent did, that would be a lot of sales.

He bit his lower lip, thinking about what Elaine said.

This show is simulcast on over a hundred radio stations across the country. We have more than a million followers on social media.

That was a lot of people.

"Lance?" Elaine said. "All that silence doesn't make for good radio. What's it going to be? Madam Love says she can find you a soulmate within two weeks. Do you disagree with her? If so, you need to accept the challenge. The world is waiting. What's it going to be?"

Lance sighed, wondering if he would regret this decision for the rest of his life.

"Fine," he finally answered. "I'll do it."

CHAPTER THREE

Lance pulled into the open parking spot in front of Noah's Bagels and turned off the engine. He glanced down the sidewalk at the businesses in the strip mall. A hardware store, a yoga studio, a burger place, a nail salon, a credit union, and a deli.

"What the hell kind of a fortune teller is located in a strip mall?" he mumbled to himself, shaking his head. "A crazy one, no doubt."

Lance was used to seeing fortune tellers, psychics, and palm reader businesses set up in converted homes, usually with flashing signs in the front window. This location had to cost a fortune and almost made her business appear legit.

She wasn't fooling anyone.

Especially Lance.

He'd already dealt with one fortune teller in his lifetime. That was one too many and something he was still trying to get over. He couldn't believe he was doing this, but what Peter had said made sense. If he proved Madam Love wrong and won the challenge, his book sales would take off and he could write whatever he wanted for his next book. He needed to be careful, though. Who knew what type of con Madam Love would try to pull on him? But he wouldn't fall for it.

Lance pushed the front door open and a bell sounded. He stepped inside Madam Love's business, taking a seat in the red leather chair in the waiting area. Nobody was at the reception counter, so he assumed Madam Love was giving another reading.

He glanced around the lobby. He had to admit it looked nice and clean. There was a standing Buddha fountain with running water against the wall. Soft music played, while the smoke of burning incense from behind the reception counter snaked up toward the ceiling. Purple hippie beads hung down from the door opening near the counter.

Lance heard footsteps and sat up, nervous. Why did he feel like this was an appointment for a root canal? Whatever the reason, he couldn't wait for this charade to be over.

A hand with bright red fingernails slipped through the beads, pushing them to the side to reveal a petite woman with long auburn hair. She wore a bright red blouse that matched her lips. With every confident step she took toward Lance, she jingled from the ridiculous amount of jewelry around her neck and wrists.

"I've been expecting you, darling," she said in a smoky, sensual voice. "Come in."

How could she be so calm and civilized after their heated discussion on the radio yesterday?

Maybe it wasn't Madam Love. It looked like she was already up to her tricks.

Nice try.

"Are you ready to get started?" Madam Love said. "Why are you staring at me that way, darling?"

"Are you the same person who was on the radio?" Lance said, wondering what kind of excuse she would come up for Madam Love not being there.

"Of course," she answered. "I'm Madam Love."

Lance studied her a little more. "You?"

She nodded. "Yes. Me. Who did you think I was, darling?"

"Quit calling me that."

Madam Love placed her hands on her hips. "Already being a pain in the butt and we haven't even started yet? You're just as obnoxious in person. Look, are we going to do this or not? Some very unlucky girl is waiting to be your soulmate."

"It *is* you."

"Of course, it's me. I was just trying to be cordial."

Lance chuckled. "Cordial. Good one. Let's get this over with so I can go back to my world based on reality."

Madam Love pulled the beads to the side for Lance. "Right this way. Your future awaits you."

"Right."

He ducked under the beads and walked to the red and purple salon in the back.

Lance plopped down on the red loveseat with the oversized cushions. He reached over and squeezed a pillow, shaking his head. "Heart-shaped pillows? So cliché." He tossed the pillow aside. "Look, this is a complete waste of time. Why don't you just pretend to sprinkle fairy dust on me and then I'll be on my way?"

"It doesn't work that way."

He glanced around the room and shook his head. "Do you

think you have enough red and purple in this room? It looks like a combined shrine to Prince and Valentine's Day."

Madam Love slid into the leather chair across from Lance and folded her hands. "I wasn't aware you were here to critique my business. Shall I take notes on how to improve things?"

Lance sighed.

"Fine," Madam Love said. "Let's get started."

"*Thank* you. Is this where I should tell you what type of woman I'm looking for?"

"No, it doesn't work that—"

"What really turns me on is a woman with an extensive thimble collection."

Madam Love just stared at Lance, which motivated him to annoy her even more.

"And there's nothing sexier than someone who can weave scarves and sweaters from dryer lint."

She crossed her arms. "Are you finished yet?"

"Not quite. Most of all, I would love to meet a girl who's a champion clogger. Someone willing to compete in local clogging contests." He did his best to keep a straight face. "Is that possible?'

Madam Love scooted up closer to the crystal ball and rubbed her hands together. "Be careful what you wish for, Mr. Parker."

She took a deep breath and let it out slowly. She held the crystal ball in the palms of her hands for few moments, and then placed it back on the table, leaning over to stare at it.

Lance pretended to check his pockets. "Can you see my car keys in that thing? I think I lost them."

Madam Love crossed her arms. "Are you going to take this seriously or not?"

"How can I take you or any of this seriously when you're dressed up in that get-up? Fake accent, fake personality, fake hair, fake eyelashes, fake—"

"Hey! My eyelashes are real. The mascara makes them look longer."

He studied her lashes for a beat. "Whatever." He gestured around the room with his hands. "I mean, come on. I know how you operate. You'll make vague statements that can apply to me or just about anyone. You'll look for subtle changes in my facial expression or body language to indicate you're on to something. Then you move in that direction with your predictions."

"I don't do predictions."

"Then you'll ask questions and repeat something I said earlier in the conversation, hoping I don't notice I was the one who gave you that info. I know how all of this works."

"It's obvious you've been searching online for info on *fake* fortune tellers, but none of that applies to me. I'm not fake."

"None of this is real."

"None of it is real to you, because you have baggage you haven't dealt with. I'm even willing to bet that your baggage involves a fortune teller."

Lance didn't answer.

How the hell did she know?

Madam Love smiled. "That's what I thought. I guess it would surprise you then when I tell you I won't ask you one single question before or after I look into the crystal ball."

Lance just stared at her.

She was right.

That was a big surprise.

"Looks like I've got your attention now," she said. "I don't know if I've ever seen such hostility before in anyone who has come in here. Typically, people hope that I can give them something useful, not hope that I fall flat on my face. Wouldn't it be wonderful if I found you your soulmate?"

"I thought it was obvious by the title of my book I don't believe in soulmates."

"If that's the case, you'll prove me wrong and sell thousands of copies of your book, right? Sorry to burst your bubble, but that's not going to happen."

Lance didn't answer. Why was the woman so confident? It made little sense.

"Now, if we are going to do this, we're going to do it right," Madam Love said. "Even if you have to fake it, you do need to play along. You don't believe in me, but *I* believe in me. And I believe there is a soulmate waiting for you. I'm sure of it. But it makes it very difficult for me to do my job when you're constantly criticizing me."

Madam Love looked away and that made Lance feel like crap. Was she going to cry? He hated when women cried. Even women he didn't like.

He leaned in, but couldn't tell if she was crying because of the dim lighting in the room.

"What are you looking at?" she asked.

Lance shrugged. "Are you crying?"

Madam Love laughed. "Please, darling. I assure you that you will not make me cry."

"Fine, then. Let's get this over with."

"That's a much better attitude. Hopefully, it lasts more than a minute."

Madam Love scooted forward in her chair, took a deep breath, and let it out slowly. She held the crystal ball in the palms of her hands for a few moments, and then placed it back on the table, leaning over to stare at it. She held her gaze there, not blinking.

Lance waited, watching her every move, her breathing, her body language. She certainly looked like she was taking it seriously, like she really believed in what she was doing. But anyone could fake that with some decent acting skills. He wasn't buying it.

Two minutes later she was still gazing down into the crystal ball. She was playing the part well, but Lance was getting impatient.

Finally, Madam Love lifted her head, took a deep breath, and smiled. "Got it." She sat back in her chair with a confident look on her face. "You need to do three things to meet your destiny. Your soulmate."

"Is that right?"

"Yes. Number one, you need to go to Little Italy for dinner."

"Tonight?"

Madam Love nodded. "Yes, but you need to go to one particular restaurant."

"Which one?"

"I can't tell you that."

"Why not?" Lance said.

"I just can't."

This woman was unbelievable.

What kind of a fortune teller was she? A horrible one, that's what kind.

Lance sighed. "Give me a hint, at least. Sodini's? Bambini's? Fettuccini's?"

"I don't know," Madam Love said.

Lance blinked. "How do you not know this? That's ridiculous. Do I just randomly choose a restaurant? Then what? I choose a random woman and she's my soulmate?" He shook his head in disgust. "What a con artist."

"This is serious. I told you yesterday on the radio, I can see a person, but not clearly. I know where they will be and what my clients have to do to meet them, but I don't have all of the info and I won't make it up. Trust your instincts. And I wasn't even finished yet!"

"You may not be, but I am." Lance stood to leave. "I'm out of here."

Emma couldn't believe what was happening. Lance was walking out on her! She should have known this was too good to be true. The only reason she agreed to give Lance a reading and find him his soulmate was because she knew it would lead to more customers. She wasn't ashamed to admit she was a little desperate for money. Especially with the rent hike coming at the end of the month. When Elaine had mentioned on the radio that she should give Lance a reading, she was initially horrified by the idea. Why would she want to help such an arrogant, hard-headed man find the love of his life? She even thought of the poor woman who would end up with him.

But then she thought of her business and her lack of money.

She had to do it—there was no other way around it.

In fact, just being on the radio yesterday resulted in two new appointments and she hadn't even done anything yet. It was amazing. She imagined how many more new clients she would have after she found Lance his soulmate. She could be booked up weeks in advance. But now it was all falling apart and she had to do something.

Emma jumped up from her chair and ran through the beads to the front lobby. "Wait!"

Lance had his hand on the door handle, ready to walk out. He let go and swung back around, waiting for her to say something. The man did not look happy.

"Get back in here," Emma said. "Now."

"Why?" Lance asked. "This was a big mistake and you know it."

"You have a soulmate. I saw her."

"I know, I know. She just happens to be at an Italian restaurant, even though you have no idea which one. I'll just go wander around the city asking every woman I meet, 'Are you my soulmate?' I wonder how many times I'll get laughed at, or even worse, slapped."

"I never told you to go wander around the city. You didn't let me finish. Be a man, get back in here, and finish what you started. Otherwise I'll call Elaine at the radio station and tell her you backed out of the challenge. Like a chicken."

Emma clucked before she could stop herself.

She felt her face heating up from the embarrassment. Sure, she'd clucked at him on the radio yesterday, but at least he couldn't see her. This was all her grandfather's fault. When Emma was a little girl he asked if she was a chicken when she was scared of doing something. Swimming in the ocean, riding the bike without the training wheels, trying out for the track team in high school, even applying for her first job. His method worked and always got her to do what she was afraid of. Emma was sure many of her successes in life were due to her grandfather's love and support. But Mr. Lance Parker wasn't going to understand that and she certainly wasn't going to tell him.

Lance studied Emma and chuckled. "Do you know how foolish you look when you do that?"

"As a matter of fact, I do!" she said, trying to recover from the embarrassment.

Lance laughed again.

Emma pointed at his mouth. "You *do* have teeth. You should smile more often."

She had no idea why she said that.

Maybe that smile caught her off guard.

"I smile when I have a reason to smile, which doesn't seem to be often." Lance studied her face for a moment. "And you need to remove that ridiculous makeup."

Emma crossed her arms and shook her head. "And here I was thinking you might not be so bad. I'll pretend I didn't hear that. Are we going to do this or not?"

Lance stared at her for a moment. "Fine."

"Fine."

Emma walked past the reception counter and stopped, pulling the beads to the side for Lance. "Right this way. Your future awaits you." She held up the index finger on her free hand. "Not a peep out of you, you got that?"

Lance threw his hands up and surrendered. "Hey, I wasn't going to say a thing." He shook his head and ducked under the beads, walking back into the room and making himself comfortable on the loveseat again.

Emma slid back into her leather chair, took a deep breath,

and looked Lance in the eyes. "Okay, let me finish this time. Got it?"

"Got it."

"Now . . . after you go to little Italy, you'll look for an Italian restaurant with a flashing, red *Amore* sign in the window."

"Amore," Lance repeated, studying Emma like he was trying to see through her.

"It means *love* in Italian," she said.

"I know what it means and this is getting cheesier by the minute. Pun not intended."

"Of course not. Speaking of cheese, you will go into said restaurant and order the baked ziti. Then, you'll—"

Lance held up a finger. "Okay, hold it right there."

Emma huffed. "What now? You said you would let me finish!"

"Don't get your knickers in a twist. I just have no idea what a baked ziti is."

"It doesn't matter!"

"Of course, it does. I don't want to order something I don't like. What if it's monkey balls? You expect me to eat it?"

"You seriously think they will serve monkey balls at an Italian restaurant?"

"You never know. Anyway, never mind. I'll get a pizza instead."

"No!" Emma said, wondering why this had to be so difficult.

Oh, that's right. Because Lance Parker was a difficult man.

"The food plays a part in all this, but not because of how it tastes. The taste doesn't matter."

"It matters to me."

This man was impossible. All Emma wanted to do was give him three simple instructions and send him on his way. She should've known it wouldn't be that easy.

She took in a deep breath and tried to summon the patience to continue. "My point is, you're not going there to eat. Yes, you'll eat, but you're going there to meet the love of your life. That should be your main focus."

"*My* point is that I can't go into an Italian restaurant and *not* have the food be the main focus. I go to an Italian restaurant to eat. Everybody does. In fact, any time I go, I *over*eat. It's expected! And, call me crazy, but I like to know what I'm eating. Do you know what baked ziti is or did you make it up? Just tell me and we can move on."

"I know it's delicious. That's not good enough?"

"No."

Emma tapped her fingers on her leg. "Hold on, Mr. Stubborn. You're impossible." She jumped up and grabbed her phone from her purse. After doing an online search for baked ziti, she sat back down to read the results to Lance. "Okay. Listen carefully. Baked ziti is a baked casserole dish made with ziti macaroni and a tomato and cheese pasta sauce. Ingredients typically can include sausage, mushrooms, peppers, onions, and then layered with a variety of cheeses. Lots of cheese. Baked in the oven and served hot. How could you not like that?"

Lance placed a palm on his grumbling stomach. "I admit it sounds tasty."

"Anything and everything that is Italian is tasty, but let me remind you it's not about the food. May I continue?"

Lance gestured with his hand for Emma to go on.

"Thank you," she said. "Just one other thing and we are done, darling."

Lance glared at her.

"Sorry. It's a habit."

"What's the other thing?"

"You need to sit in a chair that faces the front door."

"What if no chairs face the door? What if there are no chairs, only stools?"

"There will be chairs facing the door."

"How do you know if you don't know which restaurant it is?"

"It's my job to know."

Lance stared at Emma.

Too bad she didn't have the gift of reading minds.

At least Lance looked a little more relaxed—not his usual hostile self. In fact, he was quite nice when his mouth was shut. She'd even say he was handsome, but she would never tell the arrogant man that.

"Why are you looking at me that way?" Lance asked.

Emma stood, preferring not to answer his question. "We're finished here."

"So, let me get this straight . . . You're telling me all I have to do is go to Little Italy, find a place with a blinking *amore* sign, order a baked ziti, and sit in a chair that faces the front door?"

"Yes."

"And *that* will magically produce the 'love of my life'?"

She hated that he used air quotes.

"Yes," Emma answered.

"Nothing else? Do I need to hop up and down on one leg

as I eat the baked ziti? Or maybe I need to sing 'That's Amore' on a karaoke system? That will surely attract my soulmate."

"No. Nothing else. But I do expect an invite to the wedding."

Lance couldn't help but laugh out loud at that. "You'll be the first person I think of as I plan my wedding."

She pointed toward the door. "You can go now. Just remember to be yourself and everything will fall into place. And if you're ever not sure what to do at any given time during the evening, go with your instincts. Everything that happens to you when you're in Little Italy happens for a reason. Everything is connected. Go with the flow."

"Go with the flow?" Lance chuckled and turned to walk out, but then stopped himself and swung back around. "I must say . . . I'm quite impressed."

Emma looked surprised by his comment. "Don't be. I do this for a living, but I appreciate the—"

"No, not that. I'm impressed you could give me all those ridiculous instructions without laughing. You're good."

Emma hesitated. "I look forward to you losing the challenge."

He smirked. "And *I* look forward to you eating those words."

CHAPTER FOUR

Lance pulled into his driveway, his thoughts still on Madam Love. The woman thought she'd play him for a fool, but she had another thing coming. He'd been blindsided by the works of a fortune teller one time, but never again. He would go along with Madam Love's plan as a business decision and nothing more. Just like Peter had told him. He would prove her wrong and reap the rewards. As for right now, the plan was to take the dog out for a walk, then clean up a little before heading over to Little Italy for dinner.

Opening the front door, Lance was greeted by Typo, his six-month-old Jack Russell Terrier mix. Typo couldn't contain his excitement, his little tail swiping back and forth as he banged his body into Lance's shins.

"Hey there!" Lance bent down and scooped up Typo in his arms, scratching him on the head. "How's my boy? Did you miss me?"

Typo's answer was immediate—an onslaught of kisses connecting with Lance's cheek, ears, and neck.

Lance laughed. "Thanks for the bath."

He fed Typo after their walk, and got in the shower.

Forty-five minutes later, Lance hopped off the cable car and glanced up at the Transamerica Pyramid before walking down Columbus Avenue past Washington Square, in search of the infamous Italian restaurant with the flashing *amore* sign in the window. He knew it was a complete waste of time, so he would just consider this a chance to eat Italian food, since it had been a while since he'd had any.

He stopped in front of the first Italian place, inspecting the windows on both sides of the front door. They had a bright red pizza sign and a matching open sign, but nothing else. The restaurant across the street had the same signs. And so did the one a few doors up the street. The next restaurant just had one sign that said, *We Deliver*.

Lance shook his head in disbelief. "What a waste of time." His stomach grumbled again.

He continued down the street past The Stinking Rose, Franchino, and Mona Lisa. None of them had the *amore* sign in the window.

That's when he stopped in his tracks.

"You have got to be kidding me," he mumbled to himself, staring at the neon sign in the restaurant window across the street.

Amore.

The Italian word flashed back at him, on and off, almost taunting him to let him know Madam Love knew what she was talking about. Not taking his eyes off the sign, he crossed the street and was almost sideswiped by a passing taxi, the horn blaring.

Lance jumped onto the sidewalk and bumped his knee

into a fire hydrant that was painted with the colors of the Italian flag. He rubbed his knee and cursed at himself for not paying attention before crossing. He glanced at the sign one more time before reaching for the front door handle and pulling.

The door didn't open.

Lance pulled again, this time with more force.

Nothing.

He placed both of his hands against the glass, trying to see inside, but the restaurant was dark.

Odd.

He stepped back, hoping to find the restaurant hours posted. It was early, so maybe they weren't open yet. That's when he spotted the flyer taped to the inside of the window.

To our wonderful customers. We will be closed for remodeling until further notice. We apologize for the inconvenience. Please visit our Facebook page for updates on the progress and our re-opening date. We look forward to serving you again soon. The Management.

Lance shook his head. "What a joke."

So much for Madam Love's plan—not that he thought any of it was based on reality. But she could have at least gotten part of it right. She failed on the very first step. And what's worse, Lance's stomach was protesting.

He stared at the front door. "I'm so hungry."

An older man with a cane stopped alongside Lance. "Me, too."

Lance turned and nodded at the man, studying him. He must have been pushing ninety and was wearing a gray double-breasted jacket with matching cuffed pants. His tie was so wide it almost covered the shirt underneath.

The man tapped one of his black lace-up dress shoes on the sidewalk. "They won't be open for a couple of weeks." He lifted his cane and touched the glass in front of the flyer. "Remodeling and all that, but I'm not getting any younger and neither are you. Follow me."

The man took off down the sidewalk, fast for his age.

"Where are we going?" Lance asked to the man's back.

The man stopped and turned back around. "To get food. Baked ziti." The old guy swung back around and continued to walk down the sidewalk.

"Baked ziti?" Lance mumbled to himself.

He watched the man walk away. Was this a trick? Maybe the man would lure Lance into a back alley and beat the hell out of him with the cane.

Lance laughed at the thought and then remembered what Madam Love had told him.

If you're ever not sure what to do at any given time during the evening, go with your instincts. Everything that happens to you when you're in Little Italy happens for a reason. Everything is connected. Go with the flow.

Lance couldn't believe he was going to take her advice. "I guess I will go with the flow."

He glanced down the street at the old man, who had just disappeared around the corner.

"Just my luck," Lance said. "A ninety-year-old speed walker."

He crossed back over to the other side of the street, this

time looking both ways before doing so. When he got to the corner, he headed down the side street just as the old man entered a red building with a green awning that said, *Italian Deli*. Four more people walked in right behind him.

"Must be a popular place," Lance said to himself.

Lance pulled the door open, looking around. It looked like your typical Italian place with red and white checkered tablecloths, a giant shelf with cans of tomato sauce and olive oil on display, and pictures of famous Italians like Frank Sinatra, Dean Martin, Rudolph Valentino, and Joe DiMaggio. He had no idea why there was a picture of Lady Gaga on the wall. Was she Italian? It didn't matter. The only thing on Lance's mind was food and now he was going gaga over the wonderful smell of garlic in the air. He inhaled through his nose and smiled.

Lance's stomach rumbled again. He needed to eat, and fast.

The old man turned away from the counter, already holding a plate of hot food. "Baked ziti. Excuse me, I have a hot date." He winked and slid past Lance.

Lance chuckled at the man. He seemed like a good man with a sense of humor. Lance's smile disappeared when he realized the man was serious about the hot date. He kissed an older woman on the cheek, set his tray of food on the table, and sat to join her.

She also had a plate of baked ziti.

More grumbles from Lance's stomach.

He inhaled another big breath of the amazing smell.

The employee nodded proudly after noticing Lance inhale again and pointed to the *take-a-number* dispenser on top of the glass display. "Grab a ticket or you may starve to death. The evening rush will be showing up any second."

Lance chuckled. "Thanks." He looked around the deli. Just about every table and booth was taken.

Two more people entered and pulled numbers from the dispenser. Then the front door opened again, and five more people came in.

"Told you," the employee said. "You'd better hurry."

Lance quickly grabbed a number before the group of people and waited his turn, studying all the different options behind the glass displays. There were two sections: hot food and cold food. Most of the people ordering before him were going for the hot food, and in particular, the baked ziti.

He stepped closer to get a look at the dish. It looked good. Really good.

After the employee called Lance's number, he had already decided to order the dish. He stepped up to the counter and watched as another employee took the last serving of baked ziti.

"What'll it be today?" the employee asked.

Lance pointed to the empty silver tray behind the glass. "Do you have more baked ziti?"

"Is the Pope Catholic?"

Lance blew out a relieved breath. "Good. I'll have a plate."

Just then another employee swooped in and replaced the empty tray with a full one. Lance watched through the glass as the employee cut a large helping of the piping-hot baked ziti from the tray and plopped it onto a plastic plate, handing it to Lance.

The front door chimed and a few more people came in, taking up the last few empty tables without even ordering.

Great. Was he going to eat standing up?

After Lance paid and grabbed a napkin and a plastic fork,

he turned looking for a seat. After scanning the entire place, he had realized that there was one empty chair, but there was already someone sitting at that table. A woman with her back to him.

No way he would ask if he could sit there with her. Besides, maybe she was waiting for someone or the person she was with was in the bathroom.

He sighed, not knowing what to do. Yes, he could eat standing up since it was a casual place, but that might look a little strange to the others who were seated, plus he wouldn't be following Madam Love's directions to sit in a chair facing the front door.

The employee who had helped Lance glanced in his direction.

Lance shrugged and looked around.

The employee wiped his hands on a towel and came from around the other side of the counter. He walked over to the woman. "Can this kind gentleman sit with you?" He gestured back to Lance, but she didn't turn around to look.

She nodded *yes*.

"Ha!" the employee said. "Here you go. We don't want that baked ziti to get cold." He pulled out the chair for Lance.

It was facing the front door.

Lance glanced around at the other tables and realized it was the only chair in the entire deli that was facing the front door.

It's just a coincidence. Don't read too much into it.

He placed his plate on the table and sat down to eat with the attractive woman.

She had short, straight blond hair that didn't reach her

shoulders. Her big blue eyes were now open wide like she had seen a ghost.

She dropped her head down and ate her food, not saying a word.

Weird.

Maybe she was shy.

CHAPTER FIVE

Emma was on the verge of freaking out in a public place.

Lance Parker—Mr. Arrogant—just took a seat at her table.

Her table!

She jammed a forkful of the baked ziti in her mouth and continued to keep her head low as she tried to figure out what went wrong.

Lance was supposed to be at a restaurant with an *amore* sign.

This place didn't have an *amore* sign.

Plus, it was a deli, not a restaurant!

Can't the man follow simple directions?

She blamed this predicament on the baked ziti. After she had told him about it at her office, it was all she could think about. She had to have it for dinner. But having Lance show up and sit at her table was beyond crazy. What were the chances? He should be at a different place meeting his soulmate right now!

Emma took another bite and kept her head down.

"Thanks so much, I appreciate it." Lance scooted his chair closer to the table and placed a napkin on his lap. "I won't bother you at all." He took a bite of the baked ziti and moaned. He looked up at Emma for a moment. "This is amazing." He grabbed another forkful, but then paused before putting it in his mouth, glancing over at Emma. "Sorry. I said I wouldn't bother you, and here I am talking to you. Don't mind me. This entire plate will disappear in a few minutes and then I'll be on my way." He gestured to her food. "Please. Eat."

Emma just sat there in disbelief.

Her body was working overtime to control her out-of-control heart rate. If she wasn't careful her nerves would cause her to lose her appetite and the baked ziti would go to waste.

Emma couldn't let that happen.

Still, she had no idea what to do.

Calm down. He doesn't recognize me.

Emma had changed her clothes, taken off the wig and the jewelry, and removed the makeup from her face. She was now a different person. She could have been part of the FBI witness protection program and nobody would have ever known who she was. Emma was one hundred percent certain Lance had no idea she was Madam Love. Still, he must have noticed her reaction when she saw his face. She had almost jumped out of her chair.

Lance moaned again and smiled. "Well, I'll be . . . she was right. This is delicious." He continued to eat and then looked up at Emma. "You stopped eating. Am I making you uncomfortable?"

She didn't want him to be there, but she wasn't going to be

rude and say yes. She left the rudeness to Lance Parker and would not stoop to the man's level.

She shook her head no and took another bite.

It was better if she didn't speak. She'd played up her theatrics and her accent when she was Madam Love so he wouldn't recognize her voice, but she didn't want to take a chance.

"Good," Lance said. "Thank you."

Why was he so nice to her?

Right now it appeared as if he had manners and was a normal person.

Because he doesn't know who you are!

Still, something was going on with that man. Even if he didn't believe in what she did for a living, he didn't have to be so rude to her, like he had been back at her office and on the radio yesterday. There was a story behind it, and she wanted to get to the bottom of it. But right now she needed to finish what was on her plate and get out of there.

Lance glanced at her purse hanging from the side of the chair and raised an eyebrow.

She followed his gaze to see what had caught his attention.

No!

Emma's copy of Lance's book, *Your Soulmate Doesn't Exist*, was sticking out from the top of her purse! She had run out to the bookstore to grab a copy right after he had left her office. She wanted to see what kind of garbage the man was writing so she could use it against him if it ever became necessary. And she had no doubts there would be plenty of garbage in that book. But right now she needed to take his focus off her purse and the book and get it on to something else.

She pointed to his plate. "I see you're enjoying the baked ziti."

He glanced down at his plate and Emma tried to push the paperback farther inside her purse, but it didn't move an inch.

I should've gotten the Kindle version!

"Very much." Lance set his fork down, a curve forming around his lips. "How's the book?"

She decided to play dumb and moved some food around on her plate. "The cook? Well, I don't know him personally, but I think this baked ziti has got to be the best I've ever had. I guess I should thank him." She pretended to look over Lance's shoulder toward the kitchen.

Lance gestured to her purse, completely ignoring her attempt of distracting him. "I see you're reading *Your Soulmate Doesn't Exist*. Do you recommend the book?"

This was getting worse by the minute. How was she going to respond to that? If she told him the truth and said it was a bunch of crap and that the author was insane, he would most likely figure out who she was. Or not. She was willing to bet there were thousands, maybe millions of women who agreed with her.

Soulmates were real!

But the last thing she wanted was to discuss the book with him, so she took the safe route.

"I haven't read it yet," Emma answered.

He nodded, still watching her. "I heard it was fantastic, but I'm being biased since I know the author."

Know him?

The arrogant man obviously hoped she would ask how he knew the author so they could talk about him all evening. What an ego he had.

Once again she kept her comments short and to the point. "Lucky you. I should be going." She grabbed her plate and tossed it in the trash behind her.

"I'm heading out, too." Lance stood and also tossed his plate in the trash.

Emma grabbed her purse, forced a smile in Lance's direction, her signal to him that she was out of there.

"Are you done?" another woman asked, swooping down on the table like a hawk.

"All done," Lance said.

"Great!" The woman waved over a man who was standing near the cash register.

Emma moved out of the way, then took a step toward the front door.

"I'm Lance."

Emma winced, knowing she would have to turn back around to introduce herself, because she wasn't rude like him. She swung around. "Emma."

"A pleasure to meet you." Lance smiled and held her hand.

She accepted it and—

BAM!

Lance let go of her hand and then stared at his fingers, rubbing them together. His gaze met Emma's again, furrowed eyebrows and all.

"What was that?" Emma asked, knowing he'd felt what she felt. It was like an electrical shock.

"I'm not sure," Lance said, studying Emma while he continued to rub his fingers together.

"Lance Parker?" a woman called out by the olive oil display.

Lance turned around. "Yes?"

The woman's face lit up as she took a few steps toward Lance. "I'm a big fan. I'm Jessica." She held out her hand for Lance.

Lance took her hand. "Nice to meet you. I'm—well, you know who I am."

"Yes!" she said, looking out of breath.

Was she hyperventilating?

"I devoured *Your Soulmate Doesn't Exist* in less than four hours!" Jessica continued. "Amazing book, and I couldn't agree more—only delirious people believe in soulmates. And Chapter Four really resonated with me."

"Yeah?" Lance asked. "Which part?"

"The part where you talked about true love not existing and that we can learn a lot from arranged marriages. They have a success rate of ninety-six percent because they are compatible and choose to work hard, nothing more. I so agree. It really resonated with me."

"That makes me happy," Lance said.

"I also love the part where you talked about—"

Blah, blah, blah, blah, blah.

Emma tuned out their ridiculous conversation and used the opportunity to make her escape. She squeezed in between two tables and headed toward the front door of the deli.

"Hey, Johnny!" an employee called out. "The sign is not on!"

"I'll get it," Johnny said, stepping in front of Emma to push a button on the back of the sign in the window. He smiled, pushing open the front door for her. "Thanks so much for stopping by."

Emma smiled back at Johnny. "Thank you." She stepped

outside onto the sidewalk, but then stopped when she had the oddest feeling.

She flipped around to look back at the sign Johnny just turned on in the window.

Emma stared at the sign in disbelief.

It said *amore*.

CHAPTER SIX

The next morning Emma got off the MUNI electric trolley bus and walked down the street a few blocks to her office. All the businesses had back entrances, which was convenient since she liked to change out of her Madam Love outfit, and leave as someone different. Only one time had someone ever asked her if she was Madam Love as she was trying to leave. She lied, telling them she was part of the cleaning staff.

Emma inhaled the wonderful scent from Noah's Bagels before she entered.

Once inside her office, she headed straight to the bathroom to transform herself into Madam Love. She slid out of her jeans and t-shirt, and changed into her colorful gypsy-type clothes that everyone seemed to love. Next, she applied thick makeup to her face. She hated it, but it was all part of the job. She finished it off with the matte red lipstick before grabbing the wig. Emma stared at herself in the mirror, adjusting the wig and pushing her short blonde bangs underneath the front of the fake hair. She pulled a scarf over her head and wrapped the jewelry around her neck.

"I need to find lighter necklaces," she mumbled.

The weight from them was building the muscles in her neck and she didn't want to look like the Incredible Hulk.

"Hello, darling," she said to the mirror, then scratched her head. "Why does this thing always itch?" She scratched her head a few more times, then walked to the front of the building to unlock the front door.

"Another beautiful day," Emma proclaimed, looking out into the parking lot that was beginning to fill up.

Too bad most of the people were going to the yoga place and Noah's Bagels.

She lit an incense stick, hoping things would get better. At least Emma had four appointments lined up for the day. All of them resulted from that little time she had spent on the radio. It was amazing what a little publicity could do for a business. Hopefully, that meant even more customers coming her way after she found Lance Parker his soulmate.

Was that giddy fan of his from the Italian deli *the one*?

Emma hadn't heard from Lance today, so maybe that was a good sign. And even better for her since she was in no mood to talk to the obnoxious man.

Her first appointment of the day wouldn't be for another thirty minutes, so Emma had time to check her email and go through her bills before Randy came in to torture her with his latest cupcake creation. Not that she didn't love them, but Emma hoped he would be a no-show today since she had skipped her Pilates class last night after eating so much baked ziti.

Baked ziti with Lance Parker.

She pulled the copy of *Your Soulmate Doesn't Exist* from her purse and opened it, glancing at the inside flap with his picture and bio. She flipped through a few pages, stopping on Chapter Four, the chapter the woman in the deli mentioned about arranged marriages.

We can learn a lot from arranged marriages. They have a success rate of ninety-six percent because the man and woman are compatible and choose to work hard, nothing more.

She shook her head. "This is crap. They may have a higher success rate, but that doesn't mean they're happy."

Lance also failed to mention that the success rate was deceiving. Many couples stayed together because of the fear of being disowned by their families if they ever got divorced. He conveniently left out that information.

She skipped forward to the next chapter and her mouth dropped open.

Chapter Seven: You Have No Soul, So Get A Life Before You Die.

She stared at the ludicrous title of the chapter and then read more of the bull that Lance was preaching.

Think you have a soul? Dream on. The belief that we have a soul helps us deal with the fear and finality of death because we falsely believe that there will be another life after we kick the bucket. Like we are going to magically advance to the next level, learn from our mistakes, and play another round in the game of life. Wrong! You need to start living now because you don't get a second chance. That's why it's better to find someone you have things in common with instead of thinking there is someone out there among the eight billion people in the world who was placed on this earth just for you. Someone to put that sparkle in your eye. Someone who gives you that extra kick in your step. Someone to send electrical charges through every part of your body when you touch. Someone who completes you and who gets you, all the way down to the deep, dark depths of your non-existent soul. Like I said, keep dreaming. Because that's all it is. A big, fat dream and a complete waste of time.

Emma wondered what the heck had happened to Lance. She felt sorry for him. She knew there was no way he had always felt this way about life, love, and soulmates. Nobody did. Something had happened to him that left a scar. A huge scar.

Knock it off.

The last time she felt sorry for a man she ended up dating him. She tried to fix him, change his thought patterns, and his way of living. That old expression "Men Don't Change" is a much-used expression for a reason. They don't change unless they want to. Almost always, they don't want to.

One thing was for sure, this would not alter her game plan. She'd accepted the challenge and was sticking to it. Besides, this was her only hope at the moment of giving her business a boost. She needed this. And her ego and her pride wanted to prove Lance Parker wrong.

She couldn't wait to find that arrogant man his soulmate. His meeting that woman last night had to irk the man, because the last thing Lance would ever admit was that Emma was right. He had a soulmate. She wondered what Mr. Arrogant was thinking right now. She smiled, thinking he would be too embarrassed to show his face today.

The front door flew open and Lance stepped inside. "Good morning, Madam Fraud."

Emma slid her copy of *Your Soulmate Doesn't Exist* into the drawer and walked around the reception counter. Any thought of feeling sorry for him had evaporated.

"Have you always been so rude?" Emma asked.

Lance closed the door behind him. "Have you always been a fraud?"

Not in the least intimidated by his broad shoulders and confident pose, Emma took a step in his direction. "Have you always avoided questions?"

He didn't back down, moving toward Emma. "Have you always answered a question with a question?"

"Have *you*?" Emma asked.

Lance didn't answer.

He stared Emma down and she stared right back at him.

Finally, she gave in, tired of his ridiculous behavior. "Okay, enough of this childishness. Please enlighten me. How am I a fraud? Did you follow my instructions?"

She was curious if he would lie, but she had to be careful how she would call him on it, since she hadn't been there at the restaurant. At least, he hadn't known she was.

"Yes. I followed your instructions," Lance said. "First, that place you sent me to was closed for remodeling! How could you not know? Where did you get your crystal ball? Gypsies R Us?"

"Funny. If the place was closed, then it wasn't the place you were supposed to meet your soulmate. I told you that everything that happens to you when you're in Little Italy happens for a reason. Everything is connected. You were supposed to go with the flow."

He chuckled. "Right. Go with the flow . . ."

"Well, did you? What was your next move? You met no one at all?"

Try to lie. I dare you.

"Not that it's connected to anything that you may have done, but I met two women. And before you get all excited, neither of them were my soulmate."

Emma was surprised Lance told the truth about meeting both women. Or maybe shocked was more like it. Who knew the unbearable man had one good quality? Still, she had to know more about the other woman in the deli.

"How do you know they weren't your soulmates if you don't believe in soulmates?" Emma asked. "You wouldn't even know what to look for."

"I think it was obvious."

"How is that, darling?"

Lance just stared at her.

"What?"

"How long are you going to *darling* me? It's about as fake as that wig of yours. Can you take that thing off? It looks like a Chia Pet died on your head."

Emma placed her hands on her hips. "I changed my mind. I was a firm believer that every person in the world had a soulmate, but I was wrong. You're the one exception."

Lance chuckled, staring down at her hand. "You seem to be the exception, too. I don't see a ring on your finger. Where's *your* soulmate?"

Emma glanced down at her ring finger, surprised he noticed she didn't have a ring. Why would he even look? It didn't matter. He was trying to change the subject and throw everything back in her face, but it wasn't going to work.

"That's none of your business," Emma said. "This is not about me. Tell me about the woman you met last night."

"Women. Plural. There were two of them."

"Fine."

"One was a fan who had read my book and loved it, of course. The other woman was a—"

"Tell me about this fan," Emma said, not wanting to discuss the second woman since *she* was that person. "What was she like and why did you write her off so quickly?"

Lance shrugged. "She was no big deal. Tall. Slender. She had eyes that—"

Emma held up her hand. "Those are all physical attributes. Tell me about her personality."

"That's just it. She didn't have one. She was a complete turnoff from the moment she opened her mouth, because the mouth never closed after that. All she did was talk."

Emma nodded. "And that bugs you because you prefer to hear the sound of your own voice. I understand completely."

"No! She talked about mundane things like the weather and—"

Emma smirked. "Your book?"

"She *liked* my book."

"Something is wrong with her." Emma held up her index finger like she had a huge breakthrough. "Brain damage, maybe. No woman in her right mind would buy your book, let alone like it."

Obviously, since Emma had purchased his book for research only.

"Nice try, because sales are going well right now. And the other woman in the deli had a copy of my book in her purse.

Now, *she* was the complete opposite of the talker. She didn't talk at all. She avoided eye contact with me."

"Maybe she didn't like you."

"Oh, no. That's not it at all. She liked me. I'm positive of that."

Emma wanted to tell him he was out of his mind, but couldn't. "And why do you think she liked you?"

"I could tell from the moment she saw me. She was the opposite of Miss Talks-Too-Much. She was beautiful and quiet."

"Beautiful . . ."

Emma didn't mind at all when a man called her beautiful. It was odd coming from Lance. The man had a habit of insulting her whenever he had a chance.

"Yeah," Lance continued. "Not a speck of makeup, which was so natural and genuine. Almost angelic."

Emma stared at him again. Lance was calling her an angel? Maybe she'd been too quick to judge this man. Maybe she just didn't understand him. Maybe he did have some notable qualities underneath his annoying bitter shell. Come to think of it, Lance appeared more attractive when he was nice. Go figure. It was like she looked at him in a different light. She hadn't noticed before what good shape he was in, too. Lean. Well-conditioned, wavy brown hair that matched his eyes. Maybe she was being too hard on the man.

Lance studied Emma's face for a moment, then her wig, and then he dropped his gaze down to the jewelry on her neck. "You could learn a thing or two from her."

Emma wanted to punch Lance in the gut.

"What?" Lance asked.

"Is it possible for you to go at least a minute without insulting me or criticizing my business?"

Lance thought about it. "Probably not. Anyway, it looks like we're done with this charade, so you won't ever have to see me again. I followed your instructions and I don't have a soulmate. I can call Elaine at the radio station and let her know you lost the challenge. End of story."

"*Not* the end of the story. You missed something, because your soulmate was there. Last night."

"Wrong. One woman made me want to leap off a building and the other one slipped away when I turned my back. Soulmates don't walk out on each other, do they?"

Emma didn't answer because she knew it wouldn't matter what she said.

"I'll give you this much," Lance said. "The baked ziti was out of this world. It's my new favorite dish, so thank you for introducing me to it."

Emma hesitated, surprised the jerk was being nice again. "You're welcome."

"I mean, how could you not like something with so much cheese?"

"You'd have to be crazy."

"Or lactose intolerant," Lance added, getting more excited. "Those are the only two legitimate excuses."

"I agree."

"The ricotta, the mozzarella, and . . ." Lance snapped his fingers. "There was another one."

"Parmesan."

"Yes!" Lance let out a moan. "That stuff is addicting."

"Tell me about it," Emma said, smiling.

Lance jammed his hands in his pockets. "We'd better stop

talking about food. I just had breakfast an hour ago and all this talk of food is making me hungry."

"Me, too."

They both nodded and stared at each other.

What just happened there?

For that brief moment, Emma had forgotten she hated the man.

It was like they had a normal conversation.

He is driving me crazy!

One minute he was mean and next minute he was nice. She wished he would choose a route and stick with it.

"Why are you looking at me that way?" Lance asked.

"Nothing. I'm getting a vision. A signal."

"Maybe it's the mother ship ready to take you back to your planet."

Emma ignored him.

"Oh, wait . . ." Lance continued. "Let me guess . . . I need to go to Chinatown and look for a place that serves chow mein and has a flashing sign in the window that says Bruce Lee."

Emma huffed. "You need to take this seriously."

"And you need to get a real job. This is bogus."

"Bogus?"

"Yeah. Bogus."

"The eighties called and they want that word back."

Lance pointed to her head. "They also want that wig back."

Emma snorted. "You're ridiculous."

"And you're—"

Emma held up her hand. "Don't even . . . Can I finish what I was going to say earlier?"

Lance sighed and took a seat in the lobby, stretching out his legs in front of him. "Fine. Go."

"Thank you. As I said before, I had a vision and it means something." She pointed at him. "Don't move a muscle. I'll be right back."

Lance didn't argue. He just sighed again.

Emma passed through the hanging beads back into her salon, sitting down in front of the crystal ball, and closing her eyes.

"I'm bogus?" she mumbled to herself. "He's bogus." She took another deep breath. "Okay, forget about him for a moment. Focus."

She took one more deep breath and let it out. She held the crystal ball in the palms of her hands for few moments to energize it, and then placed it back on the table, leaning over to stare at it. Emma held her gaze there, not blinking. It didn't take long before she connected with the source, and it was just as she suspected.

She jumped back up and returned to the front of the building.

Lance had his feet up on the table, looking at something on his phone. "It says here on this website that the life expectancy of fortune tellers and psychics is ten years less than that of a normal person." He glanced up at her. "Killed by their disgruntled clients, I'm guessing."

"Bite me," Emma said, sitting across from Lance. "Now, listen up and put your feet down."

Lance pulled his feet back off the table and sat forward in his chair, not saying a word.

Another surprise. She'd expected another smartass

comment from him, but it never came. It was about time he changed his attitude.

"You need to be at Bark in the Park tomorrow," Emma said.

"Bark in the what?"

"Bark in the Park. It's a yearly dog festival. Exhibit booths, lots of activities, food and fun."

Lance raised an eyebrow. "Is the food and fun for the dog or for the owner of the dog?"

"Both. Last year they had over three thousand people there. Lots of dogs, too. There's even live music."

"I have a video of a dog singing along to a Bruno Mars song."

Emma crossed her arms. "What does that have to do with anything? Focus."

Lance chuckled. "Do you ever smile?"

"Are you ever serious?"

He shrugged. "Look, the festival sounds fun. Cute, even. But I don't have—"

"A dog?"

He hesitated. "I *have* a dog. I was going to say I don't have any free time."

Emma stared at him.

He was lying. There was no way that Lance Parker was a dog person. Or a cat person. She wouldn't be surprised if he hated all animals.

"You." She analyzed his face for a moment. "You have a dog?"

He nodded. "Yup."

"A *real* dog? Not stuffed."

He nodded again.

"What's his name?" Emma asked.

"Typo. He's a Jack Russell terrier mix." Lance picked up the phone off his lap, tapped and scrolled, and then handed it to Emma.

Skeptical, she took the phone and looked at the picture.

Her heart melted at the sight of the cutest dog she'd ever seen. "Awwww."

Typo was white with light brown patches over each eye. And he was still a puppy, maybe six months old at the most.

"Typo . . ." Emma said, almost instantly falling in love with the dog.

"Yup. He's my boy." Lance took the phone back from Emma.

"You need to go to the festival," she said. "She will be there. Your soulmate."

"Right. The love of my life."

"And make sure you order a strawberry smoothie."

Lance laughed. "And my soulmate will be the one serving it up?"

"I don't know."

"Of course, you don't know. You make this up as you go along, and most people fall for it. Not me."

"Go or you lose the challenge."

Lance chuckled and winked at her. "Fine." He walked out the front door, not looking back or even saying goodbye.

Emma didn't trust the man.

The way he said *fine* wasn't convincing. He wasn't going to Bark in the Park, she was sure of it. She looked out the front window and watched Lance get in his car, a black Mazda SUV with a sticker of a dog paw on the back window.

Did he really have a dog? Was the photo of the cute dog

on his phone really his? The man must have downloaded a stock photo off the Internet and showed it to women to get them into bed. Okay, maybe that was a ridiculous thing to have in her head, but she didn't know what to think when it came to Lance Parker.

One thing was for sure, she didn't trust him one bit. She had to make sure he was going along with her plan. That meant there was only one thing she could do.

Emma was going to spy on Lance.

CHAPTER SEVEN

"Settle down, Typo!" Lance laughed, having never seen his dog so excited before. "Don't worry, you'll make lots of new friends here."

Typo led Lance through Bark in the Park, to the left, to the right, to the left. Typo wanted to sniff every dog. He wanted to play with all of them. And just about every booth had free samples of dog treats. Typo would need to go on Weight Watchers by the end of the day, Lance was sure of it. At least the dog was enjoying himself. Lance, too.

Never had Lance seen so many dogs and dog lovers together in one place. There was so much to see and do. After watching dogs run through the obstacle course, Lance stopped by the makeshift corral to see the border collie sheep herding demonstration. He was amazed how smart the border collies were and how they were able to get the sheep going where they needed them to.

"Think you can do that?" Lance asked Typo.

The dog ignored Lance, his attention strictly on the sheep. His tail wagged nonstop.

"Oh," Lance mumbled to himself. "The smoothies."

Lance headed to the information booth to find out where the smoothie vendor was located. *If* there was one. He didn't expect to meet his soulmate there or anywhere, but Lance wasn't going to let Madam Love say he hadn't followed directions.

Surprisingly, the volunteer at the booth said there was a smoothie booth and directed Lance past the main stage to the food area, just opposite the Petco booth. He stared up at the menu board underneath the giant smoothie sign. They had three types of smoothies: strawberry, blueberry, and banana.

"Can I help you?" asked the man behind the counter.

Lance wasn't in the mood for a strawberry smoothie at all. The banana smoothie sounded amazing and he could see boxes and boxes of fresh bananas in the back of the booth.

He wanted that banana smoothie.

Make sure you order a strawberry smoothie.

The annoying words of Madam Love were bouncing back and forth in his head.

Why should he listen to her? The woman was a fraud, and he had no problem telling her that a thousand times. And what would be the big deal if he ordered a banana smoothie instead of a strawberry smoothie, anyway? Would the flavor of the smoothie be the difference between having a soulmate and not having a soulmate? Not that he believed in them. But still, none of this made any sense, and he wanted a banana smoothie!

"Sir?" the man behind the counter said.

Did you follow my directions, Lance? Did you order the strawberry smoothie?

"Get out of my head," Lance mumbled.

"Pardon me?" the man said.

"Nothing," Lance said. "Sorry—tough choice."

Lance wasn't sure he wanted to take a chance with a different flavor. Madam Love was looking for any excuse to call the radio station and declare herself a winner.

He glanced over at the boxes of bananas again.

"You can't go wrong with strawberry," said the female voice behind Lance. "It's my favorite."

He turned around and saw a beautiful redhead smiling back at him. She was almost as tall as Lance, wearing a white skirt and a turquoise blouse. He guessed she must have been forty-five or fifty. She had an exhibitor lanyard hanging around her neck.

"You also get the added benefit of antioxidants and vitamin C," she said.

She smiled again and this time Lance noticed how white her teeth were. She looked like she belonged in one of those chewing gum commercials on television.

"I guess I need to try one then," Lance said, smiling and turning back around toward the employee. "One strawberry smoothie, please."

The employee prepared the smoothie and placed it on the counter in front of Lance. "You're in luck. That's the last one."

"What?" the woman said, stepping forward. "How could you be all out of smoothies? It's not even noon yet."

"We're not out of banana and blueberry," the employee said. "Just strawberry. Sorry. Our supplier shorted us on the strawberries today." He pointed to the stacks of banana boxes.

"That's why we have so many bananas. Try one. If you don't like it you can have your money back."

The woman frowned. "That's okay. Thanks anyway."

Lance glanced down at the strawberry smoothie in his hand and then back up at the woman as she was about to turn away. Why did he feel guilty? It wasn't like he had done anything wrong. He just happened to be the person who bought the last one.

"Wait," Lance said, extending his hand with the smoothie. "You can have mine."

She stopped and turned back around. "What? No. Thank you, but I can't drink that."

"Sure you can. I was in the mood for a banana smoothie, anyway."

"Really? Are you just saying that?"

"No. I want a banana smoothie. Dying for one, actually."

The woman opened her purse. "Well, let me at least buy yours."

Lance waved her off. "Not necessary. Now, take this smoothie or I'll be offended."

The woman smiled and took the smoothie from Lance. "Thank you."

"My pleasure."

For a brief moment, Lance wondered if he had met this woman because of Madam Love. Was that why he was supposed to order the strawberry smoothie? Did Madam Love know Lance would get the last one and offer it to the woman?

No way. That's insane. This has nothing to do with Madam Love.

Lance wasn't going to give her credit for a random meeting with some stranger in line to buy a smoothie. This was not destiny for him to meet her. Besides, he was just talking with her and nothing more. It's not like he would ask her out or anything.

After paying for a banana smoothie, Lance swung around and took a sip. "This is heaven."

Lance stepped away from the booth with the woman.

She glanced down at Typo. "Beautiful dog. What's his name?"

"Typo."

She giggled and bent down to pet him, but Typo backed up and hid behind Lance.

"He's a little shy sometimes," Lance lied. He had no idea why Typo didn't want to be petted by the woman.

"That's okay," the woman said. "Sometimes festivals can overwhelm our furry friends."

"True," Lance said, taking another sip of his smoothie. What was supposed to happen? Was he drinking a magic potion? Was something going to happen with him and this woman? She seemed sweet and was definitely attractive, but there were a lot of sweet and attractive women in the world. He didn't believe for one minute this woman was his soulmate. In fact, he sensed she was getting anxious, like she wanted to get away from Lance.

"I need to get back to work," she said. "Thanks again for the smoothie."

Bingo.

"Of course," Lance said.

She pointed off in the distance. "See that black dog over there?"

Lance turned and spotted the large inflatable dog in the distance. It was about as tall as a two-story house.

"Yes," Lance answered.

"Stop by when you get a chance today. Our company makes organic dog treats and I'm going to sneak you a bag since you have been so generous."

"That's nice of you, but I eat human food."

She laughed.

"Oh," Lance said, pretending he didn't understand. "You mean for him?" He pointed down to Typo.

The woman shrugged her shoulders. "Why not? So, you'll come by?"

Lance chuckled. "Sounds good. Right after the K-9 unit show at noon."

"Great. See you then."

It was only after the woman walked away that Lance realized he didn't even know her name.

Where are your manners? You should have at least introduced yourself.

At least he had the banana smoothie.

He took a seat on the bench underneath the tree. Typo lay next to him on the grass, setting his head down and watching the dogs and their owners walk by. Every now and then he would lift his head and whine, letting Lance know he wanted to meet some of them.

"Hang on," Lance said. "Let me just finish this." He took the last few sips of the banana smoothie, trying to get every last bit from the bottom of the cup. Okay, now he was slurping, but he didn't care if someone heard.

He stood and tossed the empty cup in the trash, satisfied after one of the best tasting smoothies ever. And even better, he had followed Madam Love's directions. He had ordered the strawberry smoothie. Sure, he didn't have it very long, but that was beside the point. Her instructions were to order a strawberry smoothie, not drink it. And that he did.

"Okay, boy. Let's go see the K-9 show."

Typo barked and pulled on his leash. Lance knew the dog didn't understand what a K-9 show was, so why was he so excited?

The answer was right in front of Lance.

A beautiful Great Dane.

A Great Dane without a leash.

Or an owner.

Typo pulled again toward the Great Dane and the leash slipped out of Lance's hand.

Now there were two dogs loose.

Typo sprinted to the Great Dane and sniffed the dog. The Great Dane sniffed him right back. Both must have been happy with the results, since their tails were wagging. They looked like the odd couple next to each other, but they clearly had chemistry.

Lance moved closer to grab Typo's leash, but the large dog took off running, in the mood to play, no doubt. Typo took off right behind him.

"Typo!" Lance called out, chasing the dogs past the dog costume contest on the main stage, around the kids entertainment zone, and back toward the bench where he had just been sitting.

The dogs headed around for a second lap.

Lance tried to keep up with them, but it wasn't easy. "Typo!"

Emma felt as if she were at the circus, not a dog festival. Lance was chasing after his dog, who was chasing after another dog that looked more like a horse. He dodged in and out of humans and canines, like he was competing in some obstacle course. Emma had to admit it was rather amusing. If she didn't despise the man so much, she would have thought he was rather cute. Not as cute as his dog, though.

Emma had high hopes that things were going in the right direction when she saw Lance approach the smoothie booth earlier. She had been spying on him from behind the hot dog stand and had seen the strawberry smoothie he had bought, just as instructed. Why he had given it to the woman in line was a mystery, but Emma could tell they had a friendly conversation. Maybe even a connection. Considering she was the only woman Lance had met so far today, she was sure she must have been his soulmate, although she didn't recall seeing that woman in the Italian deli.

But one thing was bugging her. Why did he let the woman walk away without exchanging phone numbers? He seemed to just let her go. It made little sense. He should have been going with the flow, just like she had instructed him, and asked the woman out. Instead, he was running circles around the dog festival like a clown.

Men.

They circled around again, but this time the large dog was gone.

It was just Lance chasing Typo.

Typo snuck around the vaccination booth and was now moving in Emma's direction.

"Uh-oh," she mumbled to herself, turning her back on Typo and ducking behind the giant oak tree. She squatted down to make herself smaller and scraped the side of her knee against the rough bark of the tree. It was painful, but she didn't make a sound for fear of attracting Typo to her. Or Lance. Hopefully, the dog wouldn't see her and would just keep going on his merry, hairy little way.

No such luck.

Emma felt a lick on the back of her ankle.

And then another lick.

She giggled and tried to push Typo away, but he came back for more, now licking her toes through her sandals.

"Shooo, Typo!" Emma whispered to the dog. She peeked around the tree and could see Lance looking around for the dog, a frustrated look on his face.

"Typo!" Lance called out. "Where are you?"

Typo barked.

"No, no, no, no, no," Emma whispered. "No barking. This is a no-barking zone."

The dog continued to lick Emma and she couldn't help but giggle more. Typo was the cutest thing. She stroked him along his short white coat, then scratched him in between the ears. "You're such a cutie, you know?"

"There you are," Lance said.

Emma froze.

She kept her head down so Lance couldn't see her face. She could only see his shoes and his legs—since he was wearing shorts. He had the legs you would see on a tennis or soccer player. Muscular. Well-defined.

Very nice.

Lance squatted and grabbed Typo's leash. "Thank you for grabbing him. I—" Lance dropped his head lower, trying to get a look at Emma's face. "Wait a minute . . ."

Not good.

If he found out she was Madam Love, she would be finished. The challenge would be lost.

Relax. He doesn't recognize you.

Emma wasn't thinking clearly.

She got distracted by his legs and should've just gotten up and walked away.

Too late now.

"You're Emma, right?" Lance said.

"Huh?" Emma said, trying to play dumb.

"From the Italian deli. You know, the baked ziti?"

She didn't answer.

"Here," Lance held out his hand to help her up.

She didn't want to take his hand because she remembered what happened the last time they had touched in the deli. But she also didn't want to be rude.

Why can't I be rude?

She took his hand to stand and BAM!

There it was again, that electrical charge.

What was it with this guy?

And why did he act so different when she wasn't Madam Love?

Lance let go of her hand and then stared at his fingers, rubbing them together, just like he had done in the deli. His eyes met Emma's again and his brow furrowed. It was like a déjà vu.

"What is it with you?" Lance asked.

She fidgeted, but needed to stop. Why should she be nervous?

He doesn't know who I am, so calm down!

Lance studied her for a few seconds. "How funny we ran into each other again."

"Funny ha-ha or funny curious?" she said.

"Okay, maybe not funny, but it's a coincidence to see you again, considering Little Italy isn't even close by." He looked down at Emma's knee and his eyes widened. "You're bleeding."

Emma glanced down at her knee. She knew she'd banged it hard against the bark of the tree, but hadn't realized she had broken the skin. It seemed to hurt more now that she knew it was bleeding. But she was a big girl and had suffered far worse injuries.

"It's no big deal," she answered. "I should go."

"Just a minute," Lance said, grabbing her arm and zapping her again. "That scrape looks bad. Hold onto Typo for a minute and I'll be right back."

Before she could protest he handed her the leash and disappeared into the crowd.

Emma glanced down at Typo, shaking her head. "What am I doing?" The dog just stared at her, a confused look on his face. "Yeah. I'm just as baffled as you are."

CHAPTER EIGHT

Lance ran through the crowd toward the first aid booth he had seen near the festival entrance when he first came in. Emma's injury didn't appear to be serious, but something about the sight of blood always panicked him. It looked like she'd injured herself while trying to catch Typo for him. That was so sweet, but it also made him feel guilty.

Lance got the supplies and a bottle of water from the crew at the first aid booth and made his way back to Emma and Typo.

He smiled, thinking of how it seemed Emma had bonded with the dog. She was smiling and petting him until he approached her behind the oak tree. Then she became another person when he said something. Funny, but she acted the same way in the deli. She must be really shy.

"Over here!" Emma called out, waving from the bench.

Lance approached and smiled at the sight of Typo lying on her lap.

"Now you've done it," Lance said. "He won't ever want to leave your lap."

Emma flashed Lance a gorgeous smile and petted Typo. "I don't mind."

Lance squatted and stuck his hand out. "Okay, let me see the damage."

"I don't know why you went to all this trouble. It's nothing. Really."

Lance raised an eyebrow and kept his hand held out, waiting for the leg.

Emma sighed and extended her leg.

He scooted forward a little and grabbed her foot, resting the heel on his knee. "You're right. It doesn't look too bad from this angle. Still, it can get infected, so . . ." He twisted off the cap from the bottle and poured the water over her scrape, then set the empty bottle on the ground.

Emma winced. "Did you have to use so much water?"

"Sorry," Lance said. "I just wanted to clean it up well. Okay, we're just going to let this air dry for a couple of minutes and then I'll cover it with a gauze pad. So while we're waiting, I guess I can ask you what brings you here."

Emma stared at him. "Here?"

Was she getting shy again?

"Yeah. You know . . . I wasn't sure if you had a dog in one of the competitions or worked here or just loved dogs in general."

"I love dogs . . . in general," Emma said.

"I used to have a dog named General," Lance said. "A German shepherd."

"Is that so?"

Lance nodded. "My dad was a military man—a colonel in the Air Force. We never got along, so when I had the opportunity to name our new dog in high school, I chose the name General. I just thought it would be funny to have a dog that outranked my dad."

Emma snorted.

Her hand flew up to cover her mouth. Her cheeks turned red.

"No need to be embarrassed," Lance said, chuckling. "You snort. I think it's cute."

They held each other's gazes, not a word between them.

Emma had the most beautiful smile when she showed it. And the slight age lines around her sparkling blue eyes made her elegant and even more beautiful.

She cleared her throat and broke off whatever they had going there, pointing to her leg. "It's dry now."

"Yeah," Lance said. "Dr. Lance needs to get to work." He opened the small antibiotic ointment packet he got from the first aid station and rubbed it on the gauze pad. "This will help avoid infection and scarring. At least, that's what the guy at the first aid station told me."

He covered the wound with the gauze pad and carefully applied adhesive tape around the edges. He placed his hand under Emma's calf and lifted her leg off his knee, then placed it back down on solid ground.

"There you go," Lance said. "Good as new."

"Thank you."

"It was the least I could do." Lance pointed at Typo, who was content with his eyes closed on Emma's lap. "He's wiped out after chasing the Great Dane. So am I." Lance pointed toward the smoothie booth. "You thirsty?"

"A little," Emma said, gesturing to the empty plastic bottle on the ground. "Too bad my doctor used all the water in the bottle."

"Hey, I think I saved your life. One infection can turn into a thousand and soon an entire village is gone." He tried to keep a straight face, but he couldn't.

Emma laughed. "I wasn't aware there were villages in San Francisco."

"You have to look closely." He gestured behind him with a thumb over his shoulder. "Have you tried those smoothies?"

"No," Emma answered.

"Do you like bananas?"

"I love them."

Lance jumped to his feet. "Be right back."

"But—"

"No buts unless you're sitting on one."

Lance chuckled, picking up the empty water bottle from the ground and tossing it in the blue recycle container next to the trash. He walked over to the smoothie booth and got in line, eager to buy Emma a banana smoothie. He couldn't resist getting another one for himself. Why not? At the moment he was upbeat, although he wasn't sure why.

He smiled, thinking of the chances of running into Emma again. He was sure Madam Love would say something about it. Like she'd made it happen.

Whatever.

Then there was the other woman he met earlier. She seemed nice, too. But there was something about Emma that intrigued him. He didn't know much about her. Hell, he knew *nothing* about her, but he wanted to know more.

A couple of minutes later he returned and handed a smoothie to Emma. "This is the best smoothie you'll have in your entire life." He took a sip of his own smoothie and moaned. "So good. Try it."

"I can't believe you're having another one."

Lance was about to take another sip and stopped. "How did you know I already had one?"

"Because . . ." Emma hesitated, running her hand along Typo's coat as if she were trying to smooth out a wrinkled bedsheet. "I don't expect you to tell me it's *the best smoothie ever* if you've never tried it." She eyed his shirt and pointed to it. "Plus, you spilled some on your shirt from the first one."

Lance glanced down at his chest. Sure enough, there it was. A nice banana smoothie stain.

Embarrassing.

He laughed it off. "Looks like I did." He rubbed the spot, but it wouldn't come off. "I guess I can work on that later. Anyway, don't just sit there looking pretty, take a sip."

Emma was about to take a sip and then stopped.

"What?" Lance asked, confused.

"Why are you doing all this?" Emma asked.

"All what?"

She gestured to her bandaged knee and then held up the smoothie. "All . . . *this?*"

Lance thought about it for a moment. The truth was he had done those things without even thinking about it. It felt natural.

"Well . . ." Lance shrugged. "I guess I like you."

The temperature was going up by the second, which made little sense since Emma had been enjoying the cool breeze in the shade underneath the tree. Okay, maybe it made sense. Her cheeks were burning, and she was sure they had to be as red as a stop sign.

And that's what she needed to do.

Stop!

She couldn't be doing this with Lance—whatever they were doing. One moment she was spying on the man and the next she was having a smoothie with him and enjoying the company of his dog. Then there was that feeling she got whenever he touched her.

What was that?

Stop!

Emma needed to get herself together.

She wasn't even sure he was Lance, anyway. He had to be an imposter. The Lance she knew was an arrogant man. And bitter. A man with no heart and no soul, since he didn't believe in soulmates. This man in front of her was sweet, generous, funny, and good-looking. Okay, she would admit the other Lance was also good-looking, but it was overshadowed by all the bitterness and rude behavior that emanated from his pores like sap from a tree. A very pissed-off tree.

But this guy in front of her . . . He was something else.

First, he patched up her knee.

Then he bought her a smoothie.

Then he told her she was pretty *and* even admitted he liked her!

Emma closed her eyes and mentally cursed herself. She felt like she was in high school again, ready to tell her girlfriends she had a crush on Lance.

I hope he asks me to the prom.

This was getting ridiculous. She was forty years old!

Stop!

This was a train wreck, a car crash, and forest fire all rolled into one neatly packaged disaster.

Not good.

Not good at all.

"You look like you're having an aneurysm," he said. "Don't worry—Dr. Lance is here to help."

Emma snorted and threw her hand over her mouth.

"That's much better." He studied her for a moment. "Okay, I'll be bold and put it out there. Can I get your phone number and call you sometime?"

This was getting out of control and Emma had to put an end to this madness right now.

She shook her head. "Sorry, but I can't."

"Oh . . ." He stuffed his hands in his pockets. "You're . . . married?"

"No."

"Boyfriend?"

"No."

Lance scratched the side of his face. "Ahhh . . . I know. You've given up on men because you think they're all pigs."

She wanted to say *bingo*, but that would have been a lie. The truth was most of the guys she'd dated had been marriage material, according to the people around her. Not that she'd disagreed, but she hadn't wanted to keep seeing them to find out.

Or was too scared to keep seeing them, was more like it.

The future was a mystery for most people, but she had the ability to see things, including things that involved her. Specifically, relationships. After seeing in advance what would happen to her parents, she didn't want to know her own future. She ended relationships before she got in too deep.

Lance was staring at her and she needed to give him an answer.

"It's complicated," Emma said, petting Typo one more time before setting him on the ground and standing up. "I should go. Thanks again for everything." She turned and dropped her purse, the contents falling out onto the grass. Her keys, her phone, her wallet, her gym membership card, her Jamba Juice rewards card. Everything. "I'm so clumsy."

"I can help you," Lance said.

"That's not necessary," she said, grabbing everything and stuffing it back into her purse. She stood back up. "Okay. I need to run."

Lance stood. "You can't go now."

"Why not?"

"Because . . ." He grinned. "You'll miss the tail wagging contest."

Emma laughed. "Is there *really* a tail wagging contest?"

"Okay, maybe not, but there is a dance contest."

Emma raised an eyebrow. "A dance contest for dogs?"

He nodded and pointed to Typo. "And this little guy's going to win. You should see his moves."

Emma glanced down at Typo and then back up at Lance. "You're just saying that to get me to stay."

"I am," Lance said, chuckling. "But it's also the truth. Watch this." Lance pulled a sandwich-size Ziploc bag from his front pocket, opened it, and reached in for a treat. "Typo, do you want to dance?"

Typo barked and sat in front of Lance.

Emma laughed. "Yeah. He's a real natural. What a dancer."

Lance waved his finger at her. "Now, now . . . quiet down in the audience, please. Did you ever stop to think this might be his starting position?"

"Oh . . ." Emma couldn't tell if Lance was serious.

Can dogs dance?

They were smart, but she'd never seen one dance before.

Lance held up the treat.

"Ready?" Lance asked, one hundred percent of his concentration on the dog.

Typo barked again.

"Good boy," Lance said. "And . . . cha cha!"

Emma blinked. "Cha cha?"

Sure enough, right before her eyes, Typo jumped up on his hind legs and was dancing.

And he was doing the cha cha!

"No way," Emma mumbled to herself, pulling the cell phone from her purse. She pressed the video button and recorded. "This is crazy. I've never seen such a thing."

"Two, three, cha, cha, cha," Lance directed, his eyes focused on Typo. "Two, three, cha, cha, cha."

Typo moved in sync with Lance's commands, his balance and moves perfect.

A few people stopped to watch and clap along. A few others took out their phones and recorded the dance. Typo ignored them all and their dogs. His eyes were on the prize. The treat.

"Two, three, cha, cha, cha," Lance continued to instruct. "Two, three, cha, cha, cha." A minute later, he tossed the treat up high in the air. "Good boy!"

Typo leaped into the air and caught the treat, practically swallowing it whole before he hit the ground.

Emma clapped her hands, along with the crowd that had gathered. "He's incredible!"

"How could I not love this guy?" Lance said.

Emma bent down and kissed the dog on the head. "You're an amazing dog. How did you get those moves?"

"His dad taught him."

Emma stood back up and cocked her head to the side. "You taught him?"

"Who else?"

She analyzed him from head to toe and back up to his head. Like that would give her a clue if he was lying or not. Was the man a dancer?

"What?" Lance said. "You don't believe me? Okay, I guess you need proof." He took a few steps back and danced. "Two, three, cha, cha, cha. Two, three, cha, cha, cha."

Emma couldn't help but drop her gaze downward as Lance's hips moved back and forth with each step he took.

Good God, he could move.

Typo joined in the fun, dancing with Lance as he continued to call out, "Two, three, cha, cha, cha."

Emma was well-aware her mouth was hanging open, and she needed to snap out of it. What was she doing? Having fun with the enemy? That was not allowed! She needed to make an escape before she got in trouble and started liking the man!

Maybe it was too late.

Emma stood and gestured toward the exit. "I should go. I need to . . . get back to work."

"Okay," Lance said, cutting off his dance and tossing Typo another treat. "What do you do for a living?"

Emma was surprised by the question. How was she going to answer that?

I find people soulmates, something you don't believe in.

Right. Like she would say that.

Emma thought about it for a moment. "I work in . . . human resources."

It wasn't exactly a lie.

She was technically a resource for humans looking for love.

"Well, have fun," Emma added.

"How about if I send you a text?" Lance blurted out.

Emma stared at him. "A text . . ."

"Yeah," Lance said. "You won't let me call you, so a text is less intrusive. And after we exchange a few texts, you can decide if I'm worthy of being upgraded to phone call privileges. I do want to warn you, though. It may be very difficult to resist my charm."

His wink and grin almost knocked her over.

Lance was definitely interested in her.

This couldn't be happening.

"It must mean something that we ran into each other again, right?" he added.

Emma arched an eyebrow. "You made it clear in your book you don't believe in destiny."

He thought about it for a moment. "I think destiny is different than serendipity."

She nodded. "You think our seeing each other again was serendipity?"

He shrugged. "It could very well be. Who knows? I'm willing to explore the topic."

Emma broke eye contact with him. "My schedule is crazy busy—I don't have the time."

"Oh," Lance said. "But you have time to eat baked ziti and go to canine events?"

Wonderful.

He caught her in another lie. She needed to stop doing that, and she needed to make an escape.

"Thanks again for everything," Emma said, smiling and turning to walk away.

"Let's make a deal!" he called out from behind.

Emma stopped and turned around. "What?"

"A deal." Lance took a few steps toward her. "You and me."

She crossed her arms. "What kind of deal?"

"Simple. If we run into each other again, you give me your phone number."

Emma sighed. "Look—I'm flattered. But I doubt we will ever see each other again. It's a huge city, and this was a coincidence. The chances are better of you winning the lottery."

He grinned again. "Then you have nothing to lose, do you? If we ever see each other again, I get your phone number and we go out on a date. Deal?"

She studied him for a long beat, wondering if this would backfire on her. "Fine. Deal."

CHAPTER NINE

"This is what it has come to," Peter said, shaking his head at Lance as he took another bite of his baked ziti. "My best friend has lost his mind. Congratulations."

"What are you talking about?" Lance said.

"Crazy. Bonkers. Nuts. Do you get it now?"

"Not even a little," Lance said, grabbing a piece of garlic bread and biting into it.

"Loco."

"Spanish," Lance said, nodding his appreciation. "Nice touch."

"I'm serious."

Lance hadn't planned on telling Peter about Emma, but how could he not tell him the entire story after he saw the *amore* sign when they walked into the Italian deli today. That was a complete shock, since he was sure the sign hadn't been there the other night. Plus, they were both eating baked ziti at the same table where Lance had met Emma two days earlier.

Truth be told, Emma had been on Lance's mind nonstop

since he had seen her at Bark in the Park. There was just something about that woman. Not only something familiar, but something he was very much attracted to.

"Listen," Peter said, not getting Lance's hint that he didn't want to discuss it anymore. "By pursuing Emma, you'll lose the challenge and that won't be good for your career!"

"I would love to thank the person who invented this dish," Lance said, taking another bite of his new favorite Italian food. "Mr. Ziti is a genius."

Hopefully, Peter would take the bait this time.

"There is no Mr. Ziti, so quit trying to change the subject," Peter said. "Stop eating and look at me."

Lance swallowed, wiped his mouth, and looked up at Peter. "Yes?"

"We've got a lot riding on this."

"You worry too much."

"And you don't worry enough. What are you doing?"

Lance was about to take another bite of the baked ziti, but instead placed his fork on the edge of the plate and sighed. "You're getting all worked up over nothing. Even if anything were to happen between me and Emma, it doesn't have zippo to do with Madam Love because Emma is not and will never be my soulmate. Soulmates don't exist, remember? Haven't you read my book?"

"Very funny."

"You act like I'm getting ready to marry the woman," Lance said. "I just want to go out with her. I find her attractive, that's all. And you're forgetting I need to run into her again in order for me to get her number and a first date. The chances are slim, right? She even said it herself, this is a big city."

"Nice try. You saw her gym card. You know where she works out. I'd say the chances are good that you'll show up at her gym and find her there."

Lance wasn't going to tell Peter he had already thought of that and had it as a backup plan.

Although he was curious to see if he would run into Emma again by coincidence first.

Or by serendipity, as he had told her.

He smiled at the thought of her expression when he'd mentioned serendipity.

"Get that grin off your face," Peter said. "You need to focus. And what's so special about her, anyway?"

Lance shrugged. "She's . . . mysterious."

Peter raised an eyebrow. "If you're looking for mystery, watch a rerun of *Murder, She Wrote* and stay away from her."

"Okay, maybe she's more than mysterious. She's interesting, and smart, and attractive. Sexy. But that's all I will give her credit for." Lance chuckled and took another bite.

"People get married and spend the rest of their lives together for a lot less than that."

Lance sat up straight and looked over Peter's shoulder when he thought he saw a woman with short blonde hair enter the restaurant. Was it Emma?

No such luck.

"No way," Peter said. "Is that why you insisted on coming to this place? You were hoping to run into her again. Admit it."

"No." *Kind of.*

"Right," Peter said, shaking his head and taking a sip of his iced tea. "How long have I known you?" He took another sip of his iced tea.

"Too long. In fact, I think it's time we broke up. It's not you—it's me."

Peter coughed and threw his hand over his mouth, iced tea dripping from his chin.

Lance jumped up and smacked Peter on the back a few times. "Breathe, man, breathe."

Peter patted his own chest and cleared his throat, reaching for some water and taking a sip. "Don't say things like that when I have my mouth full."

Lance laughed and sat back down. "You get all choked up when I talk about leaving you."

"You'll never leave me. I'm all you've got."

That wasn't far from the truth.

Lance didn't have many friends at all—more like a few acquaintances. Lance and Peter had been through a lot together. High school. College. Lance was Peter's best man at his wedding. Peter would have been Lance's best man if weren't for the fact that Karla had broken up with him one week before the wedding. All because of that fortune teller.

Lance's thoughts wandered to Madam Love and then he checked his watch. "Crap." He took the last two bites of his baked ziti and stood. "Gotta run."

"Where are you going?" Peter said.

Lance wiped his mouth and dropped the napkin on the table. "I wanted to stop by Madam Love's office. She'll be there for another fifteen minutes."

"Don't tell her about Emma," Peter said. "In fact, forget about Emma."

Right.

Like it was that easy.

"I want to meet a hunky Italian firefighter who will serve me breakfast in bed in his Italian villa," the woman said to Emma. "Make sure he loves puppies and wine and chocolate. While we're at it, make sure he's got some money. I've had my eye on an amazing Dolce and Gabbana heart-patch floral dress from Nordstrom that I simply can't afford. He needs to know how much it would mean for me to have that dress."

Here we go again.

"It doesn't work that way," Emma said, opening up her appointment book for the potential client who had just walked in. "But I'll point you toward your soulmate when we get together. I promise. How's Tuesday morning at ten?"

"Sure," the woman said, losing some of her enthusiasm.

The door hadn't even closed all the way after the woman walked out when Lance pushed it back open and stepped inside.

"Stop right there," Emma said, pointing her finger at him like it was a gun.

Lance stopped in his tracks and threw his arms up in the air, surrendering.

"If you came here again to call me a fraud or to criticize me or my business, you can just turn right back around. And I'm okay if the door hits you on the way out. Preferably in the head."

That sounded harsher than Emma intended, but it was too late to take it back.

Lance grinned and took a seat in the leather chair, kicking his feet up on the ottoman. "Nice to see you, too. Do you always talk to your clients that way?"

Emma felt guilty. "Sorry. You bring it out in me."

"Well, if I bring it out in you that just means it was already there in the first place, wasn't it? Before I arrived. Before we even met. Sounds like you have some unresolved issues."

Don't let him push my buttons. He's doing it on purpose.

"Can I help you?" she said, trying to remain calm.

Lance laced his fingers together behind his head and stretched. "You already have."

What was he talking about? And why did he look so relaxed? Where was the hostile, arrogant Lance Parker she despised? She was sure it would be only a matter of time before the real Lance would surface and annoy her. Any second now.

"I'm here to thank you," he said.

"Thank me?" Emma said. "I didn't know that word was part of your vocabulary."

Lance laughed. "You need to relax more. Have you tried meditating?"

"You meditate?"

"No, but that doesn't mean you shouldn't."

She laughed, but then cut herself off when she realized she had laughed more than a few times with him at Bark in the Park. The last thing she needed was for him to recognize her laugh and figure out that Madam Love was Emma.

"Anyway, yes, I want to thank you. I met someone at Bark in the Park."

She knew he was talking about her. This could get weird. What was she going to do now? She had to think of something and fast.

"She's not the one," Emma said.

"What?" Lance said, a look of confusion on his face. "Why

would you say that? You don't even know who I'm talking about. You haven't even met her."

If you only knew.

"I know who you're talking about," Emma said. "She's not the one. Seriously. Forget about her."

Lance just stared at her. "How can I forget about her when I ran into her twice? That's a sign because you told me to go to both places. She was also in the restaurant where I ate the baked ziti. Not the obsessed fan, but the other one. I don't think we've talked much about her, but there something about her that I like. She's a little mysterious. Maybe even a little shy."

Emma snorted.

She'd been called a lot of things over the years, but *shy* was never one of them.

"I'm serious," Lance said, pulling his feet off the ottoman and sitting forward in his chair. "She's got a*mazing* blue eyes, a lot like yours, actually, but she doesn't wear that ridiculous makeup."

"Hey! Are you going to start with that crap again?"

"Sorry," Lance said. "You bring it out in me." He winked. "Anyway, I have a good feeling about her. And although she wouldn't give me her phone number, she agreed to go out with me if I ran into her again, which will happen. Where will I see her again?"

"It's best if you focus on the other woman from Bark in the Park. The one you met in line at the smoothie booth."

Lance cocked his head to the side. "How do you know about her?"

"You told me," Emma lied, hoping he would buy it. "You said you met two people at Bark in the Park."

"I did?"

"Of course," Emma lied again. "How else would I know? Anyway, forget about the one with the short blonde hair. She's not the one. Besides, you'll never see her again, so it's best not to pin your hopes on destiny."

"Well, I have a backup plan in case the destiny falls through."

"What sort of backup plan?"

"I know where she works out."

How had he found out? Emma was certain she'd never mentioned the name of the gym when they were together. She would have remembered that.

"What are you talking about?"

Lance grinned. "She dropped her purse, and I saw her gym membership card."

"You saw her . . ."

No! That's cheating!

This was getting worse by the minute and Emma had to end his hopes because she couldn't avoid the gym forever. Especially since Randy kept feeding her those amazing cupcakes!

"You can't force these things," Emma said. "You going to her gym is not allowing the universe to unfold its plan naturally."

Lance arched an eyebrow. "You said on the radio that sometimes a little help is needed in these situations. Anyway, she dropped her purse and the membership card fell out *naturally*. I didn't do anything wrong or force it to fall out. I didn't steal it or do something unscrupulous to find out where she worked out. It just happened. Sounds like it was meant for me to see that card."

"We need to do another reading."

"That's unnecessary," Lance said. "I told you. I have a great feeling about—"

"Now!" Emma said.

She passed through the hanging beads and turned on the battery-powered candles she had turned off earlier after what was supposed to be her last reading of the day. She grabbed the crystal ball and placed it on the table, taking a deep breath and waiting for Lance to come in.

A few seconds later, Lance entered the room and sat on the red loveseat. "This isn't—"

"Sit." Emma closed her eyes. "Let's begin." She took a deep breath and let it out slowly. She held the crystal ball in the palms of her hands for a few moments to energize it, and then placed it back on the table, leaning over to stare at it intently.

Emma held her gaze there, not blinking. A minute later she got the answer she had been hoping for. A very clear image of where Lance needed to be the next day.

She smiled. "Got it."

"Please tell me I need to eat more of that baked ziti," Lance said. "That stuff is addictive."

Emma shook her head. "Not even close. You need to go to the farmers' market this weekend. The one downtown. She will be there. Your soulmate."

"Emma?"

"No. Why do you think Emma is your soulmate when you don't even believe in soulmates?"

"I never said Emma was my soulmate. You did. You said she would be at the farmers' market."

"No. I said your soulmate would be at the farmers' market. Not Emma."

"Aren't they the same person?"

"No!"

"You really do need to meditate. You seem very uptight and stressed lately."

"I'm not uptight!"

"Okay, let me ask you this," Lance said. "If Emma is there at the farmers' market tomorrow, would you believe she's my soulmate? I mean, that would be three times in a row you sent me somewhere, and she was there. That has to mean something."

"It seems like you're already convinced she's your soulmate. Are you willing to admit publicly that you lost the challenge?"

Lance threw his hands in the air. "Whoa. Slow down. I didn't say that at all. I was just asking your opinion on the matter. I'm fascinated with Emma, that's all."

He had to stop doing that. It was odd hearing him use her name. Even more odd saying he was fascinated with her. Yes, a woman could get used to compliments like that, but she needed to stay focused. She really didn't understand what was going on. Was she losing her gift? It typically wasn't this difficult to find someone a soulmate. In fact, most of the time it was easy.

"Go to the farmers' market. Your soulmate will be there. Not Emma. Someone else."

And Emma would lock herself in her house to make sure she was nowhere near the farmers' market. Maybe she needed to take a red-eye out of the country. Then he would realize she wasn't his soulmate.

"I think this is a complete waste of time, but where is she going to be?" Lance said. "That farmers' market is huge."

"I can't tell you that."

Lance let out a deep breath. "Here we go again."

"Would you just go? When you're there, all you have to do is gravitate toward things that naturally pique your interest. Things you enjoy. If you see something you like, buy it. If someone offers you a sample, try it. If something seems off, follow your gut. Come back and see me on Monday with an update. And remember to go with the flow."

"Go with the flow. Right. Just like last time . . ." He sighed as he walked out.

A few seconds after the door closed, someone pushed it back open.

It was Randy, and he was carrying a Tupperware container. "I only have a minute, but I wanted you to try this. It's very important that I get your opinion."

Emma walked around the reception counter. "You really need to stop doing this."

Randy opened the container and pulled out a cupcake, holding it in front of Emma's nose.

"You're cruel," Emma said. "Have I told you that?"

Randy smiled. "Almost every time we see each other." He pointed to the cupcake. "Meet my latest creation, the apple pie cupcake. Ta-da!"

Emma licked her lips. "You're kidding me."

He shook his head. "I never joke about cupcakes. White cake with cinnamon, apple pie filling, topped with cream cheese icing. You won't be able to say no."

"You know me all too well," Emma said, grabbing the cupcake from Randy. "I'm changing the locks so you can't get in here anymore." She took a bite and moaned, talking with a mouthful. "How do you do it? This is amazing."

"Two thumbs up?"

"I would give you more, but I'm fresh out of extra thumbs this week."

He laughed and set the Tupperware container down on the counter. "Glad you like them. And you'll be happy to know I took your advice, and I got a booth to sell them at the farmers' market this weekend. I have to admit I'm a little excited about it."

"That's wonderful!" Emma said, stepping forward to hug Randy. "I have a good feeling about this. Make sure you make plenty because you're going to sell out."

"Thanks, but we'll see how it goes. I like the idea of starting small to gauge interest. If things go well, I can expand into catering weddings, parties, and corporate events."

"Believe me—you're going to be a big hit. Soon all the local shops and cafes will carry your cupcakes. I can see you going nationwide."

"Well, let's see how it goes this weekend. One step at a time. That's why I wanted your opinion. I think the apple pie cupcake is perfect to show what I can do."

Emma grabbed another cupcake from the container and took a bite. "I agree. You'll be a smashing success. I can already see it, even without my crystal ball."

"Hey, why don't you come to the farmers' market? It would be great to have you there. Especially since you have been one of my biggest cheerleaders. And my official taste tester."

Emma didn't see a problem with going to the farmers' market, as long as it wasn't the same farmers' market that Lance was going to.

"Which farmers' market?"

"The one downtown."

No way. Not going to happen!

"Are you okay?" Randy said. "You got a little pale suddenly."

"I'm okay," Emma said. "Thanks for the invite, but I need to finish up some things I've been procrastinating on. In case you haven't heard my landlord raised the rent on me."

Randy winced. "Sorry. Well, if something changes, come see me at the farmers' market."

Not in a million years.

It was six in the morning when the alarm went off, practically sending Emma into a coronary. She was clueless why it had gone off, considering she'd never set the alarm. Especially on the weekends. Maybe the power had gone out and everything reset. She reached over in her bed and tried to turn it off, but the alarm wouldn't stop. Was she dreaming?

"Stop!" Emma yelled, now banging on the top of the clock radio.

That's when she realized it wasn't the alarm, but her private cell phone ringing.

She reached over and answered it without looking at the caller ID. "Hello?"

"Emma—it's Randy. There's been an emergency and I need your help."

She sat up in bed. "Are you okay?" She wiped her eyes with one hand and then leaned over to click on the light. "Randy? Are you there?"

"Yes. I'm here and I'm okay, but the property may not be

doing so well. There was a plumbing leak, and the damage looks bad."

This couldn't be happening. Any damage to her place would be a nightmare since all of her things were there. The crystal ball, her color-coordinated furniture and decor, all of her Madam Love outfits, her laptop. Everything. And now she couldn't even remember how much of it was covered by insurance. But even if it was covered by insurance, how long would it take to get everything up and running again? The clock was working against her with the rent raise breathing down her back and the lack of funds in her bank account.

"Please tell me my office is okay," Emma said.

Please, please, please.

"Sorry—I should have been more specific. It's a different property in Los Angeles."

"Oh . . ."

Emma had no idea Randy had another property in Los Angeles. And what did it have to do with her? Why was he even calling her then? Maybe it was because it was six in the morning, but she was confused.

"Are you there, Emma?"

"Yeah . . . So, why exactly are you calling me?"

"I need your help. I spent all night baking cupcakes in anticipation of selling them at the farmers' market. All the ones you love, I made them. Now I can't go to the farmers' market. I have to fly to LA."

She still didn't get it. "You want me to eat all the cupcakes? No way, Randy."

Randy chuckled. "You're obviously still sleeping. I'm asking you the very big favor of taking my cupcakes to the farmers' market and selling them for me today."

Normally, Emma was all about helping friends who were in a pinch. She wouldn't think twice about it. But this would not happen. She had told Lance to go to the same farmers' market and she had the plan of staying a million miles away from it. No way. Plus, she needed to be available for any last-minute bookings. Call her crazy, but paying the rent was more important than helping a friend. She couldn't do it.

"Sorry, Randy. I can't. I need to work or I won't have enough money to pay the rent."

Plus, if Lance saw her again he would think it was serendipity. And she had promised her phone number and a date if it happened.

It wasn't going to happen.

Not now. Not ever.

"But this is work!" Randy said. "Of course, I will pay you for your time. You think I would send you out there and work for nothing?"

"No, but—"

"How about I delay the rent increase for another month? Does that work for you?"

Emma stared at the phone. "Pardon me?"

"You heard me. Sell my cupcakes at the farmers' market today and I will delay your rent increase for another month. Plus, I'll pay you for your time."

"But what about John? He was pressuring you to raise my rent."

"You let me handle my brother. Besides, he's not much of a business partner. He just told me he's taking off to Fiji for a month, can you believe that? Anyway, he'll be distracted, so don't you worry about him. What do you say?"

How could she say no? All she had to do was sell cupcakes

today and she wouldn't have to worry about her dwindling bank account for another month. By then she would win the challenge with Lance and have plenty of clients to make up for the rent increase. Finding Lance a soulmate was proving to be a pain in her butt. Then there was the problem of having to give Lance her phone number if he saw her at the farmers' market. She couldn't let that happen. How could Lance find his soulmate if he was going out on a date with Emma?

Wait a minute.

Emma could text Lance and tell him she had made a mistake with her reading, and that he needed to go to a different farmers' market.

The plan was genius.

"Are you in?" Randy said. "The clock is ticking and I don't have anyone else to turn to. Please help me."

"Okay," Emma said, feeling relieved. "I'll do it."

CHAPTER TEN

"What am I doing here?" Lance mumbled to himself as he wandered through the farmers' market, not sure what he was looking for.

Gravitate toward things that naturally pique your interest. Things you enjoy. If you see something you like, buy it. If someone offers you a sample, try it.

He wondered if Madam Love made up the instructions just to get rid of him. What kind of advice was that? Maybe he was supposed to spend and spend and spend until someone magically appeared in front of him with a sign that said, *Hey Bozo! I'm your soulmate!* He hoped he ran into Emma so he could prove Madam Love wrong.

Still, he would follow her advice. Again.

"What piques my interest?" Lance said to himself. "That is the question."

Lance glanced over at the gourmet pastries booth. Sure, they caught his attention. He had a serious sweet tooth, although he wasn't sure if any of those pastries would be sweet enough for him. He eyed the tall woman handing a croissant to a customer, wondering if she was the one. His soulmate.

He chuckled at the thought.

You don't have a soulmate, dummy.

A tall man dressed in black walked up and kissed the pastry lady on the cheek.

Not her, obviously.

The next booth had fresh strawberries. Sure, fresh strawberries piqued his interest, too. And they were offering samples.

Lance grabbed the end of the toothpick that was stabbed into one of the strawberry samples and took a bite of the fruit, chewing and nodding his approval, even though he wasn't that impressed with the flavor.

"They're organic," the woman said, pointing to the strawberries. "Locally grown."

Lance nodded and noticed the giant rock on her finger.

Not her, either.

Lance thanked the woman for the sample, but the strawberries weren't even sweet, so there was no way he would buy a basket. He didn't tell the woman that, though.

He walked by the handmade soaps, the farm fresh eggs, the handmade tamales, and the fresh-cut flowers.

That's when he spotted it.

The holy grail.

The booth that piqued his interest.

Lance walked toward the giant pink canvas sign that said, *Randy Dandy's Cupcakes.*

He eyed the rows and rows of one of life's greatest inventions. If nothing happened today, at least he would enjoy one of his favorite treats in the world.

"What kind are they?" Lance said to the woman who had her head under the table.

"Apple pie cupcakes. White cake with cinnamon, apple pie filling, topped with cream cheese icing."

She had the oddest voice. Nasally. Like Donald Duck with a sinus infection.

"These look amazing," Lance said.

"Thank you," she said, still under the table looking for something.

Lance opened his wallet and pulled out a ten-dollar bill. "I'll take one to start." He chuckled. "I may be back for more."

There was a loud bang, and the table shook.

"Ouch!" the woman said.

"Are you okay?" Lance said. "Do you need help with something?"

"No!" she said. "Just . . . uh . . . leave the money on the table."

Lance glanced at his ten-dollar bill and then leaned forward to see what the woman was doing. He couldn't tell because she was almost underneath the table. Maybe she spilled something.

Still, there was no way he would pay ten dollars for a cupcake. It didn't matter how good they were. The sign said three dollars for one cupcake and that's what he would pay.

"All I have is a ten," Lance said. "Do you have change?"

The woman's hand appeared above the table and moved in different directions like she was trying to swat a fly. "Your cupcake is free today. You're the five hundredth customer. Congratulations. Have a great day."

Lance stared at the ten-dollar bill, now more confused than ever. First, she said leave the money on the table and then she said it was free.

Weird.

He knew cupcakes were popular, but there was no way he was the five hundredth customer of the day. The farmers' market had just opened and he would guess that there were barely five hundred people in the entire place.

"Free?" Lance said. "Are you sure?"

"Yes. Thank you."

Lance hesitated, wondering why she was thanking him for taking a free cupcake. "Okay. Well . . . thank *you*."

There was no way he would turn down a free cupcake. He walked past the hummus and pita chip booth with the cupcake and then looked back toward Randy Dandy's Cupcakes. The woman was still under the table.

So weird.

He shook his head and then pulled back the paper from the side of the cupcake, taking the first bite. "Wow."

The cupcake was just as good as it looked and smelled. No. Better.

He took another bite and another. Then it was gone—just like that. The apple pie cupcake was out of this world and he had to have another, but this time he would insist on paying. He flipped around and took a few steps toward the booth, then stopped and froze.

The cupcake woman was no longer under the table.

She handed change to a customer and then glanced in Lance's direction.

She also froze, looking just as shocked as Lance.

It was Emma.

No! No! No! This can't be happening. What is he still doing here?

Emma couldn't believe Lance was there. He was supposed to be at the Ferry Plaza farmers' market. She'd sent him a text. Couldn't the man follow simple instructions?

She thought she had succeeded in hiding from Lance when she first saw him. She even came up with the brilliant idea of plugging her nose to disguise her voice. Her second brilliant idea was to give him a free cupcake to get rid of him. It wasn't as smooth as she had hoped since she banged her head on the table. She was sure it would bruise, but it was worth it since Lance had walked away as she peeked through the seam of the table cover from underneath. She had seen him walk past the hummus booth and figured he was on his way out of the farmers' market.

That was supposed to be the end of it.

But it wasn't the end of it.

Not even close.

Why had he come back? It didn't matter now. And it was too late to duck back underneath the table since he had already recognized her and was walking toward her with a big stupid grin on his face.

"Looks like I just won the lottery," Lance said, his grin getting wider. "Can you believe this?"

"No," Emma said. "I can't."

She blew it and would now have to give him her phone number and go out with him.

Unless he didn't mention it.

Even better, maybe he would forget.

Emma threw him a fake smile as if it was no big deal that this was the third time they had run into each other.

He pulled out his cell phone. "I would *love* another cupcake, but first I would like to get your phone number, per our deal." He chuckled. "As crazy as this sounds, I kind of had a feeling I would run into you again."

She swallowed hard. "This doesn't really count."

"What do you mean it doesn't count? Of course, it does."

"No. It doesn't." She forced a smile toward a customer who picked out a cupcake and handed her three dollars. "Thanks so much. Enjoy."

The customer walked away and Emma placed the money in the metal box. Then she arranged the dollar bills, so they were all lined up.

Lance asked again. "What do you mean it doesn't count?"

Emma crossed her arms. "I wasn't even supposed to be here. A friend asked me to help out at the last minute. I don't normally sell cupcakes."

"I know. You told me. You work in human resources."

That lie would come back to haunt her, she was sure of it.

"What friend?" Lance asked, looking up at the banner advertising the business. "Let me guess . . . Randy Dandy?"

She nodded. "If I were going about my normal life, this would've never happened. I wouldn't be here."

He grinned. "And yet you're here. Sounds like serendipity to me." He raised his cell phone again.

"What?" Emma said, playing dumb.

"Your phone number?"

She hesitated. "Oh . . . I wish I could, but I . . . lost my phone, actually. Can you believe that? Phones are so overrated anyway, aren't they? I may not even replace it!"

It had to be the most pathetic excuse, but that was all she could come up with.

"You lost your phone?"

She pretended to straighten out a few of the cupcakes that didn't need to be straightened out. "Yup. Sure did. That's right."

"Oh," he said, nodding and staring at the table. "That's why you were under the table earlier. You were looking for your phone?"

"That's right."

The lies just kept piling up.

"Why does your voice sound different now?"

Just her luck.

He was the one man in the world who actually paid attention.

"Well, I was under the table, so I'm not surprised it sounded different."

He stared at her for a few moments. "Well, how about this? Give me your phone number and I'll call it. I'm sure we can track your phone down." He winked at her and then tapped the screen on his phone.

He knew she was lying.

Someone needed to wipe that grin off his face.

"Hang on," Lance said. "I just realized my phone isn't even on." He pressed the power button and waited.

His phone wasn't on!

No wonder he was there at the downtown farmers' market.

He never got her text message this morning.

Wonderful.

He smiled again and handed her his phone. "Here you go."

All she could do now was give him the number because she was fresh out of excuses. She hesitated and then tapped her phone number into his phone, handing it back to him.

"So, how many more cupcakes would you like?" she said, trying to sound natural as he stared at the phone in his hand.

Please don't dial it now.

If he dialed her phone number, she would be caught red-handed because her phone was going to ring. She was almost certain she didn't have it in silent mode.

Don't dial, don't dial, don't dial.

"Hang on," Lance said, not looking up from his phone and tapping the screen.

A few seconds later her phone rang.

He smiled and looked over at her purse on the table. "Well, look at that. Looks like I found your phone. It was inside your purse, where most women keep their phones. Go figure."

"That's amazing," she said, trying to sound surprised, but knowing she failed miserably. She reached for the purse and pulled out the phone, but it was her business phone. She set the phone down on the table and reached inside for the other phone, pressing a button to silence it.

Lance arched an eyebrow. "You have two phones."

She forced a smile. "One personal and the other for work."

He nodded. "I don't think I've ever met anyone who had a separate cell phone for work. You must have a very important job. Who do you do human resources for? The FBI? The CIA?"

Emma smirked. "That's confidential."

Lance chuckled. "Of course. And now that we have the

mystery of the missing phone solved, I have one question for you."

"What's that?"

"What are you doing tomorrow night?"

"Tomorrow night?"

"Yeah. I would like to take you out. On a date."

Emma held up her index finger. "Can you excuse me for just one second?"

"Are you going to get under the table again?" He chuckled.

"No, I'm *not* going to get under the table again," she said, even though she had thought of it. She grabbed a cupcake and handed it to him. "Another one on the house, Mr. Smarty Pants."

Lance took a bite of the cupcake and moaned. "I should be a smarty pants more often if it means I get free cupcakes."

Emma turned around and pretended to look for something in a box while Lance was distracted with the cupcake. She needed time to figure out her options, even though she was sure she had none. Time was running out. Lance was nowhere near finding his soulmate, and she had to do something about it. Her gifts were failing her. How could that be? Her success rate with other clients was impeccable, so why weren't they working with Lance? Something about this guy was throwing her off her game. For the briefest moment she wondered if she was his soulmate since she had been everywhere she had sent him.

She immediately shook that thought from her brain.

Don't be ridiculous.

One thing was for sure, she had to find out why Lance wasn't meeting his soulmate. Maybe if she got closer to him she could see what the problem was. Was he scaring his soulmate away? She was going to find out. The sooner the better. Otherwise, she was going to lose the challenge.

Emma turned and gave Lance a smile. "Tomorrow night sounds great."

CHAPTER ELEVEN

Emma removed her Madam Love outfit and makeup and then pulled a simple, red, twenty-year-old blouse over her head. Then she slipped into an old pair of blue jeans. Well, maybe "slipped into" wasn't the right phrase for getting on her jeans. She pulled and yanked and tugged. She really needed to stop eating those cupcakes. Not such an easy task when they tasted so good. Even Lance had eaten three of them at the farmers' market.

Lance.

The man had a lot to learn about dating if he thought taking Emma to a bar for their first date was romantic. No wonder the man was single. Did he want her to sing karaoke? He was dreaming. Tequila shots? No way. The only thing he said about their date was to make sure she wore something she wouldn't mind getting a little dirty. At a bar? The only thing Emma could do was cross her fingers and give him the benefit of the doubt.

One thing was for sure, she knew she had to be clear-headed. She would only allow herself one drink. Any more than that and she risked contracting a serious case of diarrhea of the mouth, which would lead her to spill all her deep, dark secrets. She couldn't imagine what would happen if he found out she was Madam Love. What a nightmare that would be. Her ruin.

One drink.

Twenty minutes later, Emma got off the bus and walked up Mission Street to the bar. Once inside she looked around for Lance, who had agreed to meet her near the front door. He wasn't there yet.

She glanced toward the busy bar with the giant monitors overhead showing a basketball game, then over to the row of booths that lined the opposite wall. Still no sign of Lance anywhere.

Was he going to be late for their first date?

The door opened behind her and she swung around to see if it was him.

My, my, my.

It was Lance, and she had to admit the man looked good. Handsome. Stunning.

"Hey there," Lance said, taking a few steps toward Emma. "You look gorgeous."

"You too," she said, taking a few seconds to admire the designer jeans and teal polo that surrounded his gorgeous body. "Although I'm surprised you're wearing *that* since you said wear something you wouldn't mind getting dirty."

"You're right—I said that. Wear something *you* wouldn't mind getting dirty. Not me. I'm not going to get dirty."

"I don't like the sound of that. I should go." She turned and pretended to walk away.

"I'm kidding!" Lance said, grabbing her hand and pulling her back.

BAM!

Lance followed Emma's gaze down to their interlocking hands. "Don't tell me you didn't feel that again."

"I didn't feel that, again," Emma lied.

He chuckled. "Right. Follow me. We need to hurry, so we get a good spot."

A good spot? What was he talking about?

Lance led her through the throngs of people toward the back of the building. She glanced down at her hand in his, wondering why he was still holding it. Considering the tingling sensations running up and down her body, the answer didn't matter.

They entered a large room in the back of the bar.

"Welcome," the woman said at the reception table. "You're here for Paint the Town Red?"

Emma glanced over at Lance for an answer.

"Yes," he answered. "I'm Lance Parker."

Had he really brought her to a painting event? What were the chances?

Painting used to be her life until—

Don't go there.

The woman ran her finger down the length of the list, finding Lance's name and checking it off. "Okay, find two open easels and get ready for some fun. Each station has an apron, paint, and brushes. Put on the apron and wait for Tom, the artist who'll be leading you this evening. Don't paint until he instructs you. Got it?"

"Got it," Lance said.

"Oh, and the waiter will be around shortly to take food and drink orders. Have fun!"

"Thank you," Lance said, turning to survey the room.

Emma glanced around the room at the blank canvases on the easels and the people putting on their aprons. "So . . . we're going to paint?"

Lance smiled. "Yes. Follow me."

"What if I don't know how to paint?"

It was a rhetorical question since she knew how to paint very well.

"That's not a requirement," Lance said. "That's why it's going to be fun. Trust me."

Emma followed him to the two open easels underneath the giant gold chandelier. They put on their aprons, and then ordered calamari, bruschetta, and two glasses of pinot.

Lance pointed to the painting of a sunset on display at the front of the room. "Looks like we'll be painting that. That doesn't look too difficult. It's just a simple sunset on a tropical beach with palm trees and white sand. Two people holding hands." He analyzed it further. "And two pelicans. Piece of cake. Are you up for it?"

"I am," Emma said, deciding against telling Lance she had years of painting experience. She wanted him to feel relaxed on their date, not intimidated. She wondered how it would feel to pick up a paintbrush again. It had been years since the last time.

After the waiter brought their appetizers and wine, a bearded man in a bright pink sweater walked to the front of the room.

He glanced down at his clipboard for a few seconds, then looked up and smiled. "Hello!"

"Hello!" everyone called back.

"Welcome to Paint the Town Red. My name is Tom and I will lead you step by step through this fun and creative evening. If you're all ready to paint, raise your hand or your drink and say yes!"

Lance and Emma clinked their wine glasses and raised them in the air. "Yes!"

"Great," Tom continued, pointing to the sunset painting. "Let's get started then. This is an original piece I painted last year. Take a minute to study the colors and the patterns before we begin. I will let you know it is much easier to paint than you think. It's called *serendipity* and I hope it inspires you."

Lance's face turned as white as the blank canvas in front of him.

"It's just a coincidence," Emma said.

"Or maybe it isn't," Lance said, swallowing hard and analyzing the painting.

"Just remember this isn't an art class, it's an art *party*," Tom said. "You're here to have fun, socialize, and drink. And in about three hours you'll go home with your very own masterpiece. Just follow my lead and you'll do just fine! First, we will start with the sky. Grab your brush and start with a little of the blue paint just like this."

The attendees watched as Tom dipped his brush in the blue paint and painted the sky.

"Here we go," Emma said, taking a deep breath.

She grabbed her paintbrush and dipped the bristles in the paint. She paused for a few moments, enjoying the feel of the brush between her fingers, and the smell of the paint. For her, painting was therapeutic. It was like revealing a little bit of her soul. She applied a few long strokes to the top part of the canvas that would eventually become the sky. The more she stroked, the more that wonderful, zen-like feeling came back. Vincent van Gogh said the only time he felt alive was when he was painting. She couldn't agree more.

She felt alive.

Emma glanced over at Lance, wondering why the man had picked painting as their first date. There were thousands of other options in the world that he could have chosen.

Coincidences like these made her nervous. It was a coincidence, right?

Emma dipped the brush again in the paint and reached for the canvas, spilling some on her apron. She needed relax and quit thinking so much.

Lance looked over and chuckled. "You don't waste any time getting dirty, do you?"

Emma held up the brush in his direction. "Wipe that smirk off your face unless you want some of this paint on your shirt."

"Consider it wiped."

She set the brush down and crossed her arms. "Stop snickering."

"Snickering means I'm already having fun," Lance said. "That's a compliment, since I'm with you."

"Nice try," Emma said, taking another sip of her wine. "But to be honest, you surprised me already this evening."

"Oh . . . You mean with my charm and intellect?"

Emma laughed. "Can you be serious for a moment?"

"I can. Watch this." He held a straight face for her.

"Very impressive. Anyway, I wasn't expecting *this*." She gestured around the room. "Painting on a date."

Lance dipped his brush into the blue paint. "Is that good or bad?"

"Good. Great, actually. Just what I needed."

He nodded. "I think this is the ideal situation for a first date."

"Why is that?"

He dipped his brush in the paint again. "If we have any awkward moments where the conversation isn't flowing well, we can always just say we were concentrating on the painting. Although I'm sure we won't have that problem."

His wink made her heart skip a beat.

He needed to stop doing that.

Lance was right, they didn't have any awkward moments over the next hour. They laughed and joked and chatted as if they had known each other for years. They drank wine, ate calamari and bruschetta, and were enjoying the painting. She wondered if the good time was attributed to the alcohol. She blew off the thought. If anything she felt less inhibited, which was a good thing. Still, she made a promise to herself and intended on keeping it.

One drink.

Emma glanced over at her wine glass to see how much she had left.

The glass was full again.

"Is everything okay?" Lance said.

"How did my wine glass get more wine in it?" Emma said.

Lance chuckled. "Magic."

She raised an eyebrow.

"You didn't see the waiter come by with a fresh glass?" he said.

"No." Emma thought about it for a second. "I guess I was concentrating on the painting."

He grinned. "Good one." He pointed to her glass. "Sorry. I assumed you would want another. I ordered it when you went to the restroom."

She glanced over at the wine again. "I shouldn't. It doesn't take much to get me tipsy and soon I'll be yapping my mouth off. You don't want that to happen and neither do I."

"That sounds like it could be very entertaining, but I understand." He looked around the room. "I'm sure I can find someone to give it to."

Now she felt bad. She knew how much he'd paid for the wine. It wasn't cheap.

Emma waved him off. "You know what? It's okay. I'll drink it."

"Are you sure? You don't have to."

"I'm sure." She grabbed the wine and took another sip. "Thank you."

Maybe Emma was making a big deal out of nothing. It was just one more drink. All she had to do was control her mouth and keep eating.

How hard could that be?

CHAPTER TWELVE

"What do you think?' Lance said, taking a step back to admire his painting. He knew Emma would be honest, especially after her second glass of wine.

Emma turned her head sideways and pointed. "What are . . . *those*?"

"Pelicans!" he said proudly. "Of course."

Emma blinked. "They look like two slaughtered chickens dropping from the sky."

Lance chuckled and glanced at his painting again. "Okay, I admit that maybe I used a little too much red paint."

"Pelicans aren't red." She dipped her brush in the black paint and stepped toward Lance's canvas. "Hang on. I can fix it."

"Don't you dare!" Lance said, laughing as he blocked Emma's path. He pointed to a spot on the floor near her easel. "You stay over there on your side. Don't cross that line."

Emma glanced down at the floor. "What line? There is no line."

"Of course, there is. Use your imagination."

"Like you did when you painted the pelicans red?" She jumped over Lance's imaginary line with her brush. He moved to block her again, causing Emma to do a face plant into Lance's chest.

Lance reached down and grabbed Emma's waist to keep her from falling over.

She felt good in his hands.

Amazing.

They locked eyes.

He was staring at an angel.

Emma blushed and stepped back, clearing her throat. "If you don't want my help, I guess you can just continue painting slaughtered chickens. Good thing there aren't children here. They would be traumatized for life."

Lance eyed his painting again and chuckled. He loved that Emma said what was on her mind. Most people would bite their lips on a first date, or would lie and say it looked great.

Not Emma.

"Tom said to explore our artistic sides," Lance said. "Well, that was me doing just that. The red is the color of the sunset reflecting off the bodies of the pelicans. Don't you see it?"

"You can't reflect the sun off feathers."

"Sure, I can." He gestured to his painting. "Look again. Now that you know what I was trying to do, can you see it this time?"

Emma glanced at his painting again, squinting. "I still see slaughtered chickens."

Lance laughed again. "Well, they say two people can look at the same painting and see something different. This is just one of those cases. Hang on, I'll prove it to you." Lance waved

Tom over and pointed to his red pelicans. "What do you see there, Tom?"

"Hmmm." Tom took a step closer and studied Lance's painting. "Two slaughtered chickens?"

"Exactly!" Emma said. "Thank you."

Lance laughed. "I stand corrected. I guess I can touch that up a little."

"Or a lot," Emma said.

Tom glanced over at Emma's painting. "This is exquisite." He glanced over at his own piece at the front of the room and then back to Emma's painting. "Your attention to detail is amazing. I love how you added the whitecaps to the water and the palm fronds on the sand to suggest it was a windy day. Impressive, actually."

"Thank you," Emma said.

"Have you had any formal training?"

Emma hesitated. "Does paint-by-numbers count?"

Tom laughed. "Call me crazy, but I have this feeling you've had much more extensive training than paint-by-numbers. I've seen successful commercial artists with less talent."

Lance smiled and gestured to Emma. "Maybe she needs to consider changing careers and opening up her own art gallery."

"Anything is possible," Tom said. "There are other careers, too. Animator, illustrator, even an art teacher like me. Something to think about."

"I will," Emma said. "Thank you."

After Tom walked away, Lance leaned in closer to Emma and whispered. "He looked a little jealous. Your painting is much better than the original."

Emma placed her hands on her hips. "You're just saying that to score points with me."

"And if I were saying it for that reason . . . am I scoring points with you?"

"No." Emma took another sip of her wine. "Maybe." She pointed to the floor and smirked. "Get back over on your side."

Lance threw her a salute. "Yes, ma'am."

He didn't think he could ever get tired of that smile.

So beautiful. And lips so kissable.

Emma must have read his mind. She flushed and turned away again to touch up one of the palm trees on her canvas.

"Seriously," Lance said. "Have you ever considered pursuing a different career? Painting sounds a lot more exciting than HR. No offense."

"None taken. When I was younger I was actually offered a job as an animator with a Hollywood studio, but I turned it down."

"How come? You could have been the genius behind *Shrek* or *Toy Story*."

Emma shrugged. "I didn't want to move to LA. It may sound like a lame excuse, but I wanted to play it safe."

"It's not lame. That's a big deal, picking up and moving to a different city. Plus, I don't think that would have been so good, now that I think of it."

Emma cocked her head to the side. "Why not?"

He grinned. "Because then you would have never graced me with your wonderful presence."

"Are you trying to score more points with me?"

"Trying . . . Speaking of scoring points—you haven't scored *any* with me," Lance said, trying to look pouty. "None."

"What did I do?" Emma said, matching his pout and setting her paintbrush back down.

"It's what you *didn't* do. You said if you drank more wine, you would become a sloppy drunk and tell me eye-opening things that would shock and amaze me. Except for insulting my beautiful, precious pelicans, you have been rather tame."

"First, I didn't say I would become a sloppy drunk. Just a little tipsy. Anyway, my mouth is behaving this evening. But my thoughts . . . that's another matter altogether."

Lance cocked his head to the side. "Please tell me about these thoughts."

"No."

"You can tell me."

"I can't," Emma said.

"Can't or won't?"

"Won't."

Lance smiled and touched up his pelicans a little more as he thought about how much he was enjoying Emma's company. She was being playful and flirty, but he was disappointed the night would come to an end soon. He wanted to spend more time with her. Much more time.

"I have an idea," Lance said. "I'll tell you my thoughts if you tell me yours."

Emma studied him for a moment. "Deal."

Lance grinned. "You first. What do you think about us?"

"Us?"

"Yeah," Lance said. "Do you think we're . . . compatible?"

She hesitated. "No."

"Why not?"

Emma opened her mouth and closed it.

"Just what I thought," Lance said. "You think we *are* compatible." He crinkled his nose, ready to have some fun. "Too bad because I don't think we're compatible at all."

Emma arched an eyebrow. "No?"

"Of course not! I could never be with someone like you. You're ridiculously gorgeous and that's just plain wrong. How will I be able to function as a human being when all I will think about is that you're a woman who's a thousand times out of my league?"

She swallowed hard. "Glad we got that cleared up."

Lance laughed. "So, you agree with me? You're out of my league?"

"What? No!" She took another sip of wine. "Look . . . I like you."

"Oh . . ." That caught Lance off guard.

His heart rate kicked up a notch as their gazes locked on each other, long enough to know the connection between them was getting stronger.

It felt good.

Unexpected.

Emma took another sip of wine and stared inside the wine glass. "This stuff is like truth serum. I need to stop." She set the glass back down and cleared her throat. "Your turn. Tell me what you were thinking."

Lance shrugged. "I'd love to know more about you. I guess I'm curious about your family. Your siblings, if you have any. Your parents. Do they live around here?"

"I'm an only child and my parents, well, they're no longer around."

"Oh . . ." Lance caressed the side of her arm. "I'm sorry."

She glanced down at his hand. "Thanks. They died in a car accident."

"That's horrible."

"Not as horrible as knowing it was going to happen and not being able to prevent it."

Emma threw her hand over her mouth, her beautiful blue eyes going wide.

Lance blinked. "How did you know it would happen?"

Emma looked away and shrugged.

"You don't want to talk about it," Lance said. "I understand."

The only thing he could think of was she must have been in the car accident with them, but had survived.

He just couldn't imagine the hell she had gone through. He wanted to wrap her in his arms and console her, but he knew it probably wasn't the place or time. The best thing he could do for now was change the subject.

"Well, is there anything else you want to ask me?" Lance asked. "Ask away."

"What about *your* parents?" Emma said. "Siblings? Ex-wives? Children you don't know about?"

"Well, if I don't know about them, how can I know about them?"

There was that smile again.

Beautiful.

"Anyway . . . no ex-wives and no siblings. I'm an only child, just like you. As for my parents, they are divorced. My mom is probably the oldest cruise ship employee in the world. She's a lounge singer for Norwegian, on the water ten months out of the year. The other two months she shacks up with one of the many people she's met over the years."

Emma crossed her arms. "You're being serious?"

"Oh, yeah. She's got friends all around the world, in just

about every port. Alaska. Hawaii. Barbados. Australia. Greece. You name it."

"So, you don't see her often?"

"The last time I saw her was five years ago on a Mexican Riviera cruise. Hey, she's enjoying life, so I can't fault her for that, can I?"

"Not at all," Emma said. "And your father?"

"Ah . . . well, that's a different story. He remarried twice after my mom. Cheated on all three of them. I'm not sure who he lied to more, me or my mom." He sighed. "Let's just say we don't see eye to eye."

Lance couldn't believe he'd just told her that. He kept that part of his life private. His father was the reason it was hard for him to trust people.

"How's everyone doing?" Tom asked from the front, looking around the room. "We are just about out of time for this evening and you all were amazing! I hope you had a wonderful time, and that you'll come back and see us again. You're all encouraged to hang out and socialize. No need to rush out."

"Why did you write the book?" Emma blurted out.

Lance took his focus off Tom and turned to Emma. "Pardon me?"

"The book? I mean, you don't seem like the same person as the author. Are you sure you're the one who wrote it?"

He contemplated how to respond, although he was surprised the subject hadn't come up earlier.

"You sure are thinking a lot," Emma said. "It can't be that hard to answer. Let's see . . . you wrote it for the money?"

Lance shook his head.

"Okay . . ." Emma said. "You wrote it because you had

countless years of data to back up your theory and you had to share it with the public? No, we both know that's not it."

Lance laughed and gave in. "I wrote it because it was what I believed at that time."

"Interesting."

"What?" Lance said.

"You used the past tense."

"That's because I was talking about the past."

Emma shook her head. "You said you wrote the book because it was what you believed *at the time*. That means you don't believe it anymore."

Lance crossed his arms. "Wrong."

"Okay, then. Answer this question quickly . . . do you believe in soulmates?"

Lance opened his mouth and then closed it.

Emma pointed to his face. "See? You can't even answer the question! You're a fraud."

Lance's body tensed. Maybe he was confused, but he wasn't a fraud. He had called Madam Love a fraud more than a few times and now it looked like he had been wrong about her all along. Maybe he did have a soulmate. And although he couldn't be certain yet, all signs seemed to be pointing right to the feisty blonde standing in front of him.

"I can assure you I'm not a fraud."

Emma put her hands on her hips. "Okay, then . . . explain yourself."

Lance thought about it for a moment. "Let's just say I'm not sure what I believe anymore. Something seems to have changed, I'll admit that. Call me crazy, but I think it's your fault."

"Why are you blaming me? What did *I* do?"

Lance shrugged. "Honestly, I don't know, but you sure are doing it well. There's something about you that fascinates me."

"You're nuts," Emma said, shaking her head. "How can meeting me totally change your outlook on something to the point that it argues with the details that led you to write a book?"

"Fascination is a very powerful thing." He glanced down at her lips. Right on cue she licked them. His heart rate kicked into high gear. It was crazy, but he had the urge to kiss her. She glanced at his lips and didn't retreat.

He was almost certain he had been given the green light to proceed.

"Emma," Lance said. "Remember when you said you liked me?"

"Yes . . ."

"I like you, too. A lot."

She nodded and glanced at his lips again.

He closed the distance between them to kiss her and—

Emma stepped back and rubbed her forehead. "What am I doing?" She grabbed her purse, fumbling with it. "I have to go."

It was like someone had smashed a brick against Lance's head.

"I don't get it," he said. "What happened?"

Emma stopped and turned back around. "*We* happened. This was a mistake."

"But why?" Lance held his palms up, confused. "We were having such a good time."

"It has nothing to do with having a good time," Emma said.

Lance ran his fingers through his hair and blew out a deep

breath. "It has *everything* to do with it. You said you liked me. Were you lying?"

"No! But liking you has nothing to do with it, either. Look, I have to go." She threw him a smile, although it appeared tight and forced. "Thanks for everything."

"At least let me give you a ride home," Lance said.

Emma shook her head. "I'll be fine. The bus drops me off right in front of my house." She turned and walked out the door.

Lance stared at the doorway, even though he knew Emma wasn't returning.

He mentally cursed himself for trying to kiss her.

But was that what really spooked her?

He sighed, not having a clue.

One thing was for sure, he wasn't going to give up. There was definitely something between them. Lance just needed to figure out his next move.

Maybe Madam Love could help him.

CHAPTER THIRTEEN

"I'd like to meet a modern day mountain man who wears suspenders and long-sleeved plaid flannel shirts," said Debbie, Emma's client. "Lean and strong. Someone who's not afraid to get his hands dirty."

Emma opened her mouth to respond, but just didn't have the energy to stop Debbie.

"He does all the usual mountain man things like chopping wood, changing lightbulbs, salmon fishing, et cetera, et cetera, but what makes him a *modern* mountain man is that he knows his way around a kitchen. He can prepare that fresh salmon he just caught for me in a jiffy. Add a side of mushroom risotto and I'm all his. All night."

"I already told you it doesn't work that way," Emma said, tired of listening to this woman's fantasy. "You need to stick to my plan."

Debbie sighed. "I know, I know, but a woman can dream, can't she? Oh, can you at least make sure he's tall? I like tall men."

Doesn't every woman?

"And he needs to be a dog person."

Emma stared at Debbie. "You know what you need to do to meet your soulmate, darling. Do it and you'll be rewarded with the man of your dreams."

"A mountain man?"

"Not necessarily."

Debbie huffed and got up from the loveseat, following Emma to the reception area. "I wish there were an easier way to do this. Something that takes no effort at all on my part. You just snap your fingers and he appears."

Emma smiled. "If it were that easy, I would snap my fingers all day long and there would be a line out the door." She snapped her fingers twice. "See? Nothing."

The front door opened.

It was Lance, wearing a long-sleeved plaid flannel shirt.

Oh God. Debbie will think—

"Hallelujah!" Debbie said, her eyes as wide as the doorframe. "You are good, Madam Love! And he's even got a dog! You're my mountain man!" She moved toward Lance with her arms wide open.

"Mountain man?" Lance said, his eyes widening in what appeared to be horror. "Whoa."

"Ruff! Ruff! Ruff!"

Typo didn't like Debbie, obviously.

She stopped and pointed at Typo. "Tell Cujo to back off. I'm just a love machine, and you and I are soulmates."

"You're not soulmates!" Emma said, wondering why she wanted so badly for the woman to stay away from Lance. "I told you to stick to the plan. *He* already has a soulmate. Lance, can you get the door for her?"

"Sure." Lance turned and opened the door. "You have a great day."

"I will certainly try," Debbie said, inspecting Lance from head to toe and then frowning. "If things don't work out with your soulmate, Madam Love has my number for you."

"You'll be the first person I call," Lance said, closing the door after she stepped outside. He turned back to Emma and blew out a big breath. "We need to talk."

Emma wanted to curse the way her body responded whenever Lance was close by. Still, she couldn't help notice the sadness in his voice and in his eyes. She wondered if it had anything to do with her walking out on him last night. She wouldn't be surprised.

Typo pulled hard toward Emma, but Lance restrained him.

"Calm down," Lance said.

Emma was about to say it was good to see Typo again, but caught herself before she stuck her foot in her mouth. Emma had met the dog, but Madam Love had only seen a picture of him. She needed to be very careful since she was two people in one. Disaster averted this time.

"It's okay," Emma said. "You can let him go."

Lance let go of the leash and Typo sprinted to Emma, his tail wagging.

"Hey, there," Emma said. "How are you? It's good to finally meet you!" She petted Typo as the dog licked her free hand. "You're so sweet."

"He's usually not like this with strangers," Lance said. "It's like he knows you."

You have no idea.

"He just knows I'm a dog person," Emma said, now

convinced Typo recognized her from Bark in the Park, even in her Madam Love disguise. Maybe it was her scent.

Lance jammed his hands in his pockets. "Can we talk?"

"Every time we talk you call me a fraud. I'm a little busy right now for insults."

"You don't have to worry about that today," Lance said.

"No?" Emma said, wondering if it was a set up.

Lance shook his head. "Not at all. It's just . . . okay, I'm just going to say it. You have a gift."

Emma blinked.

This was something new coming from the mouth of Lance. No insults. A compliment, actually. Sure, Lance had complimented Emma more than a few times, but he had never complimented Madam Love from what she could remember.

"I'm pretty sure I found my someone special," Lance continued. "My . . . soulmate." He winced. "There. I said it."

Emma cocked her head to the side. "The man who doesn't believe in soulmates says he has found himself a soulmate? I should be recording this conversation. In fact, maybe we should head straight to the radio station to declare myself a winner."

He sighed. "Please. I need your help."

There was no doubt he looked distraught. Had she really caused it? Sure, she felt like crap for walking out on him, but she had felt guilty for leading him on. She didn't have the heart to turn him away now.

"I don't have another appointment for a couple of hours." Emma stood and pulled back the beads over the doorway. "Come in."

Lance entered the salon with Typo. The dog jumped up and plopped himself down on the loveseat.

"Make yourself at home, why don't you?" Lance said, sitting down next to Typo. He pointed to the crystal ball. "*That* is not necessary today."

"Okay, darling," Emma said, sliding into her leather chair across from Lance and studying him.

He seemed flustered, less confident than he normally was.

Something was on his mind and she was sure she knew what it was.

More guilt set in.

"What's going on?" Emma said, deciding to get right into it. "You look like you just woke up."

"Quite the opposite." Lance ran his hand through his hair. "I didn't sleep at all. It's Emma."

"Who?" she said, deciding to play dumb.

"You know who. I saw her again at the farmers' market—then we went out on a date and it was amazing until I tried to kiss her. That's when she took off in a hurry. Why would she do that?"

Emma shrugged. "Was it your breath?"

Lance gave her a look to let her know he wasn't happy with her joking at a time like this.

"Sorry," Emma said. "Bad joke. You have no idea why she left? There were no signs?"

"No. None at all."

Emma knew exactly why she had left.

She'd freaked out.

She'd been having such a great time she had forgotten all about the challenge. Had forgotten that Lance was her client. Had forgotten that she didn't want to have a man in her life because she was afraid of the future.

Lance stroked Typo, deep in thought. "I don't know. The

only thing I can think of is she's married, but she doesn't seem like the kind of woman who would do something like that."

"She's not."

Lance glanced up Emma.

"I mean . . . from what you told me, she seems like a good person."

"She is. I loved being with her. We laughed, we painted, we drank wine. People are usually not themselves on first dates. They try to be on their best behavior when they should be themselves, so the other person can see what they're getting. She was acting like herself, you know what I mean?"

Not at all. "Yeah."

"She spoke her mind, and I loved that she even made fun of my pelicans. Sure, there are still a lot of things I don't know about her."

Like maybe she's the fortune teller sitting right in front of you and that she's lying to you on a daily basis.

More guilt.

What was Emma doing? Wasn't there another way? The truth was, if there was no challenge and she didn't have a problem with a rent increase, she would be seriously interested in pursuing a relationship with Lance. But what if she was his soulmate?

"Every place you have sent me, *she* has been there," Lance said. "The same place you said my soulmate would be. It's not a coincidence I keep running into her. It can't be."

Emma couldn't explain it either. Just the thought of it made her question her own gifts.

"I want to help you," Emma said. "You have a good heart, so I'm sure things will work out just fine."

Lance just stared at her.

"What?"

"You ripped me apart on the radio. You called me bitter and arrogant and—"

"Impossible." Emma smiled.

"Right. And now you say I have a good heart?"

"I said those things before I got to know you."

"Wait. You like me now?"

Yes, I like you more than you know and I wanted you to kiss me last night.

"Let's just say . . . you're not as bad as I thought," Emma said.

"Likewise," Lance said. "Although, I still wish you would remove that makeup and that—"

"Don't push it," Emma said.

Lance laughed. "Thanks. I need a good laugh after what happened last night."

She felt what she was feeling last night—that little something between them.

Lance leaned forward in his chair. "I need to know something and I want you to be honest with me. Can you promise me that?"

Emma felt horrible lying to him and would do her best to say something honest. "Yes. I promise." She crossed her fingers, hoping the question would be an easy one.

"I know you told me before that Emma was not the one, but things keep pushing me in her direction. You have to see that now."

The more Emma thought about it, the more she believed she was Lance's soulmate. But even if she were, how could this end well? The moment he found out Madam Love was Emma it would be over. He would feel betrayed. He would despise her. She was sure of it.

But maybe that was the price she had to pay. She would win the challenge, save her business, but lose the man. On the other hand, if they were truly soulmates, wouldn't they end up together no matter what? Wouldn't they weather the storm and come out stronger because of it?

One thing was for sure, if she won the challenge, but then lost the man, she couldn't see how she could continue to be a fortune teller. Maybe she would have to shut down the business and move away. Start a new career. But if she lost the challenge she would have to shut down the business just the same. Now she was confusing herself and wanted to bury her head in the sand.

"Is Emma the one?" Lance asked.

She nodded, knowing she couldn't hide the truth any longer. "I believe she is."

Lance jumped up from his chair. "I knew it!"

"Ruff! Ruff! Ruff!"

Lance reached over and petted the startled dog. "It's okay. I got a little excited." He paced back and forth in front of the loveseat. "Great. Perfect. This is what I needed to know so I don't go crazy. I still wish I knew why she left like that."

"Why don't you ask her? I would guess she was just scared. It's common for fear to set in when people are experiencing something extraordinary or something they haven't felt in a long time. Fear of the unknown or fear of something going wrong, I don't know."

"Yeah . . ." Lance thought about it for a moment. "Hey,

how about we order pizza and brainstorm this until we come up with a game plan?"

"A game plan for what?"

Lance grinned. "You're going to help me win Emma's heart."

CHAPTER FOURTEEN

Emma was certain she had never been in a more awkward position in her entire career. In her entire life. She had just agreed to help Lance win Emma's love. *Her* love. That wouldn't have been bad if this *Emma* that he spoke of was a friend or a client or even a random person at the mall. But *she* was Emma!

She took a deep breath and tried to calm her banging heart. She still had that guilt in her gut, though. The guilt that told her everything would come crashing down on her eventually. That's why there was only one thing she could do. She had to enjoy his company while it lasted.

Because she was sure it wouldn't last long.

Lance opened the pizza box and turned it around to face Emma. "Ta-da! Brain food."

Emma pointed to Lance's half of the pizza. "Who chooses pineapple all by itself as a pizza topping? It would make sense if you ordered ham and pineapple. But just pineapple? That right there has got to be the most unoriginal pizza topping ever." She grabbed a slice of pepperoni from the other half of the pizza and took a bite.

Lance chuckled and pulled a slice from the box. "You sound like Emma the way you speak your mind like that. Sure you two aren't related?"

Emma choked on her slice of pizza.

"You okay?"

She nodded and grabbed her bottle of water, taking a sip. "I'm fine."

"You sure?"

"The pepperoni is a little spicy," she lied.

Lance rubbed his hands together. "Okay, let's get started. How should we do this?" He took a big bite of his pizza.

Emma set her slice of pizza back down on her paper plate. "I think the question should be are you sure you want to do this?"

"I'm sure. You said she was my soulmate, so why wouldn't I do it? I'm supposed to, right?"

"You do realize that by pursuing her, by ending up with her, I'll win the challenge? That could have adverse effects on your career."

He nodded. "Of course, I've thought of that. My publisher and my agent, Peter, will not be happy."

"What do you think will happen?"

"I have no idea. The sales have been pretty good, so they've made money on it. Peter says they probably won't give me another contract, which means I'll need to find another publisher or self-publish."

"And you're willing to start all over to get the girl?" Emma asked. "Sounds a little rash if you ask me."

"I thought you would have said it sounded romantic,"

Lance said. "But I'm confused why you seem to be trying to talk me out of it. If I end up with Emma, you win. Isn't that what you want?"

"I want what's right."

"Well, you already told me you believe Emma is my soulmate. And I've already concluded that Emma is worth losing the challenge over. No woman has ever made me feel this way in such a short amount of time. It's like she's a magnet and I'm steel. Everything is pulling me in her direction."

That was one of the sweetest things anyone had ever said about Emma.

Emma had the sudden urge to jump over the table and kiss the stuffing out of that man.

Control your urges.

"What's my next step with Emma?" Lance said, snapping Emma out of her kissing fantasy. "I can't just show up at her work since I have no idea where that is. All I know is she works in human resources. Should I call her?"

Emma shook her head. "No. I would suggest texting her to start. Something spooked her and that's why she ran out on you. Send a short, simple text saying you've been thinking about her. Don't go pouring your heart out. That will overwhelm her. Just something simple, then ask her out. Pursue her, but not in a stalkerish way. Make her feel wanted. Make her feel special. Seize the moment. Got it?"

"Got it," Lance said, pulling his cell phone from his pocket.

"What are you doing?"

Lance looked up from his phone. "I'm going to text Emma —something short and sweet."

"Not now!" she said, taking a quick peek over at her cell phone sitting on top of the desk.

Do I have it in silent mode?

Lance's index finger hovered over his phone. "Why should I wait?"

Emma needed to think of something good because she was sure the volume was up on her phone. If it dinged after he sent Emma the text it would raise suspicion.

She reached over and opened the pizza box, grabbing a slice of the pineapple pizza and sticking it on Lance's plate. "It's rude to be on your phone during a meal. Can't we at least finish lunch?"

"But you told me to seize the—"

"Eat! You can seize the moment after you seize the rest of your pizza. You and your soulmate will have the rest of your lives together."

"Good point." Lance slipped the phone back in one pocket and pulled a small bag of dog treats out of the other. He opened the bag, tilted it forward, and shook it until a treat fell out and onto the top of Typo's paws.

Typo just stared at the treat.

"Doesn't he like them?" Emma said.

"Yes," Lance said. "Very much. He's just waiting for the command to eat it."

Emma shook her head. "I can't believe him. What's the magic word?"

Lance mouthed the word *gobble*.

"Seriously?" Emma asked.

Lance nodded.

"Typo," Emma said, sitting on the edge of her seat. "Gobble!"

Typo dropped his chin, grabbed the treat, and swallowed it without chewing.

Emma laughed. "What a brute! You need to chew your food!"

Lance laughed with her and took another bite of his pizza, washing it down with a sip of Coke. "Thank you."

"For what?"

"You know . . . for this. For helping me find a soulmate." He chuckled. "I can't believe I'm saying that. Not that long ago we wanted to kill each other."

"I never wanted to kill you."

Lance raised an eyebrow.

"Okay, maybe I did a little." She smiled.

"Who knows? This could be the start of a beautiful friendship. In fact, the three of us need to get together some time outside of work."

"You, me, and Typo?"

"Well, sure . . . That would be great, too, but I was actually thinking of you, me, and Emma."

Emma choked on her pizza again.

A small piece of pepperoni flew out of her mouth and smacked Lance on the chest.

Five minutes after Lance had left Emma's office her phone dinged with his text. The guy didn't waste any time at all. At least he'd taken her advice to seize the moment. Lucky for her, he didn't send the text while he was still in her office, since she found out after he had left that the volume was all the way up on her personal phone. That would have been a disaster.

. . .

Lance: Hey. I was thinking about you. How are you?

Emma: I'm good. Sorry I ran out on you.

Lance: We were having such a good time.

Emma: I know. It's complicated.

Lance: How so?

Emma: It's a long story.

Lance: I have fourteen hours. Is that enough time to tell me?

Emma: LOL. Some other time, if you don't mind.

Lance: Of course. I've been thinking about you a lot.

Emma: I've been thinking about you, too.

Emma tapped her fingers on the table, feeling a little nervous that she told Lance he'd been on her mind. It was the truth. She wondered how he would respond.

She stared at the phone, waiting.

Waiting.

Waiting.

What was taking him so long to respond?

Finally, her phone dinged.

Lance: I know why you left.

Emma stared at the phone again. She wasn't expecting that response. Had he figured out who she was? She tried to think back to their conversation in her office to see if she could remember saying something she shouldn't have said. She thought she had been very careful, for the most part.

Maybe he noticed the way Typo reacted when he saw Emma? The dog obviously knew it was her. But did Lance? It didn't appear so, but he could've been hiding it. Maybe he recognized her laugh or her eyes. She had thought of buying some of those colored contact lenses. Now, she was kicking herself for not doing so. Whatever the reason, she was getting nervous and had to know.

Emma: Why do you think I left?
Lance: You were jealous of my talent for bouncing the sunset off the pelicans.

Emma shook her head and laughed. She was worried about nothing.

She did have a wonderful time last night. It was a fun and unique evening. And she would never forget that look on Lance's face as he moved closer to her. His eyes got darker and she knew he wanted to kiss her. Her heart was about to jump out of her chest in that moment and yes, she'd freaked out. How could she have so much chemistry with a man she just met last week?

Maybe because he's your soulmate, silly.

Lance: Are you still contemplating my Picasso-like painting abilities?

Emma: I told you, you can't reflect the sunset off feathers! And that's not why I left.

Lance: Okay, then. My charm was just too much for you to handle. I get it.

Emma laughed again. This guy was too much. She liked Lance's sense of humor, no doubt about that. And even though he was joking he possessed plenty of charm, although she wouldn't tell him that.

Emma: Mr. Humble.

Lance: And charming?

Emma: Maybe a little. Don't let it go to your head.

Lance: Too late. And do you know what I think of you?

Emma: Haven't got a clue, but I'm sure you'll tell me.

Lance: For starters, you're the most gorgeous woman I have ever laid eyes on.

Emma's pulse banged in her neck again. How could she respond to that? She really had no idea how. It had been such a long time since she had flirted with someone and she couldn't remember if she had ever done it through text messages. She had to admit she loved every minute of it.

Lance: Did I scare you away again? I need to quit doing that.

Emma: Still here.

Lance: Good. I want to see you again. Soon.

. . .

Emma knew he would ask her out since she had coached Lance on what to say, but still, this seemed real now. She wanted to look into her future, but was just too terrified of what she might see. She wanted to see if Lance was there with her because she could picture herself falling for him. Easily. Too bad he would be livid when he found out that Emma was Madam Love and Madam Love was Emma. She shook that thought from her head and focused on the man who was courting her through text messages.

Emma: What did you have in mind?
Lance: Are you available tomorrow during the day?

During the day? What was he planning? Maybe a hike? A trip to the zoo? Wine tasting? Better if they skipped the drinks next time. The activity didn't matter that much, now that she thought about it. The man was not boring which made things very interesting and fun.

Exciting was more like it.

She clicked the calendar button on her laptop to check her schedule. She knew she didn't have much going on, but had to make sure someone hadn't booked a consultation through her online reservation system.

"Of course not," Emma mumbled, confirming her empty schedule.

Although that meant she could see Lance, it also meant she had no money coming in for another day. It meant more than ever that she had to win the challenge. That was the only way to get more clients coming in. As for now she removed the negative thoughts from her head and thought positively.

Things will work out.

She closed her laptop and grabbed her phone to text Lance back.

Emma: Yes. Free tomorrow. No wine, please.
Lance: Great! Wear something you don't mind getting dirty.
Emma: Not again. I'm worried.
Lance: Trust me. :)

Emma trusted Lance. She was looking forward to their date, to spending more time with him. One thing was for sure, she wouldn't run away scared this time.

She would let destiny and nature take their course.

CHAPTER FIFTEEN

Emma stood near the edge of the cliff and watched a paraglider soar over the ocean below. It was a perfect day, not a cloud in the sky. Seagulls were in the air and butterflies were in her stomach. Why was she nervous?

Relax. It's only Lance.

Emma laughed at the thought.

Only Lance.

The man could be her soulmate. How could she remain calm? She didn't think it was a possibility, but she would still try.

She'd agreed to meet Lance near the wooden steps that descended down to the beach below, but still had no clue what he had planned for their second date. The first date had been wonderful if you didn't count the part where she ran from the place like it was on fire. For the second time, Lance said to wear something she wouldn't mind getting dirty. No heels. But how could she get dirty there on the cliff?

Another paraglider flew by and she had to wonder if he was planning on taking the two of them to the air in one of those contraptions. No way that would happen. She considered herself an adventurous person, but she wasn't *that* adventurous. What else could it be then? She could see getting sand stuck between her toes or maybe even getting her shorts a little wet if they went down to walk by the water, but that wouldn't necessarily get her dirty. She had no idea of the plan, but she was about to find out.

Lance approached Emma with a confident stride and a knowing smile. He wore khaki shorts and a solid black polo shirt. He looked like an older model for Banana Republic.

"Hi," he said, giving her a sweet, gentle kiss on the cheek and reaching for her hand.

"Hi," Emma said, buzzing from the contact and already at a complete loss for words. She glanced down at her hand in Lance's. "What do you think you're doing?"

That's all her brain could come up with.

Lance followed her gaze to their interlocking fingers. "What am I doing? I think it's obvious. I'm holding your hand."

"I know that, but don't you think it's a little presumptuous?"

"That depends." He squeezed her hand tighter. "Are you enjoying it as much as I am?"

Emma opened her mouth then closed it, not being able to hold back the smile. "Maybe."

Lance chuckled. "I already know that with you *maybe* means *yes*." He turned and led her toward the wooden steps that descended to the sand below. "I guess it's not presumptuous of me at all, is it?"

Emma laughed and shook her head, preferring not to respond.

Because he was right.

It wasn't presumptuous at all.

She wanted to hold his hand.

And it wouldn't have been presumptuous at all if he had kissed her on the lips instead of the cheek, but she wouldn't tell him that.

At the bottom of the steps they turned to the left and walked on the sand.

"What's the plan?" Emma admired the crashing waves and then looked over to Lance. "Just a slow, romantic walk on the beach?"

He grinned. "I'm glad you find it romantic, but no, this is not it. You'll find out soon enough."

Emma pointed to five pelicans flying by, one right behind the other. "See? Pelicans are not red!"

Lance looked in the opposite direction of the pelicans. "I have no idea what you're talking about. I don't see any pelicans."

"Over there," Emma said, laughing and grabbing Lance's waist, trying to twist him toward the pelicans. Too bad she couldn't budge him one bit.

"I told you I was reflecting the sunset off the pelicans."

"Right!" Emma laughed even louder, still trying to twist Lance around.

"What are you trying to do?" Lance said, laughing along with Emma. He pried both of her hands from his waist and lowered them behind her back. Then he pulled her up against his body. "There. Much better."

She couldn't argue there.

They were both out of breath.

There were no more words spoken between them, just the chemistry sizzling.

Emma glanced at his lips and he glanced right back at hers.

Lance moved even closer, their lips now only inches apart. "Would it be presumptuous of me to kiss you right now?"

Emma hesitated. "Maybe . . ."

Fortunately, Lance was a smart man. He pressed his lips to hers.

The kiss was electric.

Amazing.

Mind-boggling.

Emma's head grew heavy and fireworks lit up behind her eyelids.

Was she going to pass out?

Lance must have sensed it because he grabbed her even tighter and caressed her cheek. "Whoa. You okay?"

Emma nodded and blinked a few times. "Yeah. What day is it?"

"I'm not even sure of the year." His gaze didn't leave Emma's. "What just happened there?"

Emma swallowed hard. "I have no idea, but I want more." She grabbed the back of Lance's neck and hauled him in for another kiss.

Lance pulled away from Emma's kiss again, this time speechless. What had just happened was almost an out-of-body experience. He knew they had a crazy connection, but that was ridiculous. He had even forgotten where they were and why they were there. Emma looked just as dazed and confused.

They picked their shoes up off the sand and continued walking down the beach in silence, hand in hand. They glanced at each other a couple of times as they walked, but neither of them said a word. A minute later, Lance stopped and turned to her, ready to discuss what had happened between them.

"We don't have to talk about it," Emma said.

The woman was a mind reader.

"We're just two consenting adults who got caught up in the moment."

Lance nodded. "And that was a moment to remember."

"Don't read too much into it. Sometimes we have things built up inside of us. Eventually they have to come out."

"As long as you got that out of your system," Lance said, grinning.

Emma pinched Lance on the arm. "Me? I hope *you* got it out of *your* system."

"Not even close." He pulled her in closer for another kiss.

Emma pressed her palm on his chest. "Stop. We're supposed to be on a date, remember? And the kiss comes at the end. You've got everything mixed up."

"I'm glad you confirmed that there will be another kiss at the end." He winked. "I look forward to it."

"Focus," Emma said, looking around. "Are you going to tell me about the plan now?"

"I'll show you. See that path over there?" He pointed down the beach about fifty yards. "Just past the group of pine trees?"

Emma turned to look. "Yes."

"We need to follow that path around until it connects with the road. Then we cross the road, and the adventure begins."

She continued to stare toward the path. "If we need to go back to the road, why did we come down here when we were already on the road earlier before we met at the cliff?"

"I like slow, romantic walks on the beach, remember?" Lance said.

Especially when those walks were with Emma.

Emma smiled.

The electricity between them was unreal. When they walked. When they talked. When they held hands. When they were just in each other's presence.

A few minutes later, they walked past the large group of pine trees, up the path, and across the road. The real reason Lance wanted to go that way was so Emma wouldn't see the Happy Horse Ranch sign and figure out what they were doing.

"Look," Emma said, pointing to the Happy Horse Ranch sign on the opposite side of the street that Lance didn't know existed. "Are we going to see some happy horses?"

Lance frowned. "You weren't supposed to see that sign. There goes the surprise."

"That's okay." Emma smiled. "I love horses."

"Me, too."

They crossed the street and walked down the long driveway to the main office connected to the big brown barn. The sign in the window said, *Horseback Riding*.

"What if I don't know how to ride horseback?" Emma said.

Lance was about to open the door, but then stopped and crossed his arms. "Is that a rhetorical question or do you really not know how to ride a horse? Because you had the same reservations about painting and you turned out to be a closet Van Gogh."

Emma laughed. "You exaggerate."

Lance continued to stare at her, waiting for an answer.

"Okay, maybe I have ridden a horse a few times," Emma finally confessed.

"Just a few times?"

"Maybe a few more than a few."

Lance arched an eyebrow. "Why do I have a funny feeling that you're not telling me something? Like maybe you're the top female horse jockey in the world and you've won the Kentucky Derby once or twice?"

"It was the Belmont Stakes." Emma smirked. "Just once, though."

Lance laughed and squeezed her hand tighter.

There was nothing sexier than a woman with a sense of humor.

They entered the office and the owner of the ranch, Michelle, checked them both in. Then they headed back outside around the barn to the stable where the horses were.

"Here we are," Michelle said. "It will just be the three of us for this ride."

Emma stopped, her eyes growing wider. "Those are . . . Clydesdales."

"They sure are," Michelle said proudly. "Born and raised here. My babies."

"Your babies are so . . . big and tall." She looked around the ranch. "Sure you don't have anything a little smaller? Like maybe a Shetland pony?"

Michelle laughed. "All we have are Clydesdales."

"I mean, they're amazing, but I thought most people used these horses for parades and pulling wagons and Budweiser commercials."

Michelle climbed up onto the gate to scratch a horse on the bridge of the nose. "That's what they are mostly known for, but we trained them at an early age to be riding horses. We are one of the few places in the country where you can ride Clydesdales. Don't be intimidated. They're big, but they're also tender and gentlehearted. Think of your horse as a two-thousand-pound golden retriever."

"They're beautiful," Lance said.

"They sure are," Emma said, climbing up in the gate next to Michelle and petting the horse.

Twenty minutes later, Lance and Emma were back on the beach, this time riding two majestic Clydesdales side by side. Michelle led the way on her own horse in front of them.

Lance glanced over at Emma, admiring the big smile on her face. She was enjoying the ride and looked like a natural. His choice for their second date was a good one.

They hadn't said much since they left the ranch, both just enjoying the ride, the ocean, the waves. They were even lucky enough to see a few dolphins that Michelle had pointed out.

Emma caught Lance looking at her again. "What?"

"Nothing," Lance said, then changed his mind about hiding his feelings. "Well, maybe something." He thought about it for a moment. "This feels good."

Emma glanced down at his saddle. "You mean having your legs wrapped around a horse?"

Lance chuckled. "You know what I mean. You and me. I like what's happening between us. And it seems to be happening rather quickly."

"Yeah . . ."

Lance reached out, having the urge to hold Emma's hand again. He adjusted himself in the saddle to stretch his hand out farther.

Emma eyed his hand. "Are you being presumptuous again?"

He smirked. "Maybe." He reached further, squeezing the saddle with his thighs to keep his balance. "Help me out a little here."

"I don't think it's such a good idea," Emma whispered, pointing to Michelle. "You're going to get in trouble, or worse, you can fall off the horse and hurt yourself."

"Ye of little faith," Lance said, also keeping his voice low so Michelle didn't hear him. "I'm Sir Lancelot. Surely, you've heard of me? Knights of the Roundtable?"

"That's the pizza place, right?"

Lance laughed. "Come on. Give me your hand, Lady Guinevere."

"You do know that Guinevere ended up becoming a nun after her affair with Sir Lancelot? Then they both died lonely and heartbroken. Sir Lancelot may not be your best role model."

"Okay. How about if I swap this horse for a bike? I'll be Lance Armstrong." He reached out further, only an inch from Emma's hand. "Almost got you."

"Be careful," Emma said. "You're going to fall."

Too late.

Lance's foot slid out of the right stirrup, sending him backwards off the horse to the sand below. He landed with a loud thud and a sharp pain in his forehead.

CHAPTER SIXTEEN

Lance was in good spirits, considering the date with Emma had ended at urgent care. He was a little sore, but things could have been a lot worse, so he was grateful and happy for that. Why couldn't his dates end normally?

The owner of the horse ranch had insisted on Lance going to urgent care to get checked out for a possible concussion or fractures. He spent the next four hours there in the waiting room waiting for a doctor to see him, with Emma right at his side the entire time, holding his hand. That alone was worth the trip to the urgent care. It was all he had wanted. To hold her hand. If she would have given him her hand when they were riding the horses, they wouldn't have ended up in urgent care. He had blamed her for the fall, but Emma refused to take the blame, saying he fell because he was doing something stupid.

He loved how honest she was.

On the bright side, Lance had no serious injuries. No broken bones and no concussion. He had a few bruises, with the biggest being on his ego. Also, sore ribs from the impact with the sand, and a scrape on the side of his forehead where he'd hit a small piece of driftwood. They were lucky the horses didn't get spooked, otherwise it could have been a lot worse.

All in all—even considering how it ended—Lance thought it was another successful date because he felt even closer to Emma. He would have to call Madam Love later and give her an update on how well things were going.

In the meantime, he lay on his couch watching a National Geographic documentary on the largest cats in the world, trying to take it easy for a couple of days as the doctor had advised.

Lance pointed to the Siberian tiger on the television screen. "Typo, look at the big kitty."

Typo lifted his head from his doggie bed next to the couch and glanced over at the television.

"He can eat you in one bite. That's one kitty you don't want to mess with."

Typo plopped his head back down and closed his eyes, not seeming to care at all. And why should he? The dog was fearless. Lance lost track of the times Typo chased after large dogs, including that Great Dane at Bark in the Park.

Lance should have known his thoughts would travel right back to Emma. It was like he had Emma on the brain twenty-four hours a day. He grabbed his phone, eager to send her a text. As the Siberian tiger devoured a wild boar on the television screen, Lance tapped in his first message.

Lance: Guess who's thinking of you right now.
    Emma: Hmm. Not sure. You?

Lance: Bingo! How about lunch?

He hadn't planned on asking her to lunch—it just came out. The plan was to lie low, but he obviously wanted to see her again. He wanted to see her as much as possible. He was hooked on her. Going out for a quick bite to eat wouldn't hurt anybody, right? And if they ended the lunch with one of her sweet kisses, he couldn't think of a better dessert.

Emma: The doctor said you should take it easy, remember? It's only been a few days.

He should have known she would say something. He wouldn't give up easily.

Lance: I don't remember the doctor saying anything like that. How about baked ziti?

Emma: I guess your injury is worse than we thought. I may need to stop seeing you until your head is screwed back on straight.

Lance: Funny, but I suddenly remembered what the doctor said!

Emma: Good.

Lance: But seriously, do you want to have lunch with me?

Emma: You need to behave and relax. You fell off one of the tallest horses in the world, remember? Besides, I brought leftover lentils with me to work today.

Lance: You're at work, of course. I forgot. How are things in the world of human resources?

Now that he thought of it, he had no idea where she worked. It didn't seem like the most exciting job in the world, but maybe she loved what she did. That's what really mattered. He could picture employees going to her and complaining about something, and then Emma putting them in their place. The woman didn't take crap from anyone, especially Lance. And she was feisty as hell. He loved that.

Emma: Things are good. I'm getting ready to meet someone. I can check in with you later today after lunch, if that's okay??

Lance: Lunch tomorrow, then? I won't take no for an answer.

Emma: Tomorrow works.

Lance: Great! We can talk about it later. There's a new place I want to try.

A few seconds later, Lance's phone rang.

He checked the caller ID.

Peter.

He stared at the phone, not motivated to answer it. He had already avoided Peter's phone calls three times over the last twenty-four hours. Peter wanted an update on the challenge, Lance was sure of it. He was also sure Peter wouldn't like what Lance had to say.

The ringing stopped.

A few seconds later a text came in.

Peter: You're avoiding me.
Lance: You're hallucinating.
Peter: I'm going to call again in ten seconds.
Lance: Really busy right now. Talk tomorrow?
Peter: I'm calling you in ten seconds. Pick up the phone or I'm coming over. I know where you have the hide-a-key and if it's not there, I'll break a window.

Sure enough, ten seconds later the phone rang

"Time to face the firing squad," Lance mumbled to himself before answering the phone. "What's going on?"

"Why are you avoiding me?" Peter asked.

"I was in the middle of a dramatic moment in a National Geographic documentary on television. A Siberian tiger was—"

"I'm being serious here. What are you doing?"

Lance let out a deep breath, ready to come clean with his best friend. "I think it's pretty obvious what I'm doing. You want to ask me about the challenge and I don't want to talk about the challenge. That's the first rule in the challenge: don't talk about the challenge."

"You've been seeing her, haven't you? What's her name? Irma?"

"Her name is Emma. And yes, I've been seeing her."

"I don't get it," Peter said. "I told you—you'll lose the challenge and your career will suffer the consequences. You don't care?"

"I do care. About her."

"More than your career?"

"Yes," Lance said.

"You're crazy."

"That's not the first time you've said that. Maybe I am. Maybe I'm not. Only time will tell."

"But you just met her. Don't you think you're rushing things?"

"I can't help how I feel, can I? They're feelings."

Peter sighed, but didn't respond.

He wasn't happy. Not a surprise.

"You of all people should understand," Lance said. "How long did you know Ellen before you knew she was the one?"

Peter hesitated. "Ten minutes?"

"I think it was less than that. And do you remember my reaction when you told me you were going to marry her?"

"Of course. You grabbed your keys and offered to drive me to a shrink. Wait a minute . . . did you ask Emma to marry you?"

"No. My point is everything turned out perfect for you and Ellen. You've been married for over ten years. She's your soulmate. You're happy. You have a beautiful daughter."

"What happened to my friend?" Peter asked.

Lance ignored the comment.

When he thought of the perfect marriage, he always thought of what Peter and Ellen had. They were so connected and so in love. He had once hoped he and Karla would have the same, but that had ended up being a bust. He'd been convinced for the longest time that Karla was his soulmate.

Then Karla left Lance.

Then Lance wrote the book.

Then Lance met Emma.

Being around Emma was different from being with Karla. Not that he should compare the two, but he felt more alive and more excited about life when he was with Emma.

Karla obviously wasn't supposed to be the one, but he hadn't known it back then. They didn't have passion in their relationship, he could see it now. He wouldn't have been truly happy with her. He hadn't believed it until recently. All the heartache and negativity and suffering caused by Karla breaking off their engagement one week before the wedding had disappeared.

Just like that.

All because of Emma. All because of Madam Love, actually.

"I want what you have, Peter."

"Back off," Peter said. "You can't have my wife."

Lance laughed. "Thanks for setting me straight, but you went through what I'm going through right now, and everything turned out perfectly for you and Ellen. You're still madly in love with your wife after all these years."

"Yes, I'm still madly in love with her," Peter said. "But you're forgetting one very important detail."

"What's that?" Lance said.

"I didn't throw away a career to get the girl."

"But you would have," Lance said.

Peter didn't answer.

"Come on . . . If someone had told you that you could be with the woman of your dreams, but you'd have to find a new career or a new job or new place to live, you would have done it, right? Admit it."

Peter sighed again. "Yes, but this is a much different situation."

"Why is it different?"

"Because it's you we're talking about, not me."

Lance laughed. "Nice try."

"I have a great idea," Peter said. "Wait until after the challenge is over to pursue Emma."

"I can't do that."

"Why not?"

"Because," Lance said. "I don't want to win the challenge because I cheated. It wouldn't be fair to Madam Love. She deserves to win. Plus, I want to see Emma as much as possible. And who's saying my career is over after the challenge? I may have to move in a different direction or write in a different genre, but I'm not going to give up on my career and I'm not going to give up on Emma. It's crazy, but Madam Love really has a gift. She's not a fraud."

"And you've told her this?"

"Yes."

"She knows she's going to win the challenge?"

"Yes."

Peter hesitated. "If this really happens and you end up marrying your soulmate, then what? You need a backup plan."

"I'll figure it out," Lance said. "Trust me. This feels good. It feels right. And I know Emma feels the same way. We're so connected, it's scary. I wouldn't be surprised if she was thinking about me at this very moment."

Emma couldn't get Lance off her mind. She was trying to focus, but it wasn't easy. It wasn't good for business, either. That's why she'd made up the excuse that a client was coming in so she could get Lance to stop texting her. Not because she didn't like his texts. She loved them. She loved many things about the man, including his charm and sense of humor. That's another reason she had to stop exchanging texts with him.

The guilt prevented her from completely enjoying the feelings she had for Lance.

She was in too deep now.

There was no turning back, and although she was enjoying Lance's company and getting to know him, she could see there was no way their story could have a happy ending. She wanted to look into her own future. Emma wanted to see if Lance was there and if they were happy together, but she also wanted to kick herself for even considering it. She had promised herself she would never look into her future again. Not for herself and not for anyone she loved. The last time she had she'd found out her parents were going to die. She took that as a sign that maybe she shouldn't be poking her nose where it didn't belong. Emma sometimes also had visions of the future during moments of euphoria, but always cut them off when they were of her life. Her gifts were only meant to be used for others and not for herself. Yet she was being pulled in that direction.

"Are you really going to do this?" Emma whispered to herself, a little terrified of the thought.

Her heart rate accelerated as she walked through the beads in the reception area to her salon in the back.

"Here goes nothing," Emma said to herself.

Emma went through her usual routine with the crystal

ball, this time focusing on herself and nobody else. She would soon know if Lance was her soulmate. She would know if they would live happily-ever-after.

The sudden image of her parents' car accident flashed through her head, startling her.

"No," Emma said, changing her mind. "I can't do it."

She stood and paced back and forth. "Get Lance off your mind. You need a distraction. Now."

Emma's business phone dinged from the reception desk from a text coming in.

"Okay, that was scary," she said, heading back through the beads to the reception area and glancing at her phone on the desk.

The text she had received was from Lance.

Emma was certain the universe was messing with her.

Lance: Can I stop by?

Stop by? Was he kidding? She had just had a conversation with him when she was playing the part of Emma and made it very clear he should relax. What was she going to say now? She had no idea how to respond.

Men! They don't listen and they don't know what's good for them.

She hated the mixed signals her body was sending her. Her brain was telling her not to see him, but her body and heart and soul were saying, "Come on over and kiss me the way you did last time, big boy!"

Emma decided the best thing she could do is what any

grown, mature woman her age would do, given the circumstances.

She ignored Lance's text.

He would get the hint that she was busy.

She needed time to think.

It was a brilliant plan until the front door flew open twenty minutes later.

It was Lance.

"What are you doing here?" Emma said. "You should be resting."

"Resting?" Lance said, raising a scraped eyebrow and moving toward Emma. "Who told you I needed to rest?"

You fool!

Emma slipped up. And it wasn't a little slip up. This was major. Madam Love knew nothing about the date, the horseback riding, or Lance falling off the horse. How was she going to dig herself out of this Grand Canyon-sized hole?

Think of something! Anything!

"Well . . ." Emma said, hesitating as she hoped to think of something. "I had this weird feeling earlier that you had gotten in an accident." She pointed to the scrape on his forehead. "I was obviously right."

He chuckled. "I shouldn't be surprised. You're good."

"What happened to you, darling?" Emma asked, trying to pretend like she had no clue, completely in her role as Madam Love.

"I fell. Twice."

Twice?

What was he talking about?

She knew for a fact he had only fallen once. After he had fallen off the horse, they went directly to urgent care and she was with him the entire time. She would have seen if he had fallen a second time. Unless it was when he had gone to the bathroom at urgent care and hadn't said anything. And if that were the case, he should've said something.

"I don't understand," Emma said, confused. "How did you fall twice?"

Lance pointed to the side of his head. "Once off a horse." He placed his hand on his heart. "And now I'm falling for Emma."

That had to be the most romantic thing ever.

Wait a minute . . .

Emma stared at Lance, replaying the words in her head, just in case she misheard them.

And now I'm falling for Emma.

Lance was talking about her.

Falling for her.

Emma had strong feelings for him, too, but was it love?

She wasn't so sure about that.

"You look surprised," Lance said. "Believe me, I'm just as surprised as you are, but I can't hide my feelings. Emma is amazing. Wonderful. And I have to admit, it freaks me out a little. I had my doubts about you, but I was wrong. Emma gets better and better and better each time I see her. This is all happening so fast, but I'm one hundred percent certain you have won the challenge. Congratulations."

"Thank you," Emma said, still trying to process what he was saying. This was unbelievable, and she had no idea what to say or do. She was paralyzed from the mixed emotions. She needed to get rid of him, so she could proceed with her nervous breakdown. "You didn't have to come all the way down here to tell me that. A phone call or text would have been perfectly fine."

"Well, I texted you earlier, but you didn't respond," Lance said. "That's okay, because I thought it would be better to thank you in person. Plus, I wanted to give you this." Lance took a few steps toward Emma, reached his arms around her, and pulled her in for a hug.

BAM!

The electrical shock from their bodies touching was just as strong as ever. How could that be? He was hugging Madam Love, not Emma.

She prayed he didn't feel it.

Maybe it was just her feeling it.

Hopefully it was just her.

Lance pulled away from the hug and stared at her for a moment, a dazed look on his face.

God, he felt it, too. No, no, no! This is the end.

"I . . . uh . . ." Lance scratched the side of his head. "Sorry, I forgot what I was going to say."

This whole charade was on the verge of collapsing. She just knew it. That was most likely the last hug she would ever receive from Lance. And no more kisses. She wanted more of those wonderful kisses, but she knew the only thing she could do at the moment was get rid of him.

"I should get back to work," Emma said.

"Of course—I'll let you go. I just wanted to stop by and say thank you."

"You're welcome," Emma said.

"I'll see you tomorrow for lunch." Lance turned toward the door.

"Lunch?"

What was he talking about? They had never discussed lunch.

Lance stopped and flipped back around. "Yeah. You, me, and Emma? I can't wait for you to meet her." He pointed to her laptop on the desk. "I guess you need to check your schedule more often." He winked and walked out.

After Lance disappeared into the parking lot out of view, Emma quickly sat down at the reception desk and checked the schedule on her laptop. Sure enough, she had two new back-to-back bookings the next day.

Name of client: Lance Parker

Comments: Lunch with you and Emma at Finger Lickin' Chicken.

Emma shook her head in disbelief.

She was in serious trouble.

CHAPTER SEVENTEEN

Emma sat at a table with Lance at Finger Lickin' Chicken, the new restaurant located next door to Noah's Bagels in the strip mall where she had her office. She wondered how long it would be before Lance glanced over her shoulder toward the front door again, looking for Madam Love to enter. He had no idea it was impossible for Emma and Madam Love to be in the same place at the same time, but Emma had a plan that she was pretty sure would work in such a tricky situation. Her only goal was to get through the lunch without Lance finding out who she really was.

A few seconds later, Lance looked over Emma's shoulder again toward the front door, and then checked his watch. "I'm not sure what happened to her. She only has to walk a hundred feet to get here, so it can't be traffic. I can always run next door."

"Relax," Emma said, taking a sip of her iced tea. "I'm sure she'll be here soon. You're really excited for me to meet Madam Love, I can tell."

Lance nodded. "Of course. Because of her, you and I met. I'm grateful for that." He winked and pulled out his phone, probably looking to see if Madam Love had texted him.

Earlier, Lance had shared with Emma the details of the challenge with Madam Love and how it all started when she had called into the radio program. He confessed he was a little scared to share it with her, but wanted to be honest. He invited Emma to join him on the radio tomorrow with Madam Love, but she obviously had to decline, saying she had an important meeting with the entire HR department. She was tired of lying to Lance, because she truly cared about the man, but there was nothing else she could do at this point.

Lance tapped something in his phone and then set in on the table. "I just sent her a text to get an update."

Emma's phone dinged.

She forced a smile and tried to play it cool. "That could be work."

"Not a problem," Lance said, not looking at all like he was suspicious of the ding right after he sent Madam Love the text. "I'm going to run to the restroom. Be right back." He grabbed his phone and walked to the bathroom.

Emma smiled and waited for him to enter the bathroom before she pulled out her phone and glanced down at the message.

Lance: At the restaurant. Are you on your way? Looking forward to your meeting Emma.

. . .

She typed in a reply to him and then slipped the phone back into her purse.

Two minutes later, Lance returned from the bathroom, and sat back down at their table. "I got a text from Madam Love. Something came up and she's running about thirty minutes late. She said to order lunch and start eating. She'll be here as soon as she can."

"Sounds good," Emma said, waving the waiter over to order.

Fifteen minutes later, Emma and Lance were eating chicken with mashed potatoes and buttermilk biscuits. The food was tasty and the conversation lively as they chatted about horses, and painting, and life. Emma was enjoying Lance's company, but knew she would have to do something soon. She just needed a good reason to step outside so she could sneak next door and change into her Madam Love outfit. The location was an advantage for her, since it was right next door to her office. She still had no idea what to do when he wondered why Emma hadn't returned, but she would just have to figure that out on the fly.

At least she felt relaxed. This was going much smoother than she'd expected.

"Emma!" the male voice called out from behind her.

Maybe she spoke too soon.

Emma whipped her head around, knowing who it was.

Randy.

Not good.

A conversation with him could have disastrous results since he knew Emma was Madam Love. The problem was she had no escape and he was walking their way. The only thing she could do was try to get rid of him as quickly as possible.

"Hey," Randy said, stepping up to their table. "I thought that was you." He turned to Lance and held out his hand. "Hi, I'm Randy."

Lance shook his hand. "Randy as in Randy Dandy's Cupcakes?"

Randy nodded. "The one and only."

"I'm Lance Parker," Lance said. "And I must say I'm a *huge* fan."

Randy arched an eyebrow and pointed to Emma. "Did she pay you to say that?"

Lance chuckled. "I'm serious. That was a genuine compliment. I ate three of your cupcakes at the farmers' market and I could have eaten many more."

"Thank you. I appreciate that very much. Honestly, it started out as just a hobby, but Emma encouraged me to turn it into a business. And it looks like that's what's happening because the response has been amazing." He laughed. "Who would have thought a real estate investor would be selling cupcakes?"

"What type of real estate?" Lance said.

"Strip malls, mostly. Like this one."

Emma didn't like the direction of the conversation. She had a bad feeling about it and needed to put an end to it immediately.

Change the subject!

"Have you tried the chicken here, Randy?" Emma asked, hoping that would get the conversation going in a safe direction. "It is divine."

"I agree. The owners insisted I tried their food when they applied to lease this place. I drove to their other location across town and they brought me just about everything on the menu. They were either very proud of their food or they were bribing me." He laughed. "Either way, it worked! Amazing chicken and those buttermilk biscuits are to die for."

Lance looked around the restaurant and then out the window. "Oh . . . I didn't realize you meant you owned *this* strip mall."

"Me and my brother. We're partners. How do you think I met Emma?"

No, no, no!

Lance's gaze bounced back and forth between Emma and Randy. "I don't follow you. I thought you were friends."

"Well, we *are* friends," Randy said. "But we initially met because she rents—"

"His condo in Maui!" Emma lied, just in time to avoid a disaster. "It's a wonderful place right near the water in Kihei. Randy, can I talk to you for a moment? Outside? I totally forgot to update you on a couple of business things from the farmers' market."

It was the perfect excuse for her to run next door and transform herself into Madam Love. Hopefully, Randy would play along and not cause any difficulties.

Randy blinked. "Uh . . . business things?"

"Yes," Emma said, nodding when Lance wasn't looking, hoping Randy would get the hint. "Business things. Remember?"

"Oh! Right!" Randy said. "How could I forget?"

"You've got a lot on your mind, obviously." Emma turned to Lance. "Can you excuse us for just a few minutes? It shouldn't be too long."

"Take your time," Lance said, pushing his empty plate

away. "I'll order a cup of coffee and check my email on my phone. Madam Love should be here any minute anyway."

Randy opened his mouth to say something and Emma slapped him on the arm. "Let's go." She pushed him toward the front door before he could say anything that would incriminate her.

Once outside, Randy turned to Emma and crossed his arms. "Okay, you're acting mighty peculiar. What are you up to and why doesn't he know you're Madam Love?"

Emma filled in Randy on what was going on and he agreed to keep his mouth shut. He also agreed to call her in thirty minutes and pretend there was an emergency so she could escape again. The plan was perfect.

Emma quickly snuck into her office to change and then sent Lance a text to say she would be there in a few minutes and was excited to meet the woman he had been raving about.

Fifteen minutes later, Emma walked back into Finger Lickin' Chicken as Madam Love, adjusting her wig again and crossing her fingers she had everything in place. It normally took her twice as long to get ready. Hopefully there wouldn't be any wardrobe malfunctions because of the rush.

"Sorry I'm late, darling!" she said, approaching Lance a little too quickly. She lost her balance and banged into the table.

Lance jumped up to help, reaching out to grab her.

Emma stepped back, making sure he couldn't touch her. "I'm fine!"

Lance chuckled. "Okay." He sat back down. "You seem a little nervous. Is everything okay?"

"Perfect!" she said, a couple of octaves higher than Mariah Carey's vocal range. She cleared her throat. "Absolutely perfect.

I was dealing with a problem that took longer than expected and is not resolved yet." She took a seat and smoothed out her blouse.

That was a close call.

Any body contact between the two of them and she was sure they would get zapped again, like that hug yesterday in her office. Sooner or later he would figure things out. She needed to be careful.

"Where's Emma?" she asked.

Lance pointed to the parking lot. "She had to step outside to chat with someone. You didn't see her out there?"

"Oh . . ." Emma whipped around toward the front and then turned back to Lance. "Was she the cute blonde with short hair talking to Randy?"

Lance grinned. "That's her. Of course, you know Randy since he owns this property. Hopefully, she won't be too long."

Emma eyed his empty plate. "Looks like someone enjoyed his food."

"It was amazing. Fried chicken, garlic mashed potatoes, and buttermilk biscuits."

"That *does* sound amazing."

"You'll love it." Lance placed his napkin on the table and stood. "In fact, I'll go let the waiter know to bring you a plate."

"Oh . . . that's not necessary. It's getting late. I can just skip lunch for today."

She was stuffed from her first meal. How would she be able to eat a second?

It would be impossible.

"No way," Lance said. "You can't come to a place like this and not eat. The food is delicious. Besides, I said I was taking you out to lunch. I won't take no for an answer. It's the least I can do, considering everything you've done for me and Emma. You must be hungry. Just relax, eat something, and you'll meet Emma soon. Your opinion is important to me."

"But—"

"No buts. I insist." Lance walked toward the kitchen, chatted with the waiter, and returned. "He said it shouldn't take long for you to have your food."

Great.

"Are you sure you're okay?" Lance asked. "You look a little tense."

"Me? Tense?" She let out a nervous laugh. "I'm great! Never been better. It's just that little problem I was dealing with." Sweat trickled down between her cleavage. Okay, maybe she was a little tense and burning up, actually. She reached over and grabbed the iced tea, taking a long swig.

She stopped sipping when she noticed Lance was staring at her. "What?"

Lance pointed to the iced tea. "I can get you your own, you know. That was Emma's drink."

Emma glanced down at the almost-empty glass on the table and then back up at Lance. "Oh. Right. I guess I was distracted. I'll get a new one for her. You're right, I need to breathe and relax."

She didn't understand what was rattling her. She had been with Lance as Emma and she had been with him as Madam Love. This was no different than any other day they were together. Maybe she was out of her comfort zone. She rarely left the office dressed as Madam Love and some people were looking at her, probably noticing her wig, the scarf, and all the makeup and jewelry.

After the waiter brought another drink and her plate, Emma glanced down at the food, wondering how in the world she was going to eat any of it, considering how full she was.

Lance pointed to her plate. "Don't be shy. Dig in."

She forced a smile and cut into the chicken, lifting a tiny piece into her mouth. "Mmm. Good."

"Try the biscuits." He scooted the butter dish toward her. "You'll love them with butter."

She spread a little butter on the end of the biscuit and took a small bite. "Mmm. You're right. Amazing with butter."

Now knock it off! I'm going to explode!

"Don't forget the mashed potatoes!" Lance said, pointing to them.

The man was trying to kill her.

She could see the headlines in the newspaper: *Death by Comfort Food.*

Lance looked toward the front door. "I don't get it. Emma has been out there a long time. Maybe I should go check on her."

"No," Emma said. "She must have a good reason for not being here at the moment and you need to respect that. Let it be. Remember my rule? Don't force things. Go with the flow."

Lance nodded and rubbed his hands together. "Yeah, you're right, you're right. Go with the flow. I guess *I'm* the one who's nervous. I need to relax. It's just . . . I want you both to like each other. I have a feeling the two of you are going to become close friends."

Not in a million years.

"It won't hurt to just peek out the window," Lance said.

"Lance—"

Too late. The man shot out of his seat like a rocket and

was practically at the front window before she could blink. She used his absence at the table as an opportunity to get rid of her food.

She waved the waiter over and handed him her plate. "Take this, please. I'm done. Thank you."

He stared at the plate. "You didn't even touch it."

"Yes, I did. See . . ." She pointed to the chicken and the biscuit where she had taken tiny bites. "It was amazing. I'm not very hungry today."

He smiled. "No problem at all. I'll get you a box to go."

"No!" she said firmly, in a low voice. She craned her neck around to make sure Lance wasn't coming back, but he was still looking through the blinds for Emma. "Please take this away. I never want to see it again."

"You didn't like it? I'll remove it from the bill."

"Do not remove it from the bill. And I will leave an extra tip if you don't mention any of this to *him*."

The waiter glanced over at Lance and then nodded. "Mention what?" He winked and walked away with her plate.

Emma took in a deep breath, relieved she wouldn't have to eat anymore.

Lance returned and sat down, his shoulders slumping. "I don't get it. I don't see her anywhere out there. She wouldn't just leave, would she?"

"Of course not."

He frowned. "This is not going like I had hoped. I pictured the three of us having a great time and you two getting to know each other. She's an amazing woman, you'll see. Beautiful and kind and sweet. I trust her. There's a genuine side of her that you rarely find in a person. Her honesty is refreshing. What you see is what you get. Just like with you."

"Yeah," Emma said, the guilt almost suffocating her. "There are a lot of good people in the world. Even good people do bad things, but many times they do them for the right reasons."

She tried to plant that seed in Lance's head, hoping he would remember it when he found out what she had done to win the challenge.

"I guess . . ." Lance was deep in thought. "As long as you're upfront about it. Honesty is important." Lance studied her for a moment. "You look like you have something you want to say."

"No. Nothing. Honesty is a good quality—I agree. I just have other things on my mind."

Lance's initial assumption about Madam Love had been correct.

She was a fraud.

She believed she was doing it for a good reason, to keep a roof over her head, but he might not agree with her. She wanted to tell him the truth, but she knew he'd walk right out the door and out of her life forever. She couldn't let that happen.

Emma was in love with Lance.

There was no way she could tell him that now. Or ever. Who knew?

She sighed. Why did love have to be complicated?

Lance glanced down at the empty space on the table where Emma's plate used to be. "What happened to your food?"

Emma sat up. "It all went down the hatch!"

She wasn't going to clarify that "the hatch" was actually the garbage.

"You had me worried when you were picking at your food earlier."

"Well, worry no more."

And Emma didn't have to worry about eating anymore.

"Well . . . I guess that just means we need to order dessert!" Lance said.

Someone please kill me.

Emma knew it was useless to argue with the man.

When the bread pudding arrived, Lance handed her a spoon. "By all means, I want you to take the first few bites."

Emma forced a smile, took a deep breath, and then had the first bite. It was amazing, no doubt about that. Under normal circumstances she would have devoured the entire thing.

Fortunately, after the third bite her phone rang.

Thank you, Randy!

"Excuse me," Emma said. "I was expecting an important call earlier that never came in. This could be him."

"Of course," Lance said, reaching over and taking another bite of the bread pudding.

Emma tapped the green answer button on her phone. "Hello? Yes." She nodded a few times. "Okay, no problem." She ended the call with Randy and then took a few seconds to tap in a text message to Lance that was supposedly from Emma.

Lance pulled the phone from his pocket and read the text. "It's from Emma. She apologized for being gone. Randy needed an emergency ride somewhere, but she's on her way back."

Emma slid the phone back in her purse. "That's perfect. I need to run back to the office and fax a couple of important documents to my accountant. I should be back by the time Emma gets here."

Lance shook his head in frustration as he watched Madam Love walk out of the restaurant. What was supposed to be a simple lunch with her and Emma turned out to be frustrating. All he had wanted was for the two of them to meet and get to know each other. That was all. He guessed that was too much to ask because neither of them could sit still long enough to meet. He wondered if he would ever get them together in the same room. It would have been easier to bring Emma to Madam Love's office.

Lance needed to relax. Things don't always go according to plan and going with the flow was the way to go. He smiled at the thought. He was starting to think like Madam Love.

He glanced down at the empty dessert plate on the table, and then waved the waiter over.

"How's everything?" the waiter asked.

"Everything was delicious," Lance said. "I'd like to order another bread pudding dessert. My girlfriend should be back any minute and I want her to have some."

"You got it," the waiter said.

Lance smiled when he realized what he had just done. He had called Emma his girlfriend. He loved the way it sounded, but maybe he was being presumptuous again.

The truth was, Lance wanted a whole lot more than that.

He wanted everything with Emma—the sun, the moon,

the stars, and everything in between.

A minute later, Emma walked in the restaurant. Lance stood to greet her again. "Is everything okay?"

"Yes, yes," Emma said, reaching up and kissing Lance on the cheek, and zapping him good. "Sorry."

Lance touched the side of his cheek and grinned. "All is forgiven when I get those electric kisses from you. In fact, is there anything else you're sorry for? Go ahead and plant another kiss right here." He pointed to his cheek. "Or here." He pointed to his lips.

"Please sit," Emma said, shaking her head. "And where's Madam Love?"

"She had to fax something to someone. Hopefully, she'll be back soon. In the meantime . . ." Lance scooted forward in his chair and grabbed both of Emma's hands, zapping them both.

"You did that on purpose," Emma said.

"Of course, I did. It's kind of fun."

"It's kind of scary."

"That, too," Lance said. "Hey, I wanted to mention something funny that happened before you came in."

"Do tell."

"I didn't do it on purpose—it just came out. I called you my girlfriend when I was talking to the waiter."

She smiled. "Don't you think that's being a little bit—"

"Presumptuous," they both said simultaneously.

Lance laughed, while Emma crossed her arms and gave him a look. Soon, she was sharing the laugh with him.

The waiter arrived and placed the bread pudding on the table.

"What's this?" Emma asked, with a look of horror on

her face.

"Don't be scared," Lance said, chuckling. "It's just bread pudding."

Emma shook her head. "I have no room whatsoever. I can't."

"Just one bite," Lance said, spooning some in her direction. "Two bites at the most. You ate over thirty minutes ago."

"One bite," Emma said, leaning forward and taking the spoonful into her mouth.

"Good?" Lance said.

Emma nodded. "Very, but please, no more."

Lance sat up and thought about it. "Okay, we can take a break from the food until Madam Love comes back. I'd like to talk about us for a moment."

"Okay . . ."

Lance raised an eyebrow. "Are you blushing?"

"No."

He continued to stare at her until she gave him the answer he wanted.

"Maybe," she said.

Lance grinned. "There it is."

She squeezed his hands. "Quit looking at me like that."

"I can't help it. If you were me, you would be looking at you that way."

"That makes no sense."

Lance laughed, ready to put everything out there. "Okay, let me see if I can be more clear this time. Considering our feelings and the fact that we electrocute each other on a regular basis, I would like to move our relationship to the next level and consider this more than dating. And I'm ready to tell the world tomorrow on the radio."

CHAPTER EIGHTEEN

Lance was just about to enter the on-air studio to admit his defeat in the challenge to Madam Love when he was intercepted by his best friend and agent.

"We need to talk," Peter said, grabbing Lance's arm and ushering him into the first empty conference room he found. He closed the door behind them and turned to face Lance, sighing. "Are you sure you want to do this?"

"Yes. I'm sure."

"There's no turning back and there's a good possibility you'll be mocked, attacked, and ridiculed on social media. You'll also take a hit on your credibility, which can affect future book sales. This can be the end of your career."

"I doubt that. And are you telling me this as a friend or as my agent?" Lance asked.

Peter hesitated. "Your agent. You pay me to look after your career and make sure you're making the right moves. Your business and livelihood are important to me."

"What about my happiness?"

"Of course, I want you to be happy! But I also want to make sure you've really thought about this thoroughly."

Lance had thought about it, even obsessed over it, and he was certain he was making the right choice. The man who wrote the book *Your Soulmate Doesn't Exist* was going to tell the world he had a soulmate. Lance knew it was crazy and knew it could possibly affect his career—at least in the short term—but he didn't care. He was a man of his word. Madam Love won fair and square and people deserved to know how he appreciated and respected her. And even though Lance wasn't going to win the challenge, he felt like he was the one coming out ahead because he had Emma.

Wonderful Emma.

Peter pointed to Lance's face. "You're getting all googly-eyed. You're thinking of her again, aren't you?"

Lance chuckled. "Can you blame me? Wait until you meet her—then you'll understand."

"It's not too late to change your mind."

A producer knocked on the glass before sticking her head in the room. "Five minutes until air."

"Thanks," Lance said, waiting for the producer to close the door before continuing, "I told you before, I'm not going to change my mind. I understand the possible repercussions and I appreciate your concern, but I will handle whatever comes my way. Relax."

Peter leaned against the edge of the table and crossed his arms. "Relax. Right. What if it doesn't work out with Emma?"

"I'm also not going to worry about hypothetical situations. This is an exciting new chapter in my life and I want to spend as much time as possible with Emma. In fact, she's cooking me dinner this evening to celebrate my loss." He winked.

Peter shook his head. "Celebrating a loss . . . Who celebrates a loss? Have I ever told you that you're crazy?"

Lance chuckled. "More than a few times. Even in Spanish."

Maybe it was crazy that he was going to go on the air and announce with excitement that he had lost, but he felt amazing. That's what love does to a person. It makes you feel alive, excited about the possibilities, and even unstoppable. It was funny how Lance's life could change in such a short timeframe. Two weeks ago, he was single and riding high on the tail of a new book release, and now he was head over heels for a girl and didn't even care about the book.

Love was able to help him put everything in perspective and realize that life was about friends, and family, and love.

Love.

Madam Love passed by the other side of the glass. She smiled and waved to Lance, however there was something off. The smile seemed forced. Was she nervous?

Lance waved right back and gestured toward the studio, giving her a thumbs-up to let her know he would be right there.

Peter shook his head. "Don't tell me the two of you are friends now, too."

"I like her," Lance said. "She's actually a very cool person once you get to know her. I admit I judged her based on what happened with Karla and the other fortune teller, and that was wrong and unfair. Madam Love is an extraordinary woman who provides a life-changing service everyone should know about."

"Who *are* you?" Peter asked, bringing a chuckle out of Lance.

The producer swung the door open again. "We need you in the studio now."

Lance squeezed Peter's arm. "Showtime." He winked. "Don't worry. Be happy."

They followed the producer down the hallway to the studio.

After entering the studio, Lance got comfortable in the chair across from Madam Love and winked at her before slipping the headphones over his ears. He swiveled in his chair toward Elaine just as she pressed the microphone button, illuminating the on-air light.

"Welcome to the program today. I'm Elaine Stewart and you're in for a very special treat, because we're going to share the results of the big challenge between bestselling author, Lance Parker and fortune teller extraordinaire, Madam Love. Lance's book *Your Soulmate Doesn't Exist* has sparked a lot of controversy the last couple of weeks, especially with Madam Love, whose job is to find soulmates for her clients. If you were with us last time the two were on the program, Madam Love said she would be able to find Lance a soulmate in two weeks, even though she thought he was arrogant and impossible. Welcome back to the program, Lance and Madam Love!"

"It's great to be back," Lance said. "I'll try to be less arrogant and less impossible today. No guarantees, though."

Madam Love laughed. "Okay, I admit I may have been a little quick to judge Mr. Parker. He happens to be human, and he listens well for a man."

"Well, thank you very much," Lance said. "You've really impressed me."

"Thank you, darling."

Elaine glanced back and forth between the two of them.

"This is certainly not what I expected between the two of you. I had contemplated handing out boxing gloves before the show. And now you're both smiling, which doesn't make much sense since one of you has lost the challenge. Unless the two of you are now an item."

Lance chuckled. "I can assure you, that is not the case."

"Hey!" Madam Love said. "Where are those boxing gloves, Elaine?"

Elaine laughed. "By the way, I asked Madam Love and Lance to keep the winner of the challenge a secret until we revealed it on the air here today, so I'm just as excited to find out who won. Without further delay, let's find out who the winner is!" Elaine glanced over to her producer on the other side of the glass. "Do we have a drumroll for this or something?"

The producer nodded enthusiastically and clicked a button to play the drumroll.

"Okay!" Elaine said. "The time has come to find out the winner of the challenge. Lance, everyone is dying to know. Did Madam Love find you a soulmate?"

Lance grinned. "Yes. She found me a soulmate. Her name is Emma, and I love her."

Emma was at a loss for words.

Lance just admitted publicly to the entire world that he loved her.

He *loved* her!

Sure, Emma had had a discussion with Lance about having feelings for each other, but that was different. Feelings were *feelings*, they weren't love! Part of her wanted to run from the studio as fast as she could and catch the next flight to Greenland where she would live among the Eskimos in an igloo, spending her days ice fishing, dog sledding, and freezing.

Half of her was excited about his confession while the other half felt guilty. She literally didn't know what to do or say. She was frozen. Just like those Eskimos.

"Madam Love?" Elaine said. "What do you think of all this? How do you feel? I thought you'd be a little more excited, but you seem to be a tad bit reserved for such a big win."

Emma nodded. "Sorry. I always get emotional when another one of my clients finds that special someone. Don't get me wrong, I expect it to happen, but that doesn't mean I'll ever get used to it. It's a beautiful thing, really."

"Can't deny that," Elaine said. "Lance—I would imagine you must be on top of the world, but what does all this mean for your literary career? You wrote a book about the non-existence of soulmates, yet you have one now."

"Well, I do think there are still many valid points in my book, even when you take out the soulmate equation," Lance said. "As for my career, yes, this may change things a bit. Honestly, I'm not sure what I want to do next. I've always wanted to write a children's book. Maybe this was a sign for me to go in a different direction as an author. Whatever the case, I'm still optimistic about the future."

"You don't have any regrets at all? Can your ego withstand such a big hit? You're a man after all, and men have a reputation for being competitive."

Lance chuckled. "Of course. I admit I wanted Madam Love to fail miserably. I think it's human to have a belief and defend it fiercely, even a little too much so when the ego and pride get involved. I believed what I wrote at the time and I admit that I was wrong. Honestly, I'm happy to be proven wrong. I have different beliefs now, thanks to an amazing woman."

"It sounds like Emma has already taught you a lot," Elaine said.

"Well, she has, but I was actually giving kudos here to Madam Love. She has a special gift and needs to be acknowledged. I want to apologize for questioning her and for insulting her in public last time we were on air."

"Thank you," Emma said.

At least she was able to get two words in the conversation while fighting back the tears.

Tears of guilt and self-reprimand.

"Our listeners seem to think so, too. In fact, we have Ginger on the phone who would like to talk to Madam Love. Ginger, you're on the air."

"Thank you, Elaine," Ginger said. "Madam Love, I think what you did was absolutely amazing."

"Thank you," Emma said. "I appreciate that."

"Did you have a question for Madam Love, Ginger?" Elaine said.

"Yes," Ginger said. "I was wondering if you could find me a man. Tall. Dark. Handsome. Can you find me a cowboy? I love the smell of leather."

Here we go again.

"This is one thing I don't think we ever talked about, Madam Love," Elaine said. "Do your clients have any say in the matter with regards to their soulmates?"

"No," Emma said. "It doesn't work that way. You can't choose your soulmate. The universe chooses that person for you. Ginger says she would like a cowboy, but she may end up with a gynecologist."

"What in the world?" Ginger said. "Why would I want to go out with a gynecologist?"

"I'm just using that as an example," Emma said.

"Give me another example. I don't like it."

"I can't do that," Emma said. "Take Lance, for example. When we first met, he told me he preferred to meet a woman who was a champion clogger. Someone willing to compete in local clogging contests."

"I was joking," Lance said.

"But even if you weren't joking, the chances of you meeting a world champion clogger are slim to none. You can have many things in common with your soulmate or nothing at all. It's all about the connection."

"When do you know a person is your soulmate?" Elaine asked.

"Good question," Emma said. "It's not an exact science or an exact feeling, but the person can feel like your best friend. Like you could tell them anything. You're comfortable being your most authentic selves when you're together, whether you're in public or in bed. And nothing is better than being together. And for men, that means not even football on Sundays is better than being with her, unless your soulmate is just as excited about the football as you, and you're doing it together, of course. But the best answer to your question is, you just know when someone is your soulmate. You feel it. Right down to your core."

"Fascinating," Elaine said. "Well, it shouldn't come as a surprise that we have been bombarded with calls and emails from people wanting information about your services. And that doesn't even count all of the posts and messages from Facebook and Twitter. My producer has just posted your contact details on our website, so it looks like you're going to be one busy woman."

"Thank you," Emma said.

Not even thirty seconds later, her phone was buzzing in her purse. She pulled it out and could see missed phone calls, text messages, voicemails, and emails.

It was crazy.

It was just what she hoped for.

But she wasn't smiling.

Not even a little.

"She deserves every bit of the success coming to her," Lance said. "Everyone knows I thought she was a fraud when I first met her. I kept telling her I didn't trust one single word coming out of her mouth, but now I can say with one hundred percent confidence that I trust her. I trust her with all my heart and soul. I will be forever grateful for Madam Love."

A tear slipped from Emma's eye and traveled down her cheek. She quickly wiped it away before Lance had a chance to see it.

She should be happy she won the challenge.

She should be happy she would have more customers than she'll have time for.

She should be happy that she'd have no problem paying Randy the rent increase from now on. Maybe she could finally replace that clunker of a car, too.

Instead, her pulse banged in her head and her heart ached from the guilt and remorse.

It was hard for her to breathe and she wanted to shake the uncomfortable feeling from her body. How could she continue deceiving Lance? He deserved better. They had planned on having dinner later in the evening, but how could she look him in the eyes when he had just said he trusted her with his heart and soul?

That's just it.

She couldn't.

Emma needed to make this right.

She would tell him everything this evening, but after dinner so they'd have one last meal together before her irredeemable death. It wouldn't be easy, but it was the right thing to do. She knew he would walk out the door when he found out, but she just couldn't handle the guilt anymore. The sad part was she loved Lance, too.

Too bad she would lose him after he found out the truth.

CHAPTER NINETEEN

Emma lit two Yankee Candles in her family room and then straightened out the pillows on the sofa. She pulled a bottle from the case of Black Stallion 2013 Cabernet her client Brenda had brought back from Napa. Just as Emma predicted, Brenda had met her soulmate and was already head over heels for the guy who'd taken her up in the hot air balloon.

At least she'd gotten that one right.

Finding Lance his soulmate was another story.

A complete disaster.

Emma had thought she could easily find Lance someone special. She even thought she could have been the one, but she was so, so wrong. She didn't deserve Lance. He deserved someone who was honest.

"This guilt is going to give me an ulcer," Emma said to herself as she cut slices of Monterey Jack cheese and placed them on the platter next to the grapes. "Focus. Try to enjoy yourself while it lasts. Just a few more hours."

She knew it would be over after he found out she was a fraud.

Lance would be arriving in fewer than twenty minutes and Emma wanted to make sure everything was perfect for the last supper. The original plan had been to cook him a wonderful pasta dish with fresh tomatoes and mushrooms, garlic bread, and Caesar salad. That plan flew out the window when she absentmindedly bought rice at the store instead of pasta.

That's how nervous and scatterbrained she was.

Emma didn't want to take a chance on burning the meal or burning down the house, so she had baked ziti delivered from the Italian deli. He'd probably enjoy it more than her pasta, anyway.

Emma glanced over at her ringing phone on the kitchen counter to check the caller ID.

It was Randy.

He could help her relax before Lance showed up.

"Hi, Randy," Emma said, after answering.

"I heard you on the radio," Randy said his typical jovial tone. "You sounded great!"

"Good to know, because I felt like crap."

"Oh—sorry to hear that. You coming down with something?"

"Yeah. A bad case of shame and self-condemnation. I keep thinking someone is following me, but that's just the shadow of guilt. I can't handle it anymore. Lance is coming over for dinner and I'm going to come clean. I'm going to tell him everything."

"I can't say that I blame you," Randy said. "Relationships are built on trust and honesty, so it's good to get it out there in the open. Don't worry. I'm sure everything will turn out just fine with you two. This is just a bump in the road."

Emma let out a nervous chuckle. "A bump in the road? It's the world's largest pothole."

"Well . . . I'll be here if you need to talk."

"I appreciate that, but I'm pretty sure I'm going to be seeking solace in sugar and sweets after this is over. Can you be on call with cupcake support? I have a feeling I'm going to be needing lots of them over the next few days or the rest of my what-is-to-be a lonely, lonely life."

Randy laughed. "Of course. You can have as many as you can handle. In fact, I'm going to be baking pumpkin spice cupcakes for the farmers' market. They'll be topped with fresh buttercream icing, if that interests you."

"It more than interests me. Sounds amazing."

"Good. Stop by the farmers' market this weekend. I'll set aside a few of them for you."

Emma's doorbell rang.

"Thanks, Randy. Lance is at the door. I have to run for now."

"You got it," Randy said. "Good luck!"

Emma appreciated his kindness, but she would need more than luck to get through this.

She would need a miracle.

Emma took a deep breath and opened the door for Lance. "Hey, there." She glanced down toward the floor at Typo. "And what a surprise! I'm glad you came!" She reached down to pet Typo as the dog greeted her with licks on the legs.

Lance held out a bouquet of tulips in Emma's direction. "You seem to be more excited to see him than you do me."

That wasn't far from the truth.

Emma stood and took the flowers from Lance. "Thank you. These are beautiful. And it sounds like you're a little jealous."

He stepped inside and closed the door behind him. "That is not correct. I'm *a lot* jealous." He grinned and moved closer to Emma, placing his hands on her waist and kissing her on the lips.

The zap was strong and expected.

For the slightest moment Emma had forgotten that Lance was going to be hating her very soon. She had the thought of kissing him all evening to avoid the inevitable, but that would just make the breakup harder since she would miss those kisses even more.

Emma pulled off the protective plastic from around the flowers. "Let me put these in water." She grabbed a vase from the bottom cupboard and stuck it in the sink to fill. She pointed to the wine. "Do you mind opening the bottle?"

"I don't mind at all," Lance said, grabbing the corkscrew and looking around. "I love your place."

"Thank you."

"And it smells great in here."

Emma pointed to the oven. "That's the baked ziti I'm keeping warm. Unless you're talking about the pineapple cilantro candles." She pointed to the flickering flames in the family room.

Lance chuckled. "It could be a combination of both." He glanced over at the oven. "How romantic. You made baked ziti."

She waved off his comment. "I would love to take the credit, but I had it delivered."

"From our place?"

Their place? They had a place?

The guilt came back strong, jumping on her back like a giant five-hundred-pound gorilla.

She forced a smile. "Yes. Our place."

Typo jumped on the sofa and lay down.

"Sorry about that," Lance said. "I'll get him down."

Emma glanced over at Typo, who had just closed his eyes. "It's okay. Really. He looks comfortable."

Lance shook his head and chuckled, then handed Emma a glass of wine. "To us."

Emma clinked his glass, hoping he wouldn't notice her trembling hand. "To us."

To the end of us was probably a more appropriate toast.

Lance wandered through the family room, inspecting the first of the six paintings on the walls.

He swung around, his mouth hanging open. "You painted these."

It wasn't a question.

He knew.

She nodded and pulled the baked ziti from the oven.

"I can't believe you're not some famous painter. I said you were a closet Van Gogh and I was right. You should have your own gallery."

That had been the plan many years ago, or at least pursuing some type of career in the arts.

"Who are they?" Lance asked.

Emma pulled off the oven gloves and dropped them on the kitchen counter, glancing over to the family room to see what captured Lance's eye. He was standing in front of her favorite piece, the painting of her parents at the Rose Garden in Golden Gate Park.

"My mom and dad," Emma said. "They loved roses."

He nodded. "It's beautiful."

"Thank you," Emma said, her eyes starting to burn.

It was the last painting she had ever done. She was going to give it to them on their anniversary, but then they had died in the car accident. She just couldn't bring herself to paint another piece after that one. When Lance had taken Emma to paint on their first date, she was surprised how comfortable she had felt and how much she had enjoyed it. It was like she had never given up.

"You really are talented." Lance glanced at the other paintings. "No slaughtered chickens anywhere."

Emma snorted. She would miss the way he made her laugh and smile. He could snap her out of any funk.

She placed the bake ziti on the trivet in the middle of the kitchen table. "Dinner is served, Sir Lancelot."

"Thank you, Lady Guinevere." Lance winked and held his hands out. "Mind if I use your restroom real quick to wash my hands? I have remnants of a spoiled dog all over them."

"Of course," Emma said, pointing to the hallway. "It's just around the corner."

Lance headed down the hallway and pushed open the first door he came to.

"Oh," he mumbled to himself, realizing it wasn't the bathroom.

It was a large office with an oak desk, several bookcases, and a treadmill machine. He grabbed the handle to pull the door closed when something on the wall caught his eye.

It was a painting of horses, several of them running wild in the mountains.

It was gorgeous.

Lance smiled, thinking of their dates and how he happened to choose two things Emma loved: painting and horses. If that wasn't a sign he didn't know what was.

Curious, he entered the office and admired the other paintings on the wall, still amazed how well Emma could paint. Next to the horses was another painting of an outdoor cafe, maybe in France or Italy. It was brilliant and he couldn't help but think what a shame it was she wasn't doing anything with them.

Lance turned and saw a photo of Emma at Disneyland in front of Sleeping Beauty Castle. He picked up the picture frame from the desk and smiled. Emma was young, but she had that same gorgeous smile.

"Bathroom," he said to himself, ready to leave the office before he got caught snooping.

He placed the picture frame back on its place, then froze when he saw a folder on the desk that was labeled *Madam Love*.

Lance blinked twice.

Why does Emma have a folder with Madam Love's name on it?

He stared at it, confused.

Was Emma one of her clients?

Did she hire Madam Love to find a soulmate?

"No way," Lance said, his heart beating a little faster.

Madam Love had sent two of her clients to the same place so they would meet each other and think they were soulmates.

Emma and Lance had been scammed.

He shook his head in disbelief, then scratched the side of his face.

But why did Emma have a folder? Lance never got a folder from Madam Love.

And what was inside?

Lance used his index finger and thumb to slowly open the folder, peeking underneath at its contents. There was a notice of rent increase.

He shook his head. "I don't get it. Rent increase?"

Now he was more confused than ever.

Lance read the top two lines of document.

Name of Proprietor: Emma Wright

Business Name: Madam Love

He blinked again, his pulse now banging in his temples as it all started to make sense.

Emma was Madam Love.

Madam Love was Emma.

And Emma wasn't his soulmate.

He skipped the bathroom and headed straight back to the kitchen.

Emma looked up from the table. "I thought you fell in. Have a seat before it gets cold."

Lance stood there in front of the kitchen table, trying to decide if he was going to say something to her or just walk out the door without a word.

"Are you okay?" Emma asked.

He ground his teeth. "I'm fine, *darling*."

Emma's eyes grew wide, but she didn't respond.

He shook his head in disgust. "You used me to win the challenge."

Emma stood, her face turning pale. "Let me explain—"

"There's no need to explain anything," Lance said. "This was all a game to you. Me. You. Us."

"No, it wasn't. Please sit down and we can calmly discuss—"

"Why would I want to have a discussion with you? Everything that comes out of your mouth is a lie."

"That's not fair!"

"No? Human resources?"

Emma opened her mouth and then closed it.

"That's what I thought," Lance said. "You used me and manipulated me. How many people were involved in this scam? What about the old man with the cane who led me to the deli? How much did you have to pay him?"

"I have no idea what you're talking about."

"Or the employee who sat me at your table. Very clever."

"I didn't plan that," Emma said.

"Come on. You expect me to believe that? How long were you going to keep up this charade? Are you already working on your next scam, Madam Fraud?"

Emma took a few steps toward Lance. "I was going to tell you everything after dinner."

Lance laughed. "Of course, you were! After we ate baked ziti, and drank wine, and laughed, and kissed, you were just going to casually tell me that everything about us was a lie. How dumb do you think I am? Don't answer that. I'm the biggest idiot in the world because I trusted you."

Emma sniffed and wiped the tears traveling down her cheeks.

"Save the fake tears for your next performance." Lance walked over to the family room and picked up Typo, tucking the dog under his arm. He pointed to the tulips. "Enjoy the flowers." He opened the front door and turned back one last time. "And your pathetic life."

CHAPTER TWENTY

"I would like to meet a woman who is smart, compassionate, authentic, open-minded, sweet, and comfortable in her own skin," Wayne said.

Emma had to admit that caught her by surprise. Wayne was the first client in a while who actually had realistic expectations when talking about the qualities he wanted in a partner. Not that she could promise him any of those things in his soulmate, but she still found it refreshing that he didn't mention money, material things, or physical attributes.

"Oh . . . I forgot," Wayne said. "Make sure she has a nice rack."

It was business as usual at Madam Love's office with the exception of Emma having no interest in working today. In fact, she wasn't supposed to be there at all. The plan had been to cancel all her appointments for the day. Unfortunately, she couldn't get a hold of Wayne, forcing her to come in for just the one consultation with him. Then she would go back home, put on her pajamas, and kick off a marathon of movies that would make her cry. *Titanic, The Notebook, Terms of Endearment*, and *The English Patient*, for starters. A tub of ice cream or a dozen of Randy's cupcakes would also be very necessary. Then maybe she would be able to forget the look on Lance's face when he confronted her and the words that stung worse than a thousand yellow jackets. No way. She'd never forget.

You used me and manipulated me
Everything that comes out of your mouth is a lie.
Save the fake tears for another performance.
I'm the biggest idiot in the world because I trusted you.
And the worst one of all . . .
Enjoy the flowers and your pathetic life.

"Madam Love?" Wayne said.

"Sorry," Emma said, finding it hard to focus, even for a couple of minutes. She pulled the hanging beads to one side and waved him through. "Right this way. Your future awaits you."

An hour later, Wayne left Emma's office with specific instructions on how to meet his soulmate. She was certain he was going to meet the woman of his dreams. Lucky him.

Emma sat down at her desk to check her email before she headed back home. There were more new client inquiries and notifications showing new appointments booked through her online system. Things had been crazy ever since she won the challenge. The challenge she'd won by deceiving Lance.

Like a fool, she checked her phone for voicemails or text messages from him.

Nothing. Why would he talk with her again? He hated her now.

Emma massaged her temples. She was frustrated, sad, and tired. She closed her laptop and stood, ready to change out of her clothes and go home to start another round of her pity party.

The front door opened and a smiling man stepped inside.

Maybe the day wouldn't be so bad after all.

It was the man Emma needed right now more than ever, and he was holding a Tupperware container.

Emma smiled. "My hero."

Randy chuckled and placed the container on the counter. "Go ahead. Open it."

Emma pulled the top off the container and peeked inside. There were four cupcakes staring back at her, begging to be eaten. She moved her face closer and inhaled through her nose. They looked and smelled divine.

"What did you make this time?" Emma said.

Randy smiled proudly. "I call this one Chocolate Coronary. Chocolate cake filled with chocolate cream, topped with chocolate frosting. And we can't forget the chocolate sprinkles."

"It would be rude to forget them." Emma pulled a cupcake from the container and peeled back the paper. "Have I told you lately that I love you?"

Randy laughed. "Are you talking to me or the cupcake?"

Emma took a bite and moaned. "Both." She moaned again as she chewed. "Thank you—I needed this. I had a horrible night. Didn't sleep one bit."

"Sorry to hear that. So, you haven't talked to Lance?"

"No, and I don't expect to talk to him. I really hurt him."

"Does he know why you did it?" Randy said.

Emma shook her head.

"Or that you love him?"

Emma arched an eyebrow. "How do you know I love him?"

"It's as obvious as your cupcake obsession."

Emma nodded. "Well, no, he doesn't know. He wouldn't even listen to me. You should have seen how irate he was. I can't blame him at all, really."

"You need to tell him."

"I'm telling you—he's not going to listen to me. He hasn't returned my calls or text messages and I have no idea where he is. I wouldn't be surprised if he left the country to get as far away from me as possible. The message is very clear. He doesn't want anything to do with me. I respect his decision. Even if I were able to tell him, he wouldn't believe me anyway."

"I happen to know where he is right now," Randy said.

Emma cocked her head to the side. "How do you know that?"

Randy pulled a section of the newspaper from his inside jacket pocket and unfolded it, setting it on the counter next to the cupcakes. It was the Arts and Entertainment section. He pointed to the Local Literature Events column on the right side of the page. There was a picture of Lance holding his book *Your Soulmate Doesn't Exist*. The column said Lance would be signing copies at City Lights Bookstore today.

"Interesting," Emma said. "Well, I'm glad to see life goes on for him, although I doubt he'll have many people showing up for the book signing. Losing the challenge took away his credibility. I wouldn't be surprised if his book sales came to a screeching halt. All because of me."

"You should go," Randy said.

"Where?" Emma said.

"To the book signing! He won't be able to get rid of you

because he has to be there. Tell him everything, start from the beginning. Then tell him how much you love him. He needs to know."

There was no way Emma could do that. Lance would probably call security and have her removed from the bookstore for being a liar. She wished there was something she could do to help him. Not because she hoped he would take her back, but because it was the right thing to do. It wasn't fair that she broke his heart and ruined his career while her business was booming.

It wasn't fair at all.

And that's when it came to her. It was a brilliant idea that could help Lance before it was too late.

"I have to go," Emma said.

"That's the spirit! You're making the right decision. Lance deserves to know." Randy gestured over his shoulder to the parking lot. "Let's go in my car. I wanted to pick up a book from—"

"I'm not talking about the bookstore. I'm going to the radio station."

"What?" Randy said. "I don't get it. What are you going to do there?"

"Confess everything. I owe it to him and I owe it to my conscience. If I can't pay the rent I'll work two jobs, but I need to do what I should have done two days ago at the radio station."

Lance glanced around the empty bookstore from his seated position at the book-signing table and let out a frustrated breath. "What was I thinking? This is embarrassing. We should have canceled."

Peter placed another stack of Lance's books on the table. "Canceling wasn't an option."

Lance had over two hundred people waiting in line at his last book signing, so this was quite a shock to his system. Today he could have counted the number of people in line on one hand.

On one finger, actually.

A woman waited patiently, leaning against the wall, checking her phone.

"We're ready for you," Peter said, waving the woman over. "Don't be shy."

She approached the table and glanced down at the cover of Lance's book. "Pardon me?"

"Mr. Parker would be happy to sign a book for you. And feel free to take a selfie."

"Oh . . ." the woman said, gesturing back to the cash register. "I'm actually just waiting for a friend to pay for a book. Thanks, though." The woman walked away.

Peter shook his head. "I don't want to say I told you so, but—"

"You just said it," Lance said.

"No. I said I didn't want to say it." Peter removed a stack of books from the table and stuck them back in the box underneath. "I guess we won't be needing so many books."

Lance glanced around. "Or any."

"It's your own fault. I warned you. Why didn't you listen to me?"

"I had a very good reason. I thought I would be spending

the rest of my life with an amazing woman, remember? She turned out to be a con artist."

"I don't understand why you just don't go back to the radio station and tell them everything. They'll declare you the winner. At least, then you'd be able to salvage your career. There's still time."

"They would think I'm nuts, which wouldn't be far from the truth. Mr. Parker, do you believe in soulmates? Well, I used to, but then I didn't, then I did, and now I don't again." He shook his head. "They would laugh me right out of the studio. I'm not going to the radio station."

"I think you need to reconsider that," Randy said, approaching the table.

Lance stood. "What are you doing here? Shouldn't you be planning your next scam with Madam Fraud? Or do you want to have a book signed by the idiot your friend used so you can both have a good laugh?"

"I had nothing to do with what happened between you and Emma."

"Nothing? You mean to tell me you didn't know anything about her scheme? You had to be in on it."

Randy shook his head. "I had no idea what was going on between the two of you until the day I met you at Finger Lickin' Chicken. That's why she took me outside. To fill me in on everything, and it wasn't a scheme or a scam."

The revelation came as a surprise. Lance had been certain that Randy was involved. But it really didn't matter. Emma lied and used him and there was nothing more to discuss. Now he just needed to get rid of Randy.

"I'll ask you again," Lance said. "What are you doing here? If you're not buying a book, please go."

Randy placed a Tupperware container on the table. "I come in peace. And you need to get your facts straight before you start hurling accusations at innocent people. You were wrong about me and you're wrong about Emma."

Peter pointed to the Tupperware container. "What's this?"

"Cupcakes."

"I love cupcakes," Peter said.

"Lance does, too," Randy said, pulling off the top of the container and setting it aside. "And I happened to bring his favorite."

Lance licked his lips. "Apple pie cupcakes?"

"Good eye," Randy said with pride. "White cake with cinnamon, apple pie filling, topped with cream cheese icing. I brought them for you." He gestured to Peter. "Of course, you can try one, too." He held out his hand. "I'm Randy. A neutral person. A carrier of truth."

Peter shook his hand. "A pleasure. I'm Peter, Lance's agent." He pointed to the cupcakes. "Thanks for bringing these. They look amazing." Peter reached for one of the cupcakes.

Randy pulled the container away. "Hold on. You'll get to enjoy them in just a minute. I need to talk with Lance first."

"You're bribing me with cupcakes?" Lance said.

"Yes. All you have to do is listen to what I have to say. It will only be a minute or two."

"Why should I listen to you?"

"Listen to the man," Peter said, not taking his eyes off the cupcakes.

Lance sat back down. "Fine. Make it quick—I'm in the middle of a book-signing, as you can tell."

Randy looked around. "If you say so."

Peter chuckled and then stopped when Lance glared at him.

"First," Randy said. "Did you know that Emma is in love with you?"

Lance jerked his head back. "Right. You expect me to believe that?"

"You'd better believe it because it's true. Emma told me everything. There are a lot of things you don't know. Things started with the best intentions, believe me. Emma really did think she could find you your soulmate and that's why she sent you to those places. The problem was, she kept on ending up at the same places, completely unplanned. That's when she started to have feelings for you and suspect she might have been your soulmate. She was conflicted and thought about telling you a hundred times. To make matters worse, I hiked up the rent on her and she couldn't afford losing the challenge. The bottom line was, she ran out of options and had to win to survive. Emma is a good person who made a desperate choice she'll regret for the rest of her life."

Lance stared at Randy for a moment, thinking of the rent increase notice he had found in Emma's office. He was telling the truth about that. Lance wondered what he would have done if he had been in Emma's shoes.

"Why didn't she tell me any of this before?" Lance asked. "I would have let her win and we wouldn't have had any deception."

"Would you really? She wanted to tell you, but then it got complicated because somewhere along the way she fell in love. With you."

He wanted to believe it—he truly did. He professed his love for her on the radio and she'd said nothing in return.

Maybe because she was happy with the way things turned out. She won the challenge and the money was more important than a relationship with Lance.

"I still don't get why you're here," Lance said. "Emma won the challenge and now she'll have plenty of money to pay the rent. Sounds like a happy ending. At least, for her."

"That's where you're wrong. She's about to throw everything away. She's far from being happy. She's been crying and eating cupcakes for two days. Emma canceled all her appointments. That woman is a wreck. I'm worried about her."

"What are you talking about?"

"Emma went to the radio station to confess everything. She's going to get them to declare you the winner," Randy said. "She's probably already there right now."

"What?" Lance said, not understanding why she would do such a thing. "But if she does that she'll lose all the new clients coming in and she'll ruin her reputation. This will be the end of her business."

Randy nodded. "She doesn't care. She's more worried about you and said she's doing what she should have done last time you were on the air. This is how much she loves you."

"I have to go," Lance said.

"You can't just leave the book signing," Peter said.

Lance gestured around the bookstore. "There's nobody here!"

Peter nodded. "Good point. Where are you going?"

"To the radio station. I have to stop her before it's too late." Lance stood up and ran out, leaving Randy, Peter, and the cupcakes behind. He ran down the street two blocks to his SUV and got inside, a little out of breath. He started the engine, and then sent Emma a quick text before pulling out of the parking lot.

Lance: Don't do it. Don't confess.

Lance had conflicted feelings after hearing what Randy had to say at the bookstore, and Emma really had hurt him, but that didn't mean he wanted to see her lose her business.
And none of that changed the fact that he still loved her.

CHAPTER TWENTY-ONE

Lance pulled onto the street and drove to the radio station. He tuned into Elaine's radio program to see if Emma was already on the air, but a commercial was playing. It was the first time Lance had wished for a radio station to play more commercials, hoping that would delay Emma from going on the air.

"Welcome back to the program. I'm Elaine Stewart and we have a surprise guest in the studio with us today. Madam Love captured our hearts recently after finding a soulmate for author Lance Parker. She is here to give us an update on Lance and Emma. Welcome Madam Love!"

"Thank you," Emma said, sounding tired and defeated.

"I'm sure everyone is excited to hear the latest. What can you tell us? Did Lance and Emma rush off to Las Vegas to get married?"

"I'm afraid not," Emma said. "In fact, it's quite the opposite. They're not seeing each other anymore."

"I must say I certainly wasn't expecting to hear that," Elaine said. "What happened?"

"Well, it's kind of my fault," Emma said. "Actually, it's one hundred percent my fault."

"I don't understand," Elaine said. "You were the one who was instrumental in getting them together in the first place."

"I caused their breakup," Emma said. "I lied to Lance, I lied to you, and I lied to your listeners. I'm so sorry."

"Stop talking!" Lance yelled at the radio, wishing the producer would tape Emma's mouth shut. He needed to get to the radio station before she said too much, but he was stuck in traffic, feeling helpless. He tried calling the radio station while he sat at a red light, but the line was busy.

"Okay, you've lost me again," Elaine said. "What did you lie about and what does it have to do with Lance and Emma?"

"My lie has everything to do with Lance and Emma because *I'm* Emma."

"What do you mean?" Elaine said.

"Don't say it!" Lance yelled at the radio again.

"My name is Emma Wright, but I'm known as Madam Love when I'm working and finding people their soulmates. And while it was my sincere intention to find Lance a soulmate, he ended up with me instead. When I accepted the challenge, nothing went right from the very beginning. I kept running into him over and over again. It was unplanned and crazy, but it was also lovely because I got to know him and he didn't hate me when I was Emma. The problem was, I never found the right time to tell him who I was when we were together. I should have, but I didn't, and that was wrong."

"So, you're saying that Lance is not your soulmate?" Elaine said.

"I didn't want to admit it. I thought I was losing my gift," Emma said. "I kept trying to avoid him until . . ."

"Until?" Elaine said.

"Until it was too late because I fell for him. Then I had hoped that he was my soulmate, and I was his. But you can see, I was all wrong. He doesn't have a soulmate, so I didn't win the challenge. Lance Parker did. That's the reason I'm here."

"I'm your soulmate!" Lance said, sitting at another damn red light. "We fell for each other. This is not all your fault. We can fix it together. Stop ruining your career!"

If he just had let Emma explain her situation that night at her house, he would've found out the truth. He would've found out everything. She'd tried to explain, but his pride got in the way. He cut her off like a child and stormed out of her place like a jerk. Her reason for doing what she did was valid. She had no other choice, and anyone else in her position would have done the same, including Lance.

"But you love him?" Elaine said.

"Yes," Emma said. "Very much so. He's an amazing person and I was fighting my feelings for him until I thought I was his soulmate. Lance did nothing wrong. His career shouldn't have to suffer because of my mistake. He won the challenge. I encourage everyone to go out and buy his book. In fact, he's at City Lights Bookstore right now signing copies."

She's doing this for me. She loves me.

"Let's take a phone call," Elaine said. "We have Rebecca on the line. You have a question for Madam Love?"

"A comment, actually," Rebecca said. "You said you kept running into each other over and over again and it was unplanned."

"That's right," Emma said.

"I don't understand how you're in the wrong. I mean, I

could understand if you showed up wherever you knew he was going to be because you wanted him to run into you and make him believe you were his soulmate. This clearly was not the case because you were trying to avoid him. What happened between the two of you sounds like fate to me. And I think you're writing off this relationship before it's over. If you're soulmates, you'll be together in the end. There's no other way around it, so don't give up."

"That's a good point, Rebecca," Elaine said. "Thanks for the call."

Lance dialed into the radio station again and this time the line was ringing.

Come on. Pick up. Pick up.

"Mary, you're on the air with Madam Love," Elaine said.

"You need to wake up!" Mary said. "We all know he loves you, because we heard him say it loud and proud on the radio the other day. This is obviously a case of serendipity and I agree with Rebecca. Don't give up, honey."

"It sure sounds like it to me, as well," Elaine said. "Thanks for calling. Emma, Lance did say he loved you."

"I know, but that was before I betrayed him," Emma said. "He values honesty more than just about anything else and I failed at that. I hurt him deeply and I'll never forgive myself for that."

"Well, it looks like you both need to remember that forgiveness is a virtue," Elaine said. "Let's take another call. And it looks like we have the one and only Lance Parker on the line with us."

Emma's heart was about to explode out of her chest and the temperature in the studio was on the rise. Lance just called in and was on the air with her. She twisted off the cap from her bottle and took a big swig of water. Maybe she needed to pour all of it over her head.

"Welcome back to the program, Lance," Elaine said.

"Thanks for having me," Lance said. "I first want to tell your listeners to please ignore everything Madam Love has said on the radio today. She's obviously delirious."

"What?" Emma said, so nervous she must have misheard him.

"The woman has no idea what she's talking about."

"Why would you say such a thing?" Emma said. "And why are you calling?"

"Because you won the challenge," Lance said.

"I didn't win because *you* don't have a soulmate."

"Wrong!" Lance said. "I—"

Emma heard static and then silence.

"Looks like we lost Lance," Elaine said. "We'll try to get him back on the line."

"That's okay," Emma said, feeling even more deflated than before, but trying not to cry on the radio. "It's over anyway."

"I'm not so sure about that," Elaine said.

"No? He hung up on me after calling me delirious. I'd say he's had enough and is moving on."

"He also said you won the challenge."

Emma tried replaying the conversation in her head, but felt more confused than ever. Lance seemed to have something to say. Maybe he called to humiliate her on the air, but changed his mind and hung up. No. That couldn't be it. Lance was hurt, but he wasn't a mean person.

"Let's take another call while we try to reconnect with Lance," Elaine said. "Lilly is on line three. Welcome to the program."

"Madam Love. It's me, Lilliana Jones."

"What a wonderful surprise," Emma said, grateful to get her thoughts onto something a little more positive. "Lilly is one of my favorite clients. She had to take a trip all the way to Italy to meet her soulmate. How are you and Marco doing?"

"We couldn't be happier. Life is beautiful, thanks to you. And just so you know, your big prediction came true."

"No!" Emma said. "Are you talking about the babies?"

"Yes! Our lives have been turned upside down, but it's a wonderful type of crazy and I wouldn't change a thing."

"I didn't know you predicted babies, too," Elaine said.

"I normally don't," Emma said. "I sometimes get visions during moments of euphoria. That vision just came to me during their blissful wedding ceremony. I was the officiant."

"It was the wedding of my dreams," Lilly said. "Anyway, I just wanted to call and say you're being too hard on yourself. You're an authentic person, so talented, and so giving. If Lance is too foolish to realize what a good thing he's got, then he's not the one for you."

"That's so sweet of you," Emma said. "Thank you."

"I don't think we're going to have to worry about that at all," Elaine said, pointing to the window. "Emma has a special visitor standing just outside the studio here. Lance Parker. Looks like I need to grab some tissue. Beautiful love stories always make me cry."

Emma swung around in her chair and sucked in a breath.

Lance was on the other side of the glass, his eyes locked on her.

He opened the studio door and stepped inside, approaching Emma.

"I don't understand why you're here," Emma said, pulling off her headphones and standing. "You hung up on me."

Lance blinked. "We were disconnected. I called right back and got a busy signal. I was so frustrated I almost threw my phone out the window."

Emma hesitated. "Oh . . ."

"I need to tell you something," Lance said, stepping close to Emma. "I want us to have a clean slate so we can move forward with our relationship."

Did he say move forward or move on?

Her head was spinning, so she just nodded.

"I was engaged to be married, and my fiancée, Karla, broke up with me a week before the wedding. She left me because of a reading she got from a fortune teller at her bachelorette party. The fortune teller told Karla I wasn't her soulmate and that she should leave me before it was too late. So, she did. Karla called off the wedding and I never saw her again."

"I didn't know," Emma said.

Lance nodded. "I admit the heartache from that experience prompted me to write the book. That's also the reason why I judged you so harshly in the beginning, and in the end when I found out who you really were. But it wasn't that fortune teller's fault and it wasn't yours. I know now that this happened for a reason. Karla and I weren't right for each other and someone else better suited for me would be coming my way. That person is you. The universe works in mysterious ways, but I'm certain you're the one for me. You won the challenge, because you found me a soulmate. It's you, Emma. You're my soulmate and I love you."

Emma's eyes filled.

He loves me. He doesn't hate me.

"I love you, too," Emma said.

Lance put his hands on her waist and got zapped. "I miss being electrocuted by you."

"Me, too. Do you think this is going to be a problem for us in the future? Maybe we should see a doctor or wear rubber gloves when we're together."

Lance shook his head. "I don't think so. Love shows itself in many forms. Our love is electric."

He grinned, brought her closer, and pressed his lips to hers.

It was heaven.

Emma pulled away from the kiss when she heard sniffling.

She turned and saw Elaine wiping her eyes.

They were still live on the radio.

She had completely forgotten.

"That was beautiful," Elaine said, sniffling again. "Just beautiful."

Emma grabbed Lance by the hand and led him outside the studio to the hallway.

"What made you change your mind?" Emma asked.

"I'll admit I had some help," Lance said. "A kind man with tasty cupcakes opened my eyes and showed me the way."

"Randy!" More happy tears streamed down her face. "What did he say?"

Lance wiped the tears from her eyes. "He helped me see things from your point of view. I put myself in your shoes. I understood why you made the choices you made. Honestly, I would have done the same thing. I was too quick to judge you, and I was wrong. I'm sorry."

"I'm sorry, too. I should have told you everything, but I was scared. Terrified to lose you."

Lance nodded. "Fear will do that to a person, but I promise you I'm not going anywhere. I do think lack of communication is what got us into trouble though, so we need to be very open with each other from now on. Let's try again and this time have a normal relationship without your double identity. Deal?"

"Deal," Emma said. "They say when you fall off the horse, you need to get back in the saddle."

"Hmmm," Lance said, pointing to the mark on his forehead. "I don't have the greatest track record when it comes to horses. You know that."

"Don't worry. I'll show you how it's done, but we first need to seal the deal with a kiss." Emma reached up and kissed him on the lips.

His kisses were so sweet and divine.

Even better than Randy's cupcakes.

With every second of the kiss, Emma's fingers tingled more and more.

Then a vision formed in her head.

She was in a bookstore seated at a table with Lance. Peter was there, and so was Randy with his cupcakes. The table had stacks of a children's book called *My Best Friend Clyde*. The cover featured a little girl and a Clydesdale horse. She admired the colors and the beautiful animal when something caught her eye at the bottom of the cover.

Written by Lance Parker.

Illustrations by Emma Parker.

Emma broke away from the kiss, happy and excited about the future.

Lance studied her for a moment. "Why do you have that wicked expression on your face? What are you up to this time?"

Emma smirked. "I'll tell you later, *darling*."

THE END
* * * * * *

ACKNOWLEDGMENTS

Dear Reader,

I hope you enjoyed *Madam Love, Actually*. If you've read my romantic comedy *Lilliana Jones and the Temple of Groom*, you know that Madam Love had a fun part in that story. After receiving requests (demands??) from readers that she should have her own love story, I finally gave in and wrote this one. I hope you enjoyed it!

I would just like to take a moment to thank you for your support. Without you, I would not be able to write romantic comedies for a living. I love your emails and communication on Facebook and Twitter. You motivate me to write faster! Don't be shy. Send an email to me at rich@richamooi.com to say hello. I personally respond to all emails and would love to hear from you.

Please consider leaving a review of the book on Amazon and Goodreads! I appreciate it very much and it will help new readers find my stories.

It takes more than a few people to publish a book so I

want to send out a big THANK YOU to everyone who helped make *Madam Love, Actually* possible.

First, thank you to my amazing wife, Silvi Martin. She's the first person to read my stories and always gives me amazing feedback to make them so much better. Thank you, my angel! I love you!

To Becky Monson for helping me with the beautiful cover.

Thanks to Mary Yakovets for editing, and to Paula Bothwell and Sherry Stevenson for proofreading.

Thanks to Michael Hauge, Hannah Jayne, Becky Monson, Whitney Dineen, Claire McEwen, the Le Bou Bunch, and the AC for help with brainstorming this story.

Thanks to Elaine Stewart for coming with the name Elaine Stewart for the radio host. Your free copy of the book is on the way.

To Robert Roffey, Deb McNaught, Julie Carver, Maché Indelicato, and Deb Julienne for your beta feedback. Your help is invaluable.

With gratitude,
Rich

FREE romantic comedy!
All of my newsletter subscribers get a free copy of my fun story, *Happy to be Stuck with You*, plus updates on new releases and sales.
http://www.richamooi.com/newsletter.

You can also browse my entire list of romantic comedies on Amazon here:
Author.to/AmazonRichAmooi

ABOUT THE AUTHOR

Rich Amooi is a former Silicon Valley radio personality and wedding DJ who now writes romantic comedies full-time in San Diego, California. He is happily married to a kiss monster imported from Spain. Rich believes in public displays of affection, silliness, infinite possibilities, donuts, gratitude, laughter, and happily ever after.

Connect with Rich!
www.richamooi.com
rich@richamooi.com
https://www.facebook.com/author.richamooi
https://twitter.com/richamooi

CPSIA information can be obtained
at www.ICGtesting.com
Printed in the USA
LVHW092310290919
632649LV00001B/142/P

Our Seven Families

*There is nothing more painful in this world than loneliness.
Not poverty, not illness, not scorn, not imprisonment, not death.
All things are bearable when shared with others in love.
We came here to find each other,
To learn the ways of reciprocity and mutual aid,
To live abundant lives immersed in the mysteries
of unity with each other.*

Our Seven Families

Expanding and Enriching our Sense of Belonging

Elaine McCreary

GEORGE RONALD • OXFORD

George Ronald, Publisher
Oxford
www.grbooks.com

©Elaine McCreary 2018
All Rights Reserved

A catalogue record for this book is available from the British Library

ISBN 978-0-85398-612-6

Cover design: René Steiner, Steinergraphics.com

Contents

Foreword, by Janet Khan	vii
Introduction: Interwoven Social Worlds	1
1 The Global Family	28
2 The National Family	44
3 The Essential Family	65
4 The Daily Family	86
5 A Family of Friendships	104
6 The Inner Family	125
7 The Eternal Family	147
Reflections on Our Seven Families	163
Bibliography	177
Notes and References	181
Acknowledgements	191
About the Author	197

Foreword

Our Seven Families takes up the issue of the value of human social life – why we need human connections. Drawing on her experience as a social scientist and on insights derived from a deep study of the Bahá'í Sacred Writings, Elaine McCreary offers a fresh perspective on human affairs, revealing new hope and opportunities for action.

In this work, she introduces a systematic framework for gaining a deeper understanding of contemporary social reality. To highlight the complexity of human experience, she describes seven 'families' – seven human systems or planes of activity – each of which offers opportunities for personal engagement and transformation and contributes to the emergence of an organically united world.

Over the last half century, humanity's failure to establish meaningful relationships at all levels has been variously researched as problems of 'alienation', 'dislocation', or 'isolation', most recently being explored as an endemic phenomenon of 'loneliness'. In the modern world, loneliness has a devastating effect on physical and mental health, on personal well-being, on the dynamics of the workplace and society. It contributes to the very unravelling of the social fabric.

Loneliness is the subjective feeling of having inadequate

social connections, no friend or confidant to turn to for support in times of crisis or need. Loneliness is a global phenomenon. It impacts young and old, alike. Today, we live in the most technologically connected age in the history of civilization, yet rates of loneliness continue to rise.

In recent years, the reasons for the rising incidence of loneliness and the search for innovative ways to combat its destructive influences have become the subject of a plethora of media reports and increasing numbers of scientific studies.

Reporting the results of a 2014 survey from the UK Office for National Statistics, a journalist announced, 'Loneliness has finally become a hot topic'.[1] Likewise, another study conducted in the United States suggests that the number of Americans who say they have no confidant has nearly tripled in two decades.[2]

A distinguished medical scientist attributes the increase in the feeling of loneliness over the decades to such things as the fact that people are more geographically mobile and thus more likely to be living apart from friends and family, and to changes in the workplace involving new models of working, such as telecommuting and other similar arrangements. He expresses concern for the future of humankind should this epidemic of loneliness run its course: 'If we cannot rebuild strong, authentic social connections, we will continue to splinter apart . . .'[3]

While there are many approaches to redressing the issue of loneliness, most appear to focus on finding ways to help individuals establish meaningful relationships, to reconnect with each other, and to recapture a sense of community either by binding people within communities or binding different communities together.[4]

Central to the author's exposition is her conviction about the continuing role of religion in society, in particular, that the Divine teachings lead to the elevation, the advancement, the education, the protection and the regeneration of the peoples of the earth, and that the laws and exhortations of God's Messengers not only express truths about the nature of the human being and the purpose of existence, they also raise human consciousness, increase understanding, lift the standard of personal conduct, and provide means for society to progress.[5]

Her analysis expands our conception of the nature and range of human relationships, stresses the link between spiritual activities and social transformation, and suggests creative practical solutions for restoring a sense of true and loving fellowship, personal well-being and security. She skilfully weaves together the threads of a rich tapestry of social possibilities, identifying elements essential for the creation of a future society characterized by peace, diversity and justice, a society that is bound to be radically different from any established in the past.

Janet Khan
March 2018

Introduction

Interwoven Social Worlds

Just behind our noisy, cluttered, and busy social lives are clean, serene, and meaningful human connections waiting to welcome us. And why do we need those human connections? Because, no matter what we can learn about life, death, failure, and success by thinking alone our solitary thoughts, we will always learn more by testing out those thoughts through interaction with other human beings. Both our inner learning and our outer achieving are magnified through connection with others. This is the never-ending mystery, the surprise, and the value of human social life.

On a larger scale, what we think and do collectively as a society is also transformed and improved when our society interacts with and sees itself in the light of a new spiritual Revelation. Revelation, by definition, reveals a fresh perspective on human affairs. This book is written for people of all persuasions, who are curious about what new perspectives the Bahá'í Sacred Writings are bringing to human experience, revealing new hope and opportunities for action.

Each chapter describes what happens when the light of spiritual Revelation is directed toward the prism of human social life. The inner realities thus revealed seem to diffract into seven vivid and highly differentiated realms of human interaction.

These realms are more various than simply larger and smaller groups of people. They intersect each other, as do our inner life, our home life, and our work life. Through this spiritual perspective we can see that on many levels, human behaviours have important spiritual and ethical meanings. Suddenly it becomes clear that, like it or not, each of us lives on the spot where seven worlds meet.

Everyone knows that it takes two human beings to give life to a third; but not everyone understands that a new human life only grows, develops, and matures to the extent that it is bathed in the warm glow of loving human attention. As each individual life is nourished and educated by loving attention, it flourishes and all of humanity benefits. Bahá'u'lláh proclaimed:

> Regard man as a mine rich in gems of inestimable value. Education can, alone, cause it to reveal its treasures, and enable mankind to benefit therefrom.[1]

Though gifts and talents lie treasured within each of us from birth, they will only be revealed through the educational effect of social interactions. Hence the extreme importance of 'family-like' experience from childhood throughout the whole of life.

While we may readily agree on the relationship between personal development and the social context in which it takes place, there immediately arise a multitude of questions such as:

- What would the ideal family be like?
- Does anyone really live in such a family?
- What happens after we grow up?
- How is this relevant if I'm not married or parenting?
- How could we have seven families?

You are invited to take a radical departure from the usual line of thinking, and follow this unfolding tale deep into the patterns of family life, then out again and around the world of human affairs to discover other meanings of family life and how it can enable our human potentials to develop. What will emerge is the prospect that (like it or not) we all belong to seven different families at once – each of which has distinctive issues to test us and satisfying fulfilments to offer us.

Systems – worlds – families

The idea of 'system' alerts us to watch for parts that interact with each other, and have some kind of central principle or force that makes the interactions self-regulating.

The idea of 'world' suggests a whole plane of experience that is distinguished from other planes by special characteristics such as its population, its resources, its dangers, its opportunities. Within each world, the characters may be acting in harmony with each other – or not!

Now, what the notion of 'family' does is combine the features of systems and worlds in the following way: its parts are spiritual beings, who happen to be having a material experience. While it is common for us to think of ourselves as biological beings who occasionally have a spiritual experience – it is simply not true, and counter-productive to stubbornly persist in thinking so. In reality, we are spiritual beings who are temporarily having a material experience. We are moving parts interacting with each other and are potentially self-regulating by means of divinely ordained ethics. Thus, 'family' as used here is a social system, so rich and all-encompassing that it virtually forms a world unto itself.

Our human social life is so complex that we actually live on several planes of activity at once. On each of these planes we find various sets of human beings or what we will begin to call 'families'. It will be important to explore each of these family worlds to discover its respective principles of harmony and learn how to live by them. 'Learning about life' then means: learning how to live successfully in each of these 'seven families'.

Distinct human families in seven social worlds

The seven families – or worlds of experience – that we will investigate are the following:

1. The **Global Family** contains all the peoples of the earth, among whom we can see emerging the rudimentary elements of a world commonwealth and increasing degrees of equality of life for women and men.

2. The **National Family** contains all the residents within the borders of a state, where we observe the education and civilization of humanity taking place – as 'Abdu'l-Bahá described in *The Secret of Divine Civilization*. It is also at the national level that the need for peace and unity among races becomes clearly evident.

3. The **Essential Family** is a new version of the classic family. It is the fundamental, multi-generational system that embraces and sustains our human essence; it hosts our most intimate relations of marriage and parenthood; it protects children and with loving care raises them to maturity; it provides a faithful context for three or four generations to care for each other through all the stages of life.

Then we have:

4. The **Daily Family**, that cast of characters who await us every morning: the people in our building, on our bus, in our lunch-room. We don't need to watch either serialized situation comedies or ensemble dramas because there will never be a day of our lives when we are without them!

Unique among the planes of our experience is the one on which we establish:

5. A **Family of Friendships**, because this is the only plane on which we choose a family for ourselves. All the other families are granted to us by circumstance. For some people this chosen family is the only one they recognize. It forms a 'starter kit', a place to begin to understand human systems. By choosing and maintaining this system, we prove to ourselves how much we are committed to seeking and sustaining unity with others.

Most subtle and secret of all the families in which we dwell is:

6. The **Inner Family**, comprised of the living encyclopedia of our own childhood, adolescence, early-, middle-, and late adulthood, and increasing old age; it even includes everyone we have ever met! It is all inside. In a sense, the inner family contains and mirrors all the outer families. And it also craves unity. The effort to integrate our life experience into a meaningful whole is the inner work of the soul, as surely as raising the Kingdom of God on earth is the outer work of the soul.

We might easily feel that this is more than enough already: five outer families that span all aspects of concrete experience, and an inner family in which our soul undertakes unification of its experiences and rediscovers its inalienable oneness. But there is one more family membership we cannot escape, and that is our relationship to:

7. The **Eternal Family**, those who dwell in realms outside the time/space of our own historical period. They may be part of the multitude that extends backward in time into the generations preceding us, those whom we call 'the Concourse on High'. Or, they may be those who will appear in future generations, and who will remember us as champion builders struggling to bring forth a new World Order.

    The strange thing is that, in some sense, both those in the past and those in the future know who we are. Although we may not see them clearly, they have their ways of seeing us. Curiously enough, due to our mutual influence, we share certain rights and responsibilities with them, as surely as we do with our other six families.

Consider, then, how complex human experience is. Pinball games had only one set of rules and one speed, while early computer games had one set of rules and accelerating speeds as the player advanced through levels of skill – or perhaps even different rules on different levels.. But the 'divine games' of human social life have specialized rules and requirements on each plane and they all happen at once!

While this introductory chapter is not the place to treat our seven families in depth, it can at least accomplish two limited objectives:

- identify some source books from the Bahá'í Sacred Writings that seem to be especially rich in Revelation regarding each of these families;

- introduce some themes that emerge from these Sacred Writings which are particularly relevant to the search for harmony in one of the families more than the others.

The fundamental pattern which underlies all the others is the Essential Family. But in order to be able look at this family through fresh eyes, we start the book by taking the wider view first.

The Global Family

This family is of great concern to us all. Dramatic pronouncements on worldwide peace, prosperity, equality, and civilization are to be found in central Bahá'í texts such as *Gleanings from the Writings of Bahá'u'lláh*, *The Promulgation of Universal Peace*, *The World Order of Bahá'u'lláh*, *The Promised Day Is Come*, and the statement on peace addressed *To The Peoples of the World*.[2]

From these sources emerges a rich depiction of what we may anticipate will be an ever more refined and fully integrated 'World Commonwealth'. The Bahá'í Writings indicate that this ultimate planetary family will be characterized by a close and permanent political unity, and a global standard of justice. It will be fuelled by the flow of prosperity when 'all economic barriers will have been permanently demolished' and governed by 'a single code of international law'. The creativity of this Global Family will blossom forth when conflicts that have been inflamed by 'religious fanaticism . . . racial animosity . . . and militant nationalism will have been transmuted into an abiding consciousness of world citizenship'.[3] The graphic design at the start of Chapter 1 shows the yin-yang symbol superimposed on a globe, depicting both historical male domination over female world populations and northern domination over southern hemisphere populations.

Despite the cynicism of a despairing world, a common citizenship is the goal of a unified Global Family to which Bahá'ís are committed with confidence because of the thought that 'the coming of Bahá'u'lláh . . . signals . . . a fresh manifestation of the direct involvement of God in history', 'a sign of the outpouring of a heavenly grace that will enable all humanity to be free at last from conflict'[4] – free then to contribute its energies to building world peace and a divine civilization. Chief among these new contributors will be the women of the world, who, 'Abdu'l-Bahá assures us, will 'enter . . . all branches of the administration of society' and 'occupy the highest levels in the human world'.[5]

Think about it. If this faltering world were a spaceship, then for a very long time, men have stood alone on its brass and mahogany bridge trying to chart a safe course, with only half the necessary data! They can take heart now, that in all fields of cultural endeavour, women are climbing the access ladder to the board rooms of this spaceship world with the missing half of the data needed to chart a safe course into the future.

All women (Bahá'í and otherwise) are firmly encouraged by 'Abdu'l-Bahá in many of His public talks and letters, to prove that their capacities and abilities have not been lacking, but only latent and undeveloped, due to lack of opportunity. He stresses the arts, science, agriculture, and industry as areas in which women should make practical contributions. But a special light is focused on Bahá'í men in letters of the Universal House of Justice. It entrusts them with a mission to exemplify for other men 'the relationship of mutual respect and equality enjoined by the Bahá'í writings – a relationship governed by the principles of consultation and devoid of the use of force to compel obedience to one's will'.[6] With integrity and persistence, whether in the privacy of the home or in their public roles, they should see that 'the atmosphere within a Bahá'í family as within the community as a whole should express "the keynote of the Cause of God" which, the beloved Guardian has stated, "is not dictatorial authority, but humble fellowship, not arbitrary power, but the spirit of frank and loving consultation"'.[7]

We are told in no uncertain terms by 'Abdu'l-Bahá that the welfare of the entire Global Family hinges on the attainment of equality of education and opportunity for women. He says that humanity has been 'defective', 'inefficient', and 'incomplete' without the full participation of women in its affairs; that 'until the reality of equality . . . is fully established . . . the highest social development of mankind is not possible'.[8] He says that as equality of life for women becomes a reality and their qualities of 'mental alertness, intuition . . . love and service'[9] become ascendant in society, the incidence of war will gradually cease, and the very happiness for which 'mankind' has been striving will at last be realizable.

The National Family

In the World Commonwealth gradually developing on earth, Bahá'í Sacred Writings indicate that some form of nation state will continue to exist. Its autonomy will undoubtedly be modified to accommodate a universal system of justice from which no nation can exempt itself; but, for the most part, the affairs of society will continue to be managed and promoted at the level of the nation state.

In His book *The Secret of Divine Civilization,* 'Abdu'l-Bahá denounces so-called 'traditional' societies which allow their people to slip into a degenerate condition through inertia and lethargy. For societies, as for individual souls, there is no such thing as standing still spiritually. We are either striving to move forward to surpass our personal best, or we are slipping back. We cannot afford to drift, because the tendency of material reality is toward 'entropy', that is, the break-down of energy bonds by which matter deteriorates, and its energies dissipate. The only antidote for entropy in the material world is 'life', the process that 'knits up' energy units again into higher complexities. Similarly, the only antidote for degenerative tendencies in the spiritual realm of thought processes, as prescribed by 'Abdu'l-Bahá, is education – for whole national societies at a time.

From this guidance, and from the Tablets of Bahá'u'lláh which address education, the press, and many aspects of social development, we discover inspired origins to the present-day emphasis that Bahá'ís place on the importance of communication arts, literature, journalism, media, and the performing arts. These forms of creativity can have a powerful influence on the development of society. What better way to reach out and care for the education of our National Families?

Two other sources are essential to our understanding of the National Family, the statement *Individual Rights and Freedoms* by the Universal House of Justice, and *The Vision of Race Unity* published by the National Spiritual Assembly of the Bahá'ís of the United States. Not surprisingly, the life path of societies can be likened to the life path of individuals. As individuals, we grow and mature, learning to live in an ever-advancing way, as befits our immortal nature. Similarly, divinely-guided societies can expect to bring forth ever-advancing civilizations, but only if they succeed in reaching a state of societal adulthood and finding ways to continuously promote their own process of maturity and fulfilment. Unfortunately, our present period of history is 'dominated by the surging energy, the rebellious spirit and frenetic activity of adolescence'.[10] For a society to reach adulthood it must begin to develop itself through universal education, leading to widespread adoption of moderation in personal behaviour, and voluntary avoidance of extremes, for example in the realm of speech and expression.

Freedom of speech and expression are not the paramount social good if they result in harm to large portions of a society through pornography, hate literature, or racism. This balance of freedom and voluntary submission to limits is just one example of the creative tension of principles that is required for societies to mature. We are advised by the Guardian that 'nothing short of the spirit of a true Bahá'í can hope to reconcile the principles of mercy and justice, of freedom and submission', or as we see in the peace processes of the world today, 'vigilance' on one hand, and 'fellowship' on the other.[11]

One of the abiding themes of social and political theory has been the relation of individuals to the societies in which they live. The 20th century was witness to social experiments veering between the extremes of centralized decision making and unbridled individual will. For Bahá'ís, the fundamental principle which reconciles these extremes, as articulated by the Guardian, is the 'subordination of individual will to that of society',[12] a clear indication that the individual is answerable to the well-being of the community as a whole. However, this principle, in the words of the Guardian, 'neither suppresses the individual nor does it exalt him to the point of making him an anti-social creature, a menace to society'.[13]

We can chart the relationships within a well-functioning society as prescribed in the Bahá'í teachings by using a simple, two-by-two matrix of the rights and responsibilities of electors and those they elect. This set of relations is practised by Bahá'ís and their Local Spiritual Assembly, the elected governing body of their municipal unit. Such a matrix shows what support each can expect from the other and what respect each owes to the other. Its interlacing quadrants, as shown in the graphic design at the start of Chapter 2, depict the rights of electors and the rights of the elected as well as the responsibilities of the electors and responsibilities of the elected.

In all seven human systems, the web of revealed relations serves to protect both the integrity of the system as a whole, and of the individuals living within the system.

The Bahá'í commitment to interracial peace and unity has particular relevance to the National Family, since nations were once predicated on racial uniformity often brought about by effective barriers such as mountains and oceans; but history has changed all that. Today, the world over, residents of a nation may share geography, but not race. In this new age of multi-ethnic nations, Bahá'u'lláh exhorts us if we 'dwell in the same land' to 'walk with the same feet, eat with the same mouth . . .' and to be 'even as one soul'.[14] Note that He does not say 'as similar souls' or 'kindred souls', but, rather, 'as one soul'. In thinking about our adopted National Families, wherever we may live, our principal concern needs to be how we can help our nation to become one unified soul.

The soul-like nature of a nation leads to an interesting corollary: just as no two individual souls are identical, so also no two nations are identical in their composition, perspectives, creativity, and wisdom. Traditionally, we have known that each place on earth has its own special genius. We can find many statements in letters of Shoghi Effendi to the peoples of America, Germany, Britain, and many other countries praising their distinctive virtues. In a 1983 article about the missions of Japan and Australia,[15] Peter Khan restates this idea when he writes that, just as no two people have the same gifts to bring to the world, so no two nations have the same contribution to make to the emerging World Commonwealth. Those particular gifts remain to be discovered in the nation we inhabit, as we assist it to achieve a distinctive harmony, advance its cultural maturity, and fulfil its potential to serve the world community in its own unique way.

The Essential Family

So crucial is this primary human system to preparing us for all the others, that the Central Figures of the Bahá'í Faith revealed principles to help humanity revitalize the intergenerational, Essential Family. Extracts from their statements are published as compilations under such titles as: *Family Life, Marriage: A Fortress for Well-Being,* and *Women.*[16] Researchers into the Bahá'í Sacred Writings have provided additional commentaries and discussions. One example is the article 'Rights and Responsibilities in the Bahá'í Family System'.[17]

Approaching this topic, our minds are burdened with old, outworn, often mistaken ideas about the Essential Family. To prepare ourselves to read these compilations and see with fresh eyes what is revealed in them, it is useful for us to entertain a strange possibility – that the Essential Family, functioning with the perfect harmony divinely intended for it, has yet to appear on earth. No matter how good, bad, or indifferent we may judge our own family life to have been, the Essential Family as described in Bahá'í Sacred Writings will appear in history only as its prerequisite conditions appear. These include equality of life opportunity for women and men, universal education for children and adults, and enlightened institutions of local governance – to be known in the future as Local Houses of Justice. In the Bahá'í administrative system, these locally elected institutions will provide many local services, including advice and counsel on renewing the Essential Family, so that its integrity as a whole and that of the individuals within it are both equally safeguarded.

Bahá'í Sacred Writings describe a family system within

which individuals are identified by gender and by generation. The rights granted within the family system, and the responsibilities required, vary according to whether one is a child, a spouse, a parent, and, by extension, a grandparent. Furthermore, particular distinctions are made between the male and female participants in this system. Not surprisingly, mainstream social theory has moved over decades through a period of unisex thought, into a new period of gender-sensitive thought.

Bahá'ís are assured that desirable conditions can be achieved in the Essential Family without recourse to methods that have been used in the past. For example, family unity can be preserved without recourse to tyranny, and gender prerogatives can be maintained without violating equality. However, moving to this higher state will not happen of its own accord, without effort, education, and example. 'Abdu'l-Bahá declares that developing the Essential Family must be a conscious undertaking:

> . . . the family, being a human unit, **must be educated** according to the rules of sanctity. All the virtues **must be taught** the family. The integrity of the family bond must be constantly considered, and the rights of the individual members must not be transgressed.[18] [emphasis added]

Knowing that our families seldom exhibit the full degree of harmony and mutual benefit that they might, and that the essence of human 'togetherness' has yet to manifest, the natural corollary is that we do not yet know the basic principles and rules to bring it forth. Therefore none of us should assume we already know how the Essential Family is supposed to function.

'Rules of sanctity' are indicated in the Writings with regard to such functions as being a husband or wife, fathering, mothering, being a daughter or son, and relating to our parents throughout their lives. These rules of guidance are at times tender, poignant, surprising – even alarming – but they mark out relationships of 'justice' beyond anything the world has ever seen.

It is informative to draw a diagram of the Essential Family system, in the form of a five-pointed star, assigning one point for the husband/father, another for the wife/mother, a third for the son/brother, and a fourth for the daughter/sister. The farthest horizon of maturity, at the top of the star, are those family members of the age of grandfathers and grandmothers, who occupy a common point of honour. This shared point is not to deny gender difference, but rather to acknowledge that as life matures, men and women come to resemble each other more closely through attaining a more complete set of each other's virtues and becoming more whole as human beings

While the five-pointed star is a totally arbitrary diagram – we could have connected five dots with a circle – it is nevertheless intriguing to consider the human connections that are thus revealed: that of husband and wife, of father and daughter, of mother and son, and of grandchildren with grandparents.

It is also possible to connect those dots with a pentagon, and notice the other set of relations thus revealed: that of brother and sister, father and son, mother and daughter, and young parents with older parents. Now consider how much we have to learn about all these relations, and how far we have to go in discovering 'the rules of sanctity' referred to by 'Abdu'l-Bahá.

It is worth noting that reflected in the Bahá'í principles and laws guiding the Essential Family system is a pattern of ethical guidance which repeats itself in the other social families that follow. The pattern shows that we are never abandoned to moral vagueness, uncertainty, or drift. In each case, we are given a firm, clear principle, followed by qualifying statements and conditions which clarify how to apply that principle.

For example, the lines of responsibility and provision from parent to child are generally about education, and from child to parent are generally about obedience. Mothers are the first educators, and fathers are obligated to provide financially for the further education of their children; but if the father is unable to do so, the responsibility devolves to the community to ensure the education of its young. Similarly the Writings clearly state that parents are to be respected and feel contented, 'provided they deter thee not from gaining access to the Threshold of the Almighty, nor keep thee back from walking in the way of the Kingdom'.[19]

The proviso here is to offer obedience to parents *only* when it leads to the Sacred Threshold and is directed toward the Kingdom – phrases that indicate the destiny, glory, and fulfilment of the individual soul. In this first, Essential Family, we see clearly that the purpose of each human system is to develop the spiritual potential of those who belong to it. Each 'family' exposes the people within it to a larger human system in need of their assistance to achieve its particular unity and synergy. By learning to serve the synergy process of each family, they will learn the secret of overcoming their own existential separateness.

The Daily Family

In the Daily Family, all our good intentions are tested. The Daily Family is the workshop, the studio, the factory, the rehearsal hall, the gymnasium, where we will discover what it is going to take to manifest all the good we can imagine. It is the place assigned to us by God in which we are to practise being the people of Bahá. The graphic design at the start of Chapter 4 shows the globe turning through its daytime and nighttime, underlining the fact that the Daily Family is the set of down-to-earth, mundane relations we cannot avoid.

Fortunately, there is one consummate Bahá'í source to which we can turn for unfailing advice on how to cope with life in our Daily Family, and that is Shoghi Effendi's *The Advent of Divine Justice*. For all the friends who like to joke about how this life needs a 'users' manual' – well, this is it.

The key to unscrambling all our daily predicaments is contained somewhere within its central themes of 'rectitude of conduct', 'a chaste, pure, and holy life', 'complete freedom from prejudice', and gratitude for the privilege of daily life.[20] If we could step back and look in on our entire day as though looking into a hologram, and see at a glance all the people and events, and ourselves as the central character following a path through all its twists and turns, we would be able to see that only three things need to happen in order to have the perfect Daily Family.

First, we need to put straight the lines of relationship between ourselves and all the people in our social context. We do that through rectitude of conduct – through justice, truthfulness, trustworthiness, distancing ourselves from what can defile us, and submitting to the Will of God.

Second, we need to clean up what lies within our own domain (such as our thoughts, speech, clothing, possessions, and living spaces) through living a chaste, pure, and holy life. This, of course, includes practising abstinence from alcohol, the avoidance of extremes in all our choices, decency, and control of our carnal instincts. But we may be surprised to notice that it also specifies in the text, 'abandonment of frivolous conduct, with its excessive attachment to trivial and often misdirected pleasures'.[21] Wouldn't it be painful to discover that a superficial life is as offensive to our Creator as a corrupt one? 'Don't waste time!' it seems to be telling us. Life is over quickly. Soon we will have to face the court of our Creator and what will we tell Him we did with the life He gave us? Will we say:

I went shopping? I gossiped with my friends about someone else's business? I took trendy vacations?

Third, to have the perfect Daily Family, we have to fling open the gates of our hearts and lives and free ourselves completely of prejudice, so that the world can enter in, and we can venture forth from the narrow confines of what is familiar to us.

Lest all of this sound too much like work, *The Advent of Divine Justice* includes some dazzling statements about the privilege of daily life and the people we encounter there. It says: 'The holy realities of the Concourse on High yearn . . . to return unto this world . . . to render some service . . . to demonstrate their servitude.'[22] It says, 'Should a man, all alone, arise in the name of Bahá, and put on the armour of His love, him will the Almighty cause to be victorious . . .'[23] Instead of waking up with a groan because we find ourselves in yet another work day, we should, it says, 'Speed ye forth from the horizon of power, in the name of your Lord, the Unconstrained . . .'[24]

A Family of Friendships

Of all the worlds or families we will examine, this is one of the most peculiar. It differs from the others in so many ways. First, because friendships can be avoided, this is the only family which is ours entirely by choice. Second, this family seems particularly significant at this time of an emerging global culture, when travel leads us to develop many cherished friendships, some of which must be surrendered by us to separations of time and distance. Furthermore, friendships cause us to consider deeply the question of our own life, its purpose and direction in order to understand who is a true friend to us. The graphic design at the start of Chapter 5 represents our soul's journey from the periphery of understanding to the centre. As we circle the essence of Truth, trying to understand It, true friends are those who help us journey closer to the point to which we must all return, the essence of Reality, the Alpha and the Omega.

Finally, this self-selected family affords us the opportunity to address the latent question: 'Which of these is my real family?' The question causes us to consider the nature of both spiritual kinship and physical kinship. At the back of our mind, we may be thinking about this variety of families, and saying to ourselves, 'Well, this is all very interesting, but my life is organized around achieving harmony in my *real* family,' meaning the family in which one grew up, or the extended family into which one married, or the family one is creating and so on. But an examination of the Writings indicates that we have membership in at least these seven family systems simultaneously, that we have a mission to apply the Bahá'í principles in each one, and that when a value conflict appears, the Essential Family may not be the one given priority over the others. A letter written on behalf of Shoghi Effendi states the following:

> Deep as are family ties, we must always remember that the spiritual ties are far deeper; they are everlasting and survive death . . . You should do all in your power, through prayer and example, to open the eyes of your family to the Bahá'í Faith, but do not grieve too much over their actions. Turn to your . . . brothers and sisters who are living with you in the light of the Kingdom.[25]

As it happens, our Bahá'í brothers and sisters are so spectacularly diverse that it brings us to the next interesting aspect of this family. If we thought friendships were about spending comfortable time with compatible people, we're going to have to think again. Our Bahá'í friendships are so diverse that they often take us beyond our comfort zone – and we are not always willing to do that. It is ironic that in the National Family our concern is that freedom might be constrained; but in the family of potential personal friendships, there is sometimes more freedom than most of us are comfortable with, with the result that we end up retreating into the safety of our familiar groups. But it is worth the effort to venture into meeting the unknown. Dan Jordan, author of *Becoming Your True Self*, maintains that when we try to relate to the unknown, it creates an energy (an anxiety) in us which calls forth new depths of knowing and loving. Thus, each new response from within ourselves will manifest a bit more of our latent capacity, will release a bit more of our human potential.[26]

Another discovery from the Writings of Bahá'u'lláh is that the family of friendships is not so much about *having* friends as about *being* a friend to others, through our actions and not just through our conversations. Any concrete, compassionate action illumines the world through the dynamic force of example, in a way that can restore brothers and sisters who have lost hope. Bahá'u'lláh informs us that:

> One righteous act is endowed with a potency that can so elevate the dust ... tear every bond asunder ... and hath the power to restore the force that hath spent itself and vanished ...[27]

Finally, the themes of friendship, of righteous action, and the power of example bring us to consider the role of 'Abdu'l-Bahá. Whenever we need to learn how to befriend others, to find a friend who embodies a certain virtue for us, to lean on a friend who will mentor and coach us, we can turn in gratitude to the jewel in the Family of Friendships, the ultimate Friend, the Perfect Exemplar of Bahá'í character: 'Abdu'l-Bahá.

Of all the friends we could ever hope to meet, this One, who is with us now and always, will have the most radical effect upon us. Bahá'u'lláh writes of Him, 'Render thanks unto God, O people, for His appearance; for verily His is the most great Favour unto you . . .'[28] His appearance, His speech, His character draw us forward. He is an irresistible friend who summons us to follow in His footsteps in service to humanity, no matter how unready we feel.

God would not have granted us such a Friend, if He had not also endowed us with the capacity to keep company with that Friend by striving to emulate His example. 'Abdu'l-Bahá Himself assures us, 'I am with you always, whether living or dead; I am with you to the end.'[29]

And now we must briefly survey the last two worlds in which we have families, and they are intriguing worlds indeed.

The Inner Family

The Inner Family is invisible and largely inaccessible to anyone else but ourselves. Yet it is richly peopled with everyone we have ever been, and everyone we have ever met. From all of this we are expected to make a unified whole, a meaning for our life, a single, signature identity by which we will be known in the worlds to come – in other words, a soul-self. Our most mystical Bahá'í Sacred Writings speak explicitly about this world and this family, as we find when we read *The Seven Valleys and The Four Valleys,* the Arabic and Persian *Hidden Words,* and the compilation entitled *Excellence in All Things.*

Far from belittling the importance, or denying the existence, of the inner realities of human life, the sentiments confided to us by the Lord of the Age confirm that the inner realities of each soul are a treasury in the sight of God, and He urges us to turn inward, and engage with the family of realities within. While there is an ego-self, vain and vulnerable to the deceptive illusions of the world, there is also a soul-self created for a far-reaching destiny of knowing and loving God. And He wants us to raise up and educate that self. He says, 'Turn thy sight unto thyself, that thou mayest find Me standing within thee, mighty, powerful, and self-subsisting.'[30] 'On this plane, the self is not rejected but beloved; it is well-pleasing and not to be shunned.'[31] Do we hear Him telling us that there is important work to be done on a plane of action that lies within; that this work is not self-centred, selfish, or self-important after the manner of the outwardly directed ego? This work is the essential work of the soul, what the mediaeval Christians called the process of sanctification, of becoming ever cleaner and clearer within, more purified, peaceful, and focused in our intention to know and love our Lord. He wants us, even urges us, to attend to this world. He tells us to 'strain every nerve to acquire both inner and outer perfections, for the fruit of the human tree hath ever been and will ever be perfections both within and without'.[32]

The Writings acknowledge the difficulties of this Inner Family, and the oppressive resistance we may experience from many sources. Every one of these oppressive forces 'press down' our capacity to use our free will and suppress the spontaneous expression of joy, playfulness, enthusiasm, and gratitude that spring forth from the soul under natural conditions. Yet He tells us that the soul-self is a 'stronghold', that we are to 'enter therein that thou mayest abide in safety'.[33] Shoghi Effendi reminds us that the Master, 'Abdu'l-Bahá, also experienced 'the terrors of tyranny, the storms of incessant abuse, [and] the oppressiveness of humiliation'.[34]

However, we are assured that we will not be overwhelmed, but can triumph over all these forces, since He has 'ordained for thy training every atom in existence . . . that thou mightest attain My everlasting dominion . . .'[35] He urges us to retake sovereignty over our hearts – where these hearts have become preoccupied with the influence of other people through fear, infatuation, grief, anger, or any emotion that fixes the heart on another than Him alone. For Bahá'u'lláh says, 'the human heart, which I have made the habitation of My beauty . . . thou didst give . . . to another than Me . . .'[36] He tells us to shake off these tyrannies through 'justice' and to 'see with thine own eyes and not through the eyes of others'[37] because only in this way can He commune directly with each of us. He urges us to engage actively with whatever may be disturbing the peace of our dominion within. He says specifically, 'Although at the beginning, this plane is the realm of conflict, yet it endeth in attainment to the throne of splendour.'[38]

The graphic design at the start of Chapter 6 is an expanding infinity symbol designed to indicate that we can only bear witness outward to the world to the extent that we have reached inward to purify our inner holdings and move them toward harmony and unity. Many spiritual practices talk about this relationship between inner and outer. This is the world within, where the soul-self integrates and unifies all that it has experienced, so that it may fulfil its destiny and commune with its Lord.

Isn't that the ultimate? Are we done yet? Not quite. There is another invisible world that reaches beyond our own realm of experience, back into the immeasurable past and forward into the unfathomable future. And it is populated with . . . the Eternal Family.

The Eternal Family

The names of these family members are largely beyond our reach. But the inverse is not true. They know us. Both the Concourse who were here before us and who look in upon this material plane, and the generations who will follow and read about life in the days of the 'champion builders', know who we are. And they are counting on us. We are their living link in the chain of the faithful.

The graphic design at the start of Chapter 7 shows a non-symmetrical halo around the world in an attempt to demonstrate not that the world itself is shining, but that the Concourse beyond is shining in on us. If we read the prayers for the departed, examine carefully the compilation on *The Power of Divine Assistance* and the (Persian) *Hidden Words* which address wealth, generosity and service to the poor, we will find that our mission to the Eternal Family is clearly spelled out.

We are called upon to assist the ones who went before us, by praying that their souls continue to benefit from divine grace, forgiveness, and mercy. While such services have been rendered before – for example, in the tradition of Confucius which emphasizes service to one's ancestors – the Bahá'í description of those who are departed reaches beyond tribal family and specifies several different categories within the Concourse. It does speak of our 'parents', and the intercession of children on their behalf. It does speak of the extended 'kindred' of those of us who have embraced the Faith. But it also singles out 'souls in ignorance' and acknowledges that the ocean of forgiveness can surge for them. And it speaks of souls that have performed great service and asks that what they have offered will be found acceptable and receive the good pleasure of God. So in our prayerful services to those who have gone before, we can be conscious of their various conditions, discriminating about the diversity of their needs, and so adapt our prayers and mindfulness to serve them appropriately.

Then, in a stunning description of what can happen when an individual calls upon the holy ones who have gone before and enlists their aid in serving the Cause, we are told that the hosts of Divine inspiration shall descend upon him from the heaven of My name, the All-Knowing, the All-Wise. On him shall also descend the Concourse on high, each bearing aloft a chalice of pure light.[39]

And 'Abdu'l-Bahá assures us that when our acts are governed by the Teachings, we shall have 'the unfailing help of the Company on high'.[40] Bahá'u'lláh also assures us that He 'shall aid whosoever will arise for the triumph of Our Cause with the hosts of the Concourse on high and a company of Our favoured angels'.[41]

Without confidence in this assistance, the life of a soul can seem solitary and lonely, indeed. But when we are aware of the reality of the heavenly hosts – willing, powerful, ready to assist, and well acquainted with our lives from the inside out – it would be the height of arrogance and self-importance for us to feel lonely. It would be like sitting at a party with a paper bag over our head! We can try, but we will never be truly alone again – ever.

That takes care of us! Now what do we do with the rest of our lives? We are to advance in maturity and become fruitful, and provide for the members of this Eternal Family who will follow us in the near and distant future. Specifically, we are urged to undertake righteous actions, such as providing for the education of children – and for illiterate adults, who are as restricted in their capacity for freedom of action as are children. We are to be generous, not only for the sake of the initial beneficiaries, but because Bahá'u'lláh says, 'To give and to be generous are attributes of Mine; well is it with him that adorneth himself with My virtues.'[42] And we are to rouse ourselves from our comfort zones and demonstrate to the fullest those capacities which the Creator has skilfully crafted in each of us. Likening us to a 'finely tempered sword' whose value is hidden in its sheath, He encourages us to 'come forth from the sheath of self and desire'[43] and serve the world with the same skill and grace as such an exquisite instrument.

Shoghi Effendi, revered as the Guardian of the Bahá'í Faith, inspires our sense of historical significance with this pronouncement:

> The field is indeed so immense, the period so critical, the Cause so great, the workers so few, the time so short, the privilege so priceless, that no follower of the Faith of Bahá'u'lláh, worthy to bear His name, can afford a moment's hesitation.[44]

He reminds us that 'audacious must be the army of life',[45] and in such stirring terms directs us to arise and learn about life by actively serving in all the families in which we dwell.

Richer awareness and better living in all our seven families

What the Sacred Writings open for us is a penetrating vision of human social life dramatically more complex than we had previously acknowledged. Seven human systems inhabiting distinct realms or worlds of experience; each with an identity, purpose, integrity of its own; each family potentially able to nurture its many members; each poignantly in need of assistance to reach its unity. Principles embedded in the Sacred Writings address our role in assisting each family to achieve its own form of harmony and unity, and to fulfil its unique purpose in human affairs.

Individually, we each live and grow like trees, planted in the rich and varied soil of human social life, and in those settings our lives are destined to mature and bring forth the qualities of service that were always latent within us. We know it is our destiny to serve humanity in all its forms and families, because Bahá'u'lláh has revealed:

> Ye are the trees of My garden; ye must give forth goodly and wondrous fruits, that ye yourselves and others may profit therefrom.[46]

In learning to serve these families, to play our part in helping each of these social systems increase its integration, improve its degree of unity, and enrich its synergy, we will find all the satisfaction we have been seeking. We will fulfil the profound purpose for which we were created; and live each day fully to the end, ever expanding and enriching our sense of belonging.

1. The Global Family

Everyone knows the Global Family. Digital cultures have seen the image of its home shining blue and white in the light of its sun. Non-electric cultures have felt its life flowing in their hearts and beating in their drums. And all of us have wondered at its numberless members reflected in the starry night sky. Deep down, we know we are one people.

The Bahá'í Sacred Writings clearly identify a single family of planetary proportions, inclusive of every human being on earth. The future of this family is foreseen as one of profound civilization yet to be realized. As global integration takes place in technologies, transportation and commerce, and as the people of earth experience an increasing sense of their interlocking destiny in environment, health and security, the Sacred Writings foreshadow that this world will, over time, evolve an operating political economy so characterized by justice and prosperity that it will be worthy of the title '*Commonwealth*'.

The world and its nations as analogies of the family

From the globe down to its component nations; and from nations down to each region, city, and household, the paradigm of human family repeats itself at every level of our social lives. We are at all levels interacting with each other to develop awareness, to become useful, and to become more human through the fullness of our social relations than we ever could by living in isolation.

> Compare the nations of the world to the members of a family. A family is a nation in miniature. Simply enlarge the circle of the household, and you have the nation. Enlarge the circle of nations, and you have all humanity. The conditions surrounding the family surround the nation. The happenings in the family are the happenings in the life of the nation. Would it add to the progress and advancement of a family if dissensions should arise among its members, all fighting, pillaging each other, jealous and revengeful of injury, seeking selfish advantage? Nay, this would be the cause of the effacement of progress and advancement. So it is in the great family of nations . . .[1]

The emerging World Commonwealth

The unity to come does not at all appear to be a simple melting down of distinctions into one totalitarian system overseeing a single multitude. On the contrary, the future promises to unite all of Earth's diverse citizenry in a delicate balance of creative tensions among three levels of aggregation: a world-embracing governance; a continuing set of autonomous nation states, each expressing its distinctive features; and individual citizens exercising personal freedom and initiative.

At every level, we see a dynamic homeostasis, a relatively stable equilibrium among interdependent parts, capable of perpetually maintaining and advancing itself. The creative stability of our human social lives comes from finding an optimum balance between the centrifugal forces of individuation that drive us apart, and a centripetal force toward fusion with each other that is drawing us into a culture on Earth showing higher complexity and greater creativity than ever before.

> The unity of the human race, as envisaged by Bahá'u'lláh, implies the establishment of a world commonwealth in which all nations, races, creeds and classes are closely and permanently united, and in which the autonomy of its state members and the personal freedom and initiative of the individuals that compose them are definitely and completely safeguarded.[2]

Releasing creative energies

A planet that has established the unity of its Global Family will cease to squander its resources on competition and conquest between nations. Immeasurable resources will then become available and redirected to creating a commonwealth of social development in which a new economic relationship of capital and labour will benefit both. Unfolding the potential of nations will no longer be impeded by the kinds of economic barriers which until now have prohibited large segments of humanity from participating in world affairs. Prejudices of economic class, religion, and race which fragment and injure our Global Family with slander and violence will gradually be no more, so that our world community can emerge:

> A world community in which all economic barriers will have been permanently demolished and the interdependence of Capital and Labour definitely recognized; in which the clamour of religious fanaticism and strife will have been forever stilled; in which the flame of racial animosity will have been finally extinguished . . .[3]

As an expression of our rising tide of creative energy, we the peoples of the world will eventually realize and apply the essential rights and freedoms we have universally come to endorse, by turning them into standards of cultural behaviour and voluntarily creating

> a single code of international law – the product of the considered judgment of the world's federated representatives – [that] shall have as its sanction the instant and coercive intervention of the combined forces of the federated units . . .[4]

So powerful will be our desire for the fruits of united action, that our national governments will voluntarily abstain from unilateral actions of force. Each nation will seek its place in

> a world community in which the fury of a capricious and militant nationalism will have been transmuted into an abiding consciousness of world citizenship – such indeed, appears in its broadest outline, the Order anticipated by Bahá'u'lláh, an Order that shall come to be regarded as the fairest fruit of a slowly maturing age.[5]

There is nothing trivial, superficial, or partial about the change that is taking place in our sense of identity as citizens of Earth and members of the Global Family. What we are entering into is 'an organic change in the structure of present-day society, a change such as the world has not yet experienced',[6] 'the achievement of [the] organic and spiritual unity of the whole body of nations'.[7]

The appearance in history of a Manifestation of God has always signalled a sea-change in human culture, and has brought about a revolution in human nature and the springtime of a new civilization. In accord with this pattern of recurrence, the coming of Bahá'u'lláh is once again suffusing the world with God's transforming grace, the purpose of which has always been to protect the well-being and promote the welfare of its children. In the words of the Universal House of Justice:

> It is a fresh manifestation of the direct involvement of God in history, a reassurance that His children have not been left to drift, a sign of the outpouring of a heavenly grace that will enable all humanity to be free at last from conflict and contention to ascend the heights of world peace and divine civilization.[8]

Before such a commonwealth can come into existence, several barriers created by adversarial relations within the body of humanity must each be resolved. Among these barriers are animosities existing between races, creeds, and classes, prejudices which are addressed in other chapters. But the deepest-running division, the most fundamental polarity, and the most radical feature of human potential is the interacting roles of women and men in the life of the Global Family. Foremost among the distinguishing themes of the Global Family is the pressing need to promote equal development of its men and women in all the areas in which they are respectively deficient. Only as these two 'wings' are balanced in their capacities to bear burdens of various kinds will the bird of humanity soar toward ever higher fulfilment of its destined nobility.

Inequality of opportunity for the sexes

Let us not delude ourselves that thinking of equality as an inherent reality amounts to actually achieving it in the Global Family. Even in the 21st century, brutal atrocities are committed daily against millions of women, female youth, girl children, and even babies. No soul dare contemplate the full horror of this worldwide darkness.

Even in the most constitutionally 'civilized' of nations, systematic distortions in the distribution of employment, income, safety, health and dignity occur along the fault lines of gender to an even greater degree than those of race. Whatever the inequalities of social condition and opportunity between races, the divisions *within*, between the sexes, are pervasive – to the detriment of all. Most agencies of social and economic development have a surfeit of evidence to this effect. It is, as we say, common knowledge.

But what too often goes unnoticed about the perpetuation of these 'bad habits' of inequality that impose suffering and extreme disadvantage on women, is the harm they do to men and the arenas of action controlled by them.

> The denial of such equality perpetrates an injustice against one half of the world's population and promotes in men harmful attitudes and habits that are carried from the family to the workplace, to political life, and ultimately to international relations.[9]

When social discourse in the family, the workplace, and beyond is deprived of the refreshing exchange of ideas that occurs between male and female, then our mental atmosphere becomes stale and stagnant. The world's awareness of itself – which should be informed and stimulated by the complementary, bi-logical thought processes resulting from gender perspective, instead stumbles forward with mono-logical limitations. Speaking of the world of humanity and its two component halves, 'Abdu'l-Bahá says:

> In past ages humanity has been defective and inefficient because it has been incomplete ... In truth, [woman] will be the greatest factor in establishing universal peace and international arbitration ... Inasmuch as human society consists of two parts, the male and the female, each the complement of the other, the happiness and stability of humanity cannot be assured unless both are perfected.[10]

By far, the most common policy response to this self-defeating imbalance of gender in society is to attempt to mitigate the symptoms of underparticipation of women in world affairs. The approach most frequently adopted in social movements – good in itself (as far as it goes) – is to advance the welfare of women and improve their preparation to engage in social and economic decision-making.

The advancement of women

The Bahá'í Writings present an appealing image of shared adventure, the sense that we are in a new age, one that will be characterized by shared experiences of progress and comradeship, as when 'Abdu'l-Bahá states:

> In the Dispensation of Bahá'u'lláh, women are advancing side by side with men.[11]

Every person enjoys the sensation of increasing their competence in some field of endeavour, whether on the personal scale or on the societal scale. Having been required for so long to restrict themselves to personal household skills, women the world over are coming to enjoy competence in all public arenas as well:

> There is no area or instance where they [women] will lag behind: they have equal rights with men, and will enter, in the future, into all branches of the administration of society.[12]

'Abdu'l-Bahá states that the destiny of women is to join their male counterparts in every arena of human enterprise, to master the details, shoulder their share of the dilemmas, and attain the highest positions of public trust:

> Such will be their elevation that, in every area of endeavour, they will occupy the highest levels in the human world.[13]

The birthright of women to 'occupy the highest levels in the human world' will not simply come to them in the fullness of time, like an inheritance. It is an achievement to be worked for, not a legacy to be passively received. All women in the world, regardless of race, religion, or age, are summoned by 'Abdu'l-Bahá to step forward and claim their rightful place, to exercise their abilities.

> . . . while this principle of equality is true, it is likewise true that woman must prove her capacity and aptitude, must show forth the evidences of equality.[14]

Women, in all their diversity, are called upon to demonstrate their capacities, to take advantage of every open opportunity, and to relegate to the past the memory of their exclusion from fields of human achievement.

> She must become proficient in the arts and sciences and prove by her accomplishments that her abilities and powers have merely been latent.[15]

OUR SEVEN FAMILIES

Early in the 20th century, 'Abdu'l-Bahá emphasized certain essential areas of public enterprise for the special attention and engagement of women, such as design, engineering and manufacturing; food, nutrition and applied life sciences – areas that had the most direct impact on human welfare.

> Woman must especially devote her energies and abilities toward the industrial and agricultural sciences, seeking to assist mankind in that which is most needful.[16]

Without doubt, the initiative is left to women to tolerate no further delay and to advance in accomplishments on every side.

> Woman must endeavour then to attain greater perfection, to be man's equal in every respect, to make progress in all in which she has been backward, so that man will be compelled to acknowledge her equality of capacity and attainment.[17]

The sooner she demonstrates her equality in visible realms of science, art, and economy, the better, for her mate faces even greater challenges when entering the invisible realms where her achievements are already legendary. Since time immemorial woman has been known for her abilities to nurture, heal, encourage, and restore. Her uncanny awareness of the unspoken condition of others, her encompassing ability to track several processes at once, her willingness to surrender special advantage in favour of the greatest good for the greatest number, have enabled her to raise families, bind communities, and birth the elders into the afterworlds.

These nameless capacities – long unrecognized as professions and undervalued in the economy – are in this day increasingly being identified, so they can be taught in such areas as healing, recovery and resilience, learning, mentoring, encouraging, coordinating, reconciling, and self-transforming, to name only a few. The very qualities that have distinguished her from her mate now become of prime importance to him, since they are needed by him to qualify for the new day that is dawning on Earth.

The evolution of men

Every woman who has brought forth a child knows that when God sets in motion the forces of birthing, on that day, ready or not, there is no turning back. Equally so, in this day, when God has set in motion the forces of a new history, every man senses, whether he admits it or not, and certainly whether he likes it or not, that there is no turning back. In the 20th century, masses of young men in the world were singing: 'the times they are a-changing'.[18] But in the 21st century, male backlash against male/female equality has raged more savagely than ever in a futile attempt to reverse the will of God. In 2012, men with guns entered a schoolbus and after asking for a student by name, shot that student in the head, exposing their own grotesque perversion. After regaining consciousness, the youth declared: 'Extremists have shown what frightens them most: a girl with a book.'[19] Evil does not fade away of its own accord. Darkness will only be dispelled by light – by the light of good men. What men of good will are called upon to do is come to grips with the qualities and skills that women are bringing to the public domain at this time in history.

> . . . the balance is already shifting; force is losing its dominance, and mental alertness, intuition, and the spiritual qualities of love and service, in which woman is strong, are gaining ascendancy.[20]

What exactly is shifting at this moment in history? What does 'mental alertness' mean in terms of human relations? In personal relations? In global relations? What is a man to do about the ascendancy of 'intuition'? Is this a capacity that can be developed? Is this some new skill a man can learn? What is it that will link 'service' as a spiritual quality to 'love' rather than, say, to 'competence'? What are the overall implications of the foregoing passage for the evolution of men? Are men losing dominance, or is it that the traditional strategies of 'force' and domination are less valid? Is it women who are gaining ascendancy, or is it that spiritual qualities, previously associated with women, now have special relevance for men as well in order to achieve harmony in the Global Family?

Obviously, men are still the measure of certain fields of achievement, while women are in the process of attaining equality. But could this also mean that women have set the standard in certain other fields, in which men are now challenged to acquire new skills and develop latent capacities? Couldn't we just go on developing the women in society and leave 'mankind' the way it always was? Let us consider the words of 'Abdu'l-Bahá:

> The world of humanity consists of two parts: male and female. Each is the complement of the other. Therefore, if one is defective, the other will necessarily be incomplete, and perfection cannot be attained. There is a right hand and a left hand in the human body, functionally equal in service… If either proves defective, the defect will naturally extend to the other…Just as physical accomplishment is complete with two hands, so man and woman, the two parts of the social body, must be perfect. It is not natural that either should remain undeveloped; and until both are perfected, the happiness of the human world will not be realized.[21]

The 'social and economic equation' in which women 'will demonstrate capability and ensure recognition of equality'[22] takes place on an externally observable plane of action. But transformation of global culture and unification of the Global Family will result from a new commitment to learning, teaching, appreciating, and all the other forms of human communication which take place on an invisible plane of social action . It is on this invisible plane of action that men are being called to develop capacities.

If 'all virtues must be taught the family' as 'Abdu'l-Bahá says of the Essential Family, then teaching and learning are central to the welfare of all families, including the Global Family. As girls and boys both learn the same practical skills and communication skills, then they will grow into adults of the Global Family who can lead reconciliation processes and overcome the global plagues of conflict and violence. As women extend themselves outwardly into action, and men extend themselves inwardly into communication and compassion, their growing mutual communion will bring both parties into a world where inner and outer planes of action are congruent with each. These complementary processes of gender development will fill the gaps, redress the imbalances and bind us together in a shared force field of noble qualities.

> He [Bahá'u'lláh] promulgated the adoption of the same course of education for man and woman. Daughters and sons must follow the same curriculum of study, thereby promoting unity of the sexes. When all mankind shall receive the same opportunity of education and the equality of men and women be realized, the foundations of war will be utterly destroyed.[23]

While 'Abdu'l-Bahá challenged *all* women to demonstrate

their capacities, the Universal House of Justice has made a unique call to Bahá'í men to demonstrate leadership through the dynamic force of their personal example. It is by such individual example that the world will become acquainted with men profoundly refined in character and compassion – the like of which the world has not seen before. Their voluntary self-restraint, moderation, and adaptability will enable cooperation with others far beyond contemporary standards. Their skill in communication will be evidenced in consultative practices far different from the competitive world we see today.

> Bahá'í men have the opportunity to demonstrate to the world around them a new approach to the relationship between the sexes, where aggression and the use of force are eliminated and replaced by cooperation and consultation . . .[24]

Bahá'í men are called upon by 'Abdu'l-Bahá to attain a state of perfection through the refinement of their strength of heart, mind, spirit, and soul as they progress from boyhood to manhood.

> . . . the man becomes pure through his strength. Through the power of intelligence he becomes simple; through the great power of reason and understanding and not through the power of weakness [like children] he becomes sincere. When he attains to the state of perfection, he will receive these qualities; his heart becomes purified, his spirit enlightened, his soul is sensitized and tender – all through his great strength. This is the difference between the perfect man and the child. Both have the underlying qualities of simplicity and sincerity – the child through the power of weakness and the man through the power of strength.[25]

As these men show the way for others, and all people grow more accomplished in the qualities in which they have been deficient, the population at large will find itself enjoying a more complete, more humane way of life, and the resulting civilization will benefit from a new blend of salt and sweet, of yang and yin.

> Hence the new age will be an age . . . in which the masculine and feminine elements of civilization will be more evenly balanced.[26]

The greatness which might be theirs

How long has it taken us to reach this day? How long have we yearned for a happiness and fulfilment that seemed always beyond our reach? How long have the worlds of men and women coexisted in mutual ignorance, distrust, animosity, and sabotage? How long have we hungered for the companionship of the other, to end this universal loneliness and make this empty world a home filled with security, prosperity, comfort, and celebration of the unity of our differences?

> The happiness of mankind will be realized when women and men coordinate and advance equally, for each is the complement and helpmeet of the other.[27]

While the advancement of women is necessary, it is not sufficient to bring the world right. The real key to harmony in the Global Family is the evolution of men. The equality that will result from respective development of the sexes will lead to the destiny that men have been hopelessly seeking on the seas and battlefields for far too long. For men, their happiness and greatness, the fulfilment of their divine potential, hangs in the balance, awaiting the day when they share with women as co-equals.

> As long as women are prevented from attaining their highest possibilities, so long will **men** be unable to achieve **the greatness which might be theirs**.[28] [emphasis added]

The role of women in governing a peaceful planet

We have come to this conclusive connection between the welfare of the Global Family and the equality of women and men. It is not that men cannot build the bridges, plant the fields, launch the health campaigns, and compose the operas to make this world a better place. They can. But as just quoted above, even men when dominant will be unable to express fully their creative potential so long as their strengths are being drowned in the chaos of war and they experience the resulting waves of post-traumatic stress disorder, refugee displacement, disease and degradation. And men will never be able to purge themselves of war, without the resounding presence of women to help them champion peace:

> ... the achievement of full equality between the sexes, is one of the most important, though less acknowledged prerequisites of peace.[29]

Peace in turn is the prerequisite condition for all the arts of civilization to flourish. And it will require the full participation of women as voters in every nation and every level of governance to provide the critical mass of political will that is needed to make peace the global norm.

The most momentous question of this day is international

peace and arbitration, and universal peace is impossible without universal suffrage.[30]

It is not the kind of formally legislated suffrage concluded with the stroke of a pen that is needed, but the concrete reality of suffrage that is grounded in literacy, enacted by registration, transportation, and protection from violence, and concluded with the casting of a vote. Voting is not the only governance contribution of women, and women are not the only wing of humanity, but when women arise to bring forth this prerequisite condition of peace, it will prepare the way for men, thus liberated from war, to fulfil their destiny as contributors to an ever-advancing civilization.

> So it will come to pass that when women participate fully and equally in the affairs of the world, when they enter confidently and capably the great arena of laws and politics, war will cease.[31]

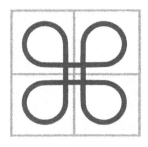

2. The National Family

The evolving definition of the National Family

In the early 21st century, we have yet to create an operational definition of the National Family. Historically, the nation consisted of one tribal people connected by blood, located in one contiguous region of lands and waters. Then, the nation became one people connected by traditions, and dispersed through many lands. Today a nation may be made up of many peoples living in a common land, gradually focusing on those qualities that will make them one nation, unique in the world. In just a few generations, millions of people have been forced to relocate from region to region, and even continent to continent due to natural and man-made catastrophes, including famine, war, epidemic, and economic collapse. In whatever country we find ourselves today, whether driven there by disaster, drawn there by opportunity, or located there since time immemorial, we are now engaged in creating a new form of nationhood and living in a new age as a National Family.

What will be the rationale of this new National Family? What will be the new mystique, ethos, vision, values, and purpose that will identify us and justify us as a nation? In the absence of historical reasons such as racial exclusivity, imperial conquest, or territorial delimitations such as island shorelines, what will become the new, compelling and more worthy reasons to exist as a National Family?

As with all 'families' or functional human systems, the composite exists to benefit the development of the members. In part, this benefit comes from the sustenance, support, and protection that the system offers its members, improving the probability of survival. But beyond mere survival lies the prospect of a nation's people being able to develop their talents and abilities better thanks to the resources of the whole. The larger context provides opportunities for members to grow by offering their services to many others, and thus to develop more capacity than they could have done by living only for themselves. This is the latent synergistic relationship waiting to be awakened between individuals and their nation state, their National Family.

In this day, identification with one's National Family is no longer as simple as belonging by accident of birth to a given region. Often the national membership 'ascribed' at birth is overtaken by another membership when one migrates to an adopted nation. Thus, a National Family cannot define itself merely by the members who were born within its borders. Formal procedures are in place for the official adoption of new members into a National Family. This is similar to the pattern in the Essential Family, in which new human families come into being through adoption or marriage – that is, by choice.

Within the borders of a nation state, side by side, may be people who have just arrived lacking a sense of the new place and people whose entire memory is of their forefathers and foremothers always living in that place. Within the borders of a nation state may be more than one race, more than one ethnicity within race, many languages, religions, classes of education, and forms of work. How could we imagine a successfully functioning National Family emerging from such a chaotic mixture?

From the time of 'Abdu'l-Bahá, when He addressed *The Secret of Divine Civilization* to the ruling Shah of Persia, Bahá'ís have contributed insights from the Sacred Writings for an emerging model of nationhood that will be capable of accommodating the modern reality of peoples with varying needs and potentials living within a national border. Two significant documents prepared by Bahá'í institutions offer an expanded understanding of the National Family. These are: *Individual Rights and Freedoms in the World Order of Bahá'u'lláh*[1] and *The Vision of Race Unity: America's Most Challenging Issue*.[2] From these two documents, a number of themes emerge that help define the National Family. These include:

- the process of human maturity as it applies to a nation;
- the reciprocity between individuals and their nation;
- the need for racial unity and harmony to benefit the nation;
- the unique contribution of each nation to the World Commonwealth.

The maturation of a national culture and society

In the next chapter we introduce the concept of maturity as it applies to the process of human development in the Essential Family from infant to child, to adult, and finally to elder; and the roles thus fulfilled in service to each other. This same process applied to a whole society would not be merely a line connecting 'young to old' or 'new to old'– in the way that folk wisdom referred to the Americas as a 'New World' when Europeans migrated west, or when commentators speak of a 'young' or an 'old' nation, referring strictly to its legal existence over time .

THE NATIONAL FAMILY

In the case of nations, 'maturity' refers to the emergence of wisdom and patterns of noble behaviour. A nation is thus considered 'immature' to the extent that it has not yet brought forth certain essential noble qualities in its culture. This is not a particularly easy process to envision, because the 20th century as a whole was so dominated by the surging energy (military, economic, psychological) of adolescence among its technologically advanced nations that a mature culture was yet to be imagined.

> In a period of history dominated by the surging energy, the rebellious spirit and frenetic activity of adolescence, it is difficult to grasp the distinguishing elements of the mature society to which Bahá'u'lláh beckons all humanity.[3]

Adolescence exhibits an abundance of energy, but rarely an equal amount of discretion. The document titled *Individual Rights and Freedoms* points out that there are many ready examples of adolescent societies. We could also search our awareness and identify national cultures that exhibit a predominance of rigid, antiquated, suffocating customs characteristic of extreme age and deterioration. To qualify as 'maturing', a set of national social and policy changes would have to occur in the direction of sustainable, benevolent lines of action, that would be in contrast to both the energetic, self-centered preoccupations of an adolescent society and the possibly well-meaning but ineffective actions of anachronistic social customs out of touch with the times.

We might prefer to hope that a social change of historic magnitude could occur spontaneously, but social evolution occurs by collective choices, consciously made through the exercise of free will. The history of the world demonstrates that radical cultural transformation comes about through the influence of divinely inspired and spiritually potent Teachings. When these Teachings enter human culture in whatever time or region, they touch the inmost depths of the human soul, awakening it to the potential life that it possesses, and empowering it to alter every aspect of its outward behaviour from the most trivial to the most significant.

'Abdu'l-Bahá tells us that the way to motivate a society to advance from an adolescent to a more mature stage is by providing education for every one of its members without exception.

> Universal education is a universal law. It is therefore, incumbent upon every father to teach and instruct his children according to his possibilities. If he is unable to educate them, the body politic, the representative of the people, must provide the means for their education.[4]

Thus, the self-governing entity of the people as a whole must provide the means if a father is unable to educate his children. This is the basis for public education, over and above exclusively private systems. It is in a society's own best interest to awaken and educate all its members (at every stage of life) to the quality of life they can enjoy through productive work, health, recreation, and service to others.

While it is the responsibility of parents to educate their offspring, who will educate the rest of a whole society? How can that be done? If advancing a nation's level of social and cultural maturity requires influencing, inspiring and 'educating' people of all ages and all walks of life, then obviously a schooling system for youth even combined with a higher education system for professionals would be insufficient. These two educational systems could only provide for a portion of that nation. For this reason, Bahá'í values emphasize the arts of communication, of theatre, literature, and music, and all those media that can and should carry life-enhancing messages. For example, Bahá'u'lláh says:

> We, verily, have made music as a ladder for your souls, a means whereby they may be lifted up unto the realm on high; make it not, therefore, as wings to self and passion. Truly, We are loathe to see you numbered with the foolish . . . Take heed . . . lest listening thereto should cause you to overstep the bounds of propriety and dignity.[5]

The statement above points to a profound attribute of maturity in general, and of a mature society in particular, one in which people implement the principle of self-chosen limits to behaviour. The principle holds that any action, including those that are essentially beneficial, can be harmful when carried to extreme. This might apply to physical actions such as exercise or driving a car, or cultural actions such as speech and literature, or other forms of personal expression such as dress or public behaviour.

> From a Bahá'í point of view, the exercise of freedom of speech must necessarily be disciplined by a profound appreciation of both the positive and negative dimensions of freedom, on the one hand, and of speech, on the other.[6]

Some nations proclaim that freedom of speech, the press and media, is an absolute right and the ultimate social good. Yet unconstrained speech includes excesses and obvious crimes against humanity such as publications promoting hatred. Many of us have found ourselves in humanities or communication arts classes debating the issue of censorship as a social tool, or exploring the conflict of values raised by the larger topic of natural or optimal limits to expression. If one has come to expect that unlimited self-expression is practically the keystone of democracy, it creates cognitive dissonance to hear that there may be natural limits to expression that it would be wise to honour. But then again, why would this be so surprising? There are natural limits to just about everything. It may be thrilling to drive a car fast, but not so fast that it overshoots the curve in the road. The case of the car is governed by the natural law of momentum which applies to concrete bodies in motion. It seems there are other kinds of natural laws pertaining to human awareness and community, such that if we exceed certain limits, what was beneficial becomes harmful. Thus, it is consistent with natural laws related to physical actions for us to identify natural limits related to social actions.

With regard to human speech and self-expression, at what point does the benefit of freedom become harmful? An expert on American constitutional law explained to the author that the whole essence of democracy is to optimize dialogue. Bahá'ís would call that the synergistic benefit of consultation. We want to maximize the collective intelligence of a group by optimizing each person's contribution to the consultation. If there is some expression of racism, sexism, classism, ageism, sectarian exclusivity, or any other form of prejudice, intolerance or hatred systematically preventing a specific group of citizens from making their contribution to the national dialogue, then that particular expression is a net evil, a net dysfunction. Such detrimental expression is counterproductive to the shared conversation. It robs the nation of the contribution that might have been made by those who were targeted and oppressed by excessive and violent speech or expression. So the point at which one person's self-expression becomes harmful to the capacity of others to make their contribution is the point at which it would be wise, and therefore 'mature', to voluntarily undertake some limits to one's freedom of speech. We practise this in our conversations with each other; we practise it in groups. Now we see that voluntary adoption of limits to speech supports the welfare of our National Family.

The subtle moral balance implied in the foregoing consideration of freedom of speech is just one of many instances of creative tension among values that a society must incorporate as it matures. It is less a question of 'this or that' and, rather, one of '*how much* of this and that?' The Guardian tells us that only the spirit of a true Bahá'í will be able to reconcile countervailing principles, such as mercy and justice, or freedom and submission.

> Nothing short of the spirit of a true Bahá'í can hope to reconcile the principles of mercy and justice, of freedom and submission, of the sanctity of the right of the individual and of self-surrender, of vigilance, discretion and prudence on the one hand, and fellowship, candour, and courage on the other.[7]

The individual in society

It is apparent that we will voluntarily choose to submit ourselves to the guidance of particular laws and principles when we recognize their value. But how will we reconcile the age-old dilemma of tension between the desires of individuals at one extreme and the needs of their culture as a whole at the other? History has produced examples of both extremes: the nation dominating the individual with its demands for conformity, and irresponsible individuals tearing a nation apart by following a self-indulgent philosophy.

The following table illustrates a Bahá'í definition of the appropriate relations pertaining between individuals and their self-governing community, their body politic. On one axis are arrayed the individual community members and the elected assembly of the society of which they are a part. On the other axis are listed the rights and responsibilities that apply between the parties. In this format, it is possible to see clearly how the principle of mutual service applies between individuals and their society. While these illustrations are taken from the case of the Local Spiritual Assembly, the council that Bahá'ís elect for their city or municipality, the same principles apply at the level of the nation state, simply 'writ large'. (The table refers to sections from the compilation entitled 'The Local Spiritual Assembly' as numbered in *The Compilation of Compilations*).[8]

	RIGHTS	**RESPONSIBILITIES**
The Elected (members of the Assembly)	❖ To be consulted on all matters . . . in the locality (No. 1393) ❖ To have LSA decisions abided by (No. 1394) ❖ To be supported and sustained (No. 1403)	❖ To consult, not to dictate (No. 1388) ❖ To approach their task with extreme humility (No. 1388) ❖ To utilize the energies of the rank and file (No. 1389) ❖ To act with justice in all cases (No. 1390) ❖ To promote harmony and fellowship (No. 1391)
The Electors (members of the community)	❖ To be heard in strictest confidence (No. 1375) ❖ To receive guidance (No. 1375) ❖ To receive assistance (No. 1375) ❖ To receive protection (No. 1375) ❖ To appeal any decision felt to be unjust or detrimental to the interests of the community[9]	❖ To actively participate in electing the LSA (No. 1394) ❖ To consult the LSA (No. 1392) ❖ To abide by its decisions (No. 1394) ❖ To cooperate with it wholeheartedly (No. 1394) ❖ To support and sustain the LSA (No. 1403)

THE NATIONAL FAMILY

For Bahá'ís, the fundamental principle on which solutions can be built is 'subordination of individual will to that of society'. 'SUB-ordination' means that the will of the individual has a place in the order of things, but that place is superseded by the principle of the community and its welfare as a whole.

> The Bahá'í conception of social life is essentially based on the principle of the subordination of the individual will to that of society. It neither suppresses the individual nor does it exalt him to the point of making him an anti-social creature, a menace to society. As in everything, it follows the 'golden mean'.[10]

In other words, the advisability of individual interests is checked against the standard of whether or not the proposed action would do harm, be neutral, or provide positive benefit for the society in which it will take place. This principle, specifying that in a conflict of interests, the individual's will accedes to that of society, does not suppress the individual by saying that individuals must do exactly thus and so, in a uniform manner, thereby stifling individual initiative. Nor does it exalt the individual to what Shoghi Effendi called 'an anti-social creature, a menace to society', who thinks that they should be allowed to do anything they want, anywhere, anytime. It reminds us that there is a living social fabric, a living body, to which we all belong. None of us can claim the right to tear apart that social fabric, or damage that living body, by our self-centred whims.

As we have seen, a set of rights and responsibilities is codified in the administration of Bahá'í communities which provides a pattern for successful larger systems such as the National Family. The agency of governance owes certain services to the people, and in turn has the right to expect cohesion and cooperation from them. Conversely, all people are responsible for establishing and maintaining the agency of governance, and have the right to receive services from the government and to appeal to it when the interests of the community seem at risk.

> The Assembly has the responsibility to guide, direct and decide on community affairs and the right to be obeyed and supported by members of the community. The individual has the responsibility to establish and maintain the Assembly through election, the offering of advice, moral support and material assistance; and he has the right to be heard by it, to receive its guidance and assistance, and to appeal from any Assembly decision which he conscientiously feels is unjust or detrimental to the interests of the community.[11]

The line of orientation is always toward the individuals who are being protected, nurtured, and developed, enabling them to offer their unique gifts to society. Government, like parenthood, exists to serve the development of individual members toward the fulfilment of their potential. Those various potentials will bring to society all the range of talents it requires for its preservation and advancement.

> This relationship . . . must allow 'free scope' for 'individuality to assert itself' through modes of spontaneity, initiative and diversity that ensure the viability of society.[12]

> How noteworthy that in the Order of Bahá'u'lláh . . . the individual is not lost in the mass but becomes the focus of primary development, so that he may find his own place in the flow of progress, and society as a whole may benefit from the accumulated talents and abilities of the individuals composing it.[13]

THE NATIONAL FAMILY

This description of self-governance resembles the Greek city-state of Athens. The body or 'polity' of its citizens (albeit comprised only of non-slave men) were so enchanted with the ideal of their self-managing community, their 'polis', that they embodied it as a goddess. Athena was the personification of the psyche or spirit of the citizenry of Athens, each of whom felt personally responsible for her, and for the quality of life within her – which could at any moment be at stake. Equally so today, as citizenry who love our city or our nation, we may find ourselves at any moment faced with the choice to serve what we love, or to turn away and default on our responsibility to 'her'.

In communities where Bahá'ís have elected a Local Spiritual Assembly, they have the opportunity to engage in a sacred relationship, a divinely established social system designed to cultivate a better quality of life not only for Bahá'ís, but for everyone within that municipality. In the foregoing table, we can see how subtle the lines of relationship are, and how carefully they must be practised to protect the social fabric of community life, and ultimately the life of the National Family.

> The happiness and pride of a nation consist in this, that it should shine out like the sun in the high heaven of knowledge. [14]

So we can see ahead to a day when our polities – our cities, regions, and nations – support each of their citizens to achieve the fullest development of their potential. And what would that be? 'Abdu'l-Bahá says there is no greater joy, no more complete delight, than to find that one has been able to serve society and become a source of social good.

> And the honour and distinction of the individual consist in this, that he among all the world's multitudes should become

a source of social good. Is any larger bounty conceivable than this, that an individual, looking within himself, should find that by the confirming grace of God he has become the cause of peace and well-being, of happiness and advantage to his fellowmen? No, by the one true God, there is no greater bliss, no more complete delight.[15]

It is true that, early in life, we are each required to pay attention to our own education, to the acquisition of skills, to income-earning, and the establishment of independence. But that is only a temporary stage. The purpose of self-sufficiency is not to continue in the same direction of self-service so that we consume more and more resources for ourselves. Rather, the purpose of satisfying basic personal needs is to move beyond them to larger aspirations, which serve as a positive asset to the larger society. The Buddhist traditions allude to the moment of development when the Bodhisattva (the devotees and aspirants, practising the way of the Buddha) realize that they can no longer increase the satisfaction of eating by eating ever greater amounts of food through their own mouth. They can only increase their pleasure by eating through the mouths of many others. As 'Abdu'l-Bahá says: the honour and distinction of the soul is through becoming the source of social good.

Racial harmony and unity

In times long past, we simply didn't have effective modes of transportation for interacting with others beyond our natural borders. Geographic boundaries, such as mountain ranges and coastlines, confined our ancestors into territories of racial uniformity. But even then, and more so as time went on, historic forces began stirring the pot. Raids upon neighbouring tribes (with the consequent abduction of slaves), floods, earthquakes, famine, and plague were among the forces causing multitudes to be uprooted from their ancestral lands and to set up homes and communities in new and foreign places. In more recent times, positive motivations such as curiosity, cultural exchange, and economic, educational and professional opportunities have enticed people to relocate in distant lands. These forces of history, both negative and positive, have moved people around the world, and mixed them together, producing the social phenomenon of many peoples living in one land, growing to be one highly diversified nation.

When Bahá'u'lláh addresses peoples who dwell in a common land, He speaks with the voice of the Creator, declaring that, since we are made of one substance, we should recognize that just as we walk with the same feet (perhaps in the same brands of shoe) and eat with the same mouth (perhaps the same brands of food), we are in fact partaking of one consciousness, one shared soul:

> Since We have created you all from one same substance it is incumbent on you to be even as one soul, to walk with the same feet, eat with the same mouth and dwell in the same land . . . that from your inmost being, by your deeds and actions, the signs of oneness and the essence of detachment may be made manifest.[16]

He categorically rejects aversion to others resulting in animalistic acts of territoriality and violence, calling us instead to our common purpose:

> All men have been created to carry forward an ever-advancing civilization. The Almighty beareth Me witness: To act like the beasts of the field is unworthy of man. Those virtues that befit his dignity are forbearance, mercy, compassion

and loving-kindness towards all the peoples and kindreds of the earth.[17]

Similarly, 'Abdu'l-Bahá specifically denounces prejudice due to variation of colour:

> This variety in forms and colourings which is manifest in all the kingdoms is according to creative wisdom and has a divine purpose. Nevertheless, whether the creatures be all alike or all different should not be the cause of strife and quarrelling among them. Especially why should man find cause for discord in the colour or race of his fellow creature? No educated or illumined mind will allow that this differentiation and discord should exist or that there is any ground for it.[18]

In another place, He draws the conclusion:

> Therefore, all prejudices between man and man are falsehoods and violations of the will of God. God desires unity and love; He commands harmony and fellowship. Enmity is human disobedience; God Himself is love.[19]

In turn, the Guardian exhorts all people intent on fulfilling the desire of God for unity and love, harmony and fellowship, to prepare themselves for the price that each one will have to pay to rid themselves of prejudice and enjoy a state of synergy born of their diversity. Addressing racism in America, he states:

> Let neither [black nor white] think that anything short of genuine love, extreme patience, true humility, consummate tact, sound initiative, mature wisdom, and deliberate, persistent, and prayerful effort can succeed in blotting out the

stain which this patent evil has left on the fair name of their common country.[20]

Diversity, with all its challenges, calls us to achieve a higher order of unity, since unity is the very law of life itself. Speaking of biological life, 'Abdu'l-Bahá states that 'the spirit of life . . . establishes such a unity in the bodily organism that if any part is subjected to injury or becomes diseased, all the other parts and functions sympathetically respond and suffer'.[21] Taking this as an analogy for the social and cultural life of a society, *The Vision of Race Unity* states: 'Bahá'ís see unity as the law of life; consequently, all prejudices are perceived as diseases that threaten life'.[22] But what is the solution for such a state of disorder and disease? Again, the answer comes from 'Abdu'l-Bahá:

> the world of humanity is a composite body, and the Holy Spirit is the animating principle of its life . . . we must strive in order that the power of the Holy Spirit may become effective . . . may confer a new quickening life upon the body politic of the nations and peoples . . .[23]

Distinctive national contributions

So glorious is the World Commonwealth foretold in the Bahá'í Writings that we are at times tempted to forget that there is a continuing place for nation states to make their distinctive contributions to that whole. Shoghi Effendi characterizes the future role of patriotism, in the world order envisioned by Bahá'u'lláh, in the following way:

> Its purpose is neither to stifle the flame of a sane and intelligent patriotism in men's hearts, nor to abolish the system of national autonomy so essential if the evils of excessive

centralization are to be avoided. It does not ignore, nor does it attempt to suppress, the diversity of ethnical origins, of climate, of history, of language and tradition, of thought and habit, that differentiate the peoples and nations of the world. It calls for a wider loyalty . . . It insists upon the subordination of national impulses and interests to the imperative claims of a unified world.[24]

At many points, 'Abdu'l-Bahá alluded to the diversity later described so eloquently by Shoghi Effendi, highlighting the particular strengths that a country, region, or continent brings to the world. Regarding the Arabian Peninsula, He said:

When the light of Muḥammad dawned, the darkness of ignorance was dispelled from the deserts of Arabia. In a short period of time those barbarous peoples attained a superlative degree of civilization which, with Baghdád as its centre, extended as far westward as Spain and afterward influenced the greater part of Europe.[25]

During His travels to Canada, 'Abdu'l-Bahá stated:

I see before me souls who have unusual capability and the power of spiritual advancement. In reality, the people of this continent possess great capacity; they are the cause of my happiness, and I ever pray that God may confirm and assist them to progress in all the degrees of existence. As they have advanced along material lines, may they develop in idealistic degrees, for material advancement is fruitless without spiritual progress and not productive of everlasting results.[26]

And while in the United States of America, He remarked:

The American continent gives signs and evidences of very great advancement; its future is even more promising, for its influence and illumination are far-reaching, and it will lead all nations spiritually. The flag of freedom and banner of liberty have been unfurled here, but the prosperity and advancement of a city, the happiness and greatness of a country depend upon its hearing and obeying the call of God.[27]

Highlighting distinctive characteristics and endowments, Shoghi Effendi wrote the following description of the historic diversity of Europe:

A continent [Europe], occupying such a central and strategic position on the entire planet; so rich and eventful in its history; so diversified in its culture; from whose soil sprang both the Hellenic and Roman civilizations; the mainspring of a civilization to some of whose features Bahá'u'lláh Himself paid tribute; on whose southern shores Christendom first established its home; along whose eastern marches the mighty forces of the Cross and the Crescent so frequently clashed; on whose south-western extremity a fast evolving Islamic culture yielded its fairest fruit; in whose heart the light of the Reformation shone so brightly, shedding its rays as far as the outlying regions of the globe; the wellspring of the American culture; whose northern and western fringes were first warmed and illuminated, less than a century ago, by the dawning light of the Revelation of Bahá'u'lláh . . .[28]

And in a manner both reverent and respectful, Shoghi Effendi praised the qualities that Africa had preserved, and which were in decline in other parts of the world:

I feel particularly gratified by the substantial participation in this epoch-making conference of the members of a race dwelling in a continent which for the most part has retained its primitive simplicity and remained uncontaminated by the evils of a gross, a rampant and cancerous materialism undermining the fabric of human society alike in the East and in the West . . .[29]

More recently, another Bahá'í scholar has developed the notion of national complementarities introduced by Shoghi Effendi, and provided the following thoughts on the cultural counterpoints of Asia and Australasia:

The Asian believers bring to the Bahá'í community the richness of their cultural traditions rooted in the wisdom of the great religions of the Prophetic Cycle, while the Australasian Bahá'ís are, in many ways, relatively free from the fetters of religious orthodoxy and ecclesiastical authority and can thus freely surrender themselves to the Bahá'í way of life. The individualism that is so dominant in much of Australasia is balanced by the emphasis on social cooperation and collective action in much of Asia. The spiritual axis acts as a bridge joining together the best qualities of the peoples of the world's largest continent and the world's largest oceanic area, for the construction of the new World Order.[30]

That every great region and every nation within it has a unique place in the scheme of things reiterates the pattern of the Essential Family (see Chapter 4), in which every member's place is reserved, their rights assured, and their responsibilities expected. Obviously the large nations control vast resources and, even though slowed by the very scale of their self-governance, have an important contribution to make to global decision-making.

Of equal significance is the fact that small nations have the flexibility to undertake social innovations on a national scale very rapidly. Thus, each one becomes a leader in its own distinctive way. Since all nations have something distinctive to contribute to the whole commonwealth, their autonomy must be safeguarded by the whole, just as the nations themselves had guaranteed personal freedom to their respective citizens.

> The unity of the human race, as envisaged by Bahá'u'lláh, implies the establishment of a world commonwealth in which all nations, races, creeds and classes are closely and permanently united, and in which the autonomy of its state members and the personal freedom and initiative of the individuals that compose them are definitely and completely safeguarded.[31]

Between nations, contentions will give way to peace. Within nations, racial tensions will give way to harmony and cohesion among all the peoples in a National Family:

> National rivalries, hatreds, and intrigues will cease, and racial animosity and prejudice will be replaced by racial amity, understanding and cooperation.[32]

Bahá'u'lláh Himself declared that the freedom from prejudice which guarantees cohesion at the national level is so powerful that it will also weld together the nations of the world:

> So powerful is the light of unity that it can illuminate the whole earth.[33]

Thus, each individual citizen and each nation is urged to respond to the opportunities of this propitious time in history.

Each nation has its unique contribution to make, and will thus attain its share of Divine good pleasure.

> He Who is your Lord, the All-Merciful, cherisheth in His heart the desire of beholding the entire human race as one soul and one body. Haste ye to win your share of God's good grace and mercy in this Day that eclipseth all other created days.[34]

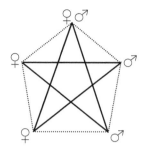

3. The Essential Family

How many ways have we tried to name the most essential of all human systems? Every day in casual conversation we hear it called: 'the immediate family', 'the nuclear family', 'the extended family', 'the traditional family', 'the birth family', or 'the family of origin'; more recently, we hear 'the adopted family' or 'the blended family'.

It is important to keep in mind that the idea of an Essential Family as we will use it here is not a sociological one, an empirical one obtained from observing daily life. Rather, the Essential Family is a prototype, or pure form, derived from guidance and insight found in Bahá'í Sacred Writings. What we are looking for in all the 'families' of this series is how a pure form (comprised of rights, responsibilities and relationships) manifests itself in a distinctive setting for human life, experience and action. These social systems or 'families' have a spiritual purpose: to provide us with a variety of dynamic settings in which to practise becoming united.

> Bahá'u'lláh came to bring unity to the world, and a fundamental unity is that of the family. Therefore, we must believe that the Faith is intended to strengthen the family, not weaken it.[1]

In the case of the Essential Family, relevant principles are to be found in the compilations of Sacred Writings on women,[2] marriage,[3] and family life;[4] insights are also to be found in the article entitled 'Rights and Responsibilities in the Bahá'í Family System'.[5]

Another critical point for understanding the ideal of the Essential Family is that it results from a set of cultural features that do not yet exist worldwide. It will gradually come into being as a new civilization takes shape in the world. As described, this Essential Family has never been seen before in its entirety and perfections, because the conditions required to bring it forth have not yet become common.

Many of these required conditions would be beneficial, but three critical ones come to mind: the first is realization of the equality of women and men, whose perspectives on reality are as different as those of the right and left eye, and whose complementary perceptions are equally vital to navigating this world successfully. The second is universal education for children and adults alike, because an illiterate adult is as constrained in society as an unschooled child. In future, everyone will be provided access to educative experiences that will keep them growing and learning throughout their lives. The third condition is the establishment of local, elected councils, not only to coordinate the affairs of the community, but also to serve as local Houses of Justice. Every community needs such a forum within which to examine spiritual laws and principles of guidance, so that we may all be assisted to find options and guidance when we are struggling to resolve complex issues.

The Essential Family system, as described in Bahá'í Sacred Writings, exhibits a subtle balance of values in creative tension with each other. The Essential Family exhibits both centrifugal forces that push things apart and centripetal forces that pull them together. Balancing these two tendencies is crucial, because if either one becomes ascendant, the system will not survive. If the outward-pushing one is dominant, the system will blow apart; people will become estranged or indifferent to each other. If the inward-pulling one is dominant the system will implode upon itself, suffocating individuality in an overbearing conformity. To sustain a family that protects its own cohesion, as well as the rights of its members to exhibit individuality, is the ultimate challenge to our skilfulness in serving any complex architecture of human relations, be it a corporation, community, space station, or basketball team. Learn these skills once, and they will serve us wherever else we live and work collectively.

Bahá'í communities are beginning to provide, through their Local Spiritual Assemblies, some of the assistance that will characterize the local Houses of Justice. These centres of guidance will be sought by people in distress to help unravel human dilemmas and predicaments, and to point out some simple paths to peace and harmony, by providing reference to appropriate passages from the Sacred Writings. For Bahá'ís, the purpose of consulting the institution of the Local Spiritual Assembly is to obtain its prayers and protection as well as its assistance in finding, understanding, and applying relevant guidance from the Revelation of Bahá'u'lláh.

The Sacred Writings have very specific things to say about marrying, fathering, mothering, being a son or daughter, and having ageing parents. The interlacing of these roles with each other is described through Revelation with such clarity that we will not be able to complain to God, 'You didn't tell us how this is supposed to work!' However, we are not born to this knowledge. It must be acquired with considerable conscious effort:

> the family, being a human unit, must be educated according to the rules of sanctity. All the virtues must be taught the

family. The integrity of the family bond must be constantly considered, and the rights of the individual members must not be transgressed.[6]

To the extent that the foregoing conditions of gender equality, universal education, and Local Spiritual Assemblies pertain, we will have the potential to see the new, classic, Essential, family system come forth and operate in this world.

The Essential Family will occupy a special role in the new civilization that is emerging, as the world finds its way toward a pragmatic peace – what Bahá'ís call the Lesser Peace. The term 'civilization' refers to a society that is ruled by law. Whatever else it will be (since we are speculating), the family will serve as a mediator for the individual, providing an environment that will naturally shape and educate him or her to take part in establishing a lawful society.

To understand how the family serves as a prototype for larger social systems, we can use the rational technique of modelling one system with another. One example of parallels is found in the 'centre-periphery' model. By studying a planetary system in which the sun is the central influence, providing energy to its dependent bodies, we can understand how the soul, as a person's essential reality, manifests its influence through the physical body, speech and behaviour of the person. Similarly, each historical appearance of a Manifestation of God becomes the central defining influence of an Age, inspiring whole new societies through the radiating effect of new Teachings. Thus by starting with the model of a planetary system, we find parallel sets of relations in those between a soul and its human expressions, or between a Manifestation and the civilization that is brought forth by Divine Teachings.

Consider then the parallels existing among the following three systems: a society, a family within that society, and a pregnant mother. Each of these systems nourishes and develops the individuals within it. For example, when a mother eats a bowl of strawberries rich in iron, the iron comes through the mother's digestive system, and fans out into the circulatory mesh of the placenta, from which the baby's circulatory system receives it. The baby cannot eat the strawberries directly. Rather, the iron must be digested and passed to it. Similarly, a family system serves as a protective buffer for a little human being, enabling it to reach the sustenance provided for it in the larger society. A toddler cannot go and benefit from the resources of society directly. A two-year-old cannot get on a bus and go to the library and bring home books. It needs an adult to go to the library, get the books, bring them home, and read the story in the book to the child. In this way, the family surrounds the emerging individual, protecting and supporting its growing capacities.

Furthermore, we will see that it is not just children who are nurtured by the family. The system seems to be set up so that each individual in the family, whether child or adult, will receive something that they need from the arrangement. Remember that this series describes not one, but seven different families, each of which contributes in some way to the growth of all the individuals within the system.

Within the ideal Essential Family, the Bahá'í Writings distinguish between individuals by generation and by gender; every person's location in the system is identified by these two coordinates. The husband/father, wife/mother, son/brother, and daughter/sister, as well as the grandparents, each have a distinguishing set of relations. Grandparents have an interesting role that emphasizes age while downplaying gender difference, perhaps because, as time goes on, we all develop a broader set of human virtues, and become more complete human beings, entering a rank of 'elderhood' that is shared by both men and women.

In order to locate each of these five gender/generational focal points in a diagram, one way would be the five-pointed figure of a pentacle. The pattern of the pentacle highlights these strong, primary relations: the husband and wife, the father and daughter, the mother and son, the grandparents and their grandchildren. Now this may not be true objectively, nor what we have personally experienced subjectively, but instinctively it does seem that these are often the less problematic relations. The others, which we find by drawing a pentagon around the dots, tend to be more demanding: fathers and sons, mothers and daughters, brothers and sisters, new parents, and parents from the previous generation. By drawing up one of these diagrams, it becomes easy to analyse what our own personal experience has revealed about each of the many lines of relation in the Essential Family.

The Writings have very particular things to say about each of these relations. We can see by the pentacle/pentagon diagram just how complex the family system is, because each of these pairs in relation is 'busy' with interactions. Consequently, to the extent that we can get the family system working for us, we will all be able to travel this life with improved safety, security, encouragement, and reinforcement when they are needed. So it is really worth the effort to work on building this vehicle according to divine specifications.

Marrying

The Sacred Writings liken the bond between husband and wife to that of intimate friends. It says there will be a 'tenderness' and connection between them. The chosen word 'tenderness' as a quality or state of being came into English in the 13th century, from the French 'tendre', itself from Latin 'tener' meaning tender, young, and delicate.[7] Then in the 14th century the English word 'extend' appeared from the Latin 'extendere' to stretch out, built from 'tendere' to stretch.[8] So two people who experience tenderness for each other can, in some sense, stretch out to delicately perceive one another at a distance. Isn't that remarkable? The Writings extol this noble relationship that can express an affinity, a natural gravitation, an attraction, deference, courtesy, and preference given by each to the welfare of the other.

> Women and men have been and will always be equal in the sight of God . . . Verily God created women for men, and men for women.[9]

We are told that the partner for life must be suited for both the spiritual and material aspects of living.

> Among the people of Bahá . . . marriage must be a union of the body and of the spirit as well, for here both husband and wife are aglow with the same wine, both are enamoured of the same matchless Face, both live and move through the same spirit, both are illumined by the same glory. This connection between them is a spiritual one; hence it is a bond that will abide forever. Likewise do they enjoy strong and lasting ties in the physical world as well, for if the marriage is based both on the spirit and the body, that union is a true one, hence it will endure.[10]

The refinement of such mutual affection is the source not only of our welfare and happiness in this world, but of our ability to benefit from the bestowals of grace in the worlds to come.

> The Lord, peerless is He, hath made woman and man to abide with each other in the closest companionship . . . two

intimate friends, who should be concerned about the welfare of each other.

> If they live thus, they will pass through this world with perfect contentment, bliss, and peace of heart, and become the object of divine grace and favour in the Kingdom of heaven. But if they do other than this, they will live out their lives in great bitterness, longing at every moment for death, and will be shamefaced in the heavenly realm.[11]

The bond of affection and loyalty thus created between the man and woman becomes in some sense a third entity, a oneness through which the nature of God in all Its worlds is perceivable.

> When, therefore, the people of Bahá undertake to marry, the union must be a true relationship, a spiritual coming together as well as a physical one, so that throughout every phase of life, and in all the worlds of God, their union will endure; for this real oneness is a gleaming out of the love of God.[12]

In fact, all things in creation can be understood as the union of two entities into a third. And in achieving union, the creatures become endowed with the capacity to experience the unifying nature of love in the spiritual realms.

> And above all other unions is that between human beings, especially when it cometh to pass in the love of God. Thus is the primal oneness made to appear; thus is laid the foundation of love in the spirit.[13]

Practising this union through all the exigencies of daily life will require the couple to demonstrate for the others in their family that, in the final analysis, their union is of greater value than their separateness. This will challenge them to bring out the uniqueness of their relationship through creatively applying certain principles and guidance.

> For example the principle that the rights of each and all in the family unit must be upheld, and the advice that loving consultation should be the keynote, that all matters should be settled in harmony and love, and that there are times when the husband and the wife should defer to the wishes of the other. Exactly under what circumstances such deference should take place, is a matter for each couple to determine . . .[14]

Over time, their practice of preference and deference will demonstrate that divine Teachings produce a loving and sustaining bond, a 'tie between them [that] is none other than the Word of God'.[15] In this way they will create a domain of ever-increasing joyfulness that is at once a home to both of them, and a sanctuary to all who know them.

> Thus the husband and wife are brought into affinity, are united and harmonized, even as though they were one person. Through their mutual union, companionship and love great results are produced in the world, both material and spiritual. The spiritual result is the appearance of divine bounties. The material result is the children who are born in the cradle of the love of God . . .[16]

Fathering

Given that it is only the mother who can bear babies for nine months, give birth to them, and nurse them in infancy, it becomes evident why in the Essential Family system, the father is assigned by Sacred Writings the primary economic responsibility for the family; it would be unreasonable to predicate family life on the mother's earnings, over and above her demanding physical role in reproduction and responsibility for the care of her newborn children. The father's crucial role in providing for his dependent children and for the mother who is caring for them is not treated lightly; rather it is articulated clearly, especially in Sacred Writings pertaining to the situation of 'intestacy', where the Writings provide for the situation in which a father dies without leaving a final will, and assigns special responsibilities and rights to the eldest son.

A man's responsibility is to prepare himself to fulfil this role, and offer this service to his wife, children, and thereby to the world. Thus, in the balance of head and heart required to protect and sustain a family, the father may be regarded as the 'head'.

> [While] the Research Department has not come across any statements which specifically name the father as responsible for the 'security, progress and unity of the family'. . . it can be inferred from a number of the responsibilities placed upon him, that the father can be regarded as the 'head' of the family. The members of a family all have duties and responsibilities towards one another and to the family as a whole, and these duties and responsibilities vary from member to member because of their natural relationships.[17]

The inference concerning 'head' of the family was based on 'the clear and primary responsibility of the husband to provide for the financial support of the wife and family'.[18] Thus, the designation 'head', as used here, connotes a specialized function among equally important functions and not one of dominance as in earlier systems.

The description of the husband as 'head' of the family does not confer superiority upon the husband nor does it give him special rights to undermine the rights of the other members of his family.[19]

The mother, in her tender, unconditional affection for her offspring, is predominant in being the 'heart' of the family.

> This does not mean that the father does not also love, pray for, and care for his baby, but as he has the primary responsibility of providing for the family, his time to be with his child is usually limited . . . As the child grows older and more independent . . . the father can play a greater role.[20]

And again, as the children attain some independence from her affectionate nurturing, the mother can expand her roles as financial provider and rational strategist for the family.

> Similarly, although the primary responsibility for supporting the family financially is placed upon the husband, this does not by any means imply that the place of woman is confined to the home . . .[21]

Conversely, the father is not solely a provider, but is also involved in raising his children, preparing them for a useful, fruitful life of service by being a positive role model, and through his encouragement and support for their education.

> . . . the father also has the responsibility of educating his children, and this responsibility is so weighty that Bahá'u'lláh has stated that a father who fails to exercise it forfeits his rights of fatherhood.[22]

In fact, the fathering and mothering roles, while physically based, are to some extent also archetypal constructs, and can be fulfilled by the complementary parent.

> This by no means implies that these functions are inflexibly fixed . . . Rather, while primary responsibility is assigned, it is anticipated that fathers would play a significant role in the education of the children and women could also be breadwinners.[23]

On the exclusively male side of the family equation, intergenerational relations between fathers and sons have been known at times to deteriorate into competition. But the growing strength of one is not at the cost of the strength or rank of the other; far from it. In fact, the glory and renown of fathers is attributed to how well they succeed in dedicating themselves to passing on and nurturing in their offspring the very best qualities and resources they have.

> The father must always endeavour to educate his son and to acquaint him with the heavenly teachings. He must give him advice and exhort him at all times, teach him praiseworthy conduct and character, enable him to receive training at school and to be instructed in such arts and sciences as are deemed useful and necessary. In brief, let him instil into his mind the virtues and perfections of the world of humanity.[24]

Mothering

In all of creation, God chose only one venue for His own habitation, and that was the human heart. He endowed it with the hidden potential to reflect ALL of His names; yet it can be tarnished, obscured and buried alive by the deceptions and delusions of the world. To whom then did He entrust the early care of these vulnerable wee treasures of His heart? – to mothers.

> O ye loving mothers, know ye that in God's sight, the best of all ways to worship Him is to educate the children and train them in all the perfections of humankind; and no nobler deed than this can be imagined.[25]

In the nursery/classroom/studio/workshop of the home, she sets out the toys, tools, and tasks of each child's early training.

> The task of bringing up a Bahá'í child, as emphasized time and again in Bahá'í Writings, is the chief responsibility of the mother, whose unique privilege is indeed to create in her home such conditions as would be most conducive to both his material and spiritual welfare and advancement. The training which the child first receives through his mother constitutes the strongest foundation for his future development.[26]

Which brings us back to the father of the child: how ever could she fulfil her primary responsibility to tenderly train and raise up the child, unless he, by his labour, makes provision for both of them and cares for their needs?

> A corollary of this responsibility of the mother is her right to be supported by her husband – a husband has no explicit right to be supported by his wife.[27]

Being a daughter

Not surprisingly then, given the weighty responsibilities attributed to motherhood, daughters are accorded a special role in the family commensurate with their future.

> The capacity for motherhood has many far-reaching implications which are recognized in Bahá'í Law. For example, when it is not possible to educate all one's children, daughters receive preference over sons, as mothers are the first educators of the next generation.[28]

This statement not only guarantees the education of daughters but, if resources are scarce, actually gives them priority in access to education. What was at the time a revolutionary injunction to the followers of this new Revelation has since been borne out as the wisest of commands. Contemporary research by such agencies as the World Health Organization, UNESCO, the International Labour Organization, or the World Bank has repeatedly shown that the most effective and efficient investment that can be made to increase the domestic welfare of a nation is to invest in the girl child.

But this priority with regard to the potential of her mind does not abandon the girl child to fend for herself. Her tender vulnerability is also recognized, and the need to protect her against those who would abuse her is directly acknowledged.

> As they do not allow themselves to be the object of cruelty and transgression, in like manner they should not allow such tyranny to visit the handmaidens of God . . . He is the Protector of all in this world and the next.[29]

Being a son

As each generation builds on the achievements of the previous one, the young man has the opportunity to extend the noble qualities of his father, while leaving behind the qualities that should not be carried forward. This selective process is not a matter of genetics; rather, it is a matter of choice and free will, and therefore a spiritual process.

> Be the son of thy father and be the fruit of that tree. Be a son that hath been born of his soul and heart and not only of water and clay. A real son is such a one as hath branched from the spiritual part of man. I ask God that thou mayest be at all times confirmed and strengthened.[30]

In doing so, it is expected that the son will adopt and embody the very best of what his father was and tried to be; to emulate the good his father manifested and fulfil the truest part of him. To be the 'fruit' of a tree is not just to be born of it, be produced by it, but to carry within oneself the seeds of a generation that will follow even the fruit itself. The fruit thus carries a trust not only to be noble in its own lifetime, but also to raise up many others resembling its forbear. Thus, the fruit sacrifices itself in the process of enabling the next generation to emerge and flourish.

So it follows, in a natural, reciprocal way, that the role of the son is to care for and provide for his loving parents, and to be the epitome of the spirit of service where their welfare is concerned.

> The son, on the other hand, must show forth the utmost obedience towards his father, and should conduct himself as a humble and a lowly servant. Day and night he should seek diligently to ensure the comfort and welfare of his loving father and to secure his good pleasure. He must forgo his own rest and enjoyment and constantly strive to bring gladness to the hearts of his father and mother, that thereby he may attain the good pleasure of the Almighty and be graciously aided by the hosts of the unseen.[31]

After describing the duties of a father to encourage his son in the attainment of human perfections, we see the above reference to the son reciprocating with the 'utmost obedience'. A discussion of this principle of obedience and the conditions that limit its application will be seen in the later section on grandparents. Suffice it here to point out the limitations that are implied by the word 'servant' with regard to the son. First, the son is exhorted to provide for the welfare of his 'loving' father. There is no expectation that the son should provide comfort for a tyrant, for one who deceives his family, or for one who steals from the dignity of the son or any other member of the family. Explicitly, 'Abdu'l-Bahá states:

> Kindness cannot be shown the tyrant, the deceiver, or the thief, because, far from awakening them to the error of their ways, it maketh them to continue in their perversity as before.[32]

So to return to the 'loving father': the Writings state that the son is to put others before himself, forgoing his own 'rest and enjoyment' if that be necessary in order to bring 'gladness' to the hearts of his father and mother. One assumes that the son will not run himself ragged responding to malicious whims, or minor tasks that are within his parents' capacity. He is expected instead to provide for their 'gladness' with acts of respect, kindliness, inclusion, acknowledgement, and gratitude to his parents. They would undoubtedly be acts not only of efficiency, but of heart-melting love.

In the reference to water and clay, one might infer some mortal, limited, and perhaps not entirely inspired aspects of the father. Every human being has limitations, qualities that are less than perfect, perhaps less than admirable. The son is exhorted to be more than that: to model himself not after the failings, but after the essence of the heart and soul of the father.

Indeed, the Writings even go so far as to suggest that being born of the spiritual part of a man is what constitutes a 'true son'. This leaves open the possibility that one can *choose* to be the son of any great exemplar, by emulating him to the best of one's ability. And conversely, they suggest that any man may have *true sons* to the extent that he gives of the spiritual part of himself to encourage and uplift younger ones who are in need of his strong example of service.

Intergenerational relations

As we have seen, some distinctive rights are accorded to members of the family system by their gender and generation. The obligation to provide education or to be obedient or supportive is not necessarily equally bestowed, or reciprocal between any given two parties. For example:

> the parents have the inescapable duty to educate their children – but not vice versa; the children have the duty to obey their parents – the parents do not obey the children . . .[33]

There is a potential for discord to occur as adult children surpass their parents in education and opportunity while they 'carry forward an ever-advancing civilization'.[34] Parents may not share in their adult child's broader experience, nor come to their conclusions; nor yet have chosen to learn from their adult child. Ageing parents however have their own life experience, their own relationship to sacred wisdom, and may not in fact conclude that the adult child has a better understanding. In such a situation of divergence, adult children do not have the right to expect their parents to obey every request or conform to every expectation. The parents are pursuing their own journey toward wisdom. At the same time, adult offspring cannot abandon the new wisdom they have acquired and instead return to blind imitation of, or obedience to, their ageing parents.

How then can we resolve these intergenerational relations? It is true, in broad terms, that what flows from young children to the parents who are providing for their education is 'obedience'. It is clear that the absence of obedience in any relationship of learning would be counterproductive, whether one has that relationship with a tutor, coach, choirmaster or spiritual guide. If one wants to be tutored and trained, one has to respond with obedience to instructions, until one has learned the skills and developed the judgement to guide oneself. The usefulness of the principle of obedience is abundantly clear, especially in the years before 15, by which time youth are deemed spiritually responsible for their own conduct.

It should be noted, however, that the Writings offer an interesting caveat on obedience. This pattern recurs throughout Bahá'í ethics: on the one hand, guidance is neither vague nor equivocal; but along with the clear principle there appears a condition in the qualifying statement specifying how to apply the principle. We read that adult offspring do owe obedience to their parents, at least in the sense of ensuring their contentment in later life. Arbitrary demands, vicious whims, demands that truly benefit neither the father nor the son would obviously not qualify for obedience.

> . . . for parents must be highly respected and it is essential that they should feel contented, **provided** they deter thee not from gaining access to the Threshold of the Almighty, nor keep thee back from walking in the way of the Kingdom.[35] [emphasis added]

Thus obedience is owed *'provided'* that what the parents are requiring is not in conflict with the spiritual progress of their adult child, who is endeavouring to reach spiritual attainment through walking a righteous path. For example, a demand to follow a criminal path out of respect for ancestors and obedience to parents would be clearly discounted. In every case the standard of behaviour, whether for parents, adult children or grandchildren, is what will enable the soul to advance, walking in the way of the Kingdom.

Grandparenting

While the term 'grandparent' as such is not mentioned in the Sacred Writings, we can infer a few things about this period of life from references to the generations succeeding one another. For example, the law of parental consent for marriage is one of the cornerstone social laws of Bahá'í life, and difficult to understand in itself if taken out of context of the goal of strengthening the bonds of love through extended families.

> Bahá'u'lláh has clearly stated the consent of all living parents is required for a Bahá'í marriage . . . This great law He has laid down to strengthen the social fabric, to knit closer the ties of the home, to place a certain gratitude and respect in the hearts of children for those who have given them life and sent their souls out on the eternal journey towards their Creator.[36]

Willing submission to this law by adult Bahá'í children, placing their trust in the potency of divine guidance in the Revelation, has been known to send them in search of estranged parents, or long-lost birth parents in the case of adopted children. Time and again, we have seen demonstrated the power of this great law to melt the frozen hearts of parents tragically distanced from their adult children. Recognition, gratitude, and respect from their adult children has awakened these fallen parents to their crucial role in the fabric of the family, and assured them of the satisfactions that come from continuity with future generations.

Coming into a period of history when inter-cultural, inter-ethnic, and inter-racial marriages would become so much the norm, it becomes even more evident that there is wisdom to requiring all living parents (not siblings or other family) to pledge their support in writing for the proposed marriage, before the couple proceeds.

> For both Bahá'u'lláh and 'Abdu'l-Bahá never disapproved of the idea of inter-racial marriage, nor discouraged it. The Bahá'í Teachings, indeed, by their very nature transcend all limitations imposed by race . . .[37]

How tragic if a couple in love were to marry without that support and endure years of their parents and extended families trying to undermine their union. By choosing to support their adult children in writing, the ageing parents are bringing the full weight of their life and stature to bear and thereby sending out an expectation to the extended family to support the new couple. Of course, if the parents do not think the marriage is wise, they do not have to sign their consent. And yet again, if consent is withheld unjustly, there is recourse.

When this law is functioning with wisdom, abundant benefits follow. The prior consent of both sets of parents indicates their endorsement of the marriage as the means of happiness and well-being not only for their adult children, but also implies their moral support of future grandchildren to follow from that union.

Great as is the humility required of parents to learn

voluntarily from their adult children who have overtaken them in the vanguard of spiritual quest and social service, still, the role reserved for parents is to be content with their advancing age and the new horizons of spiritual growth that continue to open for them through their family association with adult children and growing grandchildren.

Conclusion

It is valuable for us to remember that the Essential Family system foreshadowed in Bahá'í Sacred Writings is truly archetypal and not merely physical. Any one of us may take on the role of adult sister or brother, and thereby of aunt or uncle to another's children; similarly, we may see ourselves as the adult child of a childless elder, or as grandparent to children other than our own progeny. The roles described herein are defined in social terms by gender and generation, not physically by genetics. In this way, the social fabric is strengthened and all members enjoy the satisfactions of extended connectedness with each other.

When we imagine the Essential Family as it will come to be – operating according to an inspired code of behaviour, protecting rights and allocating responsibilities to each member, balancing centrifugal and centripetal forces, enabling the individual to gain from others while growing through service to them – in such a resplendent model we find the guiding prototype for all other family-like social systems in which we will inevitably participate.

4. The Daily Family

Of all the Seven Families in this series, the Daily Family is the least favourite for some people, because it is the very epitome of the ordinary, the necessary, the mundane. For others, the Daily Family is the very one that appeals to them most, because it is the final proof, the 'bottom line' of our ethical, our spiritual maturity.

During an early implementation of Seven Families as a class series, a woman came up to the speaker exclaiming enthusiastically, 'This is the topic I've been waiting for! This is what interests me most about religion because this is what happens when "the rubber hits the road", when the principles have to be applied in action.' The principles of any religion worthy of our interest should surely make our lives better. The Daily Family is therefore often a favourite simply because it is comprised of the people we cannot avoid: the people we see in our everyday life, in our down-to-earth, daily rounds, the people we work with on the job, the people we travel with on the bus or meet repeatedly when we do our shopping.

> Wherever a Bahá'í community exists, whether large or small, let it be distinguished for its abiding sense of security and faith, its high standard of rectitude, its complete freedom

from all forms of prejudice, the spirit of love among its members, and for the closely knit fabric of its social life.[1]

For each of the Seven Families, passages have been selected from Bahá'í Writings that are particularly focused on that human system. For this Daily Family, there is a preeminent source and that is the work of Shoghi Effendi, the Guardian of the Bahá'í Faith, entitled *The Advent of Divine Justice*. In this work, he challenges all Bahá'ís to present a model to the world of a coherent, recognizable, and absolutely distinctive way of life.

Some people like to joke that there is no 'users' manual' for being human, no handbook to consult. It isn't a very good joke any more, because in fact there *is* a handbook we can consult, and that is *The Advent of Divine Justice,* which contains both the Guardian's narrative and his translation of passages of Revelation regarding the family of characters that we encounter daily.

As with each family system, for which specific themes are introduced, the Daily Family comes with the overall theme of right conduct, coupled with the concept of contingency or correct response to particular circumstances. While our daily lives may bring unpredictable incidents over which we have little control, what *is* within our control is the response we choose to make to those events.

Four principles for daily life

With each family we have found distinctive principles of conduct that will ensure the harmony and stability of that human system. In the case of the Daily Family, four relevant principles are to be found in *The Advent of Divine Justice*:

i) committing to rectitude of conduct;
ii) striving for a chaste, pure and holy life;
iii) freeing ourselves from the constraints of prejudice; and
iv) yearning for the privilege of daily life.

Looking at this particular 'family', one can see a lot of hard work coming. Only unrelenting vigilance will keep us alert to behave every minute of every day in a manner that praises God and serves humanity.

If we could rise above the world – at about the level of a hot air balloon – we could cruise silently and look down into the places we frequent on a typical day. We could watch ourselves move through our home, along the street, into our places of work, and so on. We might find that our day ran smoothly, But more likely, it would have bumpy spots and times of turbulence.

Perhaps some days are even chaotic. Our overview of the day would most likely read like a mixed report, with some aspects of our behaviour in need of redress or repair. Like a garden in need of weeding, none of it might be quite the way we want it to be. This is probably the most difficult working lesson of the entire series of Seven Families, because there isn't any part of the foregoing formula that comes easily. This formula is the entire curriculum for being and behaving well as befits a human being.

Committing to rectitude of conduct

The first order of business is for each of us to cease causing harm in the world; and instead to become a source of benefit. In some Eastern traditions, this is referred to as ceasing to be the source of 'bad karma' or harmful consequences and instead becoming the generator of 'good karma' or beneficial effects. Bad karma is comprised of those waves of offence that are caused by bad behaviour and which eventually redound upon the perpetrator, while good karma is generated by righteous actions that are stored in the cosmic system as positive potential for benefit. The Bahá'í Sacred Writings say that such righteous actions are 'treasured up'.

Some interpretations of these Eastern traditions also say that there is just simply 'karma', that is, the result or consequence of our actions; and this may be neither good nor bad, as it is all going to be part of the soul's learning experience. Similarly, the Bahá'í teachings say that all things serve the Covenant, the binding of the individual to universal law, as provided by God.

In any case, how do we align ourselves with universal law? What will enable us to become morally upright with regard to others? Some phrases are found in *The Advent of Divine Justice* to help us develop 'rectitude of conduct' as we pass through the world. The first few are from Shoghi Effendi himself:[2]

- an abiding sense of undeviating justice
- equity, truthfulness, honesty, fair-mindedness
- reliability and trustworthiness

Such qualities governing behaviour toward others build upon more profound, spiritual qualities that Bahá'u'lláh revealed:[3]

- perseverance
- remaining undefiled from whatever things can be seen in this world
- resignation and submission to the Will of God

An abiding sense of undeviating justice

In the same way that the hallmark of Lord Buddha's revelation may be 'peace' or 'tranquillity', and that of Lord Jesus may be 'love' or 'compassion', the distinguishing theme of the Revelation of Bahá'u'lláh is undoubtedly 'justice' which opens the way to unity, both with one another and with God. Justice marks the emerging maturity of human beings individually and collectively. For individual souls, justice protects the path to their highest development as sentient beings. What the seeker desires most is to find the Supreme Being with whom they can commune. We are told that if we desire the Best Beloved of the world, and wish Him to commune with us, then we must approach Him through justice.

> The best beloved of all things in My sight is justice; turn not away therefrom if thou desirest Me, and neglect it not that I may confide in thee.[4]

What kind of 'justice' is indicated here? It must be something quite other than what is implied in common usage. Bahá'u'lláh says that justice is the essence of scientific practice, and involves seeing accurately the world around us. Justice in perception is the very essence of being a sentient being. He warns us to ponder the centrality of justice to our unfolding development.

> By its aid thou shalt see with thine own eyes and not through the eyes of others, and shalt know of thine own knowledge and not through the knowledge of thy neighbour. Ponder this in thy heart; how it behoveth thee to be.[5]

He concludes by emphasizing the profound significance of justice as part of our spiritual endowment, our divine protection, and a light of guidance for our exercise of free will: 'Verily justice is My gift to thee and the sign of My loving-kindness. Set it then before thine eyes.'[6]

A very forceful statement is made to the effect that the entire creation is protected and sustained by justice, and that civilization and the welfare of humanity as a whole depends upon justice, not forgiveness. This is, indeed, a dramatic departure from cultural traditions that emphasize either forgiveness or revenge. What new thought is being introduced here? It may take us a long time to contemplate the nature of this justice:

> The canopy of existence resteth upon the pole of justice, and not of forgiveness, and the life of mankind dependeth upon justice and not upon forgiveness.[7]

In time, society will become characterized by justice for all, as more and more individual citizens develop their sense of justice, implement it by acting in a just manner and by advocating justice for all. The cultural fruit of pervasive justice would then begin to appear. For justice is only the means to yet another, even greater purpose.

> The purpose of justice is the appearance of unity amongst men.[8]

This great word 'unity' contains within it many realities that come forth only after deep contemplation. Unity as the absence of prejudice and estrangement. Unity as the presence of loyalty and belonging. Unity as the absence of violence and stress. Unity as the presence of peace and abundant energies to direct toward creativity, productivity, and fruitful pursuits. Such unity is only possible when each of the participating partners experiences a justice in their circumstances that promotes development of their particular nature. It is helpful to consider the cultivation of plants as an analogy for this kind of justice. Some plants need a lot of moisture; that is their justice. Other plants need dryness to flourish. Thus, justice may be that set of conditions that will help something perfect its inherent nature. The quotation about justice we have been examining refers to a 'sense' of justice, that is, a keen perception to guide our actions. It also says 'undeviating' meaning never to compromise, but to be absolutely direct in one's sense of what justice is in a given situation.

Bahá'í principles are not stated in vague or ambiguous terms. They are stated, as it says, in an 'undeviating' manner, and are then followed by caveats on how to implement them. A principle is not applied in a uniform, prescribed manner, but rather in a manner that is both adaptable and consistent. This is justice by contingency or specific circumstance, not justice by blind repetition of precedent. Therein lies the daily challenge to probe deeply in one's heart and soul in order to behave in a just manner in ever new and novel situations.

Equity, truthfulness, honesty, fair-mindedness

How elegant would be the equality of all people, if each one knew they would be treated with equity and truthfulness, with honesty and fair-mindedness. How brightly these qualities gleam in our estimation, especially when compared with the murky goings-on of much of our daily experience without divine guidance. There is a cleanliness to these standards which has the power to restore and dignify relations between ourselves and others.

Reliability and trustworthiness

Both these terms refer to something that abides over time. The quality of reliability belongs to someone who has a sound and consistent character on whom we can depend with confidence, a person worthy of being relied upon or trusted. Curiously, the root of 'reliable' or 'rely' is the same as that of 'religion', from the Old French 'relier' to bind together, which in turn comes from the Latin 'religare', meaning to bind.[9] Such a person can be bound together with another person in a bond of trust.

Similarly, the term 'trust' has come to mean a confident expectation due to a firm conviction that the one in whom we trust is reliable. The roots of this word run very deep in human cultural history, conveying strength and dependability shown more clearly in a related word 'trussed', as in a bridge that has been firmly reinforced. The transitional Middle English 'trost' comes from the Old Norwegian 'traust' meaning agreement or pact.[10] All our societal undertakings, our economic or contract law, depend on a strong confidence that promises given will be redeemed. Trustworthiness is clearly, as Bahá'u'lláh pronounced, the foundation of all human prosperity. We should be mindful in an age when lawlessness, violence and terror live side by side with lawfulness, peace and reassurance, that the Sacred Writings do not state that we should be 'trusting' in anything save God. But in matters of human daily affairs we are to prove ourselves 'trustworthy'.

Perseverance

Among other qualities, this term also refers to something abiding over time. In a universe that moves through time, unfolding a narrative we call 'history', an admirable quality is only as good as its power to last, to endure through time.

Perseverance is thus the steadfast pursuit of an objective; to persevere is to follow through with determination, however severe the conditions.

Undefiled from whatever can be seen in this world

This arresting phrase confirms that we cannot avoid seeing things in the world that are not good for us. But it also implies that we can see them without being defiled by them, if we do not touch them, or allow them to touch us.

Resignation and submission to the Will of God

So far, rectitude of conduct has been defined by our relationship to each other. Now this last point refers to our relationship to God. Far beyond our perception and ken is the All-Knowing and the All-Wise. We do what we can to pursue worthy paths of action in our lives; sometimes the desired results come; sometimes they don't. As Hindu traditions teach, the results of action do not rest with us. That is the purview of God alone. But the responsibility to undertake right action as faithfully as we can resides with us. After we have done what we can, we commit ourselves to the care of God and make peace with whatever conditions may come. As folk wisdom has it: 'the will of God will never put you where the grace of God cannot reach you.' Bahá'í Sacred Writings exhort us to 'cling to the cord' of faithfulness and trust, resignation and radiant acquiescence, so that our connection to God remains firm. Ours is the choice to cling to the cord, and let Him carry us where the will of the All-Knowing, the All-Wise, the Ever-Forgiving, and the Most Generous would have us go.

Striving for a chaste, pure and holy life

Following the first order of business for each of us to cease being a cause of harm to others, the second turns our attention on ourselves and charges us to clean up conditions within our own thoughts, feelings, speech and behaviour, to become master of our own domain and to bring it to a state of refinement. Once again, the Guardian draws from many sources of Bahá'í Revelation to distil several aspects of guidance for us on living our lives well.[11] These are:

- modesty, purity, temperance
- decency and clean-mindedness
- daily vigilance in the control of one's carnal desires
- abandonment of frivolous conduct
- abandonment of trivial and misdirected pleasures
- total abstinence from all alcoholic drinks and habit-forming drugs

It is worth getting a dictionary and looking up some of these words, because very often they do not even denote what we thought they did, let alone connote the images we carry of them.

Modesty, purity, and temperance

These first three words may refer to the body and to its condition in the world. Modesty of appearance indicates avoiding both the extreme of exhibitionism that would demand attention or demean the body, and the extreme of restrictiveness such as excessive covering of the face, limbs, skin, or hair. Modesty implies simply self-respect and moderation. Purity addresses both outward cleanliness and inward health, since avoiding contaminations and nourishing the cells with water and pure nutrients will promote health. Temperance is an interesting word that can be linked to such related terms as temperament, bad temper, or a 'well-tempered sword'. Where 'temperament' refers to one's habitual mental disposition, 'temperance' refers to self-chosen moderation in the food and drink that one puts into the body. The point of modesty, purity and temperance with regard to the body is to free oneself from attachments and from preoccupation with aspects of life that are instrumental to life, not its purpose.

> A race of men, incomparable in character, shall be raised up which, with the feet of detachment, will tread under all who are in heaven and on earth, and will cast the sleeve of holiness over all that hath been created from water and clay.[12]

Decency and clean-mindedness

These two words may refer to mental rather than bodily aspects of life since 'decency' in one's actions comes from conformity to what is correct or befitting to the well-being of all, and clean-mindedness protects the thoughtful from anything which would defile or degrade them. Our state of cleanliness is vital since our capacity to find our Lord, and live a noble life, depends upon our being receptive and prepared for His guidance. Bahá'u'lláh writes:

> He hath chosen out of the whole world the hearts of His servants, and made them each a seat for the revelation of His glory. Wherefore, sanctify them from every defilement, that the things for which they were created may be engraven upon them.[13]

Daily vigilance in the control of one's carnal desires

'Carnal' means, of course, 'meat'; and since we are in the flesh, the word 'carnal' brings two things immediately to mind: one is sex, the other food. But other things are implied as well: laziness, as a habit, is an admission that a carnal desire is out of control. Basically, the body is responding to gravity, is surrendering to torpor, and not responding to the will of the one who inhabits it. So who is in charge here? Who is in control? The higher nature of our soul's awareness, or the lower nature of our body's material tendencies?

Abandonment of frivolous conduct and trivial and misdirected pleasures

Among the behaviours that the Guardian specifies as part of a 'chaste, pure and holy life' is 'abandonment of frivolous conduct' and of 'trivial and misdirected pleasures'. What if we were to get to the life after this one and find that, in addition to the really horrible things we might have done with ourselves and our lives, one of the worst offences we committed was to be superficial? Is that not what the foregoing words suggest? The terms 'frivolous' and 'trivial' suggest shallow ripples on the waters of life. They indicate that, rather than undertaking great journeys, we just frittered our time away. Lest we think we qualify for a 'chaste, pure and holy life' simply because we do not commit the worst abominations imaginable, this admonition informs us that we are at risk if the days are going by and nothing deep or significant or evolutionary is happening for us. It may turn out that a superficial life is as odious and offensive to God as a corrupt life.

Total abstinence from all alcoholic drinks and habit-forming drugs

Individuals and whole societies are drowning in the de-humanizing effects of addictive substances. We know that all human nobility – to learn, to work, to love, to serve – is rendered helpless by addictions. The means of recovery from addictions is an enormous field of social practice dealt with in depth elsewhere. Here just a few thoughts are added as relevant to the larger theme of a chaste, pure and holy life.

The pervasive availability of mind-altering, judgement-impairing, will-enslaving substances is a defining feature of our contemporary society. Furthermore, mass media carry misleading messages that intoxicated states are attractive – messages paid for by the companies that sell legal drugs and alcohol. Since those influential messages are everywhere, they would inevitably gradually shape our own mindset if we did not undertake to shape our own thinking and programmes of self-improvement according to divine guidance.

While we have latitude to set our own programme of self-improvement; we do not have options outside the prime directive to live a chaste, pure and holy life. It can be quite shocking for us to ponder that it is we ourselves who are being called upon to be 'holy'. It is much easier for us to accept that someone else is holy, such as angels, or beings from the spiritual world, or even our saintly friends and neighbours. Our own holiness can be both a surprise and a burden to us. But it is our destiny. We were created to be whole and sanctified, that is, to be holy.

In reading the Sacred Writings of Bahá'u'lláh and reflecting deeply upon them, we begin to grasp that this present era truly is the Day of God, the Day when knowledge of what is 'right', and 'right to do', from both the scientific and the sacred perspectives, will fill the whole world. With that realization comes another even more astounding one: that God has appointed each one of us to be here exactly at this time. Is it possible that we are the army of light, the ones called upon to bear witness to spiritual truth by the example of our inner character and personal behaviour?

If not us, who? If not now, when?

Freeing ourselves from the constraints of prejudice

Prejudice means pre-judging, that is, coming to a conclusion before examining something, or becoming familiar with it. For example, children are very habit-bound in the things they like. Have you ever seen, or been, the parent who prepared food that was unfamiliar to a child who at first sight declared 'Oooooh, I don't like *that*!' More often than not, the poor parent replied, 'Just one forkful. If you take just one forkful, then you don't have to eat any more.' In reality, what the parent is trying to do is loosen that child's grip on prejudice, jumping to a conclusion based on lack of familiarity. Either the food is too soft, or the little piles are mixed together, or the child takes exception to some other detail such as colour. What the parent is trying to do is expand the child's preparedness to experience different things.

In adult life, the impact of choice is greater. Rejection based on ignorance does more damage than in childhood, and freedom from prejudice yields more significant benefit both for the adult and for society. Perhaps the most common excuse for prejudicial avoidance of each other is race, when in fact this distinction is intended to be a source of attraction, association and joy. 'Abdu'l-Bahá told a Western audience:

> Bahá'u'lláh hath said that the various races of humankind lend a composite harmony and beauty of color to the whole.

> Let all associate, therefore, in this great human garden even as flowers grow and blend together side by side without discord or disagreement between them.[14]

Just as we see the benefits of diversity in landscaping a garden, we also find it in musical composition, bringing us back again to the human diversity that beautifies our daily lives.

> This variety in forms and colourings, which is manifest in all the kingdoms, is according to creative Wisdom and hath a divine purpose... The diversity in the human family should be the cause of love and harmony, as it is in music where many different notes blend together in the making of a perfect chord.[15]

In his essay *Becoming Your True Self,* Dan Jordan describes a very nice algebra that explains the dynamics of prejudice, calling it a cognitive error compounded by an affective error. When we are in a state of prejudice, he writes, we believe something to be a fact which is objectively not true; furthermore, we make an emotional commitment to that error. Thus, we super-charge a mistake with an emotion. 'A prejudice is a belief (a kind of knowing) in something that is not true, coupled with an emotional confirmation (a kind of loving). In other words, a prejudice is an emotional attraction or commitment to falsehood or error.'[16]

These combined errors cripple the brain and the heart. But the good news is that this formula specifies that we can go about undoing such 'prejudice' by unhooking either A or B; that is, either the emotional commitment, or the cognitive error. When we work to dissolve a prejudice, we can apply an intervention to either the error in thought or the error in feeling. But instead we may continue to deny ourselves the freedom to know or feel something new, as Jordan points out: 'Bigoted persons are in a tragic position because they always avoid exposing themselves to any situation which would confront them with the fact that they may possibly have a prejudice.'[17]

One effective way to undo the error in feeling is to surprise the emotionally averse person with a pleasant experience. Bahá'í communities are rather good at this, sponsoring a unity feast or a cultural evening in which we suddenly find ourselves experiencing an unexpected feeling of comfort, solidarity, and unity. We may not even know what to call this pleasant, surprising emotion.

Far from condoning the self-made prison of prejudice, Bahá'u'lláh calls us to a different order of life. He foresees for us such a degree of mutual acceptance, welcome, identification, and concord, that our life together will feel like living as one soul, one fully integrated being.

> Since We have created you from one same substance it is incumbent on you to be even as one soul, to walk with the same feet, eat with the same mouth and dwell in the same land, that from your inmost being, by your deeds and actions, the signs of oneness and the essence of detachment may be made manifest.[18]

From our inmost being will emanate a certainty that we are one; and our freedom from fear and estrangement will enable us to achieve the same resonance as the harmonic complementarity produced by an orchestra emitting a perfect musical chord.

Yearning for the privilege of daily life

Towards the end of *The Advent of Divine Justice*, after labouring through all the instructions on what it will take to create a harmonious daily life, Shoghi Effendi offers an outpouring of reassurance, like sunshine after a storm. The trials of this world are seen in the perspective of the worlds to come. We are informed that it is not just a pilgrimage here and a vacation there. Rather, we are told that the souls who have passed on now look back into this world and wish they could return. Conditions in the worlds to come do not afford the same opportunities as this earthly one to show forth noble qualities and live in service to others. Without death, how can we be brave? Without scarcity, how can we be generous?

> The holy realities of the Concourse on high yearn, in this day, in the Most Exalted Paradise, to return unto this world, so that they may be aided to render some service to the threshold of the Abhá Beauty, and arise to demonstrate their servitude to His sacred Threshold.[19]

The ones who are in the spiritual world 'yearn' to be once again in the material realm. We are given to understand that they can see us, know what we are doing, and yearn to participate, 'to render some service'. From what the Writings tell us of the reality of the spiritual realm, it seems that there are not the same kinds of limitations and constraints as pertain here. We learn that it is impossible to be thirsty there, or to be hungry, or to have any such basic cravings. Even striving to know and understand, as we do here, is relieved by a sudden clarity of awareness. In such circumstances, if we wanted to give a gift, and found there was no hardship in giving it then it would feel as though it were missing some of its value. This, apparently, is why the souls in the hereafter wish they were here, so they might also strive with us. And that is why they are willing to support and assist us. So we should ask them to supercharge our efforts and to give us the grace and the ability to complete what we begin.

Bahá'u'lláh assured us that 'should a man, all alone, arise in the name of Bahá, and put on the armour of His love, him will the Almighty cause to be victorious . . .'[20]

One Bahá'í teacher amused us by joking about the souls in the spiritual world, saying 'you think we have an unemployment problem on earth? Consider the spiritual realm. There, hundreds of thousands of holy souls are unemployed, unless and until we arise and call on them, giving them an opportunity, a conduit into the world, to contribute their aid.' The seventh 'family' in this series is entitled the 'Eternal Family' and describes the rights and responsibilities we have in relation to those who passed on before we arrived in this world, and those who will arrive after our time on earth. Suffice it here to acknowledge that our daily lives are not lived in isolation from those who look in from beyond and who are empowered to assist us. We can, and indeed must, arise to spread abroad in the world whatever glad tidings and good will have been granted to us. We are being called to greet every new day with gratitude and enthusiasm.

> Speed ye forth from the horizon of power, in the name of your Lord, the Unconstrained, and announce unto His servants, with wisdom and eloquence, the tidings of this Cause, whose splendour hath been shed upon the world of being.[21]

Unlimited power is ready to come roaring through us like Niagara Falls as soon as we open ourselves as a conduit for that intense, life-giving power to flow into the world. Life is short. We have so little time, so few years, to impart to the world the precious gifts which have been entrusted to us.

Life passes by so quickly, and the opportunities to serve are GONE. Let us then celebrate this day with service, for it will never come again.

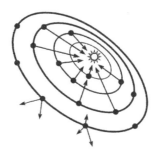

5. A Family of Friendships

Life is long . . . and throughout the length of its ages and stages – no matter whether we find them to be interesting, arduous, dangerous, or enjoyable – the worst thing we will ever have to endure is loneliness. All our other trials and tribulations – poverty, sickness, violence, humiliation – become bearable when the experience can be expressed to, and acknowledged by, another friendly soul. The best that we can ever have (second only to the nearness of God) is friendship; the best we can ever be (in the course of serving our God) is a friend.

The nature of friendship

Friendship is a choice

While the Romance languages base their terms for 'friend', such as *amigo* and *ami* on the Latin verb *amare* meaning 'to love', quite a different light is shed on friends and friendship when we search the Old English 'frēond': we find its origins in such German words as *freund* (friend), *frein* (freedom), *frei* (to be free), and *befreien* (to set free).[1]

Let us imagine for a moment the social restrictions of medieval feudalism, a social system in which a man and his family laboured as though they were the domestic cattle of their landlord. In that age, each class of society was restricted in the interactions that custom allowed them to have – both within and between classes. Among slaves, indentured labourers, and serfs, social relations were rigidly predetermined. The serf had no choice regarding those to whom he owed loyalty. Only when one became a freeman could the question of choice arise. As a serf, each man surrendered both his hands inside the grasp of his liege lord; as a freeman he could reach out one hand to grasp the hand of another 'frēond' in a station of equality.

The definitive characteristic of friendship then, is freedom to choose. No one can demand friendship from another, expect it, or require it. And no one can force their friendship upon another. It can only be offered to another; or invited from another. Reciprocity is not guaranteed, as the lives of great exemplars of love attest. It becomes evident that no one can oblige your membership in a family of friendships. No one can ever say: 'We must be friends!' A bridge of friendship is only built when both sides build toward the middle.

Alone among all the human systems represented by these Seven Families, the Family of Friendships is entirely self-chosen and, as such, reveals a great deal about the workings of the heart of the one who is choosing. All the other families have their membership specified by definition. The distinction of a Family of Friendships then, is that it will reveal to us those with whom we choose to associate closely, and those whom we choose to avoid.

Friendship promotes well-being

How are we to distinguish the meaning of true friendship from all the careless meanings that are tossed around in daily conversation? One person will say 'I have lots of friends'; another says 'I have difficulty making friends'; yet another boasts 'Everyone is my friend'. In a prayer that begins 'O God, refresh and gladden my spirit', 'Abdu'l-Bahá chooses to end with the words 'Thou art more friend to me than I am to myself', indicating that there is a profound qualitative difference between these two innermost types of friendship. If friendships were all the same, we would not find in the Sacred Writings such phrases as 'pure friendship' or 'unalloyed friendship', clearly indicating that there may also be unpure, alloyed or compromised friendships, and qualitative differences among those people who would claim to be friends. What then are the signs by which we can recognize true friendship?

'True' friendship (also found as 'real friendship' and 'genuine friendship') is associated in the Sacred Writings with concepts such as *peace, harmony, affection, kindness, love, tenderness, sincerity, unity, loyalty,* and *good cheer.* It might help us to appreciate the potency of these qualities if we consider them together in a composite image. In this image, true friendship is like a dwelling place somewhere in a deep wood that provides safe shelter and with it *peace* for all those who gather there. In this shelter they move about in *harmony*, at ease, compatible, neither giving offence nor being offended – rather being complementary to each other and companionable. The presence of *affection* and *kindness* in that dwelling place is like sunshine on the windowsill and glowing coals warming the welcoming hearth. The nearness of *love* and *tenderness* is like the caress of a hand or the reassurance of an arm around the shoulders, the look of *sincerity* in the eye and the smile of acknowledgement that assures the heart and comforts the soul of a friend. Around the table of shared experiences reigns an open-hearted *sense of unity* achieved through mutual effort and a deep *loyalty* safeguarding against all adversity, which taken together, yield the *good cheer* of friendships aged to perfection.

A FAMILY OF FRIENDSHIPS

Friendship is expressed in actions

In this day, our 'communion' with God – and our 'community' with each other – have once again come into alignment. Whereas in ages past the most intimate and sacred conversations with God might have been confined to solitary worship, in this day we are called upon to turn again to the world, to offer something that is pleasing to Him, and to carry into the world actions that will be worthy of His presence.

> The days when idle worship was deemed sufficient are ended. The time is come when naught but the purest motive, supported by deeds of stainless purity, can ascend to the throne of the Most High and be acceptable unto Him.[2]

Indeed, when we faithfully serve His kingdom and His creatures, our life of service to God comes to resemble the life of a creative artist who daily crafts new beauty and delight. We no longer just talk about virtue or the value of friendship, but understand that these have no reality until they are expressed and embodied in actions. Otherwise we are worthless stand-ins for the noble life we could be leading.

> The essence of faith is fewness of words and abundance of deeds; he whose words exceed his deeds, know verily his death is better than his life.[3]

Person-to-person, we are urged to express friendship in tenderhearted, practical actions.

> Do not be content with showing friendship in words alone, let your heart burn with loving kindness for all who may cross your path.[4]

And on the scale of person-to-humanity, the exhortation to action likewise applies:

> What profit is there in agreeing that universal friendship is good, and talking of the solidarity of the human race as a grand ideal? Unless these thoughts are translated into the world of action, they are useless.
>
> The wrong in the world continues to exist just because people talk only of their ideals, and do not strive to put them into practice. If actions took the place of words, the world's misery would very soon be changed into comfort.[5]

But are all deeds equally worthy? What kinds of deeds would qualify to ascend to the 'throne of the Most High'? Surely the answer is: those deeds that are guided by divine Teachings as recorded in Sacred Writings on how humanity can attain to its well-being; indeed, the Teachings themselves become the very means to heal, to sanctify, to awaken, and to restore humanity from all that has oppressed it or befouled its dignity.

Let's pause for a moment to consider the fundamental purpose of Sacred Writings. What could they possibly be for, except to encourage and guide souls in the direction of discovering their own greatest good? And what would that greatest good be except something that resonates with their very essence. And where would that essence be found except back at the beginning at their source of being? If we knew our source of being, we'd know our essence; and if we knew our essence we could attain our greatest good by aligning ourselves to the purpose of our existence. So where is it (our origin)? And what is it (our essence)? (This is going to take some time and effort on our part.) If we have emerged into existence *WITH* consciousness, then logically we came from an Origin that *HAS* consciousness, or possibly *IS* Consciousness Itself. If It is conscious, then we can try to talk to It. If It is Consciousness Itself then It will likely be trying to communicate with us. So it seems reasonable for us to call a text a Sacred Writing (whether ancient or historically recent), that communicates to us in Its Voice, that conveys to us the most expansive, illuminating, consoling, inspiring, motivating, pure guidance.

Back to friendship: If Sacred Writings are the elixir of essential guidance that can get us back on track with the purpose of our life and our greatest good – then one of the most potent of all actions for expressing friendship would be to include a jewel-like phrase from Sacred Writings in the course of a deep, personal conversation. In this way, we would enable a friend to experience the powerful, creative Word – perhaps for the first time – and thereby awaken to a new and better reality and range of possibilities. Those sacred phrases that guide our own hearts will equally guide other hearts and are meant to be shared.

> The things He hath reserved for Himself are the cities of men's hearts, that He may cleanse them from all earthly defilements, and enable them to draw nigh unto the hallowed Spot which the hands of the infidel can never profane. Open, O people, the city of the human heart with the key of your utterance. Thus have We, according to a pre-ordained measure, prescribed unto you your duty.[6]

Friendship requires noble qualities

'Abdu'l-Bahá provides explicit guidance concerning what will equip us to serve others in a spirit of true friendship:

> Should any one of you enter a city, he should become a centre of attraction by reason of his sincerity, his faithfulness

and love, his honesty and fidelity, his truthfulness and loving-kindness towards all the peoples of the world, so that the people of that city may cry out and say: 'This man is unquestionably a Bahá'í, for his manners, his behaviour, his conduct, his morals, his nature, and disposition reflect the attributes of the Bahá'ís.'[7]

No shadow of deception or dissimulation could hide among the radiant qualities of *sincerity*, *honesty* and *truthfulness*. No whim or fickleness would ever tarnish or weaken relationship with a person who exhibited only *faithfulness* and *fidelity*. And no harm would ever come from a person whose responds to everyone with *loving-kindness*. 'Abdu'l-Bahá then goes on to specify the dimensions of action by which one can assess the character of a potential friend. He mentions such things as *manners* or their general outward bearing; *behaviour* toward themselves and others; *conduct* as the ways in which they direct or manage their affairs; *morals* as the rightness and justness of choices they make; *nature* as the most fundamental of their innate qualities; and *disposition* as the prevailing moods and temperament that colour their every moment. These elements provide evidence of the *selfless love* that qualifies someone to be a friend and the *attraction* which that selfless love exerts on the hearts of others.

The limits of friendship

In the early years of our soul's journeying, we search everywhere and among all sorts of people for the meaning of life, for a clue to the truth, for a trace of the traceless, faceless divine Friend.

On this journey the traveler abideth in every land and

dwelleth in every region. In every face, he seeketh the beauty of the Friend; in every country he looketh for the Beloved. He joineth every company, and seeketh fellowship with every soul, that haply in some mind he may uncover the secret of the Friend, or in some face he may behold the beauty of the Loved One.[8]

But a willingness to be friendly to others does not guarantee that others will respond to us in kind. Not every heart contains a conscious wisdom equal to or greater than our own. Consequently, the early set of friends we gather, trying to create for ourselves a Family of Friendships, may be contentious, subject to mood swings or power struggles – not unlike the early stages of other Families.

Given the likelihood of strife in the Family of Friendships, how then are we to respond? In ages past, Jesus directed the loved ones of God to 'turn the other cheek' rather than respond to hurt with another unkindness. In the same spirit, 'Abdu'l-Bahá also clearly directs us not to degrade ourselves by returning hurt for hurt. Rather, we are to carry on, faithful to our own code of conduct, governed only by good will.

> When ye meet with cruelty and persecution at another's hands, keep faith with him; when malevolence is directed your way, respond with a friendly heart.[9]

Especially we are admonished not to sink to the level of hurting another, even if that person feels malice toward us, or wishes us harm:

> Beware lest ye harm any soul, or make any heart to sorrow . . . Beware, beware, lest any of you seek vengeance, even against one who is thirsting for your blood. Beware, beware,

lest ye offend the feelings of another, even though he be an evil-doer, and he wish you ill.[10]

HOWEVER, we are not required to keep subjecting ourselves to the presence of those who knowingly or unknowingly do us harm. As Bahá'u'lláh says: 'The company of the ungodly increaseth sorrow . . .'[11] When circumstances allow, we are to take advantage of the opportunity to get out of their range and seek better company. God has granted us the option of withdrawing from the influence of those who are so full of themselves and the stuff of the world that they are unfitted either to befriend us, or to receive the friendship we offer them. Instead we are permitted and even encouraged to seek out companions who have found higher ground and learned to roam beyond the boring limitations of lower worlds.

> [The] seeker . . . should treasure the companionship of them that have renounced the world, and regard avoidance of boastful and worldly people a precious benefit.[12]

Thus, by seeking the company of one and avoiding the company of another, we gradually reconstruct the Family of Friendships around us – a possibility unique among all the social systems or Families that we inhabit. The Family of Friendships is a select flock of co-travellers through life that we cherish deeply. Even if we are separated from some people by hundreds or thousands of miles; even if we are separated by years or decades; even if we lose contact with them due to changing circumstances or historic events, STILL they remain in more than our memory, they remain in the active firmament of our Family of Friendships – people whose personality, character, moral behaviour, noble qualities inspire us and remind us of who we also can strive to be.

Then there are those who are physically near, but who have chosen to become something quite distant from what we are choosing for ourselves. We are never to delude ourselves into thinking that our good will can somehow override the dark or deluded will of another. We cannot bribe or cajole or indulge another person into right choices. Fires of addiction, violence, incest, gambling, or rage are not quenched by trying to drown them in kindness, forbearance, indulgence or other forms of enabling. Rather, such indulgence serves only as fuel to feed the fires of self-destruction even further, and to multiply the number of victims consumed therein.

> Strive ye then with all your heart to treat compassionately all humankind – **except** for those who have some selfish, private motive, or some disease of the soul. Kindness **cannot be shown** the tyrant, the deceiver, or the thief, because, far from awakening them to the error of their ways, it maketh them to continue in their perversity as before. No matter how much kindliness ye may expend upon the liar, he will but lie the more, for he believeth you to be deceived, while ye understand him but too well, and only remain silent out of your extreme compassion.[13] [Emphasis added]

The world contains many instances of those who have chosen degradation for themselves. For each of us to stay true to our own self, our purpose, our mission, our spiritual quest, we will eventually regard *avoidance* of such persons as a precious benefit; we will prefer withdrawal of ourselves from such harmful interaction; and will instantly eschew or shy away from, indeed abstain from, those who would sadden our hearts or sicken our souls. As Bahá'u'lláh says: 'Treasure the companionship of the righteous and eschew all fellowship with the ungodly.'[14]

At the same time, He prepares us to appreciate the benefits

of associating with true friends, who help us cleanse our own hearts, hear the Words of God, and receive bounties from the Holy Spirit:

> ... fellowship with the righteous cleanseth the rust from off the heart. He that seeketh to commune with God, let him betake himself to the companionship of His loved ones ...[15]

Spiritual friendships
Spiritual friendships are profound and enduring

In many communities of faith we hear speakers address the gathering with a phrase such as, 'Good morning, friends.' It is natural to find in a community of faith that there are loyal ties of friendship which reflect a primary loyalty to God. These are the true bonds of affection that we would hope to find, but may not necessarily enjoy, in our family of origin, or even in the family we create for ourselves through marriage. We are indeed fortunate, and it is a great achievement to attain to spiritual bonds of friendship within the intergenerational Essential Family. That happy condition is indeed light upon light.

> There is no teaching in the Bahá'í Faith that 'soul mates' exist. What is meant is that marriage should lead to a profound friendship of spirit, which will endure in the next world, where there is no sex, and no giving and taking in marriage; just the way we should establish with our parents, our children, our brothers and sisters and friends a deep spiritual bond which will be everlasting, and not merely physical bonds of human relationship.[16]

The trusted ties of spiritual friendship are thus the most sustaining of all, since they are in harmony with the essential nature of life, even as it continues beyond this world. Bahá'ís find appreciation for spiritual friendship expressed in the following statement:

> Deep as are family ties, we must always remember that the spiritual ties are far deeper; they are everlasting and survive death, whereas physical ties, unless supported by spiritual bonds, are confined to this life . . . Turn to your Bahá'í brothers and sisters who are living with you in the light of the Kingdom.[17]

Spiritual friendships dissolve barriers of prejudice

Homogeneity has a way of creating stagnation, the opposite of growth. And yet, despite the danger of stagnation it is easy to attribute 'friendship' to people who are very much like ourselves. We find an easy harmony with them that can lead us astray, if that so-called harmony results simply from our group's sameness or uniformity.

In the essay *Becoming Your True Self*, author-educator Daniel Jordan contrasts the drabness of uniformity with the stimulus of diversity in our choice of friends. 'We tend to choose for our friends others who think the same as we do, who feel the same way about other things as we do, who have similar tastes, and who like doing similar things. Within such a homogeneous group, one's transformation can easily come to a halt, for a set repertoire of responses is developed and there is no stimulus to develop new ones. That is why one of the most precious attributes of a Bahá'í community is its diversity.'[18]

By contrast with the stagnation of homogeneity, social diversity stimulates growth. Immersing ourselves in a socially diverse community may put us off balance at first, but provides the stimulus to lift us out of our predictable groove, and awakens us from the boredom of a social life that often keeps us in a rut. Jordan says, 'trying to relate to those unknowns creates energy (anxiety) which sets [in motion a] reciprocal process of knowing and loving, through faith and courage. Defining a legitimate goal which will constructively utilize the energy from that anxiety will call forth a new repertoire of responses. Each new response is a bit of one's latent capacity made manifest – a release of human potential.'[19]

In effect, we can set ourselves up for growth by intentionally widening our circle of friends, seeking out those who differ from us in age, race, education, and experience. Making room for surprises will bring delight and in some cases distress; and this, in turn, will prove the greater bounty when we stretch our hearts to encompass the realities of new friends. 'It is for this reason', writes Jordan, 'that the struggle for world unity takes place more within the Bahá'í community than outside it.'[20]

Thus, as we allow ourselves to leave behind the familiar and the superficial, to reach out and become acquainted with the stranger, and most importantly, to look past superficial details of tradition and culture to the very heart of those we befriend, we will find ourselves on common ground with all humanity.

> If we abandon these timeworn blind imitations and investigate reality, all of us will be unified. No discord will remain; antagonism will disappear. All will associate in fellowship. All will enjoy the cordial bonds of friendship. The world of creation will then attain composure.[21]

The perfect exemplar of spiritual friendship – 'Abdu'l-Bahá

The most significant friends for assisting our development are the ones we call 'mentors', those who can perform three services for us: model aspects of what we want to become; challenge us to aspire to our own nobility; and support us in getting there. Bahá'u'lláh Himself has presented 'Abdu'l-Bahá to us as the very embodiment of all those qualities to which we would aspire; the potency of His inspiration is such that it can revive the weakest heart, and revitalize the faintest spirit.

> Render thanks unto God, O people, for His appearance; for verily He is the most great Favour unto you, the most perfect bounty upon you; and through Him every mouldering bone is quickened.[22]

Known as the 'Mystery of God', 'Abdu'l-Bahá stands somewhere above even the most inspiring heroes and saints; yet He denies all comparison to the Christ-like Manifestations of God. He occupies a unique spiritual station never before seen in the spiritual history of humanity. While setting a standard of behaviour beyond the attainment of the most devoted believer, He yet provides – as would the greatest human friend – a fortress of security for all who would seek shelter with Him. He then raises us aloft to fulfil aspirations beyond our highest hopes.

> We have made Thee ['Abdu'l-Bahá] a shelter for all mankind, a shield unto all who are in heaven and on earth, a stronghold for whosoever hath believed in God, the Incomparable, the All-Knowing. God grant that through Thee He may protect them, may enrich and sustain them, that He may inspire Thee with that which shall be a wellspring of wealth unto all created things, an ocean of bounty unto all men, and the dayspring of mercy unto all peoples.[23]

He Himself reaffirmed His mission to befriend all humanity

when He explained the meaning of His title 'Abdu'l' (Servant of) 'Bahá' (the Glory of God). His purpose, He explained, is to be the voice of friendship from God to humanity, calling in the name of transcendent truth, bringing within our grasp a reconciliation or homecoming reunion for all humanity, and a revitalizing new life for all people:

> The Voice of Friendship, of Truth, and of Reconciliation is he, quickening all regions. No name, no title will he ever have, except 'Abdu'l-Bahá. This is my longing. This is my Supreme height. O ye friends of God![24]

Abdu'l-Bahá, this ultimate friend and spiritual Master, takes the service of friendship beyond time and space, into everlasting life, by making us this solemn vow: 'I am with you always, whether living or dead, I am with you to the end.'[25]

Just as Jesus had promised in ages past, 'Lo, I am with you always, even unto the end of the world,' the limits of friendship are raised by 'Abdu'l-Bahá into the realms of eternity. He fills to overflowing our most profound longings for the bestowals of a friendship that never fails, for qualities and actions of heroic magnitude. His very appearance on earth among us – a human being of such monumental nobility – signifies that our lives can no longer be lived on the small scale of former times: 'That God has favored man with the gift of a Perfect Exemplar testifies to the greatness of this day and to the heights of perfections which man is summoned to attain.'[26]

The ultimate purpose of friendships

The further we go in our life explorations, the closer we get to seeing the journey's goal, then the clearer our vision becomes of who is actually accompanying us, who are those persistent

Spiritual friends heal and restore each other

As soon as we realize that the life of the soul has a direction, it suddenly becomes easier to distinguish those people whose effect on us is 'friendly' from those whose effect is negative. Friends are those who assist us in the direction of our soul's fulfilment; those who deter, delay, or distract our soul from its destination are not acting as its friends. Conversely, true friends share with each other those Teachings that revive our sense of conscience, that is, our sense of orientation and direction. Friends satisfy each other's hunger for belonging when we enable each other to recognize ourselves within the community of the love of God.

> O ye friends of God! True friends are even as skilled physicians, and the Teachings of God are as healing balm, a medicine for the conscience of man . . . They waken those who sleep. They bring awareness to the unheeding, and a portion to the outcast, and to the hopeless, hope.[27]

The dust of daily ordinariness is the soil from which our soul longs to spring upward, bloom and bear fruit. But we can be weighed down by that ordinariness, lose our way, lose our strength and even lose hope. Even at that point, service from one friend to another can help to renew our hope, reverse conditions, enable us to overcome our limitations and reach our divine potential.

> One righteous act is endowed with a potency that can so elevate the dust as to cause it to pass beyond the heaven of

heavens. It can tear every bond asunder, and hath the power to restore the force that hath spent itself and vanished . . .[28]

Spiritual friends remind each other of life's purpose

We are reminded that while we have freedom of choice in our associations, we are also on a quest that has purpose and value; this means that we are watching for companionship that will lead to advancement, both for us and for those whose company we choose to keep. The graphic design at the start of this chapter represents our soul's journey from the periphery of understanding to the centre. As we orbit the essence of Truth, trying to understand It, we are enabled through true friendships to journey closer to the Point to which we must all return, the essence of Reality, the Alpha and Omega.

The soul comes into being with a mission, a longing that it will take a lifetime to satisfy ever more deeply. The short obligatory prayer deftly and beautifully summarizes this great destiny. The believer says: 'I bear witness, O my God, that Thou hast created me to know Thee and to worship Thee.'[29]

Finding the truth of our identity, the point of origin of our journey, the goal of our devotion is our primary directive, our life's purpose. Concomitant with that search is our desire not only to draw near, but to establish a relationship of praise and gratitude. Relationship with the divine Friend is the destiny and destination of every soul. That is its reason for being. In the depths of each soul is the awareness that it is homeward bound to the radiant court of its Beloved, its point of origin, its Alpha and Omega point, the Primal Point; and each soul calls on God to pour blessing upon that One.

> Do Thou bless, O Lord my God, the Primal Point, through Whom the point of creation hath been made to revolve in

both the visible and invisible worlds, Whom Thou hast designated as the One whereunto should return whatsoever must return unto Thee . . .[30]

Spiritual friends share the ultimate journey

Our exodus out of mortality and material degradation, our pilgrimage to purity and paradise, is a form of 'return', this time to our Point of Origin.

To aid with this journey, it seems as though our souls were created as a kind of two-directional 'transponder'. We are able to perceive and receive an inspiring thought, thus fixing our direction on the homing beam of Divine love; at the same time, we are able to send out a message, beseeching assistance, expressing praise and gratitude, and calling out in affirmation, as we make our exodus homeward. Upon receiving inspiration, we are drawn forward:

> I beseech Thee, O my Lord, by Thy Name through which Thou hast enabled Thy servants and Thy people to know Thee, through which Thou hast drawn the hearts of those who have recognized Thee towards the resplendent court of Thy oneness, and the souls of Thy favoured ones unto the Day-Spring of Thy unity . . .[31]

And in sending our cry to God to assist us in this wilderness, we remind Him that we are only responding to His nearness, in the immensity of this creation, as announced by His Prophets.

> I entreat Thee by Thy footsteps in this wilderness, and by the words 'Here am I. Here am I' which Thy chosen Ones have uttered in this immensity . . . to ordain that I may gaze on Thy beauty and observe whatsoever is in Thy Book.[32]

As spiritual friends, we keep each other company while each one makes a unique journey across an entire universe of distractions. Our common goal is the holy mountain of communion, the Mount Sinai of our soul's inner journey homeward. Our final destination is the court of our ultimate Friend, our divine Beloved. Spiritual friends undertake righteous actions together in order to make their souls' ascent more directly and effectively. Among the actions of self-sacrifice and ascent to the Beloved, the two most effective are daily prayer and annual observance of the 19-day Fast ordained by Bahá'u'lláh. While undertaking this Fast during daylight hours, many benefits occur for the soul; but its highest wish is to turn all benefit wholly into praise for the Beloved Friend:

> I beseech Thee to grant that I may be assisted to observe the Fast wholly for Thy sake, O Thou Who art full of majesty and glory![33]

Each one of us must make the journey on our own. But to our left and right, before us and behind us, is the company of friends equally determined to succeed in this exodus, their gaze and their willpower immovably fixed on the Object of their devotion. In truth, this is my tribe, my people, my companions, my company of friends, my ultimate Family of Friendships; and God is our Lord.

> Empower me, then, O my God, to be reckoned among them that have clung to Thy laws and precepts for the sake of Thee alone, their eyes fixed on Thy Face.[34]

A FAMILY OF FRIENDSHIPS

Together, friends return to the divine Friend

What we are searching for together is the face of the ultimate Friend, the divine Beloved. To assist us we have friends in this world and the next: believers, pilgrims, saints, and the Manifestations of God who have joined us here on earth from age to age.

> If thou be a man of communion and prayer, soar up on the wings of assistance from Holy Souls, that thou mayest behold the mysteries of the Friend and attain to the lights of the Beloved, 'Verily, we are from God and to Him shall we return' [*Qur'án 2:151*].[35]

All paths lead homeward, so all guides become one, all friends a foretaste of the one Friend.

> After passing through the Valley of Knowledge, which is the last plane of limitation, the wayfarer cometh to the Valley of Unity and drinketh from the cup of the Absolute, and gazeth on the Manifestations of Oneness. In this station he pierceth the veils of plurality, fleeth from the worlds of the flesh, and ascendeth into the heaven of singleness.[36]

All friendships have led us to this, the journey's goal, the final Friend.

> With the ear of God he heareth, with the eye of God he beholdeth the mysteries of divine creation. He steppeth into the sanctuary of the Friend, and shareth as an intimate the pavilion of the Loved One.[37]

Eventually, even the lover's love for the Beloved becomes too much separation to bear, and in a conflagration of love, all that remains is the Friend.

> For when the true lover and devoted friend reacheth to the presence of the Beloved, the sparkling beauty of the Loved One and the fire of the lover's heart will kindle a blaze and burn away all veils and wrappings. Yea, all he hath, from heart to skin, will be set aflame, so that nothing will remain save the Friend.[38]

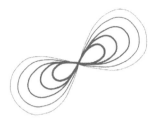

6. The Inner Family

Hidden within us is a living encyclopedia of our own childhood, our adolescence, our early, middle, and late adulthood – and, should we be so fortunate, the experience of increasing years as an elder. Intertwined with this personal, ever-present cast of characters is the entire multitude of everyone we have ever known, or even met. Added to all the foregoing are the personages and role models we have internalized from all the forms of media through which we learn. This inner world, mirroring all we have ever seen of ways to be and ways to behave, makes for a crowded and rambunctious Inner Family, which may explain why we often try to ignore it. We may try, but it tends to keep asserting itself to get our attention.

When we begin to look within, our sporadic efforts discover that the Inner Family is inexhaustible. We may find ourselves saying things like: 'I've been trying to know myself for years, and I never seem to get to the bottom of it. I keep discovering more, understanding more maybe, but never finishing. It seems that I will never be able to say that I've even accounted for all the parts, much less that I've been able to make sense of it, or establish peace within.' Undertaking to know the Inner Family is so consuming of time and effort that even to make a start requires that we first see the spiritual value of such a laborious exploration.

The inner realities of human life

Mystical literature of all spiritual traditions concerns itself with the inner life, and this is certainly so in the Revelation of Bahá'u'lláh. But as Bahá'ís, we are often so committed to the observable world, to social justice, to freedom from prejudice, and the elimination of extremes of wealth and poverty, that we tend to forget the sacred work associated with our inner selves. A competition of loyalties arises between outward service and how much attention we feel we should put on our inner life. People are heard to say, 'Well you know, we are told to be selfless. Maybe I shouldn't be focusing so much on my "self". Maybe I shouldn't be spending time on introspection and the psychological aspects of the Faith. Perhaps I should only concentrate on the spiritual and social aspects.'

Our first concern, then, is to discover what Bahá'u'lláh has to say about the inner realities of human life and their importance, and how much He values the invisible part of us, the essence of us: our soul. When we examine the Sacred Writings, we find that everything a heart could ever want to hear about being cherished has been said to us by our Creator in the Revelation given to us by the Lord of the Age. Consider the following excerpts from a passage in *Gleanings*:

> Whatever is in the heavens and whatever is on the earth is a direct evidence of the revelation within it of the attributes and names of God . . . Methinks, but for the potency of that revelation, no being could ever exist . . . To a supreme degree is this true of man, who, among all created things, hath been invested with the robe of such gifts, and hath been singled out for the glory of such distinction. For in him are potentially revealed all the attributes and names of God to a degree that no other created being hath excelled or surpassed . . .

THE INNER FAMILY

Manifold are the verses that have been repeatedly revealed in all the Heavenly Books and the Holy Scriptures, expressive of this most subtle and lofty theme. Even as He hath revealed: 'We will surely show them Our signs in the world and within themselves.' Again He saith: 'And also in your own selves: will ye not, then, behold the signs of God?' And yet again He revealeth: 'And be ye not like those who forget God, and whom He hath therefore caused to forget their own selves.'[1]

Bahá'u'lláh first stresses that each soul is a unique treasure, a frontier of free will. In fact, each soul is a microcosm of all creation. The implications of this are enormous. So valuable is the individual soul that, in one sense, we could put that soul into a balance on one side and everything else in existence on the other. No one of us can possibly get 'lost in the crowd' with the Creator. Lest we doubt the value of our soul-self, we are instructed by Bahá'u'lláh: 'Turn thy sight unto thyself, that thou mayest find Me standing within thee mighty, powerful and self-subsisting.'[2] Where will we find Him, in all of creation? – Standing within our 'self'.

Thus, what is going on within us is a great and noble process that has been studied, codified and named variously by observers from many cultural contexts. Some schools of psychology refer to the process of soul development as 'maturing', as 're-parenting', as 'integration of the self', or as the search for 'gestalt', meaning an integrated understanding of our life and self. Some therapies refer to the process in a double negative as 'detoxification'. The mediaeval Christian mystics wrote extensively about this process of extricating the soul from its worldly wounds, attachments, and preoccupations; they termed the gradual dedication of that soul to the high road of worshipping God and seeking to please Him as the process of 'sanctification'.

OUR SEVEN FAMILIES

If there is one theme of significant overlap between contemporary psychology and the Sacred Writings of the Bahá'í Faith, it is found in the theme of emergence of the soul 'self':

> If the travelers seek after the goal of the Intended One . . . this station appertaineth to the self – but that self which is 'The Self of God standing within Him with laws'.
> On this plane, the self is not rejected but beloved; it is well-pleasing and not to be shunned.[3]

In pondering selflessness, we must be careful to discriminate between the ego self and the self of the soul. The ego is attached to the finite, mortal world and is, therefore, vulnerable to becoming ensnared in selfishness or the cravings of a lower nature; the self of the soul is an artefact of the Creator and the true identity of each of us. While the universe may be richly endowed with aspects and entities ready and even eager to assist each soul to grow, primary responsibility for releasing the potential of the soul lies within the soul itself. No one else can do the job of developing our soul for us. No one else in all the world, of the millions and millions of people roaming the planet, will be able to complete the job the Creator started when he planted the seed of our soul – except ourselves. Bahá'u'lláh conveys the following assertion of our Creator:

> Out of the wastes of nothingness, with the clay of My command, I made thee to appear, and have ordained for thy training every atom in existence and the essence of all created things.[4]

He also provides assurance of how very precious our soul and its development are in His sight. In even more poignant language He says:

THE INNER FAMILY

> Veiled in My immemorial being and in the ancient eternity of My essence, I knew My love for thee; therefore I created thee, have engraved on thee Mine image and revealed to thee My beauty.[5]

Our origins are hidden, cloaked in cosmic forgetfulness, in a place out of time, steeped in the heart essence of our unknown Creator. Yet we know by His word that something stirred in Him, and He first experienced a love for the idea of us; then created us in faithful expression of that pre-existent love. Inherent in the faithful creation is the signature, nay more, the entire image of the Creator, in such manner that we are endowed with the capacity to reciprocally recognize His Supreme Beauty. Searching for that Beauty is thus our prime directive. No mere mortal force can ever, ultimately, deter us from that mission. Although this world may distract, detour, detain, or delay us, we are divinely destined to arise and succeed as He has commanded us.

> O Son of Spirit! Noble have I created thee, yet thou hast abased thyself. Rise then unto that for which thou wast created.[6]

The soul's search for the image of God within itself is the primordial instinct of every human being. Some contemporary Christian friends call the process 'absorption into God'. By whatever name, it is the individual soul freeing itself of all that holds it down, and becoming dissolved into remembrance and recognition of God. Some Hindu sources affirm that 'Atman' (the individual soul) is 'Brahman' (Spirit, or God). In this sense, yoga is the process of unveiling the eternal relationship, bond, or 'yoke' of the individual soul with its God, its Origin and Source. Both cultural precursors and contemporaries of the Bahá'í Revelation confirm that the inner life is the scene of important work. We are doing important work when we attend to this; we are not avoiding work; we are not wasting time; we are doing the work that God has entrusted to us as of primary importance, actually taking precedence over what we would accomplish externally or visibly. In fact, we are told to get on with this work, with our utmost effort.

> Strain every nerve to acquire both inner and outer perfections, for the fruit of the human tree hath ever been and will ever be perfections both within and without.[7]

The double imperative of perfections within and without does not mean that we spend fifty per cent of our day inside the self and fifty per cent outside. We may spend only five per cent of our day inside in prayer or introspection. But that may be enough to balance the outer demands and preoccupations. The directive simply states that we have to attend to both frontiers of perfections; and in this nothing has changed. It has ever been so that half of human life is visible outwardly, and its mirror image is visible inwardly.

Therefore, the Inner Family is comprised of every human image that a person has witnessed externally. It is everyone the person has ever been: infant, toddler, child, adolescent, young adult, mid-adult, older adult, and elder. It is everyone the person has ever seen, including all examples of how to be a mother or brother, aunt, or grandchild. And it is every impression of humanity the person has ever felt and absorbed through science, art, and literature. The Inner Family is the comprehensive and exhaustive assemblage of images depicting all human beings and all human doings that a person has encountered in an entire lifetime. Extreme contrasts are bound to exist among these images, and those contrasts of purity and perversion create a painful dissonance within the person, who then tries to sort, categorize, evaluate, prioritize, and reconcile their inner mess into something resembling a single integrated picture. Each person, knowingly or not, is trying to achieve a gestalt within the universe of their experiences. Each person is trying to reconcile the tensions within. This is life in the Inner Family and there is only one sure guidance, one transcendent standard by which to find the inner resolution, and that is the revealed Word of God.

The existence of oppression

If development of the soul is what the Creator wants for us, why doesn't it just happen? Why don't we just 'blossom forth' in all of our individual beauty? As the analogy suggests, blossoming and 'the fruit of the human tree' entails gradual unfoldment of qualities and capacities of the soul. In the meantime, life presents every soul with conditions which, at first glance, seem to be holding back or restricting its unfoldment. 'Oppression' refers to all of those conditions and experiences that figuratively 'press down' on the soul and seem to work against the natural tendency of the soul to expand and develop.

Anticipating that life would encompass us with trials and tribulations, the Sacred Writings tell us where to withdraw for safety. We may imagine how nice it would be to withdraw to the desert or the mountains – anywhere – to get away from life's harassments. But we might go there and find that we had taken all the oppressive effects with us. Instead, we must stand firm in the midst of oppression and withdraw deeper within our soul self than the oppression has reached. We have to withdraw into the presence of God.

> Thou art My stronghold; enter therein that thou mayest abide in safety.

> My love is in thee, know it, that thou mayest find Me near unto thee.[8]

'Stronghold' is such an interesting and imaginative word. Dating from the early Middle Ages, fortified castles all over Europe usually included an architectural feature called a 'keep'. It was most often designed in the form of two stone cylinders, one within the other, with a set of stairs binding the two. The keep was used as the final refuge in a human settlement. If the settlement was under attack, the women and children and old people would go inside the inner ring of this stone keep, and the able-bodied men would run up or down the stairs between the two walls, shooting from window slits at the attackers. It was called a keep because it was designed to keep you safe. So, in this difficult world God has provided a keep, and it is the soul self. He calls to us to enter therein, to abide in safety, and find Him near to us.

While the Sacred Writings acknowledge just how hard this life is, and how difficult the world, we sometimes make things worse by being very hard on ourselves, judging ourselves harshly for our performance in life. We sometimes say to ourselves, 'If I were doing this right, life would be a lot smoother, wouldn't it? Wouldn't my days be a lot easier? Wouldn't my whole life be a lot better?' Maybe not. Perhaps the world is set up to be like an exercise machine. The whole point is that as you get a little bit stronger, it puts up a little more resistance, so that we will continue to advance in strength.

> For everything there is a sign. The sign of love is fortitude under My decree and patience under My trials.[9]

It seems that the world is like a teaching machine. More than even the most sensitive computer, it knows the entire 'development profile' of each one of us. Consequently, just when we get one situation mastered, it seems to increase the stakes and make the whole situation more difficult. In casual conversation about spiritual matters we may refer to this series of increasing challenges as the 'tests' in life. But this is hardly inspiring or useful because most of us don't actually enjoy tests. We would be better off remembering the joy of learning a new activity, such as the skill of playing the piano, of managing money, of learning a language, of skiing, or of driving a car; there is a grace and a power as our skills improve, and with practice they become fun, joyful, exhilarating. And we think: this is great! I'm getting better at this!

Perhaps if we learned to think of the increasing pressures of life in this way we would experience them with joy and increasing satisfaction instead of dread. We would be able to give thanks for such changes and make sense of the passage in the Sacred Writings in which Bahá'u'lláh says that the true lover 'yearneth for tribulation', because in truth, we all long for that which will prepare us, equip us, and provide us a bridge back to the Beloved.

> The true lover yearneth for tribulation even as doth the rebel for forgiveness and the sinful for mercy.[10]

The rebel perversely runs as far and fast as needed to arouse the object of its desire to overwhelm its rebellion with reunion. The rebel seeks forgiveness (as the renewal of giving and receiving), the end of estrangement and the return to reciprocity. The sinful have withheld mercy from others and themselves in the hope that Mercy will one day find them and take them home. 'Yearning for tribulation' does not mean that we are masochists and are simply looking for trouble. What enables us to welcome tribulation is knowing that through the terrible challenge it presents, we will experience the kind of education and attract the kind of assistance we need to grow strong. The lover here desires a means to prove the desire for the beloved – a quest, a great undertaking that will measure what the lover is willing to expend to be deserving of the presence of the Beloved. Shoghi Effendi writes:

> We can prove ourselves worthy of our Cause only if in our individual conduct and corporate life we sedulously imitate the example of our beloved Master, whom the terrors of tyranny, the storms of incessant abuse, the oppressiveness of humiliation, never caused to deviate a hair's breadth from the revealed Law of Bahá'u'lláh.[11]

Examine the key words: tyranny, abuse, and humiliation. Consider what can happen in a state of terror: we are stressed to the point of panic; we cannot think straight; we make mistakes, then feel badly and say: 'Oh, I failed because I wasn't calm in that situation.' Shoghi Effendi goes so far as to indicate that terror imposed by tyranny was a constant circumstance for 'Abdu'l-Bahá. We know that terrible pressures have been contrived by tyrants to break a human being's will. But Shoghi Effendi says that the Master, as our Perfect Exemplar, was not made to compromise His will or behaviour from the revealed Law, even by the experience of terror.

How relentlessly the Guardian layers on the qualifiers to the Master's experience of oppression. The Guardian specifies 'the storms of incessant abuse' in which the emphatic descriptor is 'incessant'. We can tolerate a bad day, and even a bad week, but when abuse goes on incessantly, a person's strength becomes drained away. Every human being has to rest. And yet abusive periods of life can go on for months and years as though it will never end, or as though there will be no escape.

Another form of persecution that is identified by the Guardian is 'the oppressiveness of humiliation'. Humiliation, like ridicule, can be harder to bear than an aggressive, overt attack. Ridicule works like psychological warfare, which is a strategy designed to undermine the will of the other side to resist. Humiliation is more than merely loss of face in public. It can cause us to doubt our own goodness, and our own worthiness to succeed, or to strive, or even to survive.

In the same manner, guilt works as an insidious instrument to suppress the sense of our innate and inalienable nobility, to make us feel essentially tainted and unable to achieve our divine goal. While we are charged to exhibit righteous conduct at all times, the sense of guilt is useful only for alerting us to make amends should we fail, and other than that has no further usefulness. Certainly, guilt is not to be prolonged in ourselves or in others, or it generalizes into an all-consuming sense of shame.

The ultimate stage of oppression occurs when the external oppressor becomes internalized, causing any of us to feel that we don't basically like our self any more. At that moment, the oppressor has reproduced itself. It has expropriated our survival machinery and turned it into self-sabotaging machinery. The Sacred Writings acknowledge that this dreadful turn of events can befall any soul, and has throughout the course of history; but that God has not abandoned us, and will provide for our recovery:

> And if thou art overtaken by affliction in My path, or degradation for My sake, be not thou troubled thereby. Rely upon God, thy God and the Lord of thy fathers . . .[12]

Displacing oppression by sovereignty and dominion

Bahá'u'lláh has very specific instructions and promises concerning how we are to counteract oppression. The two words that He uses regarding how to turn back oppression are 'sovereignty' and 'dominion'. Sovereignty refers to the inviolability of a soul's borders. Each soul has been created as an independent territory in which dwells a self-determining free will. And although that independence or self-possession may be undermined or compromised temporarily by an oppressor, the loss can be reversed because God the Creator has endowed each soul with an ultimate sovereignty that it can reclaim. Dominion in turn refers to the soul's exercise of self-determination over all of its properties, attributes, experiences and activities.

Divinely revealed Text explains to us how we were created, how we are to be trained, and what the purpose is for this exercise – that we might attain to a state of integrity and worthiness.

> Out of the wastes of nothingness, with the clay of My command I made thee to appear, and have ordained for thy training every atom in existence and the essence of all created things . . . And My purpose in all this was that thou mightest attain My everlasting dominion and become worthy of My invisible bestowals.[13]

The good news is that although oppression is allowed to operate in the world, it is not allowed to crush us. Bahá'u'lláh says, 'I have ordained for thy training every atom in existence and the essence of all created things.' Look what these statements are saying: I created thee and caused thee to appear. And everything else in existence is here for your training. This is a very interesting combination of statements. It was once expressed by a lecturer on yoga, who said there is a level of consciousness at which it is correct to understand that you are alone with God, and everything else in existence is part of His teaching machine, designed for you, to bring you forth as a soul.

And where are we going with this training? 'That thou mightest attain my everlasting dominion and become worthy of My bestowals.' Where is He taking us? He is taking us into a level of 'dominion'. What is the meaning of this?

We don't need to fear an experience of oppression, because the Divine knows the exact dosage we can bear. It will never give us such an experience of oppression that we cannot come back from it like eternal Springtime. The hidden benefit of a tribulation is like homeopathic remedies – they are essentially the same poisons from which the patient is already suffering, and they are administered to cause the immune system, or the corrective systems, to kick in and counter-balance the condition – to bring back a healthy balance.

> My calamity is My providence, outwardly it is fire and vengeance, but inwardly it is light and mercy. Hasten thereunto that thou mayest become an eternal light and an immortal spirit. This is My command unto thee, do thou observe it.[14]

Is it not remarkable that He says 'hasten' to 'My calamity'! This doesn't mean seek out trouble that isn't there. But it may mean that if a great challenge is coming at us, or has suddenly arrived, we are to do more than just be stoic and endure it. He says we are to <u>willingly</u> submit to it, <u>eagerly</u> take it on. <u>Hasten</u> unto it. While we may well be saying, 'I don't want to deal with this!', He is saying, hasten unto it. Go engage with it! Wrestle with that thing! Because you are going to win. It only exists to advance your strengthening.

What is it that He wants for us? Why is He bringing us

forth through the means of calamity? What is it that He or we stand to gain? In the first place, He says that this is the way for us to become an 'eternal light', to step beyond time and history to become 'an immortal spirit'. But more than this, what He indicates is that it is possible to achieve a condition in which we can commune with Him. We can rise to be near Him if we can just trust Him enough to let Him lead us through these stages of development.

> I desire communion with thee, but thou wouldst put no trust in Me. The sword of thy rebellion hath felled the tree of thy hope. At all times I am near unto thee, but thou art ever far from Me. Imperishable glory I have chosen for thee, yet boundless shame thou hast chosen for thyself. While there is yet time, return, and lose not thy chance.[15]

Everywhere we see analogies: take space travel for instance. When you see the rocket leaving the earth, it's pushing up through the atmosphere. The early stages require the greatest force. Once it gets up, it's free of all that atmosphere, and it just cruises, freely, effortlessly.

> Burst thy cage asunder, and even as the phoenix of love soar into the firmament of holiness.[16]

Spiritually, we are like a spacecraft trying to break free of the earth's gravitational pull. In the early stages, when we are first learning to respond to the Creator, we really have to put out an effort. But the closer we get to Him, there comes a simplicity, an ease and easiness – as when the pilot says, 'We have reached 35,000 feet, our cruising altitude.' Bahá'u'lláh says, 'I desire communion with thee.' We are invited into keeping company with Him, and in that condition we will find a degree of certitude, of confidence, and of tranquillity. By the grace of God we can soar into the realms of His loving kindness and the celestial firmament of His holiness.

Returning to the words 'sovereignty' and 'dominion': Sovereignty is composed of two parts, the original Latin words 'supra' meaning over and 'regnum' meaning rule. Hence, to rule over or to reign over. When we speak of 'national sovereignty' it means that a country governs itself within its own borders. So when I personally have sovereignty, I have achieved controlling power over my own life. We know that we will never be able to place blame on our neighbour for the deeds we ourselves have committed. I will always be held accountable for my own decisions. YET, as much as I am held responsible for my decisions, at the same time I am a prisoner of habit. I may have developed certain habits of self-doubt or self-sabotage under the influence of oppression by other people, and now, although I really should know better and behave with better judgement, I'm still acting like a puppet to these old habits.

What Bahá'u'lláh prescribes is that we learn to become 'just'. The process of attaining sovereignty over one's own life and over one's own decisions requires a difficult exercise of justice, but it is the means of attaining His presence and His guidance.

> The best beloved of all things in My sight is Justice; turn not away therefrom if thou desirest Me, and neglect it not that I may confide in thee. By its aid thou shalt see with thine own eyes and not through the eyes of others, and shalt know of thine own knowledge and not through the knowledge of thy neighbour.[17]

Justice then, by this usage of it, is the means of seeing the exact nature of things, and the precise actions to take that are appropriate. It is a quality first of perception (to see with thine own eyes) and second of decision-making that is absolutely appropriate to the situation. So what we have here is almost an identity between the word sovereignty, which is rule over myself, and the power of justice, which is to see cleanly and clearly with my own eyes and to judge with my own thought and not with the thought of my forefathers or cousins or neighbours or oppressors.

It's very difficult to attain this degree of sovereignty and He knows it. He says, I made everything in creation for you except one thing: that one thing is the human heart, and inside the human heart I have secreted away My beauty and My glory. But He asks, What have you done? You've gone and given my one resting place to another.

> All that is in heaven and earth I have ordained for thee, except the human heart, which I have made the habitation of My beauty and glory; yet thou didst give My home and dwelling to another than Me . . .[18]

What does He mean by this, that we have given His home to another? It may mean that we have gone and clogged up the heart that should be clean and ready for His occupancy; filled the rooms of the heart with junk. This could imply obsessions about things or people to which we are attracted. It could equally mean obsession with an activity like skiing or dancing or worse, gambling or other degenerative pursuits. Yet again it could be that the heart is full of grief, anger, sorrow, or fear. When we read His accusation, we should not necessarily interpret it to mean that the heart has been given to another in only the sense of loving someone or something more than we love Him. It may mean also that negative things are filling the heart.

THE INNER FAMILY

It's very difficult to clean the heart of sadness or anger, or fear. However, He is telling us that we must TRY to do just that.

Added to the key words of sovereignty and dominion is the notion of 'enlightenment'. With the most romantic imagery, reminiscent of desert breezes fluttering the door of a tent, He says that our hearts are being wakened and called to free themselves from the fanciful preoccupations that have detained them. We may now leave all that behind and hasten to His court and earn the right to be with Him beyond death and the downward trends of the material world, free and finally worthy to live in unlimited realms.

> . . . the spirit of enlightenment hath breathed in the Sinai of thy heart. Wherefore, free thyself from the veils of idle fancies and enter into My court, that thou mayest be fit for everlasting life and worthy to meet Me. Thus may death not come upon thee, neither weariness nor trouble.[19]

In the time of the Bábís, it was considered that a prayer would not be acceptable if there were any stain on our clothes. How much more unacceptable or inadequate is our prayer when there are so many stains on our hearts? We have to clean our hearts 'to be fit for everlasting life', to be worthy to meet Him. Thus may death not come upon us, neither weariness or trouble. As we unload the grievances we have held, we will not even feel tired. We will be 'fit' for everlasting life – for the rest of forever.

Living to celebrate excellence in all things

Finally, the teachings on the Inner Family end with the uplifting theme of excellence: excellence in my outer life, and excellence in my inner life. The logo for this family system bridges the inner and outer worlds with a balanced infinity symbol. In the same way that the expanse of a tree's branches is perfectly balanced by the expanse of its root system, the image indicates that we can transform our outer world only to the extent that we have transformed our inner world. This is an equation that our brothers and sisters in other periods of religious history have also discovered.

In the Four Valleys, Bahá'u'lláh says that at the beginning, this plane of self-discovery (and self-recovery) is the realm of conflict, yet it ends in 'attainment to the throne of splendour'. The throne of splendour re-echoes the theme of sovereignty. A sovereign sits on the throne, surveying and commanding all things from that vantage point.

> Although at the beginning, this plane is the realm of conflict, yet it endeth in attainment to the throne of splendour . . .
>
> This is the plane of the soul who is pleasing unto God. Refer to the verse: 'O thou soul who art well assured, return to thy Lord, well-pleased, and pleasing unto Him . . . Enter thou among My servants, and enter thou My paradise'.[20]

'O thou soul who art well assured . . .': what music this wafts to the ears of anyone who has engaged in a therapeutic process of recovery. The struggle is so profound, so elemental – the very notion of attaining consolation and assurance is the highest, sweetest state imaginable. Furthermore, it states unequivocally that we are coming to Him NOT as a first-time achievement, but are returning home to the palace and paradise where we belong. How tranquil then would be the heart that discovered it was both well pleased with what its Lord had ordained for its education, and by the same token had become pleasing to Him in the quality of its attainment of self. The lonely struggle ends in a welcome home, among a company of His refined and noble servants ... and to the surrounding delights of His paradise.

What can it possibly mean, 'excellence in all things', when our every day is full of less than perfect experiences? One possible meaning is that we should continuously improve the quality of behaviours we exhibit toward others, and the way we act in response to the less-than-excellent actions directed toward us by others. But another meaning must surely address how we review and transmute the darker memories of earlier years when we were even farther from the shores of 'excellence in all things'.

For these purposes, memory is more important for the soul than future intent. Memory contains within it every bit of experience that the soul has collected. We are like vacuum cleaners, or video cameras. Our whole lives, in all the years we've spent on earth, we have gone around monitoring and recording human experience, unconsciously vacuuming in even that which slipped past our conscious awareness.

The work of transmuting memory apparently involves two phases. One phase selects the good things and concentrates on them – a function that produces gratitude in us so we can praise our Creator, and supplies us with fresh courage and confidence so we can face the rest. The second phase selects the bad things, the things that made us afraid, the things that hurt us, the things that tarnished and contaminated our sense of our own goodness, and enables us to see through those experiences to the sustaining divine grace that was just behind the experience and brought us through it.

Many fairy tales, like the one about Rapunzel who spun straw into gold, are about transmuting the raw first substance of memory into something fine and lasting. One of our favourite folk wisdoms states, 'If you find yourself with a bunch of lemons, make lemonade.' This is a very gentle way of referring to what may have been devastating human degradation. But again and again, from war zone to concentration camp to pornography to domestic violence, individual human beings have survived and healed and renewed themselves to bear witness to the amazing powers of the soul to recover its innocence, purity and integrity.

Recovery is a divine form of artistry, transmuting the raw material of memory into something that embodies and communicates significant positive meaning. Anything that is ultimately beautiful starts with raw material, and the raw material of the soul is memory. Bahá'u'lláh tells us that in the beginning, this process of self-discovery is a realm of extreme conflict. But the more we transmute these experiences, we come to a place of quiet, of tranquillity. He says in the Four Valleys: 'O thou soul who art well assured . . .!' Isn't that nice? 'Return to thy Lord, well pleased and pleasing unto Him.' Isn't that what we all long for – that He will be pleased with us and what we have become. Just as it is recorded in the Christian scriptures, what we want most is for the Creator to say to us: 'This is my beloved son, in whom I am well pleased.' That's all we want, that when we get back home, that He will say 'well done'.

> Live then the days of thy life, that are less than a fleeting moment, with thy mind stainless, thy heart unsullied, thy thoughts pure, and thy nature sanctified, so that, free and content, thou mayest put away this mortal frame, and repair unto the mystic paradise and abide in the eternal kingdom for evermore.[21]

Having attained a state of rest and tranquillity within the soul, we are then urged to live on with the mind stainless of all that had troubled it, the heart unsullied, the thoughts pure, and the nature sanctified. Just as the mediaeval Christians had said regarding this transmutation of the soul's contents, it becomes in the end a process of sanctification or conversion to a state of holy consecration. 'Free and content' are the attributes of the little soul that gave its all to come forth in a world that seemed to have been ranged against it. We are told it has the capacity to get free and to live on with its yearning satisfied – in a state of contentment. Thus it reaches its crowning moment.

> From amongst all mankind hath He chosen you . . . and blessed by abounding grace, your hearts and souls have been born into new life. Thank ye and praise ye God that the hand of infinite bestowals hath set upon your heads this gem-studded crown, this crown whose lustrous jewels will forever flash and sparkle down all the reaches of time.
> To thank Him for this, make ye a mighty effort, and choose for yourselves a noble goal.[22]

The gem-studded crown encircles each enlightened soul like a gothic cathedral in which are framed great windows of vibrantly coloured transparency. Such are the brilliant lights around each soul. In a sense the tracery of memories provides the lattice work in which are positioned gem-like moments transmuted from suffering into transcendent victory. From massive pressure, coal is transformed into diamond. From moments compressed by the pain of oppression are transmuted imperishable, glorious insights. Each moment thus transformed becomes an enormous coloured gemstone that flashes and sparkles with rejoicing, gratitude and praise – down all the reaches of time. The promise is that as we advance this work of unifying the Inner Family of experiences, we don't achieve it just for a moment. We win it for all eternity. We will enjoy eternal life in this soul which has emerged from its long journey into an unassailable self.

Having attained this unqualified victory, a new horizon opens for the soul on a higher level of being. It is invited to bring forth from itself some artefact of gratitude to express its victory. Having attained a level of celestial peace but still inhabiting a body, it is invited to choose a noble goal for itself, something of great magnitude as a worthy celebration of the excellence of its Creator.

> To thank Him for this, make ye a mighty effort,
> and choose for yourselves a noble goal.[23]

7. The Eternal Family

Since ages past, peoples in most parts of the world – except perhaps the most urbanized and secularized – have sensed a connection between the welfare of their lives in the present, and the well-being of those who have gone before them. The methods by which they honour and activate that connection, and what they understand it to mean, has varied from place to place and age to age. Some cultures have emphasized connection to only the blood line of direct ancestors. Others have paid tribute to all great figures and noble souls who were forbears and protectors of the community as a whole. As with so many of the eternal truths renewed in this Dispensation, the Bahá'í Sacred Writings bring a fresh understanding and new insight to the meaning and method of these ancient wisdoms concerning both the ones who went before and the ones who will come after us in the flow of history.

Time and eternity

We who are here on this planet now are here at a place 'in history' so to speak. Positioned invisibly around us in some unidentifiable placeless place are the souls of those who have gone before, who have lived on this planet and left it before we got here, whom Bahá'í Sacred Writings call the Concourse on High or the Company on High. It would seem that they are also here now, but 'outside of history'. We are within the flow of time, whereas they are in eternity; hence the reference to them here as our Eternal Family.

Eternity seems to function something like an infinite 'present'. But how can we poor, time-bound mortals relate to an eternal, infinite present? Whatever it is, it would not seem practical for it to be a sort of spatial presence where everything, everywhere and 'everywhen' could be perceived at once, as that would make for a very crowded picture. Perhaps eternity is more like a database that is potentially present to perception and that responds to scanning by our focused and selective attention. That would also mean that eternity operates something like a city that is networked for reciprocal communication. Perhaps we can call on others within eternity at a moment's notice. But whatever the details yet to be experienced when we ourselves leave time and enter eternity, the main point is that, by definition, the immutable, incorruptible aspect of eternity renders it more like an infinite present than a fleeting, changeable, corruptible, and irretrievable present in the way we experience 'moments' within time.

Future and past

Within time, what makes any fleeting moment 'momentous' and significant is precisely its transitory nature. We have an all-too-brief experience of the 'present' as just an instant. Positioned as we are on this sliver of time known as the present moment, we tend to forget that 'history' is not only rolling out behind us in the record of time, but is also flowing towards us from the mists of the future. The future is as much a part of history as the past. The future is history moving toward us with all its potential, its possibilities, its probabilities, and most importantly its unanticipated unknowns. The future portion of history is unknown until the moment we shape it, that is, until we exercise our free will upon it. Thus, the formlessness of the future takes shape like a photograph, in a flash, in that very moment when history passes through us from the future into the past. Even though we may reinterpret it many ways, as the artist redevelops the photo many ways, still, the formless has taken form. In the flow of time, the future becomes the past right on this very spot.

The potency of the present moment

Even more powerful than the thought that we connect the future to the past in the flow of time, is the thought that we also stand on the point that connects time and eternity. That stunning thought reveals the immeasurable potency of the present moment. We humans occupy the great crossroads of the cosmos. This infinitely small intersection of time and eternity is the artist's workshop, where we create history out of the stuff of the unknown. We put our mark on history, moment by moment. It is in the flash of a moment, as when sperm penetrates egg, that life begins. It is in the flash of a moment that great thoughts are spoken and become the rallying point of nations. It is in the flash of a moment that genius perceives the form of the ingenious device, the medical cure, the healing balm of forgiveness. All things become possible in the glory of a moment. That is why the present moment is endowed with immeasurable potency to attract the confirmations of all the beings who inhabit it, including all those who occupy the limitless present of eternity. They can hear our cry, as surely as our cry can be heard by a multitude assembled in a plaza. Because they are among those present, at every moment, everywhere, they can respond, and lend the assistance of their creative will to our efforts to create an art form from every moment of our lives.

Our place in the Eternal Family

In each of the families we have described, we could draw a little arrow, to say: 'You are here.' You have your place, here, in each of these families. For Bahá'ís, when we speak of the ones who went before, we don't just mean the ones in our tribe, our clan, our bloodline; we mean all the ones who went before. Every mother, father or child who went before us is ours. And when we speak of the ones who come after, we don't just mean our physical children, grandchildren, and great-grandchildren but all the ones who will come after us and are influenced in some manner by the choices we make today.

It is interesting to think, as we walk through the world, and pass by the landmark of a hill or a body of water, about the people who passed that way before us, and who will pass that way after we are gone. What were they like? What were they thinking? Were they walking? Riding a donkey? What will the ones who will be walking here three hundred years from today think about us? Will they curse me or bless me for the world I left for them? So the Eternal Family causes us to consider the relation of the visible and the invisible, and especially to appreciate the glory of this present day, because this moment is the spot upon which hinges everything else that will ever be.

Assisting the ones who went before

When we begin to turn our attention to all those who have gone before us, the obvious place to look in the Sacred Writings for the means of understanding and communicating with them is the revealed prayers that enable us to supplicate God on their behalf. As we read the prayers for the departed, we discover that the Concourse is not just an undifferentiated mass. The prayers actually identify four groups within the Concourse: our parents, our kin, souls in ignorance, and souls who have achieved great things during their days on earth.

On behalf of our parents, the following prayer was revealed:

> O Lord! In this Most Great Dispensation Thou dost accept the intercession of children in behalf of their parents . . . Therefore, O Thou kind Lord, accept the request of this Thy servant at the threshold of Thy singleness and submerge his father in the ocean of Thy grace, because this son hath arisen to render Thee service . . .[1]

Ultimately, the success of everything depends upon its acceptability to God. The last 'yes' always belongs to God alone. So it is noteworthy that in this portion of His Writings, 'Abdu'l-Bahá announces that God accepts the intercession of children on behalf of their parents. However, He goes on to stipulate that the opportunity to intercede at the threshold of our Lord will be predicated on our first having arisen to render God our service. In other words, first we show up; then we can intercede.

Perhaps the parent–child relationship is the one that comes most readily to mind when we think about assisting the ones who went before. However, a special relationship is also indicated between ourselves and all those in the Concourse who are our kindred.

> One of the distinguishing characteristics of this most great Dispensation is that the kin of such as have recognized and embraced the truth of this Revelation . . . will, upon their death, if they are outwardly non-believers, be graciously

invested with divine forgiveness and partake of the ocean of His Mercy.

This bounty, however, will be vouchsafed only to such souls as have inflicted no harm upon Him Who is the Sovereign Truth nor upon his loved ones. Thus hath it been ordained by Him Who is the Lord of the Throne on High and the Ruler of this world and of the world to come.[2]

This seems to say that to the extent that we arise (recognize) and engage (embrace) on behalf of the Cause of God, there will be favourable impact upon those who knew us, or know us, or are connected to us. But there is a caveat: as we have seen earlier, Bahá'í principles are very clear; but they come with conditions that guide their applications. Here, it says that those kin of a believer will partake of the ocean of grace only if they have inflicted no harm upon Him Who is the Sovereign Truth, nor on His loved ones. Such people who during their lifetimes have simply responded to the direct grace of God, and have lived 'good' lives, without knowing the Manifestation of God in this day, and are connected to a family member who has recognized the Revelation, will after their departure from this world partake of the bounties of the Lord of the Age.

There is yet a third category among the hosts of the Concourse of whom special mention is made: these are 'souls in ignorance', the ones who have done terrible mischief or damage, to the extreme of their ability, their whole lives, to the last minute. While we may not know what actually happens to them and what the self-created consequences of their actions are, the following passage suggests that eventually even they can be liberated from the alienation their lives produced.

> O Thou forgiving Lord! Although some souls have spent the days of their lives in ignorance, and became estranged and

> contumacious, yet, with one wave from the ocean of Thy forgiveness, all those encompassed by sin will be set free.[3]

Perhaps this requires some pondering. Perhaps we'd like some of them to have to wait. We know that Dispensations before this one have made provisions, such as 'purgatory', a place of waiting, a place of working things through. But it is not for us humans to measure the price of forgiveness; that ocean belongs to God. This passage affirms that it is within the almighty power of God to free every soul, no matter what its ignorance. Since we are all in some sense ignorant, we are all in need of the ocean of forgiveness; and, trusting in the ability of that limitless ocean to reach us, we already affirm that it can reach everyone. Someday, we too will be in the worlds beyond this one; and, more likely than not, we will have left behind some who feel we have harmed them. Let us hope, when that day comes, those incarnate ones will say this prayer for us. That being the case, we can understand exactly why it is incumbent upon us to pray for the release of others from the clutches and consequences of their ignorance.

And then there are those special ones, who have modelled for us noble qualities we want to emulate. For them we can pray for special recognition and reward.

> I ask of Thee by the splendour of the Orb of Thy Revelation, mercifully to accept from him that which he hath achieved in Thy days . . . Grant, then, O my God, that Thy servant may consort with Thy chosen ones, Thy saints and Thy Messengers in heavenly places that the pen cannot tell nor the tongue recount.[4]

Perhaps in this world we really do not recognize what counts as an achievement. It is not possible to visit the Holy Places where members of the Holy Family received pilgrims without wondering such things as: 'How much tea did the Greatest Holy Leaf make? How many pilgrims did she welcome and comfort after all the trials of their life and journey?' She must have made a lot of tea, in conditions which were at times excruciatingly difficult. What counts as an achievement may not be outwardly very impressive. How many centuries have Jewish mothers put the Sabbath supper on the table – against all odds. Getting that supper on the table may have been the most heroic act of that week, in that place, at that time. As difficult as it is for us here to recognize the value of true achievements, it seems that such achievements are deeply appreciated on the other side.

> No goodly deed was or will ever be lost, for benevolent acts are treasures preserved with God for the benefit of those who act. Blessed the servant and the maidservant who have fulfilled their obligation in the path of God our Lord, the Lord of all worlds . . .[5]

These few extracts from the Sacred Writings tell us that we need to refine our understanding of the members of the Concourse and the way we relate to them. It would serve us well to pay more attention to what we do for them here – while we are still able – because as we develop that friendly relationship with the Concourse, there is much that they can do for us.

Calling upon the ones who went before

We are so lovingly encouraged to call upon the ones who went before. How could we ever say, 'I wish someone would care for me; I wish someone would look after me; I wish someone would help me,' when in fact there are unnumbered hosts who exist now ready and able to fulfil that purpose as part of their continuing development in service to humanity for the glorification of God.

The Writings say that each one of us can become like an army, that thousands will come to our aid if we arise. We cannot even remotely appreciate the number of those who know exactly where each of us is located, what each of us is doing, and what each of us needs. Consider what the Writings say about the assistance available to us when we make mention of God in this world:

> Whoso openeth his lips in this Day and maketh mention of the name of his Lord, the hosts of Divine inspiration shall descend upon him . . . On him shall also descend the Concourse on high, each bearing aloft a chalice of pure light . . .[6]

All that is required is for us to step forward, with them in mind, and the capacity to serve the world will flow through us by the loving assistance of our Eternal Family now resident beyond the reaches of this world.

> If in this day a soul shall act according to the precepts and the counsels of God, he will serve as a divine physician to mankind . . . and such a virtuous soul hath, to befriend him, the unfailing help of the Company on high.[7]

They passionately care for us, and love to join in our community gatherings as anyone would love to be enfolded in an ideal family reunion. They live to empower our work, and so rejoice in doing this that we are submerged in the ocean of their bliss.

> If a small number of people gather lovingly together . . . the deeds they do, will unleash the bestowals of Heaven, and

provide a foretaste of eternal bliss. The hosts of the Company on high will defend them, and the angels of the Abhá Paradise, in continuous succession, will come down to their aid.[8]

So many phrases describe wave upon wave of assistance: ' the hosts of divine inspiration shall descend'; 'the Concourse on high, each bearing aloft a chalice of pure light'; ' the unfailing help of the Company on high'; 'unleash the bestowals'. This last phrase sounds like something very small, just a little ripcord that we pull, and it releases an avalanche of giant, soft, rose petals, heavenly bestowals tumbling down upon us, angels of the Abhá Paradise tumbling head over heels in continuous succession to our aid.

We would be foolish to attempt anything – to get up in the morning, to cross the street, to write a letter, not to mention teach the Cause of God – without imploring the help of the Concourse. When credit cards were first introduced to the masses through advertisements on television, there was one that warned the user 'Don't leave home without it'. Well, we don't dare leave home without inviting talented and insightful members of the Concourse to come along with us! This is a dangerous world. We are well advised to call upon their protective company.

Providing for the ones who follow

Day by day, our positive actions are building, not only for ourselves, but for all who will follow. Though each action may be small in itself, its effect is cumulative, like children on summer vacation, throwing stones into the water day by day to build a causeway. At some point, the path of stones starts to become visible through the water; and later, with time, the pathway emerges above the water line. Each generation that comes into the world will add a few marker stones of spiritual conviction and cultural benefit, to raise the pathway for humankind above the water line of material disorientation and despair.

The question we each have to ask ourselves is: what should those contributions be? For some of us, it has to do with the reconstruction of society and the raising of the Kingdom of God on earth. Perhaps in our lifetimes we will begin to see the constellation of agencies of social and economic justice that are described in the Sacred Writings as being arrayed around the House of Worship in each community. The place of worship and its agencies of common welfare together comprise an institution called the Dawning Place of Worship (Mashríq'ul-Adkhár in Arabic). We anticipate that in every locality of the world in which Bahá'í governance will be in place, we will begin to provide for all from birth to death: maternal health, education for the children and others all their life long, shelter for travellers, comfort for the aged, hospital and hospice care – the full set of services that a human being needs in order to blossom as a moral, spiritual being. Some of us will choose to contribute to such civilized developments, so that those who come after us will not have to begin life as we did, with disadvantages, obstacles, deprivation and ignorance. Our satisfaction will lie in this service, as every parent and every Bahá'í is enjoined to labour in dignity, earn from our handiwork, and contribute to the well-being of all those who follow.

> Ye are the trees of My garden; ye must give forth goodly and wondrous fruits, that ye yourselves and others may profit therefrom. Thus it is incumbent on every one to engage in crafts and professions, for therein lies the secret of wealth . . . Trees that yield no fruit have been and will ever be for the fire.[9]

We all know the story of how Lord Jesus, when He came to an olive tree that had produced no fruit, pronounced that it was fit only for the fire. Perhaps this was not meant as a punitive and unforgiving judgement, but rather a simple statement of fact. Apart from sheltering birds or providing shade, the essential purpose of an olive tree is to provide fruit that can propagate other trees and prolong the life of those creatures who are nourished by its fruit. Shelter and shade will end with the finite life of the tree, which then disappears as wood into the fire; while infinite continuity is attained through the life of other trees and creatures sustained by its fruit.

The wonderful analogy of 'trees' is used in many different ways in the Sacred Writings. There is the 'Divine Lote Tree' beyond which there is no passing, the Prophet of God who marks the ultimate destination of the path to God. There is the 'Tree of Life' which lives from age to age, drawing from metaphysical inspiration and producing moral beings in the visible world who will one day fall to the ground and yield their lives to nourish the next ones who will come after them. And each of us is like a tree, not in the literal sense, but because our inner yearning is to constantly seek upward for spiritual inspiration, so that our creative energy can rise up and bring forth righteous acts specific to our own gifts. And the world, we are told, needs the particular fruits that each of us can yield. If we do not contribute our unique gifts, no one else can. Creation will lack those embellishments, those critical components. Not one other person in all the world can bring forth the exact fruit that the Creator has given each one of us to manifest.

At the very least, we can each arrange, at the time of our departure, to return to God what belongs to God for the provision of education for His children:

Everyone, whether man or woman, should hand over to a

trusted person a portion of what he or she earneth through trade, agriculture or other occupation, for the training and education of children, to be spent for this purpose with the knowledge of the Trustees of the House of Justice.[10]

We are tested and evaluated by the breadth of heart we show toward our fellow beings, both those who are with us in the present and those who will follow us in the future. As we expand the range of our compassion to include those who are beyond us in the future, we expand our heart to resemble more closely our Creator, who like a mighty and fruitful tree, provides for all.

> Tell the rich of the midnight sighing of the poor, lest heedlessness lead them into the path of destruction, and deprive them of the Tree of Wealth. To give and to be generous are attributes of Mine; well is it with him that adornest himself with My virtues.[11]

At first, it appears that the purpose of being fruitful and generous is to provide services that will benefit the generations who are to come after us. And while a service, by definition, must benefit others, its deeper purpose is to help us to develop divine perfections. It seems that our Creator longs to see us fulfil our potential, and develop those qualities of His that are inherently our own. In this way, He becomes known to the world, through us, by virtue of our willingness to become the evidences of His nature. Thus, He says:

> Thou art even as a finely tempered sword concealed in the darkness of its sheath . . . Wherefore come forth from the sheath of self and desire that thy worth may be made resplendent and manifest unto all the world.[12]

We are called to come forth from the sheath of self and desire. We are informed that we cannot have a satisfactory 'balance sheet' at the end of our lives if we have only looked out for ourselves and our own needs; or even if we have cared only for those of our own kin. Neither of these services is the full measure of our capacity. We are, however, capable of transcending our smaller selves, in an unbounded service to God and humanity that reaches beyond present sight and time. The command says that our worth should be made manifest 'unto all the world'. Our earthly lives are actually designed to prepare us to break out of the confinement of the smaller, finite shell of self, by living in service to the unbounded well-being of others.

There is so much to be done to raise up the world, that our greatest service cannot just be the work we do with our own hands. Opportunity to uplift humanity is open to everyone in the world, most of whom are as yet unaware of the vision of humanity unveiled in its most recent Revelation. Therefore, our best service to humanity yet unborn is to attract more and more souls into that service by sharing with them the message of human dignity and destiny contained in Bahá'u'lláh's Revelation.

> The field is indeed so immense, the period so critical, the Cause so great, the workers so few, the time so short, the privilege so priceless, that no follower of the Faith of Bahá'u'lláh, worthy to bear His name, can afford a moment's hesitation.[13]

Shoghi Effendi imparts such a sense of urgency to this call. He does not say that we should wait until some later more appropriate stage of life, when we graduate, or when our children graduate. He states, without qualification, that no follower of the Faith worthy of the name can afford a moment's hesitation.

How many opportunities do we carelessly delay? How many times do we say, 'Yes, I'll do that, but not right now.'

In serving the worldwide children of the future we are urged to be audacious, lest these precious children suffer for want of having had benevolent forbears. In this noble cause nothing is beyond the combined power of those of us serving in this world assisted by our limitlessly resourceful Eternal Family.

> The Kingdom of God is possessed of limitless potency. Audacious must be the army of life if the confirming aid of that Kingdom is to be repeatedly vouchsafed unto it . . .[14]

And in the end, whatever tasks we shoulder, and risks we take, there is really only one thing to remember and to do: Bahá'u'lláh says that all God wants us to do is to make mention of Him on His earth. By this action, He will, in turn, recognize us as His own, and welcome us home, and we will both be glad.

> Make mention of Me on My earth, that in My heaven I may remember thee, thus shall Mine eyes and thine be solaced.[15]

There are so many distractions in this world. Yet, under all circumstances, He wants only that we remember Him, and make mention of Him, that we live in mindful remembrance of Him, so that others may also come to remember Him. This is the victory He wants us to achieve.

Surely, our worst fear would be of disappointing Him – of there being no remembrance of Him in us by which He could recognize us as His own. Wouldn't it be dreadful to arrive in the Abhá Kingdom, and calling out to Him at last, 'I'm home!', have Him respond with the question 'Who?' Would it not be unimaginably dreadful if we had lived so faint-heartedly, had become so pale, so listless, faded of the signs of His glory that He did not even recognize us as His own? Instead, what we desperately desire is that when we return and call out to him, He will reply, 'Welcome Home . . . I've been waiting for you.'

What we actually want from life is not the satisfaction of whatever we accomplish here (such as it is). What we really want is that our life will evoke recognition and acknowledgement from Him. There is an amusing and touching story, told by a gifted counsellor, about a little boy on the way home from school. He finds a dead bug on the street, and bursting with pride in his achievement, scoops it up in his hand. Arriving home, he calls to his father, saying, 'Hi Dad, I'm home, and I brought you a dead thing!' The father bends over it, with an arm around his child, and, staring intently, pronounces, 'That's the BEST dead thing I've seen all day!'

Everything hinges on His acceptance of our meagre offerings. His acceptance is within our 'hope', though not within the range of our 'doing'. We've been promised that it is within His grace, that one day we will know the moment, when He says to us, 'This is My beloved [one] in whom I am well pleased.'

And we will fall into the welcoming embrace of our patient Creator, for He has promised that, after all we have been through on this journey with all our human Families and with all our relations with every living being, by living in remembrance of Him there will come a time of soul-satisfying reunion. His rejoicing will be reflected in our own, and it will be just as He promised, when He said: 'thus shall Mine eyes and thine be solaced.'[16]

Reflections on Our Seven Families

Just by being born ...

On the day of our birth, we drew breath and opened our eyes on a social reality comprised of only a few voices and moving forms. At that moment, we did not know that over time we would grow into an awareness of our connection with other human beings on many interwoven layers of social reality.

In this book, the interwoven social worlds have been described as families containing distinctive populations, resources, dynamics, challenges and principles to guide successful life and action. Each of these social system 'families' exhibits distinguishing features while still maintaining similarities that identify it as sharing a common order of reality with the others: populations governed by spiritual principles and revealing dynamic patterns that resonate on all levels of social reality. We will now look back to contemplate the patterns we have seen, as the book draws to a close.

Themes from the Global Family

The Global Family contains all the peoples of the planet and within it we can see emerging the rudimentary elements of the global commonwealth foretold in the Bahá'í Sacred Writings, a commonwealth that will provide both the material and spiritual basis for a world civilization. The Global Family is charged with protecting the diversity and enhancing the synergy of all those who dwell on earth. In this perspective, globalism is a threat only when it violates the prime operating principle of protecting cultural diversity, because diversity sustains life and promotes creativity, as was illustrated in the discussion of nations which make their distinctive contributions to the Global Family.

Uniformity has its place in technical standards for such common global needs as food safety, postal services, air travel, telecommunications, and so forth. But diversity is our cultural safeguard offering the prospect that somewhere on the planet, among our highly diverse peoples, we have the capacity to meet and respond successfully to all contingencies that may arise. The Global Family illustrates themes of:

a) cultural diversity as a protection for global sustainability;
b) emergence of a world civilization from a global commonwealth;
c) a new age releasing the collective creative energies of humanity;
d) increasing equality of life opportunity for the sexes; and
e) the decisive role of women in governance of a peaceful planet.

Themes from the National Family

The National Family contains all the residents within the borders of a state and demonstrates that health and wealth, peace and creativity are unattainable in a nation which does not invest in the life and talents of its people. It is in the National

Family that we see what has been called the social contract – the reciprocity between people who have the crucial role of electing their public servants and those who were elected to shoulder the burden of governance.

Here we observe the complete reliance of civilization, as the creative flowering of human potential, upon the cultivation of human gifts and capacities through universal education and lifelong learning. Human beings do not complete themselves by simply growing physically. We must learn and develop socially, mentally, and spiritually to realize our latent potential. Nations do not succeed merely by fostering material well-being, which is usually not fairly distributed. It is within the nation that people, whether at the regional or local level, develop their unique perspective on life, where they produce crafts, create arts, investigate the universe, write literature, make music, embrace nature, and praise God. From the life of National Families several themes emerge:

a) the process of maturing over time writ large in the life of nations;
b) the reciprocity and mutual reliance of the individual and the nation;
c) the fundamental need for race unity to benefit the progress of a nation; and
d) the unique contribution of each nation to an emerging world civilization.

Themes from the Essential Family

The Essential Family is a new version of the classic family, the fundamental system that embraces and sustains us over the course of our lifetime. It hosts our most intimate relationships. This set of people dance the dances of marriage, of parenting, of reunions, anniversaries, and passages. Like clan members who have known each other always, these hearts travel together as they make their way into this life; pass through the arches of the years, and out of this world into the life to come. While unique in many ways, this Essential Family also provides the prototype of certain fundamental principles of human relationship that recur with variations in all other family systems of humanity such as:

a) the whole is comprised of parts interacting with each other;
b) successful interaction has to be consciously learned;
c) there is a need to balance inward-drawing and outward-expanding forces;
d) rights and responsibilities are attributed to each individual taking part in the whole;
e) the purpose of each system is to promote development of the individuals taking part in it; and
f) individual development comes through reciprocity with others and the whole.

Themes from the Daily Family

The Daily Family is that cast of characters that awaits us every morning: the people in our building, on our bus, at our place of work, in our lunchroom. We do not need media dramatizations to have situation comedy or tragic story-telling by instalments. There will never be a day of our lives when we are without one or the other or both! Comedy, tragedy, and petty annoyance are with us day after day in our Daily Family. Here we find principles of universal guidance, good for all people, everywhere, that take us to the highest standards of detachment and transcendence, by showing us how to navigate the mundane, concrete events of our daily lives. In the Daily Family we learn the power and importance of:

a) rectitude of conduct;
b) a chaste, pure, and holy life;
c) complete freedom from prejudice; and
d) thankfulness for the privilege of daily life on this material plane.

Themes from the Family of Friendships

Unique among the planes of our experience is the one on which we establish a Family of Friendships. This is the only plane on which we choose a family for ourselves; all the others are given to us by circumstances. And it is precisely because this family is freely chosen, that it is where we prove to ourselves just how much we are committed to seeking and sustaining unity in relation to a variety of people. In the Family of Friendships we discover many recurring spiritual dynamics:

a) freedom of choice;
b) promotion of well-being;
c) commitments expressed in action;
d) the prerequisite of noble qualities;
e) limits imposed by lack of reciprocity;
f) relationship that is profound and enduring;
g) relationship that dissolves barriers of prejudice;
h) the power of example and 'Abdu'l-Bahá as our Perfect Exemplar;
i) relationships that heal and restore;
j) relationships that remind us of life's purpose;
k) the joy of sharing the spiritual journey; and
l) ultimate reunion with the Friend.

Themes from the Inner Family

Most subtle and secret of all is the Inner Family which houses the encyclopedia of our personal childhood, our adolescence, our early, middle and late adulthood, and increasing old age, until becoming an elder; along with the entire multitude of everyone we have ever met! It is all inside.

In a sense, the Inner Family contains and mirrors all the outer families. And like them, it also craves unity. The effort to integrate our life experience into a meaningful whole is the inner work of the soul, as surely as raising the Kingdom of God on earth is the outer work of the soul. In the Inner Family, we discover the dynamic force of:

a) the inner realities of human life;
b) the high value placed on our inner life;
c) the damaging effects of oppression;
d) displacing oppression with 'sovereignty' and 'dominion'; and
e) the motivation to strive for excellence in all things.

Themes from the Eternal Family

The Eternal Family surrounds and observes all our other families. It is comprised of those souls who dwell in realms outside of our own historical period. They may be part of the multitude that extends backward in time into the long procession of generations preceding our lifetime, the ones whom we call 'the Concourse on High'. They may have recently left the flow of history and passed into the eternal present. Or they may be among those who will appear in future generations, and who will remember us as champion builders in a period of history struggling to bring forth a new World Order. From the Eternal

REFLECTIONS ON OUR SEVEN FAMILIES

Family we learn about:

a) living at the intersection of time and eternity;
b) history experienced as both future and past;
c) eternity experienced as the present;
d) how to assist the ones who went before;
e) how to call upon the ones who went before to assist us; and
f) how to provide for those who will come after we are gone.

Some comments from spiritual companions

You will no doubt draw your own conclusions about these domains of social life and the spiritual dynamics that power them. You may make mental notes about what actions you want to take to help each of these families improve their quality of life and manifest more of their inherent potential. In the course of such reflections, it may help you to see comments that were made by others who have studied *Our Seven Families* as a series of classes and workshops.

When asked for a personal reflection on the human systems revealed by these passages from the Sacred Writings, your fellow travellers made observations that included the following:

- Every person in every system has a job description.
- The roles of son and daughter prepare them for their future roles.
- We need to see the entire system, not one element at a time.
- It's an organic whole; it's alive.
- True happiness comes from caring for others in the system.
- Everyone knows his duty, and failure to fulfil it will affect the whole family.

- There are rights and responsibilities for each member.
- Traditional families seem to be contrary to what the Essential Family should be.
- Children in rebellion sometimes try to take on the parents' roles.
- Problems arise when there is no clarity about who has the ball.
- Any variations can be arranged by consensus (mother earning, father educating).
- All roles are held together by spiritual commitment, not physical discipline.
- The family structure can become the object of divine grace and favour.
- Each family is like a total life-support system, a vehicle.
- No wonder marriage is a sacred, social 'institution', instituted by God.
- You can see that each 'family' is a coherent, cohesive whole.
- Seeing the families changes my sense of both the world and the Sacred Writings.

From the sublime to the practical

Multiple interconnecting layers of human interaction are revealed in the Sacred Writings. The deepest and most mystical of these are anchored in profound levels of reality from which has emerged the history and evolution of our species as a whole, our species soul as a single entity – humankind.

> We desire but the good of the world and the happiness of the nations . . . That all nations should become one in faith and all men as brothers; that the bonds of affection and unity between the sons of men should be strengthened; that diversity of religion should cease, and differences of race be

annulled – what harm is there in this? . . . Yet so it shall be; these fruitless strifes, these ruinous wars shall pass away, and the 'Most Great Peace' shall come . . . and all men [will] be as one kindred and one family . . . Let not a man glory in this, that he loves his country; let him rather glory in this, that he loves his kind . . .[1]

We are reminded that even the Manifestations of God themselves had families. Despite the fact that some family members were tempted to reject and even persecute the divine Person among them, others arose to support and sustain Him; and those faithful members of the Holy Family continue to this day, from their vantage point in the Concourse, to praise and encourage us to carry forward their work of serving the Cause revealed by Him.

Verily, thy Lord assisteth and watcheth over thee at all times and under all conditions. The blessings of the Concourse on high surround thee, and the kindred and the leaves of the holy family . . . extol thee with a wondrous praise.[2]

We are reassured that we are being carried forward on a tidal wave of human evolution encompassing our planet and preparing it for the unity and synergy that will enable the luminous qualities of a mature humanity to shine forth.

In this day . . . means of communication have multiplied, and the five continents of the earth have virtually merged into one . . . In like manner all the members of the human family, whether peoples or governments, cities or villages, have become increasingly interdependent. For none is self-sufficiency any longer possible, inasmuch as political ties unite all peoples and nations, and the bonds of trade and industry, of agriculture and education, are being strengthened every day. Hence the unity of all mankind can in this day be achieved. Verily this is none other but one of the wonders of this wondrous age, this glorious century. Of this past ages have been deprived, for this century – the century of light – hath been endowed with unique and unprecedented glory, power and illumination.[3]

These ideas, principles, and holy teachings make a great claim upon us. This is no time to be faint-hearted. We are the ones who have been born into the long-awaited day of global convergence in spiritual awakening, when everyone on earth would come to realize that we are one people, one planet, reliant upon One God.

Let there be no mistake. The principle of the Oneness of Mankind – the pivot round which all the teachings of Bahá'u'lláh revolve – is no mere outburst of ignorant emotionalism or an expression of vague and pious hope. Its appeal is not to be merely identified with a reawakening of the spirit of brotherhood and good-will among men, nor does it aim solely at the fostering of harmonious cooperation among individual peoples and nations.[4]

The implications of being born into this age of global convergence are awe-inspiring. The way we conduct the business of our families, our communities, and our world, is about to change profoundly and forever due to this singular principle of the Oneness of Mankind.

Its implications are deeper, its claims greater than any which the Prophets of old were allowed to advance. Its message is applicable not only to the individual, but concerns itself primarily with the nature of those essential relationships that must bind all the states and nations as members of one human family . . . It implies an organic change in the structure of present-day society, a change such as the world has not yet experienced.⁵

From this time forward, we will begin to conduct our affairs through the force released by our united hearts.

> Unification of the whole of mankind is the hall-mark of the stage which human society is now approaching. Unity of family, of tribe, of city-state, and nation have been successively attempted and fully established. World unity is the goal towards which a harassed humanity is striving. Nation-building has come to an end. The anarchy inherent in state sovereignty is moving towards a climax. A world, growing to maturity, must abandon this fetish, recognize the oneness and wholeness of human relationships, and establish once for all the machinery that can best incarnate this fundamental principle of its life.⁶

We, the peoples of the world, are the bearers of unlimited human potential to manifest spiritual dynamics in family-like relations all over the world. Despite evidence to the contrary, we are, in fact, learning to conduct ourselves in these various levels of family-like human systems, and to move our global culture toward justice and reciprocity, fair trade, human rights, and world peace.

The Universal House of Justice (the elected body that guides, guards, and governs the multitude of Bahá'ís who have turned to it from every imaginable corner of the planet) provides some encouraging reflections on the prospects for our common future. It based its observations on the experiences of Bahá'í communities throughout the globe, and addressed its reflections in an open letter to the peoples of the world as follows:

> Together with the opposing tendency to warfare and self-aggrandizement against which it ceaselessly struggles, the drive towards world unity is one of the dominant, pervasive features of life on the planet during the closing years of the twentieth century.
>
> The experience of the Bahá'í community may be seen as an example of this enlarging unity. It is a community of some three to four million people drawn from many nations, cultures, classes and creeds, engaged in a wide range of activities serving the spiritual, social and economic needs of the peoples of many lands. It is a single social organism, representative of the diversity of the human family, conducting its affairs through a system of commonly accepted consultative principles, and cherishing equally all the great outpourings of divine guidance in human history. Its existence is yet another convincing proof of the practicality of its Founder's vision of a united world, evidence that humanity can live as one global society, equal to whatever challenges its coming of age may entail. If the Bahá'í experience can contribute in whatever measure to reinforcing hope in the unity of the human race, we are happy to offer it as a model for study.[7]

From the most sublime visions of the future of humanity to the most practical requirements of our life today, our unity as one people and one planet becomes abundantly clear through contemplating even the few extracts from Bahá'í Sacred Writings presented in this small volume.

REFLECTIONS ON OUR SEVEN FAMILIES

Understand this: No one of us is alone, free-floating, or isolated. We are inextricably intertwined with each other through at least these Seven Families, in a meaningful life drama. In each family we have an important role to play to help it achieve its cohesion and synergy. It is in service to these sacred human families that we will directly experience the fulfilment of our life's purpose, and the satisfaction of our ancient hunger to belong.

Bibliography

'Abdu'l-Bahá. *'Abdu'l-Bahá in London* (1912, 1921*)*. Comp. Eric Hammond. London: Bahá'í Publishing Trust, 1982.

— *Paris Talks: Addresses given by 'Abdu'l-Bahá in 1911* (1912). London: Bahá'í Publishing Trust, 12th ed. 1995.

— *The Promulgation of Universal Peace: Talks Delivered by 'Abdu'l-Bahá During His Visit to the United States and Canada in 1912* (1922, 1925). Comp. H. MacNutt. Wilmette, IL: Bahá'í Publishing Trust, 2nd ed. 1982.

— *The Secret of Divine Civilization.* Trans. M. Gail. Wilmette, IL: Bahá'í Publishing Trust, 1957.

— *Selections from the Writings of 'Abdu'l-Bahá.* Comp. Research Department of the Universal House of Justice. Haifa: Bahá'í World Centre, 1978.

— *Tablets of 'Abdu'l-Bahá* (etext in the Ocean search engine; originally published as *Tablets of Abdul-Baha Abbas.* 3 vols. Chicago: Bahá'í Publishing Society, 1909–1916). Wilmette, IL: National Spiritual Assembly of the Bahá'ís of the United States, 1980.

Bahá'í International Community. *Ending Violence Against Women: Statement to the 51st Session of the UN Commission on Human Rights.* Geneva: BIC, 1995.

Bahá'í World Centre. *The Proclamation of Bahá'u'lláh.* Haifa: Bahá'í World Centre, 1967.

Bahá'u'lláh. *Gleanings from the Writings of Bahá'u'lláh*. Wilmette, IL: Bahá'í Publishing Trust, 1982.

— *The Hidden Words of Bahá'u'lláh*. Trans. Shoghi Effendi. Wilmette, IL: Bahá'í Publishing Trust, 1990.

— *The Kitáb-i-Aqdas: The Most Holy Book*. Haifa: Bahá'í World Centre, 1992.

— *Prayers and Meditations by Bahá'u'lláh*. Trans. Shoghi Effendi. Wilmette,IL: Bahá'í Publishing Trust, 1938, 1987.

— *The Seven Valleys and The Four Valleys*. Trans. Marzieh Gail, in consultation with Ali-Kuli Khan. Wilmette, IL: Bahá'í Publishing Trust, 1986.

— *The Summons of the Lord of Hosts*. Haifa: Bahá'í World Centre, 2002.

— *Tablets of Bahá'u'lláh Revealed after the Kitáb-i-Aqdas*. Comp. Research Department of the Universal House of Justice. Trans. Habib Taherzadeh et al. Haifa: Bahá'í World Centre, 1982.

Bahá'í Prayers: A Selection of Prayers Revealed by Bahá'u'lláh, The Báb, and 'Abdu'l-Bahá. Rev. ed. Wilmette, IL: Bahá'í Publishing Trust, 1991.

Barber, Katherine (ed.). *Canadian Oxford Dictionary*. 2nd ed. Oxford: Oxford University Press, 2004.

Clark, M.; Thyen, O. (eds.). *Oxford-Duden German Dictionary*. 3rd ed. Oxford: Oxford University Press, 2005.

The Compilation of Compilations. Prepared by the Universal House of Justice 1963–1990. 2 vols. Maryborough: Bahá'í Publications Australia, 1991.

Dylan, Bob. *The Times They Are a-Changin'*. Studio recorded album. New York: Columbia Records, 1964.

Esslemont, J. E. *Bahá'u'lláh and the New Era*. Wilmette, IL: Bahá'í Publishing Trust, 1998.

Gove, P. B. (ed.-in-chief). *Webster's Third New International Dictionary of the English Language, unabridged*. Springfield, Mass.: Merriam-Webster, 2002.

Herrmann, Duane L. *Fasting: The Sun and Its Moons: A Bahá'í Handbook*. Oxford: George Ronald, 1987.

Lights of Guidance: A Bahá'í Reference File. Comp. Helen Hornby. New Delhi: Bahá'í Publishing Trust, 1994.

BIBLIOGRAPHY

Jordan, Daniel C. *Becoming Your True Self.* London: Bahá'í Publishing Trust, rev. ed. 1993.

Khan, Peter. 'The Spiritual Axis between Japan and Australia', in *Bahá'í News*, May 1983.

Mahmoudi, Hoda; Dabell, Richard. 'Rights and Responsibilities in the Bahá'í Family System', in *The Journal of Bahá'í Studies*, vol. 5 (1992), no. 2, pp. 1–12.

Maxwell, May. *An Early Pilgrimage.* London: George Ronald, 1969.

Nábil-i-A‡am (Muhammad-i-Zarandí). *The Dawn-Breakers: Nabíl's Narrative of the Early Days of the Bahá'í Revelation.* Trans. and ed. Shoghi Effendi. London: Bahá'í Publishing Trust, 1975.

National Spiritual Assembly of the Bahá'ís of the United States. *Marriage: A Fortress for Well-Being.* Wilmette, IL: Bahá'í Publishing Trust, 1993.

— *The Vision of Race Unity: America's Most Challenging Issue.* Wilmette, IL: Bahá'í Publishing Trust, 1991.

— *The Dynamic Force of Example*, in *Comprehensive Deepening Program*. Heltonville, IN: Special Ideas, 2001.

Shoghi Effendi. *The Advent of Divine Justice* (1939). Wilmette, IL: Bahá'í Publishing Trust, 1990.

— *Bahá'í Administration: Selected Messages 1922–1932.* Wilmette, IL: Bahá'í Publishing Trust, 1974.

— *Messages to America, 1932–1946.* Wilmette, IL: Bahá'í Publishing Trust, 1947. Published online by the Project Gutenberg.

— *Messages to the Bahá'í World 1950–1957.* Wilmette, IL: Bahá'í Publishing Trust, 1971.

— *The Promised Day Is Come* (1941). Wilmette, IL: Bahá'í Publishing Trust, 1980.

— *Unfolding Destiny: Messages from the Guardian of the Bahá'í Faith to the Bahá'ís of the British Isles 1922–1957.* London: Bahá'í Publishing Trust, 1981.

— *The World Order of Bahá'u'lláh: Selected Letters by Shoghi Effendi* (1938). Wilmette, IL: Bahá'í Publishing Trust, 1982.

Taherzadeh, Adib. *The Revelation of Bahá'u'lláh.* 4 vols. Oxford: George Ronald, 1974–88.

The Universal House of Justice. *Framework for Action: Selected Messages of the Universal House of Justice, and Supplementary Material 2006–2017.* West Palm Beach, FL: Palabra Publications, 2017.

— *Individual Rights and Freedoms in the World Order of Bahá'u'lláh.* Letter of 29 December 1988. Wilmette, IL: Bahá'í Publishing Trust, 1989.

— *Messages from the Universal House of Justice 1968–1973.* Wilmette, IL: Bahá'í Publishing Trust, 1976.

— *Messages from the Universal House of Justice 1963–1986.* Comp. Geoffrey W. Marks. Wilmette, IL: Bahá'í Publishing Trust, 1996.

— *To the Peoples of the World: A Bahá'í Statement on Peace by the Universal House of Justice.* Ottawa: Association for Bahá'í Studies, 1986.

— 'Violence against Women and Children', in *American Bahá'í*, 23 Nov. 1993, pp. 10–11.

— *Wellspring of Guidance.* Wilmette, IL: Bahá'í Publishing Trust, Wilmette, 1976.

Yousafzai, Malala. *I Am Malala.* New York: Little, Brown and Co., 2013.

Notes and References

Foreword
1. Natalie Gil, in *The Guardian*, 21 July 2014, https://www.theguardian.com.
2. George Monbiot, in *The Guardian*, 20 February 2018, https://www.theguardian.com.
3. Vivek H. Murthy, in *Harvard Business Review*, 12 October 2017, https://hbr.org/.
4. David Brooks, in *New York Times*, 16 February 2018, www.nytimes.com.
5. Letter on behalf of the Universal House of Justice, 19 April 2013, in *Framework for Action: Selected Messages of the Universal House of Justice, and Supplementary Material 2006–2017*.

Introduction: Interwoven Social Worlds
1. Bahá'u'lláh, *Gleanings from the Writings of Bahá'u'lláh*, CXXII, p. 260.
2. Bahá'u'lláh, *Gleanings from the Writings of Bahá'u'lláh*; 'Abdu'l-Bahá, *The Promulgation of Universal Peace*; Shoghi Effendi, *The World Order of Bahá'u'lláh* and *The Promised Day Is Come*; The Universal House of Justice, *To the Peoples of the World: A Bahá'í Statement on Peace*. For publication details see the Bibliography.
3. Shoghi Effendi, 'The Goal of a New World Order', in *The World Order of Bahá'u'lláh*, p. 41.
4. The Universal House of Justice, *Individual Rights and Freedoms in the World Order of Bahá'u'lláh*, para. 10, pp. 16–17.
5. 'Abdu'l-Bahá, quoted in 'Women', in *The Compilation of Compilations*, vol. II, no. 2114.
6. Letter from the Universal House of Justice, 22 July 1987, quoted ibid. no. 2344.

7 Letter from the Universal House of Justice, 28 December 1980, quoted ibid. no. 2340.
8 'Abdu'l-Bahá, *The Promulgation of Universal Peace*, pp. 108, 76.
9 'Abdu'l-Bahá, quoted in Esslemont, *Bahá'u'lláh and the New Era*, p. 149.
10 The Universal House of Justice, *Individual Rights and Freedoms in the World Order of Bahá'u'lláh*, para. 21, p. 20.
11 Shoghi Effendi, quoted ibid. para. 30, p. 24.
12 Letter on behalf of Shoghi Effendi, 21 November 1935, quoted in *Lights of Guidance*, no. 1354.
13 Shoghi Effendi, quoted in The Universal House of Justice, *Individual Rights and Freedoms…*, para. 49, p. 30.
14 Bahá'u'lláh, *Hidden Words*, Arabic no. 68.
15 Khan, 'Spiritual Axis between Japan and Australia'.
16 For further information about these publications, see the Bibliography.
17 Mahmoudi and Dabell, 'Rights and Responsibilities in the Bahá'í Family System', in *Journal of Bahá'í Studies*, vol. 5, no. 2, pp. 1–12.
18 'Abdu'l-Bahá, *The Promulgation of Universal Peace*, p. 168.
19 'Abdu'l-Bahá, quoted in *Lights of Guidance*, no. 767, see also 'Family Life', in *The Compilation of Compilations*, vol. I.
20 Shoghi Effendi, *The Advent of Divine Justice*, pp. 22–3.
21 ibid. p. 25.
22 'Abdu'l-Bahá, quoted ibid. p. 47.
23 Bahá'u'lláh, quoted ibid. p. 57.
24 Bahá'u'lláh, quoted ibid. p. 76.
25 Letter on behalf of Shoghi Effendi, 8 May 1942, quoted in 'Family Life', in *The Compilation of Compilations*, vol. I, no. 881.
26 Jordan, *Becoming Your True Self*, p. 42.
27 Bahá'u'lláh, *Gleanings from the Writings of Bahá'u'lláh*, CXXI, p. 287.
28 Bahá'u'lláh, quoted in Shoghi Effendi, *The World Order of Bahá'u'lláh*, p. 135.
29 'Abdu'l-Bahá, quoted in Maxwell, *An Early Pilgrimage*, p. 40.
30 Bahá'u'lláh, *Hidden Words*, Arabic no. 13.
31 Bahá'u'lláh, *The Seven Valleys and the Four Valleys*, p. 50.
32 Bahá'u'lláh, quoted in 'Excellence in All Things', in *The Compilation of Compilations*, vol. I, no. 560.
33 Bahá'u'lláh, *Hidden Words*, Arabic no. 10.
34 Shoghi Effendi, *Bahá'í Administration*, p. 132.
35 Bahá'u'lláh, *Hidden Words*, Persian no. 29.
36 ibid. Persian no. 27.
37 ibid. Arabic no. 2.
38 Bahá'u'lláh, *The Seven Valleys and the Four Valleys*, p. 50.
39 Bahá'u'lláh, *Gleanings from the Writings of Bahá'u'lláh*, CXXIX, p. 280.

REFERENCES AND NOTES

40 'Abdu'l-Bahá, *Selections from the Writings of 'Abdu'l-Bahá*, no. 8, p. 23.
41 Bahá'u'lláh, quoted ibid. no. 5, p. 18.
42 Bahá'u'lláh, *Hidden Words*, Persian no. 49.
43 ibid. no. 72.
44 Shoghi Effendi, *The Advent of Divine Justice*, p. 46.
45 Letter from Shoghi Effendi to the National Spiritual Assembly of the United States and Canada, 28 January 1939, in Shoghi Effendi, *Messages to America 1932–1946*, p. 17; also quoted in 'The Power of Divine Assistance', in *The Compilation of Compilations,* vol. I, no. 1683.
46 Bahá'u'lláh, *Hidden Words*, Persian no. 80.

1. The Global Family

1 'Abdu'l-Bahá, *The Promulgation of Universal Peace*, p. 157.
2 Shoghi Effendi, 'The Unfoldment of World Civilization', in *The World Order of Bahá'u'lláh*, p. 203.
3 Shoghi Effendi, 'The Goal of a New World Order', ibid. p. 41.
4 ibid.
5 ibid.
6 ibid. p. 43.
7 Shoghi Effendi, 'The Unfoldment of World Civilization', ibid. p. 163.
8 The Universal House of Justice, *Individual Rights and Freedoms . . .*, para. 10, pp. 16–17.
9 The Universal House of Justice, *To the Peoples of the World*, p. 13.
10 'Abdu'l-Bahá, *The Promulgation of Universal Peace*, p. 108.
11 'Abdu'l-Bahá, quoted in 'Women', in *The Compilation of Compilations*, vol. II, no. 2114, p. 367.
12 ibid.
13 ibid.
14 Abdu'l-Bahá, *The Promulgation of Universal Peace*, p. 283.
15 ibid.
16 ibid.
17 'Abdu'l-Bahá, *Paris Talks*, no. 50, p. 171.
18 Bob Dylan, 'The Times They Are a-Changin''.
19 Malala Yusafzai, *I Am Malala*.
20 'Abdu'l-Bahá, quoted in 'Women', in *The Compilation of Compilations*, vol. II, no. 2116, p. 369.
21 'Abdu'l-Bahá, *The Promulgation of Universal Peace*, p. 134.
22 ibid. p. 283.
23 ibid. p. 175.
24 The Universal House of Justice, 'Violence Against Women and Children', in *American Bahá'í* (23 Nov. 1993), pp. 10–11.
25 'Abdu'l-Bahá, *The Promulgation of Universal Peace*, p. 53.

26 'Abdu'l-Bahá, quoted in Esslemont, *Bahá'u'lláh and the New Era*, p. 149.
27 'Abdu'l-Bahá, *The Promulgation of Universal Peace*, p. 182.
28 'Abdu'l-Bahá, *Paris Talks*, no. 40, p. 136.
29 The Universal House of Justice, *To the Peoples of the World*, p. 13.
30 'Abdu'l-Bahá, *The Promulgation of Universal Peace*, p. 134.
31 ibid. p. 135.

2. The National Family

1 The Universal House of Justice, 29 December 1988.
2 National Spiritual Assembly of the Bahá'ís of the United States, 1991.
3 The Universal House of Justice, *Individual Rights and Freedoms*, para. 21, p. 20.
4 'Abdu'l-Bahá, quoted in 'Women', in *The Compilation of Compilations*, vol. II, no. 2137, p. 376.
5 Bahá'u'lláh, *Kitáb-i-Aqdas*, para. 51, p. 38.
6 The Universal House of Justice, *Individual Rights and Freedoms*, para. 24, p. 22.
7 Letter from Shoghi Effendi to the Bahá'ís of North America, 23 February 1924, quoted ibid. para. 30, p. 24.
8 The Universal House of Justice, 'The Local Spiritual Assembly', in *The Compilation of Compilations*, vol. I, pp. 39–60.
9 The Universal House of Justice, Individual Rights *and Freedoms*, para. 19, p. 20.
10 Letter from Shoghi Effendi to an individual, 21 November 1936, quoted ibid. para. 49, p. 30.
11 The Universal House of Justice, ibid. para. 19, p. 20.
12 ibid. para. 50, p. 30.
13 ibid. para. 51, p. 31.
14 'Abdu'l-Bahá, *The Secret of Divine Civilization*, p. 2.
15 ibid. pp. 2–3.
16 Bahá'u'lláh, *Hidden Words*, Arabic no. 68.
17 Bahá'u'lláh, *Gleanings from the Writings of Bahá'u'lláh*, CIX, p. 215.
18 'Abdu'l-Bahá, *The Promulgation of Universal Peace*, p. 113.
19 ibid. p. 300.
20 Shoghi Effendi, *The Advent of Divine Justice*, p. 40.
21 'Abdu'l-Bahá, *The Promulgation of Universal Peace*, p. 321.
22 National Spiritual Assembly of the Bahá'ís of the United States, *Vision of Race Unity*, p. 2.
23 'Abdu'l-Bahá, *The Promulgation of Universal Peace*, p. 321.
24 Shoghi Effendi, 'The Goal of a New World Order', in *The World Order of Bahá'u'lláh*, pp. 41–2.
25 'Abdu'l-Bahá, *The Promulgation of Universal Peace*, p. 368.

26 ibid. p. 302.
27 ibid. p. 104.
28 Shoghi Effendi, Message to the European Intercontinental Conference, Stockholm, Sweden, 21–16 July 1953, in *Messages to the Bahá'í World, 1950–1957*, p. 161.
29 Shoghi Effendi, Message to the African Intercontinental Conference, Kampala, Uganda, 12–18 February 1953, ibid. p. 136.
30 Khan, 'The Spiritual Axis between Japan and Australia', 1983.
31 Shoghi Effendi, 'The Unfoldment of World Civilization', in *The World Order of Bahá'u'lláh*, p. 203.
32 ibid. p. 204.
33 Bahá'u'lláh, *Gleanings from the Writings of Bahá'u'lláh*, CXXXII, p. 288.
34 ibid. CVII, p. 214.

3. The Essential Family

1 Letter on behalf of the Universal House of Justice, 1 August 1978, in 'Women', in *The Compilation of Compilations*, vol. II, no. 2160, p. 383.
2 'Women', ibid. pp. 355–405.
3 'Preserving Bahá'í Marriages', ibid. pp. 441–459.
4 'Family Life', ibid. vol. I, pp. 385–416.
5 Mahmoudi and Dabell, 'Rights and Responsibilities in the Bahá'í Family System', in *The Journal of Bahá'í Studies*, vol. 5, no. 2, pp. 1–12.
6 'Abdu'l-Bahá, *The Promulgation of Universal Peace*, p. 168.
7 Gove (ed.), *Webster's Third International Dictionary*, p. 2355.
8 ibid. p. 804.
9 Bahá'u'lláh, quoted in 'Women', in *The Compilation of Compilations*, vol. II, p. 379.
10 'Abdu'l-Bahá, *Selections from the Writings of 'Abdu'l-Bahá*, no. 84, p. 117.
11 ibid. no. 92, p. 122.
12 ibid. no. 84, p. 117.
13 ibid. no. 87, p. 119.
14 Letter on behalf of the Universal House of Justice, 16 May 1982, in 'Women', in *The Compilation of Compilations*, vol. II, no. 2163, p. 385.
15 'Abdu'l-Bahá, *Tablets*, vol. 3, p. 605, quoted in 'Family Life', in *The Compilation of Compilations*, vol. I, no. 839, p. 391.
16 ibid.
17 Letter from the Universal House of Justice, 28 December 1980, in 'Family Life', in *The Compilation of Compilations*, vol. I, no. 916, pp. 413–14.

18 Letter from the Universal House of Justice, 25 July 1984, in *Messages from the Universal House of Justice 1963–1986*, no. 402, p. 633.
19 ibid.
20 Letter on behalf of the Universal House of Justice, 23 August 1984, in 'Women', in *The Compilation of Compilations*, vol. II, no. 2166, p. 386.
21 Letter on behalf of the Universal House of Justice, 28 December 1980, in 'Women', in *The Compilation of Compilations*, vol. II, no. 2162, p. 385.
22 Letter from the Universal House of Justice, 28 December 1980, in 'Family Life', in *The Compilation of Compilations*, vol. I, no. 916, p. 415.
23 Letter on behalf of the Universal House of Justice, 9 August 1984, in 'Women', in *The Compilation of Compilations*, vol. II, no. 2165, p. 386.
24 'Abdu'l-Bahá, quoted in 'Family Life', in *The Compilation of Compilations*, vol. I, no. 849, p. 393.
25 'Abdu'l-Bahá, *Selections from the Writings of 'Abdu'l-Bahá*, no. 114, p. 139.
26 Letter on behalf of Shoghi Effendi, 16 November 1939, in 'Family Life', in *The Compilation of Compilations*, vol. I, no. 876, pp. 402–3.
27 Letter from the Universal House of Justice, 28 December 1980, in 'Family Life', in *The Compilation of Compilations*, vol. I, no. 916, p. 414.
28 Letter from the Universal House of Justice to an individual, 24 July 1975, in 'Women', in *The Compilation of Compilations*, vol. II, no. 2121, p. 370.
29 Bahá'u'lláh, quoted in 'Women', in *The Compilation of Compilations*, vol. II, no. 2145, p. 379.
30 'Abdu'l-Bahá, *Selections from the Writings of 'Abdu'l-Bahá*, no. 117, p. 140.
31 'Abdu'l-Bahá, quoted in 'Family Life', in *The Compilation of Compilations*, vol. I, no. 849, p. 393.
32 'Abdu'l-Bahá, *Selections from the Writings of 'Abdu'l-Bahá*, no. 138, p. 158.
33 Letter on behalf of the Universal House of Justice, 28 December 1980, in 'Women', in *The Compilation of Compilations*, vol. II, no. 2162, p. 384.
34 Bahá'u'lláh, *Gleanings from the Writings of Bahá'u'lláh*, CIX, p. 214.
35 'Abdu'l-Bahá, quoted in 'Family Life', in *The Compilation of Compilations*, vol. I, no. 843, p. 392.
36 Letter on behalf on Shoghi Effendi to the National Spiritual Assembly of the United States and Canada, 25 October 1947, in 'Family Life',

in *The Compilation of Compilations*, vol. I, no. 892, p. 406; see also Bahá'u'lláh, *The Kitáb-i-Aqdas*, note 92, p. 207.
37 Letter from Shoghi Effendi to the National Spiritual Assembly of the United States and Canada, 27 January 1935, quoted in *Lights of Guidance*, no. 1288, p. 386.

4. The Daily Family

1 The Universal House of Justice, Message to the First Oceanic Conference, Palermo, Sicily, August 1968, in *Messages from the Universal House of Justice 1963–1986*, no. 63, p. 137.
2 Shoghi Effendi, *The Advent of Divine Justice*, p. 23.
3 Bahá'u'lláh, quoted ibid.
4 Bahá'u'lláh, *Hidden Words*, Arabic no. 2.
5 ibid.
6 ibid.
7 Bahá'u'lláh, quoted in Shoghi Effendi, *The Advent of Divine Justice*, p. 28.
8 Bahá'u'lláh, *Tablets of Bahá'u'lláh Revealed after the Kitáb-i-Aqdas*, p. 67; quoted in Shoghi Effendi, *The Advent of Divine Justice*, p. 27.
9 Gove (ed.), *Webster's Third New International Dictionary*, p. 1917.
10 ibid. pp. 2456–7.
11 Shoghi Effendi, *The Advent of Divine Justice*, p. 30.
12 ibid. p. 31.
13 Bahá'u'lláh, *Gleanings from the Writings of Bahá'u'lláh*, CXXXVI, p. 297.
14 'Abdu'l-Bahá, *The Promulgation of Universal Peace*, p. 69; quoted in Shoghi Effendi, *The Advent of Divine Justice*, p. 37.
15 'Abdu'l-Bahá, *The Promulgation of Universal Peace*, p. 113; *Paris Talks*, no. 15, p. 45; quoted in Shoghi Effendi, *The Advent of Divine Justice*, p. 38.
16 Jordan, *Becoming Your True Self*, p. 17.
17 ibid. p. 18.
18 Bahá'u'lláh, *Hidden Words*, Arabic no. 68.
19 'Abdu'l-Bahá, quoted in Shoghi Effendi, *The Advent of Divine Justice*, p. 47.
20 Shoghi Effendi, ibid. p. 57.
21 Bahá'u'lláh, quoted ibid. p. 76.

5. A Family of Friendships

1 See for example, Barker (ed.), *Canadian Oxford Dictionary*; Clark and Thyen (eds), *Oxford-Duden German Dictionary*.
2 The Báb, Address to the Letters of the Living, in Nabíl-i-A*z*am, *The Dawn-Breakers*, p. 93.

3 Bahá'u'lláh, Words of Wisdom, in *Tablets of Bahá'u'lláh Revealed after the Kitáb-i-Aqdas*, p. 156.
4 'Abdu'l-Bahá, *Paris Talks*, no. 1, p. 2.
5 ibid.
6 Bahá'u'lláh, *Gleanings from the Writings of Bahá'u'lláh*, CXXXIX, p. 304.
7 'Abdu'l-Bahá, *Selections from the Writings of 'Abdu'l-Bahá*, no. 35, p. 71.
8 Bahá'u'lláh, *The Seven Valleys*, p. 7.
9 'Abdu'l-Bahá, *Selections from the Writings of 'Abdu'l-Bahá*, no. 7, p. 21.
10 ibid. no. 35, p. 73.
11 Bahá'u'lláh, *Hidden Words*, Persian no. 56.
12 Bahá'u'lláh, *Gleanings from the Writings of Bahá'u'lláh*, CXXV, p. 265.
13 'Abdu'l-Bahá, *Selections from the Writings of 'Abdu'l-Bahá*, no. 138, p. 158.
14 Bahá'u'lláh, *Hidden Words*, Persian no. 3.
15 ibid. no. 56.
16 Letter from Shoghi Effendi, 4 December 1954, in 'Preserving Marriages', in *The Compilation of Compilations*, vol. II, no. 2332.
17 Letter from Shoghi Effendi, 8 May 1942, in 'Family Life', in *The Compilation of Compilations*, vol. I, no. 881.
18 Jordan, *Becoming Your True Self*, p. 41.
19 ibid. p. 42.
20 ibid. p. 49.
21 'Abdu'l-Bahá, *The Promulgation of Universal Peace*, pp. 344–5.
22 Bahá'u'lláh, quoted in Shoghi Effendi, 'The Dispensation of Bahá'u'lláh', in *The World Order of Bahá'u'lláh*, p. 135.
23 ibid. pp. 135–6.
24 'Abdu'l-Bahá, Tablet to the Bahá'ís of New York, 1 January 1907, as reported in *'Abdu'l-Bahá in London*, p. 109, note. A slightly different translation is given in *Tablets of 'Abdu'l-Bahá*, vol. 2, p. 430.
25 'Abdu'l-Bahá, quoted in Maxwell, *An Early Pilgrimage*, p. 40.
26 National Spiritual Assembly of the Bahá'ís of the United States, *The Dynamic Force of Example*, p. 226.
27 'Abdu'l-Bahá, *Selections from the Writings of 'Abdu'l-Bahá*, no. 8, p. 23.
28 Bahá'u'lláh, *Gleanings from the Writings of Bahá'u'lláh*, CXXXI, p. 287.
29 Bahá'u'lláh, *Bahá'í Prayers*, p. 4.
30 Bahá'u'lláh, *Prayers and Meditations*, CLXXVIII, p. 300.
31 ibid. pp. 298–9.
32 Bahá'u'lláh, *Bahá'í Prayers*, pp. 13–14.
33 Bahá'u'lláh, *Prayers and Meditations*, CLXXVIII, p. 299.
34 ibid.
35 Bahá'u'lláh, *The Seven Valleys*, p. 17.

36 ibid.
37 ibid. pp. 17–18.
38 ibid. p. 36.

6. The Inner Family

1 Bahá'u'lláh, *Gleanings from the Writings of Bahá'u'lláh*, XC, pp. 177–8.
2 Bahá'u'lláh, *Hidden Words*, Arabic no. 13.
3 Bahá'u'lláh, 'The Four Valleys', in *The Seven Valleys and the Four Valleys*, p. 50.
4 Bahá'u'lláh, *Hidden Words*, Persian no. 29.
5 ibid. Arabic no. 3.
6 ibid. Arabic no. 22.
7 Bahá'u'lláh, quoted in 'Excellence in All Things', in *The Compilation of Compilations*, vol. I, no. 770.
8 Bahá'u'lláh, *Hidden Words*, Arabic no. 10.
9 ibid. Arabic no. 48.
10 ibid. Arabic no. 49.
11 Letter from Shoghi Effendi to the National Spiritual Assembly of the Bahá'ís of the United States and Canada, 12 April 1927, in Shoghi Effendi, *Bahá'í Administration*, p. 132.
12 Bahá'u'lláh, Tablet of Aḥmad, in *Bahá'í Prayers*, p. 211.
13 Bahá'u'lláh, *Hidden Words*, Persian no. 29.
14 ibid. Arabic no. 51.
15 ibid. Persian no. 21.
16 ibid. Persian no. 38.
17 ibid. Arabic no. 2.
18 ibid. Persian no. 27.
19 ibid. Arabic no. 63.
20 Bahá'u'lláh, 'The Four Valleys', in *The Seven Valleys and the Four Valleys*, p. 50.
21 Bahá'u'lláh, *Hidden Words*, Persian no. 44.
22 'Abdu'l-Bahá, *Selections from the Writings of 'Abdu'l-Bahá*, no. 17, p. 35.
23 ibid.

7. The Eternal Family

1 'Abdu'l-Bahá, in *Bahá'í Prayers*, p. 65.
2 Bahá'u'lláh, in 'Family Life', in *The Compilation of Compilations*, vol. 1, no. 823.
3 'Abdu'l-Bahá, in *Bahá'í Prayers*, p. 47.
4 Bahá'u'lláh, ibid. pp. 43–4.
5 Bahá'u'lláh, in 'Ḥuqúqu'lláh', in *The Compilation of Compilations*, vol. I, no. 1138.

6 Bahá'u'lláh, *Gleanings from the Writings of Bahá'u'lláh*, CXXIX, p. 280.
7 'Abdu'l-Bahá, *Selections from the Writings of 'Abdu'l-Bahá*, no. 8, p. 23.
8 ibid. no. 39, p. 81.
9 Bahá'u'lláh, *Hidden Words*, Persian no. 80.
10 Bahá'u'lláh, *Tablets of Bahá'u'lláh Revealed after the Kitáb-i-Aqdas*, p. 90.
11 Bahá'u'lláh, *Hidden Words*, Persian no. 49.
12 ibid. Persian no. 72.
13 Shoghi Effendi, *The Advent of Divine Justice*, p. 46.
14 Letter from Shoghi Effendi to the National Spiritual Assembly of the Bahá'ís of the United States and Canada, 28 January 1939, in Shoghi Effendi, *Messages to America 1932–1946*, p. 17.
15 Bahá'u'lláh, *Hidden Words*, Arabic no. 43.
16 ibid.

Reflections on Our Seven Families
1 Words of Bahá'u'lláh as recorded by E. G. Browne, quoted in Esslemont, *Bahá'u'lláh and the New Era*, pp. 39–40.
2 Bahá'u'lláh, *The Summons of the Lord of Hosts*, p. 150.
3 'Abdu'l-Bahá, *Selections from the Writings of 'Abdu'l-Bahá*, no. 15, pp. 31–2.
4 Shoghi Effendi, 'The Goal of a New World Order', in *The World Order of Bahá'u'lláh*, pp. 42–3.
5 ibid.
6 Shoghi Effendi, 'The Unfoldment of World Civilization', in *The World Order of Bahá'u'lláh*, p. 202.
7 The Universal House of Justice, *To the Peoples of the World: A Bahá'í Statement on Peace*, pp. 23–4.

Acknowledgements

from my personal journey

The substance of this book is guidance found in Bahá'í Sacred Writings on a constellation of human systems. But our capacity to hear the Revelation, to recognize some of the limitless meanings in the sacred Word as we read it, is enabled by life experience that penetrates and prepares our souls as the plough penetrates and prepares living soil. Some of the people who aided my journey of discovery are honoured here.

Global Family: This can only begin with Berit Bergstrom who first invited me to research this field on behalf of the Swedish Bahá'í community which was looking for a way to honour the United Nations Year of the Family in 1994. As we travelled together, I began to absorb a Scandinavian way of viewing the world. Before that experience were my travels in Western Siberia and European Russia, in the days when they were still known as the Soviet Union, for a UN conference on development. The lead translator for the team became a true friend and mentor as she coached me through how to appreciate the efforts that were being made by local people on my behalf. Later, on a return visit to the region, as we stood hand in hand in the museum commemorating the millions who died of starvation in the three-year siege of Stalingrad, we both acknowledged that our younger years had been stained by propaganda against each other, and that we had conquered all that to become friends. Perhaps the first eye-opener for me on the global family happened when the Computer Centre of a university in Malaysia invited me to share expertise in the earliest years of Internet teaching. My hosts were family members of the Centre's Director. An observant Muslim family, they had four little boys, the smallest of whom would burst into giggles every time I turned to look at him. When I asked the mother why, she said he had never seen anyone with green eyes and thought I was joking. It was my turn to be the strange one. Slowly I came to see that every place thinks of itself as the centre of the world and our perspectives integrate like a kaleidoscope.

National Family: Growing up in the eastern woodlands of Canada, just north of the Great Lakes, it was normal for me to know and love what I learned of Huron, Mohawk and Algonquin peoples. They were the definition of the Canada I loved. It was only much later that I realized there was a national scandal of cultural and physical genocide lurking below the surface of my national history. Like any family evil passed down from generation to generation, this one broke my heart. I came to know that the country famed for its mountains, forests and waterways had wounded and usurped the millennial trustees of those wonders. Now we are passing through a period of truth-telling and reconciliation in which some fitting repentance and restitution must be made. The same country that raised me up with a doctoral fellowship is trying to raise up the

ACKNOWLEDGEMENTS

members of our national family that it harmed. Every family has done some wrong; every family has to learn ways to heal itself and restore its members. I still love Canada.

Essential Family: There are so many reasons to honour my parents William Prescott McCreary and Phylis Kathrine Dobbyn. The central duty of parents is education of the young. My father taught me for years about world history, monarchy, and governance. My mother taught me by her own creativity about music, live theatre and the creative kitchen. What they both passed on to me was knowledge of their prior generations who had made the migrant's journey of desperation from Ireland six generations before me and whose love of learning and education had produced my father as the first college graduate and me as the first doctorate. But my parents were the bearers of intergenerational trauma before their own passages through the poverty of the Dirty 1930s and the following world war. So I entered with the 'baby boom' generation and its post-war optimism. Now I am learning continually from my three grown daughters, Casey, Joanna, and Sara who demonstrate through their diversity the most remarkable mutual loyalty – maintaining the integrity of the whole while guarding the individuality of those within it.

Daily Family: These are the numberless people who have been fellow students or colleagues in six universities and co-workers in 12 years of bureaucratic labour for government. Given the peculiar person I am, these families have responded to me with a mix of attraction and rejection, with celebration and ostracism determined in large measure by those desiring novelty and innovation and those requiring stability through conformity. I was like a flux to them. But the best co-workers who must be honoured are the 600 from 56 countries who were serving in the same years of wonder as I did at the Baháʼí World Centre. Only veterans of service there really understand its atmosphere – like living on a space station – no longer of this world but neither is it the world yet to be. It's like being on site at the birth of a planetary people. While being blessed daily by the place, we also endured intense pain as each of us was purified of our attachments. For me it was the loss through market pressures of the home I had raised up against all odds for my children. When the pain was too intense – like having my foot in a bear trap – one couple offered to pray with me in the Shrines; and the pain went away. Then another co-worker told me of several others including himself who had also lost their homes while serving, and what he said to me was a wake-up call. He said, 'Now at least I can look some of the Persian friends in the eye' – those who had suffered and sacrificed so much. It was the honour of my life to be with all those people as my daily family.

Family of Friendships: These people shine in the firmament of my heart like stars in the night sky. With some I shared years of comradeship. With others our communion was as brief as an international conference. But they all had something in common. With them there was an intense mutual recognition. They saw the 'me' I want to be, the one crying to become, and as they spoke to that person, I knew I was real. I hope I did the same for them. Returning again and again to visit their signature vibration, I live in hope that we will meet again in the worlds to come and share with laughter and tears the adventures of the lives we did not share on earth.

Inner Family: Now this one is a tour-de-force, as my inner family has been over-populated with clear memories from way back before the verbal years. It has been my burden to be

ACKNOWLEDGEMENTS

conscious pretty much from the beginning. So the inventory of my inner family is enormous and three people were significant in helping me sort it out. Dr James Bartee, Dr Eli Somer, and Dr Richard Bauman (who was my direct report authority at the time). All three of these men contributed to helping me bring harmony and unity to the moving parts within my inner family. That they are *men*; that they respect this inner work of the soul as the counterpart to the external work of raising a civilization worthy of being called the kingdom of God on earth, gives me enormous hope that we are seeing a new race of men arise. For me, these men embodied the unity of virtue/virility and showed me that the inner victories are key to all external ones.

Eternal Family: While the eternal family may seem elusive to many, I want to thank some of mine by sharing with you that I have actually seen them, and they taught me something. It was at a large garden party that went on all day honouring the 50th wedding anniversary of my Aunt Eunice and Uncle Bob. Aunt Eunice could have been a general because she could marshal resources and people like nobody's business! Following an afternoon of barbershop music and storytelling, about 200 of us were about to enter two white gazebo tents for a formal dinner at round tables with careful seating plans. I had been contemplating that after six generations, we cousins were now scattered around the continent, and this aunt was the last remaining elder who had the authority to call us back to this village which had been the centre of our tribe. All the family reunions would now end with this reunion, and all those generations who had held the place before us would never again be able to convene like this around us who are the succeeding generations. At the moment when a family piper in full regalia began to call us to rise from our lawn chairs and move toward the tents, with inner vision I suddenly saw them in their own plane, arm-in-arm, promenading with solemnity and dignity in the direction of the tent. They were dressed in their Sunday best, coming for the last time to finish the story they had started for us. And I wondered, 'how come they look so good?' I know for sure they were farmers, working hard with no electricity, no indoor plumbing, and no central heating. And then I realized, they were showing me how they live now. They were showing me that they are living eternally in the refinement of their finest aspirations. They have become their own highest hopes . . . and the power of it all was almost beyond bearing.

Which brings me to a final acknowledgement of Dr Peter Khan and Dr Janet Khan, who together did more to educate me to this world and the next than any other people I could mention. He taught me to function in a multicultural environment as we move into a world culture that will be like 'nothing we have ever seen, and no where we have ever been'; and she taught me that researching the Sacred Writings requires accepting that all words have been infused with new meanings and now have new relations to each other. Together they modelled for me how to live at the World Centre, do daily chores at the vortex of human evolution, and walk steadfastly lifelong – even when the ground is shaking as eternity comes thundering into time to transform our world and our many families.

About the Author

Elaine McCreary is a globally-oriented educator, published by NATO for online learning and the Soviet Academy of Scientists for methods and techniques of mass public education. Her professional work spans many fields of lifelong learning including a tenured Associate Professorship for graduate studies in international development, work in the administrative development of secondary and post-secondary institutions, and funding policy analysis in a Ministry of Advanced Education. The highlight of those careers was service at the Bahá'í World Centre (1991–97) focusing on staff and organizational development at the direction of the Universal House of Justice. Elaine holds a B.A., M.A. and Ed.D. in fields related to lifelong learning. She is currently President and Creative Director of Harvest Home Lifelong Learning, Inc. (www.harvesthome.ca) creating courses for online delivery, and publications related to life skills in the 21st century. Elaine's teaching work has taken her from Iceland to Malaysia and from Western Siberia to Hawaii. She was made her home on the west coast of Canada; and is Mother to three grown daughters and Nanny to four inspiring grandchildren.